THE ART of BEING REBEKKAH

By Karoline Barrett

e·LITBOOKS

This book is a work of fiction. Names, characters, places and incidents either are products of the author's imagination or are used fictitiously. Any resemblance to actual events or locales or persons, living or dead, is entirely coincidental and not intended by the author.

THE ART OF BEING REBEKKAH

Cover Art and Design by Martin Blanco

For information on subsidiary rights, please contact the publisher at info@e-litbooks.com

ISBN 978-0615920566

To my husband, Aaron, the rest of my family, especially Kyle and Joey—so happy to be your mom, authors Kelly McClymer and Kathryn Johnson, and, of course, to Literary Counsel for making my dream come true.

ONE

Rebekkah wandered through the narrow stacks with a list of book titles in her hand. It was warm in the library, and the lazy ceiling fans barely stirred a breeze. It would be even hotter at home. Until it reached eighty-five degrees outside, her husband, Avram, insisted on opening the windows instead of turning on the air conditioning, even though she had allergies and breathed better with it on. Here in the library, the warmth hardly registered with her. She loved the smell and feel of the old books, the display of the latest best sellers, and the librarians who knew most of the neighborhood patrons by name.

She found the section she was looking for and scanned the titles. So many books about fertility and help with getting pregnant! She pulled the first book on her list out of its place on the shelf and flipped open the cover. Good, it had been recently published so it was likely to have the most up-to-date information.

Tucking the book into her bag for easy carrying, Rebekkah refused to think about Avram's reaction when, once again, she brought up the subject of why she hadn't become pregnant yet. He'd told her he didn't care whether or not they had children, that maybe it was God's will that they didn't. But *she* cared, and couldn't believe it was God's will to deny her what she wanted most.

She strolled to the center of the library where couches were neatly arranged in a square. Sitting with her legs folded underneath her, she flipped open the book. Within minutes her mind was totally focused on the words in front of her. So much so that when she finally looked up she was shocked to see that it was four-thirty.

Snapping the book shut she jumped to her feet. She had to stop at Freling's Super Market and shop for dinner before Avram got home. It would ruin his mood for the evening if she was late getting dinner on the table, and she didn't want his mood ruined. Not tonight.

Rebekkah waved to Jenna, the clerk who was checking out books, but bypassed her in favor of the self-check-out stand. Jenna was sweet, but a gossip. She didn't want Jenna telling everyone that Rebekkah Gelles was, maybe, having problems getting pregnant. She pushed the library door open, trotted down the steps, and tossed the bag with the book in it onto the back seat of the Mini Cooper she and Avram shared.

When she arrived at Freling's Rebekkah gathered her shopping bags from the back of the car and joined the throng at the deli counter. She reached over the lined-up shopping carts then yanked out number thirteen from the dispenser on top of the counter. According to the neon number hanging high on the wall, five people were ahead of her. She pocketed her piece of paper and headed for the bakery. A big black-and-white cookie for her and a small apple pie for Avram for dessert.

By the time Rebekkah made her way back to the deli counter, she had planned her dinner menu in her head and, when her number was called, she ordered a fat rotisserie chicken and potato salad. The green beans and corn she could pick up at the small market a block away from her house.

Twenty minutes later she pulled up in front of her Park Slope brownstone, maneuvered the Mini Cooper into a parking space with just enough room for it, and made her way on foot to the market for the rest of her items.

"There you are," Avram called to Rebekkah when she came through the front door. "I was wondering where you were. I was afraid I'd have to make my own dinner. Are those bags I hear? You need help?"

As if making his own dinner would happen, Rebekkah thought, and smiled, picturing her husband trying to cook. It's a good thing she loved to do it; otherwise, they might starve. "No, I got them all in one trip. I got a close parking space, too." She left the groceries on the kitchen counter and joined him in the living room.

She dropped the bag with her library book in it on the coffee table, already piled high with other yet-to-be-read books and magazines. "I've been at the library most of the afternoon. I didn't think you'd be home yet. I'll have dinner ready soon."

"Mark and Amy have everything under control at work, so I came home." Avram studied her. "Find anything interesting at the library?" He folded the *New York Times* and dropped it to the floor beside the chair.

Pulling off his reading glasses he nodded his head toward the couch across from where he sat. "Sit with me?"

Rebekkah threw him a smile, but evaded his question for the time being. She didn't want to tell him about the book until she finished reading it. "I should work on dinner. I bought a chicken from Freling's."

"Good, I'm starved. Call me when it's ready." He picked up his paper again and reached for his glasses.

Busy with dinner preparations, she jumped when Avram yelled from the living room a few minutes later. "Rebekkah?"

"What is it?" she called back. She was startled to see him standing in the kitchen doorway when she pulled her head out of the refrigerator.

At almost six feet tall, with broad shoulders, trim waist, and long, muscular legs, Avram cut an imposing figure. He still wore the clothes he had put on that morning, minus the suit jacket. His dark hair was cut short, and the sleeves of his dress shirt were rolled three quarters of the way up his arms. His tie hung loose around his neck. She noticed a few threads of gray growing among the brown when the light hit his hair just right.

Rebekkah swung the refrigerator door shut. "Why don't you go change your clothes? You have time to put your sweats on before dinner."

"I'll change later. What is this?" Avram brought his hand around from behind his back and thrust the library book at her.

Her heart skipped a beat. He could see what it was, obviously. "Why did you take it out of..." She let her sentence die. She should have hidden the book as soon as she got home. She didn't want to get into this now. Pushing her hands into the twin pockets of her apron she murmured, "It's a book," and tried out a weak smile on him, hoping the humor would relax the moment.

He tossed the book onto the kitchen table, where it landed with a thud, and crossed his arms in front of his chest. "I know it's a book. I'm asking why you took this particular book out of the library. I told you there's no reason to worry because you aren't pregnant yet."

The last time she brought up the subject of the lack of children in their almost four year-old marriage Avram had told her she was worrying unnecessarily, and a huge argument ensued. Rebekkah tried again to keep the mood light. "I want to read about the possible reasons for my not getting pregnant yet. You put me off every time I bring it up, but I'm getting nervous. I want a baby."

He pulled out a kitchen table chair and sat. "Do you think there's something wrong with me because you aren't pregnant? I thought I pleased you in bed."

"That's exactly what I've been trying to tell you. I am worried there might be something wrong with one of us. You pleasing me has nothing to do with it," Rebekkah replied, pulling plates and glasses from the kitchen cabinets.

"So, do I please you in bed?" he asked as if that mattered above all else.

"Yes, you know that." She lowered her voice as she turned back to him. "Can we drop it?"

To her relief, his expression softened. "That's better. Then you'll take the book back? I can take it back for you tomorrow morning, on the way to work."

"I'll take care of it," she assured him. It wasn't exactly a lie. She would take care of it, just not immediately. If she kept it out of his sight he would forget about it. Once she'd read it, and did some research into their specific situation, she would appeal to his intellect. Maybe he'd listen if she logically presented facts about fertility problems. She was becoming convinced something physical was standing in their way of getting pregnant. If she found out what that something might be, maybe they could correct the problem.

"Believe me when I say there is nothing wrong with us," Avram continued as if reading her thoughts. "You don't need a book when I've already assured you of that. These things take time, and we have plenty. Besides, I don't know that I'm ready to share you with a baby. Listen, if I thought we had something to worry about I'd be at the library taking books out myself."

Rebekkah swallowed the argument that immediately came to mind. They didn't have a lot of time. Avram was forty-five, twenty years older than she. She didn't regret marrying him, and most of the time she didn't think about their age difference, but she wanted children while he could still be an involved father. Rabbi Weissman teased her about not doing her job of populating their synagogue's day school, but for her it was no laughing matter. Was he trying to tell her she was a failure because she was childless?

"Speaking of making babies, tonight's your mikveh night, isn't it?" Avram interrupted her musings. "I can't wait to have you back in our bed later. I hate not sleeping with you. I toss and turn all night. I miss kissing you, touching you, making love with you."

"I miss you too," she told him as she took the potato salad from the refrigerator. She checked the corn and green beans then turned off the stove. "I can't wait until tonight, either." How ironic a confrontation about her desire for children would be headed off by thinking about the sex they would have later. The very thing that should be making her pregnant, but wasn't.

Rebekkah put a placemat at her place at the table, leaving Avram's place without one. The missing placemat looked wrong, a reminder to each of them that until she came home from the mikveh, she was a *niddah*; a menstruating woman, and according to Jewish law, unable to come into contact with Avram in any way, including sleeping in the same bed with him, kissing, or even passing a plate to him lest they touch accidentally.

She became a niddah from the first sign of her period. According to the family purity laws—*Taharat Ha-Mishpachah*— Rebekkah must immerse herself in a mikveh, the ritual bath Jewish women used for purification, as soon as possible after nightfall of the seventh post-menstrual clean day. Only then would she be free to touch and enjoy Avram's body, in and out of their bed.

It had been fourteen days since she had been in bed with Avram, and let him make love to her. At the beginning of their marriage, she had loved going to the mikveh. She felt renewed and refreshed, both spiritually and physically. Now, it was an unwelcome reminder of her empty womb.

She finished setting the table, and put Avram's plate of food at his place while he washed his hands, careful not to brush up against him. She poured iced tea for both of them, washed her own hands, and sat with him.

"How was work?" Rebekkah asked after the blessing was recited and they were enjoying their meal together.

"Busy," Avram replied without looking up. "We have the Botwick and Kadden funerals tomorrow afternoon."

She was amused at the way Avram barely stopped shoveling in food long enough to answer her. Mark Bender and Avram owned Gelles & Bender Funeral Home. They had met in mortuary school and gone into business together right after graduation.

"You'll be over later, won't you?" he asked her.

"I'll be there around one. I told Katie I'd finish the filing for her." She laughed. "It's the job we both hate the most, so it piles up."

Rebekkah's job at Gelles & Bender was answering the phone and taking care of other duties when Katie, their receptionist, was off—three mornings a week and vacations. She enjoyed working there, helping Katie keep everything organized for Mark, Avram, and Amy, who was also a funeral director. The best part was spending extra time with her husband and watching Avram calm grieving families. He was so good at it. As were Mark and Amy.

"You aren't having any?" Avram asked when Rebekkah got up and served him the apple pie she had bought earlier.

"I got myself a cookie for later. I want to get to the mikveh." She glanced at the clock on the microwave. "My appointment's at six-thirty. You know how traffic can be."

"Wait. I'll take you. I don't want you to drive there and back alone."

"It's not as if it will be dark out yet," Rebekkah replied. "Or as if I haven't driven by myself before."

"I know, but let me drop you off. I'll come back for you in half-an-hour or so." He gulped his pie down and dropped his fork on the plate. "Humor me."

"All right. Thank you." Avram was always so considerate and attentive. He looked after her as if she were the most important thing in the world to him. Sometimes his attention was a little stifling, but maybe that's the way all husbands were. Rebekkah told herself she really had nothing to complain about.

"Ready?" he asked after she had cleared the table and loaded the dishwasher.

Rebekkah turned and waved to Avram as she entered Beth Israel synagogue. She breathed in the stillness and cool air, then was greeted by the mikveh attendant. Yanna had been there as long as Rebekkah could remember and was like an aunt to her. She knew anything she told Yanna would never leave the mikveh. Rebekkah told her things she didn't tell her own family. Yanna was truly Ann Landers for the women of the mikveh.

"There's my Rebekkah, right on time as usual." Yanna came toward her with a fresh, thick, cream-colored towel.

She followed Yanna. Candles gave off a sweet lavender scent. Yanna guided Rebekkah into the prep room. "Come out when you're ready," she said.

Rebekkah nodded then sat at the dressing table and was again struck by the simple beauty of the blue-and-white tiles and cherry cabinets. She took off her simple gold wedding band and placed it in a velvet pouch. She picked up the nail trimmer and trimmed her nails. Nothing must stand between her body and the water.

She pulled off the scarf she was wearing, dragged the brush through her thick hair, and closed her eyes for a moment before undressing. She forced herself to relax and tried to let go of her anger toward Avram for being so stubborn. Now was the time to focus on God and why she was here.

Rebekkah's period was a nexus point between life and death. Because she had her period, a child would not be born. The mikveh was a sign of life, and when her body became one with Avram's tonight, there was hope that a child would be conceived. Now was the time for Rebekkah to nurture that hope in her heart.

She finished her preparation, slipped out of her clothes and stepped into the pre-immersion shower. The hot water felt good on her body, and she once again mourned the babies that hadn't been conceived. As she dried off and wrapped a sheet around herself she called for Yanna.

"Your cheeks are nice and rosy, but your eyes have no sparkle, Rebekkah," Yanna said.

"Am I the only one here?" Rebekkah looked around. She loved talking to Yanna, but didn't want others to hear them.

"There's no one else for another hour, so you have my undivided attention. Sit for a minute."

"It's Avram," she confided. "I think it's time to determine why I'm not pregnant. I want to make an appointment for us to see Rabbi Weissman. I've told Avram not all rabbis are against alternatives to getting pregnant the conventional way, if it comes to that for us. Rabbi Weissman wrote a paper for the *Jewish Element* stressing it is not as important how a woman gets pregnant, as it is that she conceives."

"And he hasn't agreed to see the rabbi?" asked Yanna.

Rebekkah frowned. "I haven't told him that I want to do that. He'll want nothing to do with it. He's the most stubborn man in the world."

Yanna smiled. "Most of them are, yet we manage to love them despite that, don't we? You will have to be more stubborn than Avram. If anyone can change his mind, you can."

"I hope so," Rebekkah let out a long breath. "He can quote *Halacha* like some men quote baseball statistics. But when it comes to what Torah says about being fruitful and multiplying, he turns a deaf ear."

Yanna patted Rebekkah's arm and gave her a sympathetic smile. "It's good, though he knows Jewish law, no? Be patient. The babies will come. Here, let me inspect you."

Rebekkah dropped her sheet and hoped Yanna was right. When Yanna said she was ready for her immersion, she descended the steps into the blue-and-green tiled mikveh. The majestic tile mosaic of Jerusalem on the walls surrounding the mikveh was a reminder to Rebekkah of her heritage, and made her feel a kinship to all other Jews.

She ducked under the water, and felt her soul go still as she offered prayers to God. She spread her arms and legs and left her eyes open. Her hair floated around her like seaweed, and she heard nothing from the outside world. This must be what it feels like to be in the womb, Rebekkah thought.

Yanna left her alone to recite in Hebrew as she immersed herself, "Praised are you, Adoshem, God of all creation, who sanctifies us with your commandments and commanded us concerning immersion." She ducked beneath the water twice more, and took a few minutes to ask God to open her womb.

When she was through she returned to the prep room to dress. Thinking of Avram, she slipped on her new lace teddy. She knew he would love it. The rest of her anger seeped out as she thought of his body joining with hers to create a new life. Just as her body was now ready for him, she wanted her spirit to be ready. She didn't want anger to serve as a barrier to a new life.

"See you in nine months?" Yanna asked, knowing that if Rebekkah got pregnant she wouldn't need to come back any sooner.

"God willing," Rebekkah smiled. "Thank you, Yanna."

Avram was pulling into the parking lot when the door shut behind Rebekkah. "I've already immersed in the mikveh," she announced as soon as she slid in the car. If she didn't tell him, he must consider her still a niddah.

He took her hand and kissed the back of it. Rebekkah shivered in delight. She couldn't wait until they got home. "I hope tonight will be the night." She laid her hand on his leg and felt the muscles flex as he shifted gears in their little car.

Rebekkah would change the sheets on their bed as soon as they arrived home. She loved the smell and feel of crisp, clean sheets. They made the rest of the ride in silence. She sensed he was as excited as she that they were finally going to make love again.

When they arrived home, Avram took care of turning off the lights in the living room. Rebekkah left on one small lamp in the bedroom so that they wouldn't be in total darkness. She liked to see Avram's face when they made love.

He came into the bedroom as she was stepping out of her skirt and unbuttoning her shirt. Every time she and

13

Avram came together after her visit to the mikveh, she felt like a nervous bride, making love for the first time. Avram watched her undress, his eyes raking up and down her body. His sharp intake of breath as she came to him and kissed him gave her goose bumps.

Avram's arms came around her as he returned her kiss. He picked her up and deposited her on their bed. It was her turn to watch as he undressed. He's beautiful, thought Rebekkah as he joined her. He kissed her again as he entered her, and her body arched toward him.

"Now, Avram, please," she whispered against his lips after a few minutes. When his seed spilled into her she willed her body to open to new life.

"No, don't move," she protested as he started to pull away.

"I'm too heavy for you."

"I love how your body feels on mine." She tangled her hands in his hair and kissed him again and again.

"I hope I have given you a child."

"No more than I."

Avram's body finally slipped from hers. Rebekkah turned over on her side, and he held her so tightly that she could feel his heart beating against her back.

She was sure she could feel life sprouting inside her already. It had to be! Giddy with hope, she promised God if she were pregnant, she would strive to be a perfect wife and mother. She would do her best not to think about the fiancé she had loved so desperately before Avram.

Avram knew about Jonathan, but they never spoke of him. Avram wouldn't allow it. His attitude after they married had changed. Before they were married, he listened to whatever Rebekkah wanted to talk about. She had unburdened herself to Avram many times, especially about losing Jonathan. Now that subject was off-limits.

She understood that, on some level, her husband was insecure about her past relationship with Jonathan, even though Jonathan no longer existed as part of her life. To Avram, it had to be as if Jonathan never existed at all. He was possessive and jealous, but Rebekkah took that as a sign of his love for her. So only in her mind did Jonathan exist, and from time to time she thought of him.

If she was pregnant, she vowed, Jonathan would never again have a place in her heart, or thoughts. As she drifted away in sleep, she silently assured God of this, half-afraid that maybe because sometimes she thought of a man who wasn't her husband, He had been offended and closed her womb.

TWO

"Bekkah! To what do I own the honor of your visit so early this morning?" Shira Goldman's face beamed as she held the screen door open for her daughter.

"What happened to you?" Her mother's cheek was smudged with dirt, the faded blue sweatshirt she wore had a hole right in the middle of it, and more of her hair hung out of her pony tail then in it.

Shira laughed. "I've been cleaning out the attic. Our neighborhood association is having a block party next weekend and, wouldn't you know, at the last minute decided to include a yard sale. Your father has encouraged me to I get rid of whatever I can. Want to help with the attic?"

"I can help for a few hours, but I have to work at the funeral home this afternoon. I'm here because I could use your advice, Ima," Rebekkah answered, slipping comfortably into the Hebrew word for mother. She followed Shira through the house, two yellow Labradors on their heels, until they ended up in her mother's kitchen.

Shira pulled a cake from one of her ovens. Like many observant Jews, and Rebekkah herself, her mother had two ovens, two refrigerators, and two dishwashers. Rebekkah had inherited her excellent cooking skills from her mother.

Rebekkah inhaled. "Smells good. Chocolate?"

Shira closed the oven door. "You wouldn't expect anything else around here, would you? I still have the spoon and the beaters." She pointed to a small plate on the counter. "Remember how you hovered beside me waiting for these when you were little?"

"Hmmm," replied Rebekkah as she eagerly licked off the chocolate.

"You've got good timing," said Shira. "I was up early to start this for us. Your brothers and sister are coming for dinner tonight. I promised them cake. You and Avram want to join us?"

"No, I've got dinner thawing, but thank you. That explains the cake. I thought I'd missed someone's birthday," said Rebekkah, thinking of her two older brothers and their endless appetites. Even her sister ate more than most girls yet managed to stay skinny as a branch.

Not for the first time Rebekkah was struck by her mother's beauty. Shira never wore makeup, yet at fifty-five there were no obvious lines in her face. She still weighed 119 pounds, as she had on her wedding day. "Aba loves your chocolate cake, doesn't he?"

"It's his favorite thing," Shira agreed.

Rebekkah rinsed off the beaters and spoon under the faucet. "You know, I think Avram likes it better than mine, he just won't admit it."

"Nonsense. Your cake is every bit as good as mine," Shira insisted, but she looked pleased at the compliment. "I'll make some tea, and you can tell me what kind of advice I can give you. I could use a break from the attic. I'll cut the cake for us after it cools. Never too early for cake, right?"

Rebekkah agreed wholeheartedly and wandered into the living room. She thought of how she and Avram had made love again that morning with wild abandon before she made him breakfast. Another chance for a pregnancy.

"So, what is it? Are you ill? Is it Avram? What's wrong?" Shira joined Rebekkah and handed her a cup of tea as she rattled off questions.

Rebekkah took her cup and sat. "It's nothing like that. We're fine. I'm worried that I'm not pregnant yet. Do you think I should be? Worried, I mean."

Shira put her tea on the coffee table and joined Rebekkah on the couch. "I know children mean a lot to you. I still have all the dolls you played with when you were little. I don't have the heart to get rid of them."

Rebekkah sipped her tea. "I hope someday my daughters will play with them."

"Have you talked to Dr. Gavin?" Shira asked.

Rebekkah shook her head. "Avram doesn't want me to pursue it. I don't want to go behind his back to my gynecologist. Avram only laughs and says nothing is wrong

18

with us. It's been almost four years, Ima. I don't think he really cares if we have children."

"I'm sure he wants children. But maybe he's right. Just relax and enjoy your married life together. I wouldn't worry yet. Give it a few more months."

Rebekkah stood and went to the window, staring out into the street. "Avram's not getting any younger. If I..."

Shira joined Rebekkah at the window and laid a hand on her arm. "You're wondering if things might be different if you had married Jonathan. You still miss him?"

"Sometimes," Rebekkah admitted, "but it's not as painful anymore." Why was she thinking of Jonathan now? Hadn't she promised God last night that she would try not to? Of course, she didn't know if she was pregnant, so maybe it didn't count. It wasn't as if she thought about him daily. She was usually successful in blocking thoughts about the car accident on the Long Island Expressway six months into their engagement.

Rebekkah had been in the car with Jonathan, and had miraculously emerged with nothing more than some stitches in her head and a broken leg. Her physical injuries healed, but at times her heart reminded her that it was still bruised. Then her conscience would prick her because she had come out of the accident intact, and he hadn't.

"I hope your father and I weren't wrong to encourage a relationship and marriage to Avram," Shira said. "You were so lost. And what could we do for you? We couldn't make Jonathan come back. I remember meeting Avram at Aunt Charlotte's funeral. He was interested in you right away. He seemed rather lonely, too."

Rebekkah wrapped her arms around herself and turned to face her mother. "You weren't wrong. Avram was what I needed to shake me out of my depression. Eventually, it worked, didn't it?"

Shira's eyes twinkled. "I think he fell in love with you the first night he saw you. We didn't have to do much nudging to get him moving in the right direction."

The long walks she and Avram had taken in the parks around the city soon after he had made his interest in her known flashed through Rebekkah's mind. The museums he took her to, the movies, and the fun they had at the Bronx Zoo. She hadn't been to the zoo since she was a child. Avram was always there for her, always listening. He gradually drew her out of her self-imposed cocoon of misery and made her smile, even laugh again.

Rebekkah's thoughts led her to the clear fall night Avram had asked her to marry him. It was after their dinner at Pretoria near the Plaza Hotel. From there had gone on a chilly ride in one of those horse-drawn carriages in Manhattan. Avram had bundled her up tightly in a blanket, and she had leaned against him, his arm around her. His warmth, and the steady clip-clopping of the horse's hooves, had lulled Rebekkah almost to sleep. He asked her to become his wife just before the ride was through.

In the end, she hadn't been able to resist Avram's charm and persuasive arguments for marriage. He promised her he'd be the best thing that ever happened to her, and most of the time he was. She did love him in return. Yes, in a very different way than she had loved

Jonathan, but it was still love. Rebekkah remembered wanting to stay with him in that carriage forever that night.

Shira's voice brought Rebekkah back to the present, and they sat back down on the couch together. "Your father and I were so worried. You moped around and lost so much weight. Weight you didn't need to lose, mind you."

"I do love Avram. But sometimes I can't help it...I wonder what if—"

"I know," Shira cut in. "We all have our 'what ifs.'"

Rebekkah blinked. "Do we?"

"Of course." Shira's eyes widened. "Mine was Aaron Green. Of course, I never had contact with him. I only saw him from afar. He was tall, and so handsome! Ah, you wouldn't believe. I dreamt of marrying him for over a year." She batted her eyelashes and burst into laughter. "Your father's still jealous, even though when I laid eyes on David Goldman, any other man ceased to exist for me. I haven't told your father that Aaron Green weighs about three hundred pounds now and smells." She held her nose for effect.

Rebekkah burst out laughing. "I can see why Aba would be jealous then."

Shira patted Rebekkah's knee. "Finish your tea. Come up to the attic with me. I want to show you something you've never seen before. It's your great-grandmother Rebekkah Ruth Kantor's 'what if'. She's the relative you were named for, in case you've forgotten. I don't know why I never showed any of this to you before. It's been up there since your grandma Susan moved to Florida years ago."

"I'll be up in a minute." Rebekkah squeezed her mother's hand.

Understanding dawned in Shira's eyes and she squeezed her daughter's hand back.

Rebekkah took their tea cups to the kitchen and rinsed them for Shira, then made her way upstairs to her old bedroom. At first glance, nothing had changed, from the white furniture with gold accents, to the ruffled pink curtains on the windows, to her old dolls on the bed.

Rebekkah pulled open a dresser drawer. Shira used that drawer for storage now that Rebekkah's things were gone. Buried underneath old pictures and souvenirs from family vacations to Florida and Europe, her hand found the velvet box. Avram's marriage proposal faded and was replaced by the memory of Jonathan kneeling in front of her in her parents' living room. *Will you marry me Rebekkah Ruth Goldman?* His deep voice seemed to echo in her old bedroom.

Rebekkah had flown into Jonathan's arms as he stood up, almost knocking him down. Her heart had been bursting with love for him. "Ima! Aba!" she screamed up the stairs. "I'm engaged!"

Her parents and siblings had pounded down the stairs and more screaming, tears and hugs flowed between them all. Rebekkah couldn't wait to become Mrs. Jonathan Mindell. He was the love of her life and she adored him. Jonathan was her whole world.

After the accident, Rebekkah's life came to a devastating halt. She sobbed herself dry, was unable to eat, or bring herself to face Mr. and Mrs. Mindell. She couldn't bear imagining what they were going through, or how they must hate her for coming through the accident virtually unscathed. The only thing Rebekkah wanted to do after she came home from the hospital was lie on her bed with the shades and curtains closed.

Even drawing breath was an effort she'd rather not bother with. Rebekkah had been so angry at God. "Why Jonathan? Why him?" she would cry out, but no answer came. She tried turning her back on God and cursing Him, but she couldn't. Something in her soul whispered that He would be the only way she could make it through her agony. And she had made it.

Rebekkah prayed Jonathan understood her marriage to Avram. She knew he wouldn't expect her to actually lie in her bed forever, closed away from everyone and everything. She eventually had to face the fact that the man she loved no longer existed, but she still did, and she would have to go on.

She flipped open the lid of the box and slipped off her wedding ring. Her hand trembled as she slipped on Jonathan's engagement ring. You can't change it, she told herself. Stop thinking about him. He isn't coming back. Rebekkah pulled the ring off and put her wedding ring back on. It felt right. Avram's ring belonged there.

She shuddered inwardly. If Avram ever found out she had kept Jonathan's ring, or worse, the reason she still had it, his anger would be like a thundering avalanche of rocks. Her mind refused to go down that road. There was no reason to suspect he would find out. Ima and Aba, and the Mindells, of course, were the only ones who knew she still had Jonathan's ring. They understood, and would never mention it if that was what Rebekkah wanted.

She put the engagement ring back in its box and tucked it back into its place, then quickly made her way to the attic, accessible through a door in Lilly's old bedroom. "You've made a lot of progress," she told Shira when she arrived. "Where did that come from?"

Shira turned toward the easel behind her. "It's your great-grandmother's easel. Her 'what if' I was telling you about."

"I didn't know she was an artist," exclaimed Rebekkah, making her way to the easel.

"She had a lot of talent. I'll show you her paintings in a minute."

"Did my great-grandfather encourage her?" Rebekkah asked.

Shira stretched her back and placed her hands on her hips. "No. Not at first. They were living in the Depression. Money had to go for food, clothing, and heat. There was nothing left over for frivolities. Your great-grandmother announced one day she wanted to paint. At least that's how my own mother tells the story. Once she got something in her mind, God help the person who tried to deny her."

Rebekkah sat down on one of the sturdier boxes. She wanted to hear more about the great-grandmother she had never known. "What happened?"

"Max, your great-grandfather, tried to discourage her. That upset her and she became even more determined to paint. But she also knew there was no money, so there was nothing she could do about buying equipment. Of course, Max couldn't stand to see Rebekkah Ruth so sad, so he took an extra job during the night." Shira paused and took a breath. "Your great-grandmother thought he was out gambling, or drinking."

"Why didn't he tell her he was working a second job?" Rebekkah asked.

"He was working to buy her what she wanted. It was to be a surprise." Shira walked over to where the easel stood and dug around in a crate. She held up a small wooden box.

Rebekkah leaned forward, her chin on her fists. "What is it?"

"Paints. Twenty colors. Max worked at the tailor shop his brother-in-law owned to earn the extra money to buy Rebekkah Ruth the paints and the easel."

Rebekkah put her hand over her heart. What a touching story. She could just picture her great-grandfather working hard, then surprising his wife with the means to achieve her dream.

"Rebekkah Ruth felt so bad for being suspicious," Shira continued. "All that time she had been accusing her humble, devoted husband of gambling, and who knows what else. And here he was, working to buy her artist's supplies, just to satisfy her notion she that could paint even before she'd tried it."

"He must have loved her very much," said Rebekkah.

Shira nodded. "She loved him, too. Great-grandma Rebekkah did have talent after all. But sadly, she completed only a few pieces before Max died. She was heartbroken when he went. She never picked up her paints again. What if she had continued?" Shira shrugged. "Who knows. It's too bad she died right before you were born. So you see, we all have our 'what ifs'. We have to learn to live with them."

Rebekkah thought for a moment. "I guess we do. You were going to show me her paintings?"

"Oh, yes." Shira went to a pile and pulled out a canvas in a stretcher and held it up. "She never finished this."

Rebekkah gasped. It was a partially completed painting of the Brooklyn Bridge in the rain, a beautiful wash of blended grays. After all these years the color was still so vivid she could almost hear the rain. "May I have it?" she asked, surprising herself. "And the easel? I want to finish it. It needs to be finished."

"Really?" asked Shira. "You want to finish it?"

"Yes," said Rebekkah. "It's not right that it sits up in an attic, unfinished."

"If you really want to try."

"Please, Ima. I won't ruin it. I promise," Rebekkah pleaded.

"I didn't know you still had interest in painting. You were good when you were young, but then you never pursued it."

"I always loved it. I don't know why I put it aside." The painting pulled at Rebekkah's heart, demanding that she claim it and finish the vision that had been her namesake's. She hugged her mother. "Thank you for trusting me with it. You won't be sorry."

Shira pulled out the other four paintings that Rebekkah's great-grandmother had completed. Each seemed to Rebekkah more breathtaking than the one before it, the details and colors of each painting stunning, even after all this time.

"Ima, why didn't anyone in the family try to show these to a gallery? They're gorgeous."

"I thought so, too," said Shira. "But they were packed away and forgotten long before I became aware of them, and it never happened."

"Not only am I going to finish this painting," Rebekkah declared, "I am going to find a gallery that will take all of them. Don't sell them to anyone, whatever you do."

Shira promised not to, and she and Rebekkah spent the next three hours working side-by-side until Rebekkah announced she had to go home and clean up so she could get to the funeral home. Shira helped carry the easel and unfinished painting down to the first floor.

"Are you sure you want to do this?" asked Shira as she watched Rebekkah place the easel and painting, now tenderly wrapped in scads of tissue paper, in the car.

"Absolutely."

"Wouldn't it be wonderful if they were displayed in a gallery? Your grandma Susan would be so proud of her mother. So would the rest of the family."

Rebekkah climbed into the car and waved as she backed out of the driveway. She was glad Avram had left the car for her today since he frowned on her riding the subway to work, or anywhere else for that matter. It would have been difficult walking home the six blocks lugging a painting and easel.

She put the old easel and painting in the living room once she got home and ran a hand up and down the easel's smooth wooden surface. It was splattered with paint, and Rebekkah could easily imagine her great-grandmother using it to create art on. She left the items where they were and hurried to clean up so she could get to the funeral home.

"What are you doing with that old thing?" asked Avram when he came home later that evening and joined Rebekkah in the living room.

She hadn't mentioned her treasures to Avram all day as they'd worked, except to say she had something to show him. "The easel? It's my great-grandmother's. The one I was named after. That's the surprise I told you about at work earlier. She was an artist." She went over to the bag that held the unfinished painting, un-wrapped it, and held it up.

Avram studied it and frowned. "The colors are exceptional, I'll say that, but it doesn't look finished."

"I know. I want to finish it." Rebekkah flipped the canvas over and gazed at it.

"Finish it?" echoed Avram, his tone suggesting that Rebekkah had announced she was going to perform brain surgery that very evening.

"I was very good at art in school," she informed her husband.

He grinned at her. "Let me guess. Your mother displayed it all on the refrigerator."

"Well, yes, of course, but I also won a contest when I was in eighth grade. I'd forgotten about that until Ima showed me my great-grandmother's work."

"Eighth grade?" Avram laughed.

Rebekkah ignored his response. "I'm going to set up a studio in the attic. We've been thinking of making it into an extra bedroom, or reading room, anyway. There'll be plenty of room for an easel, paints and other supplies. If I do a decent job of finishing the painting I want to take it, and my great-grandmother's other pieces that Ima has, to a gallery."

Avram draped an arm over Rebekkah's shoulder and gave it an affectionate squeeze. "I see no harm in you trying to paint a little, but I wouldn't take your great-grandmother's paintings, or the one you're determined to finish, to a gallery. Chances are they'll turn you away. I don't want you to be disappointed when that happens and come home crushed."

She bristled at his attitude. He already had her failing. "I won't be crushed, Avram. I bet if she had finished this one and taken the others to a gallery my great-grandmother would be a famous name in art now." She chewed on her bottom lip. "I hope I don't ruin this painting, but I want to try. Maybe I do have talent, but it's been lying dormant."

"The only talent I care about is your cooking talent." Avram rubbed his stomach. "I'm going to relax and watch TV while you make dinner. If it makes you happy to take up a little hobby, I don't have a problem with it. Remember, not everyone can be Picasso. I'm only trying to save you from heartache."

"You don't have to save me," Rebekkah huffed. "I'm not going to fall apart if nothing comes of this."

"Maybe not, but it's my responsibility to protect you, and save you from getting hurt."

She opened her mouth to argue that she could handle being hurt. Hadn't she in the past? But Avram was speaking again, and she couldn't get a word in.

"Until we get the attic in order I'll make a place for you to paint in the dining room. The light coming in from the window should be good for that."

Their dining room was huge, and they rarely used it, choosing instead to eat in the kitchen. Rebekkah instantly forgave Avram for treating her like a delicate piece of porcelain, which he was prone to doing, and decided not to argue with him. It was nice of him to offer to make her a place to try painting. She was eager to get started. "That's a good idea, thank you."

"You're quiet. What are you thinking so hard about?" Avram asked Rebekkah a half hour later while they sat in the kitchen together, eating the dinner she had hastily put together.

Her fork paused midway to her mouth. "The painting. I already have an idea of how to start. Tomorrow I'm going to go get paints."

"How do you know what kind to get?"

"I don't," Rebekkah admitted. "I'm going to find a good paint shop and take my painting with me so they can help."

He studied his plate, frowning.

"Something wrong?" she asked when he didn't reply.

"Not really. I want you to have a hobby. I hope you'll still have time to tend to the house and pay attention to me. Mark and I depend on your help at work."

He sounded like a little boy, Rebekkah thought. She got up and stood behind Avram, wrapping her arms around her his neck, then sliding her hands down his chest. Her chin rested on his head. "Of course I will. I won't be painting twenty-four hours a day. I love keeping our house in order. That won't change. Some women sew or knit, or I don't know, watch TV all day, I guess. I'm going to paint."

Avram kissed the back of Rebekkah's hand. "Then I can't wait to see it when you're done."

Glad that he seemed satisfied, she sat and ate the rest of her dinner. When she and Avram headed for bed later and he reached for her, the last thing on her mind after they made love was her great-grandmother's painting.

THREE

"You should have all you need to finish that beautiful painting," the man waiting on her at Ullman's Art Supply told Rebekkah as he scooped up her paints and brushes and put them in a bag.

It had been two weeks since Rebekkah had taken her great-grandmother's unfinished painting home, and she was excited to finally have a chance to get the supplies she needed to finish it.

"Now, I suggest you use a pane of glass to mix your paints. The plastic and wood palettes can be hard to clean," he continued.

"Do you carry them?" she asked as she wrapped the painting back up and fished in her purse for her wallet.

"Sure do. Be right back."

"Thank you." She smiled at him as she pulled out two twenty dollar bills.

He was back a few minutes later. "Here you are." He put a finger to his lips and his brow furrowed. "Let's see. You got the grays you need and the red, we picked your

33

brushes. Anything else I can help you with? Canvas? Pencils? Paper?"

She laughed. "No, this will be fine for now. I'm finishing this before I attempt anything else. My great-grandmother's painting reminded me of how much I used to love painting, but I'm afraid I haven't done any of it since before high school."

The man leaned toward her. "From what I saw of that piece of work there, if painting's in your genes, you'll be better than good. We offer lessons if you're interested."

"You do? Do you mind if I ask your name? You've been so helpful."

"Glad to be of help. I'm Bill. My wife, Edith and I have owned this store for almost thirty years. I hope you'll be a repeat customer, Miss?"

"Mrs." she automatically corrected. "Rebekkah Gelles. But please, call me Rebekkah."

"Pleased to meet you, Rebekkah. Here, take one of our business cards in case you want to call about the lessons."

She took the card from him. "I'll keep them in mind, thank you."

Bill handed Rebekkah the bag with her supplies in it and the pane of glass he had wrapped in newspaper. "Glad you stopped in. Have yourself a good day."

"Thank you so much. Have a good day yourself," she answered as she made her way out of the store.

When she got home she changed into old clothes. She and Avram had rearranged the dining room furniture a few nights ago, so she had a comfy niche in the corner for her easel and chair. He had retrieved an old bookcase from the basement for storing her supplies. The sun spilling in through the dining room window provided excellent light as she got to work.

"Looks like you've made a good start," said Avram when he came home from work a few hours later and found Rebekkah in the kitchen cleaning paint brushes.

She yanked a paper towel from its roll and laid her brushes down to dry. Turning off the faucet she turned around to give him a lingering kiss. "Did you look at it?"

"I certainly did. You've done well."

Rebekkah was gratified to hear the approval in his voice, until he spoke again.

"Don't be disappointed if you can't finish it."

Her heart sank. His words stung. "Of course I'll finish it. Why would you say that? You can see I'm almost done." Rebekkah waved toward her easel in the dining room. "I may take art lessons from that little store around the corner. I want to continue to paint. This one should be done in a couple of days."

To her surprise, he didn't look too pleased at the thought. "You don't think I should take lessons?"

"What if you aren't any good? Will lessons help?"

"What if I am good?"

35

"I'm trying to protect you." He ran a hand through his hair. "I can tell by the unhappy look on your face you're going to accuse me of treating you like a child again."

"Wrong. I'm going to accuse you of treating me like a fragile child."

He ran a hand across his chin and gazed toward the painting. "You're right."

"I am?"

"Yes, I suppose so. If you want lessons, take them. If you don't have talent, you'll find out soon enough. If you do, maybe you'll stop worrying about having children. So you have my blessing. I'm headed to the living room. Want to join me?"

Rebekkah nodded. "For a bit."

"You took that book on fertility testing back, didn't you?"

"Avram," Rebekkah came to an abrupt halt at the entrance of their living room. "Painting isn't going to make me not want to have children. But, yes, before I went to the art store I went to the library to find a couple of art books I needed, and I dropped off the book on fertility issues."

He dropped to his recliner. "Good girl. I'm glad you decided I was right. You're a good wife. What's for dinner?"

"Meatloaf and a salad. It'll be ready in about a half an hour. I didn't decide you were right. I read the whole book before I took it back. I want to tell you what could be preventing us from becoming parents."

Avram glared at her, but said nothing.

Rebekkah didn't let the dark look on his face deter her, even though her heart pounded. "I know you think we have time, but you're forty-five and—"

"And what?" he interrupted. "You want someone younger, is that it?"

It was hard to hide her frustration. "No, that's not my point. I wouldn't have married you if I wanted someone younger. I want children while you can still enjoy them."

"So, this is about my age."

"I admit it's about your age as far as children are concerned, not as far as my feelings for you are concerned."

Rebekkah thanked God when Avram's expression lightened a little. "Come on, sit down. Aren't you happy just being my wife? Caring for our home?"

"Of course I am." She moved to the couch facing him and sat on the edge. "Children will complete my happiness. Please don't put me off this time. This means a lot to me, and I need you to listen to me. Please."

Blood rushed to Avram's face. He had a temper at times and she could see he was struggling to control it. She had to be careful not to say anything that would make him shut her out.

"I didn't know I married such a spitfire," he finally said. "Okay. You win. I'll listen to you. You'll listen to me.

Then the issue will be closed. I love you, Rebekkah, but I am your husband, and with my many years of life experience I think I know more about the world than you."

What that had to do with anything Rebekkah didn't know, but since he had allotted her time to speak about the subject, she chose not to go down that road, and quickly gathered her thoughts, feeling as if she were on trial with only a few minutes to make her case. She pulled a piece of folded paper out of the pocket of her skirt and smoothed it out.

"You took notes?" Avram asked, a smile twitching on his lips. He pulled the lever on the recliner's side so the footrest kicked out and stretched out his legs. "Go ahead." He motioned at her with a grand gesture. "I'm listening."

Rebekkah cleared her throat and gave a last glance at Avram to make sure he was truly listening. "For women there could be ovulation issues, damaged fallopian tubes, or menstrual irregularities. Men can have issues with their sperm, like the count, the volume, and the shape." She put her notes on the coffee table and her eyes held Avram's. "We'd have to have blood tests, ultrasounds of my uterus and fallopian tubes. They would analyze your semen."

"Is that it?" he asked.

"That's the gist of it."

"What if there is something wrong with one of us? Will you then accept that it's God's will we don't have children?"

38

"No, I won't," she replied, trying not to lose patience. "Finding out if there is a problem is just the first step. Do you have any idea how many options are out there? How many ways there are to get pregnant?"

"If you mean other than the natural way, I consider them against God's will," he informed her.

"No, Avram, they're not. I've done research and have read nothing that indicates fertility testing, or in vitro fertilization, are against God's will. I don't understand why you are so sure it's sacrilegious to consider conception assistance," Rebekkah pressed. She wouldn't be able to believe in such a cruel God.

He didn't answer her question and instead asked his own. "What happens if we do in vitro fertilization and there's a lab mix up, God forbid? What if we end up with a child who is not really Jewish because of that?"

"I don't want a lab mix up, either. We could work out all those issues with Rabbi Weissman and my gynecologist. Can't you at least try to see my point of view?"

"Human interference with conception is wrong for us. I'm not going to masturbate so they can collect my ejaculation. You know that's forbidden."

"You don't need to do that, there are other ways to collect your sperm that are in accordance with Halacha."

He kicked the footrest of the recliner down then rose and joined Rebekkah, taking one of her hands in his. "My sweet, innocent wife. Before we consider all that, maybe you should pray harder. Like Sarah, Rebekah, and Samson's mother."

Was Avram suggesting that her failure to conceive was her fault because she hadn't prayed enough? Rebekkah prayed all the time. She was a good wife, like Avram himself had just said, and he couldn't doubt she would be a good mother. What man is going to marry a woman he thinks wouldn't be a good mother to his children?

"The Talmud says Isaac was the one with fertility issues," she argued, hoping Avram would relax a little, not be so rigid and unyielding with his rhetoric.

"Rebekkah, these women prayed and God opened their wombs."

"When you're ill, Avram, don't you seek medical treatment?"

He ignored her question. "Look at Hannah, Rachel, and Michal. 'God desires the prayers of the righteous,' say the rabbis in the Talmud. And in Genesis, when Rachel pleads with Jacob to give her children or else she will die, he responds, 'Am I in the place of God who has withheld from you the fruit of your belly.' Then it goes on to read, 'God remembered Rachel and God heard her and God opened her womb.'"

"You're telling me I'm not righteous enough?" cried Rebekkah in disbelief.

"No, I'm telling you to try praying harder. Your problem could be with God, not with me. Look at it as a way to become more observant. It couldn't hurt, could it?"

Rebekkah was fed up with Avram lecturing her. "Stop talking about ancient biblical people. I want to have a discussion about conceiving children in the 21st century, not participate in a history or religion class."

Avram looked as if Rebekkah had stuck him. She sucked in a breath, afraid for a moment she had gone too far.

"I was the one who suggested you practice family purity, was I not?" he asked. "You told me you were grateful, that it made you closer to God. Now I suggest you spend more time in prayer to help you get pregnant, and you act as if I'm punishing you. I'm trying to do things that are for your own good. Things that may help you conceive."

More and more often Avram was telling her he was doing things for 'her own good.' At first, it was sweet, and Rebekkah loved being taken care of. After the raw emotion of losing Jonathan it was a relief to let someone take charge, to feel loved and cherished. What Avram continually failed to see was that she was a grown woman with her own mind. Another reason for children, she thought, so he would stop treating her like one, and start treating her as a wife, as his equal.

Rebekkah had indeed started practicing family purity at Avram's suggestion after they were married, and she loved it. Her parents were Conservative Jews, but her mother had never gone to a mikveh. At least as far as she knew. But Rebekkah couldn't accept Avram's opinion that failure to be righteous enough was why she hadn't become pregnant.

She wondered if she had married Avram too quickly, before she knew enough about him. She certainly knew next to nothing about his family. He rarely spoke of them. About the only thing she knew was that they lived somewhere in the Midwest, and that Avram had ended up in New York for college.

To give them some credit, they had come back East for her and Avram's wedding, but they seemed aloof and cold to Rebekkah in contrast to her own family. They had gone home immediately after the reception. Attempts by Rebekkah to get to know them in the limited time she had with them were met with bland indifference on their part. She found it odd they didn't seem at all interested in the woman their son had chosen for his life partner. Wasn't it a joyous occasion for them, as it was for her parents? When Rebekkah approached Avram about their attitude he advised her not to take it personally. "That's the way they are," he'd said.

Avram had told her he had been brought up as a Conservative Jew, but lately she noticed him becoming more observant. Now, it certainly sounded as if he also wanted her to become more observant, too. He had made comments lately about her wearing skirts and dresses instead of jeans and pants. He was suddenly wearing his yarmulke every day, and occasionally expressed the desire that they go to an Orthodox synagogue instead of the Conservative Beth Israel. The synagogue where they had been married and the one she was used to. Her family and friends went there.

Settling back on the couch, Rebekkah focused her attention on Avram again. "Soon you'll have me wearing a sheitel." She couldn't imagine covering her hair with a wig like some very religious Jewish women did. She respected their reasons for doing so, but still, the wigs looked hot and uncomfortable.

Avram leaned toward Rebekkah and caressed her face. His fingers entwined in the long, dark blond hair he loved. "Would you wear one if I asked?"

"I hope you aren't going to ask," she retorted. "I already wear a scarf when I go out. We're way off the topic here. Since you seem to be so taken with the law, let's talk to Rabbi Weissman. I'll agree to abide by his word if you will."

This was the first serious stumbling block in their marriage. If he refused to see the rabbi, refused to go for testing, what future did they have?

Deflated when Avram didn't reply, Rebekkah got up. "I'll get dinner." Dinner she was in no mood to eat. They hadn't resolved anything. Tears gathered in her eyes.

"Wait!" Avram stood up and called before she disappeared from his view.

Rebekkah turned and looked expectantly at him.

"Okay. I'll go see Rabbi Weissman."

She flew into his arms. "Thank you," she whispered, hugging him. "I'll call him now. It's still early, maybe he can see us after dinner."

"Whoa, not so fast," protested Avram. "I don't have to be at the funeral home until tomorrow afternoon, why don't you ask if he can see us tomorrow morning."

"And you promise to abide by what he says?"

"I told you I'll go see him," replied Avram, laying his chin on Rebekkah's head.

She settled for that, sure in her heart Avram would be persuaded by the rabbi to go for fertility testing. She went into the kitchen to finish dinner and call Rabbi Weissman.

"I know many Jews still shun technological assistance with conception." The rabbi picked up a book from his desk, flipping the pages. "But I believe that Judaic philosophy encourages it." He read from the book: "The Lubavitcher Rebbe quoted the previous Rebbe as saying that 'a person should actually give up his existence in order to have children.'"

Rebekkah was riveted by what he was saying. He sounded so wise.

"The first Commandment from God to Adam was 'Be fruitful and multiply.' Not conceiving in three years is no reason to panic, but there is a big concern." The rabbi leaned toward Rebekkah. "You aren't the first couple I've spoken to with this problem. And we men have our pride, don't we?" He threw Avram a conciliatory smile.

"I've done extensive research, but before we talk about the options that are acceptable to the ethics of Halacha, such as artificial insemination and in vitro fertilization, the first step is for both of you to be diagnosed and treated."

Rebekkah slanted her eyes sideways while the rabbi was speaking to see how well the rabbi's words were sitting with Avram. Her heart plummeted. It didn't matter that

Rabbi Weissman had explained that thousands of Jewish children had been born as a result of in vitro fertilization, Avram's stony look told her he wasn't buying any of it. She reluctantly turned her attention back to Rabbi Weissman, wishing she could read her husband's mind.

"Rebekkah, if no problem is found in you, Avram would be evaluated. As your rabbi, I strongly recommend doing just that. You can rest assured I will be more than happy to guide you through it."

"I find the idea of in vitro repugnant. The thought of a baby coming from a test tube, of masturbating to create a baby, seems too cold and scientific," Avram burst out.

Rabbi Weissman leaned back and chuckled. "If you're trying to shock me, you've failed. I've heard all this before."

"How can I bring myself to masturbate when I have such a beautiful wife?" he continued.

"Avram!" Rebekkah's loud exclamation would surely let him know how deeply he had embarrassed her.

Rabbi Weissman continued, not in the least disturbed by Avram's statement. "Some more liberal Orthodox and Conservative Halachists allow for masturbation if the doctor deems it to be the best way to get the most accurate results. They base it on Halachic precedents allowing one to follow a doctor's advice even if it contradicts Torah values. Of course, most traditional Orthodox rabbis strictly limit ejaculation, requiring the woman to undergo a full battery of testing before any of the semen collection strategies are used.

45

"Once semen testing is deemed necessary, Orthodox Rabbis set rules on which mode of sperm collection is preferable. Do you want to discuss that now?"

"No." Avram sprang from his chair. "I think you've given us enough information, Rabbi. We appreciate your time very much. Rebekkah, let's go."

She rose, further embarrassed that Avram was not trying to hide the fact that he couldn't wait to get out of there. Not wishing to cause a scene, she stood up, too. "Yes, thank you, Rabbi. You've given us a lot of good information."

"My pleasure. Call me if you need anything at all. I'm here for both of you. I can tell you from my own experience that children are indeed a special blessing."

"I refuse to set foot in that place again," Avram snapped as soon as they'd entered their car.

Rebekkah went cold. "What?"

"I really do want us to go to an Orthodox synagogue."

"Oh, Avram, no. Why? Just because you disagree with the rabbi? You didn't even try. You were completely closed off to his words. He was giving us the Orthodox viewpoint anyway, so what use would going to an Orthodox synagogue do? Face it, the problem is not me, or what synagogue we attend, the problem is you. You don't want children."

His fingers gripped the steering wheel and he closed his eyes, saying nothing. Rebekkah's stomach churned.

He finally looked at her. "I want you. Is that so bad? Don't you think I haven't thought of my age? If you got pregnant tonight, I'll be sixty-six when my child is twenty. That's too old."

Avram's words shocked Rebekkah. Why hadn't he said anything before they were married? Tears welled and she brushed them away. "You knew I wanted children. You also knew there were more than just a couple of years between our ages. You could have been honest before now. You led me to believe you wanted children, too."

"I didn't lead you to believe anything."

Rebekkah's mind scrambled to recall the conversations she and Avram had had before their marriage. She had been adamant about wanting children. Surely, he had been also. All she remembered was talking about her and Jonathan's plan to have as many children as they could. That was back when Avram was still working to make her fall in love with him. Before he decided certain subjects were off limits.

Avram's deep voice filled the car. "I let you have your say. I saw Rabbi Weissman, and now I am finished discussing this. Don't make a tsimmes out of it."

"Don't make a big deal out of it? Are you kidding?" Rebekkah cried. "It is a big deal."

"So, what do we do?" he whispered hoarsely. "My God, I love you so much, Rebekkah, but what's done is done. You're my wife now. You aren't going to change that, and I can't change my age. I can't magically make you pregnant. It is what it is."

47

"That's the end of it then?" She couldn't believe that Rabbi Weissman had failed to change Avram's mind.

He started up the car and they headed toward home. "For me, yes. As I told you before, reach out to God for your children. Using science to manipulate God's will is wrong."

Rebekkah turned to face him. "It's not the end of it for me, Avram."

"What does that mean? Are you saying you would divorce me over this?"

"No, I'm not saying that right now."

Avram grabbed her hand from her lap and squeezed it.

She yelped and pulled her hand away, rubbing it.

"I'm sorry. I didn't mean to hurt you. You won't divorce me. You love me. I don't intend on ever letting you go. I would go crazy without you."

She shivered. Avram's words sounded like a threat. Instinct warned not to say anything more, but at that moment a thick wall had been erected between them. In Rebekkah's mind it was made of heavy square brown stones piled one on top of the other.

By the time they arrived home, Avram was chatting about other things, totally oblivious to Rebekkah's distress. He had no clue to the feelings of disappointment raging in her. When he kissed her goodbye and left for work, she felt nothing but relief.

She truly didn't want their marriage to end over this, but how long could she love Avram if her feelings meant so little to him that he refused to get tested. Maybe she wouldn't divorce him right now, but what if she refused to make love to him? Let him think she would divorce him? How far would he go to keep her? Might he agree to testing? Rebekkah almost laughed, thinking of herself as a woman scheming to get what she wanted. It was so unlike her. But it would only be for a little while. Avram, and God would surely forgive her.

An hour after Rebekkah had seen Avram off to work she was in a taxi, on her way to the Upper West Side in Manhattan. A visit Avram had no idea she made at least once a month. She had her cell phone if he needed to contact her, and she would be home long before he was.

FOUR

When the taxi dropped her off, Rebekkah trotted up the steps of the Mindells' townhouse and rang the bell.

"Darling!" Pamela Mindell swung the door open and greeted Rebekkah. After exchanging kisses on each other's cheeks, Pamela studied Rebekkah. "How are you? How's Avram?"

Rebekkah took in Pamela's perfectly coiffed hair, the make up so well done it was barely discernible, and her impeccable peach-colored suit. Even though she probably wasn't going to leave the apartment, Pamela looked perfect, as if she had stepped out of the *New York Times* society page, in which she and her husband, Alex, appeared occasionally. Only those who knew her well could see the lingering sadness over Jonathan that had dimmed her blue eyes.

Rebekkah had finally reached out to the Mindells two months after the accident. Since then, she had been coming to visit once or twice a month. She and Pamela had grown even closer. There was no resentment on the

Mindell's part that Rebekkah was unmarked by the accident.

She didn't want to burden Pamela with her problems with Avram. They were miniscule compared to what Pamela had endured. "We're both fine. What about you and Alex?"

Pamela smiled faintly. "You know how it is. We have our bad days and good days, but the good usually outweighs the bad. We haven't seen you in a while. Alex and I thought maybe you had decided not—"

"No," Rebekkah broke in, reading Pamela's mind. "I'll never do that. I'm sorry it's been so long since I've come over."

"Darling," said Pamela gently, stroking the back of Rebekkah's head. "I can't imagine not having you drop by either. But you have your own life. We understand."

"You'll always be a part of my life," insisted Rebekkah. "Nothing can change that."

Pamela nodded imperceptibly. "I'm glad. Alex and I would miss you terribly. You're like another daughter to us. Go on up. I'll have a snack with you when you come down. Julia made brownies."

Rebekkah's stomach grumbled reminding her she hadn't eaten lunch. Julia was Pamela's cook, and she made the best brownies Rebekkah had ever eaten. "And you're like a second mother to me."

Pamela hugged Rebekkah. "May it always be so. Go on." She glanced toward the staircase and pressed a finger to the inside corner of her eye. "Before you make me cry."

Rebekkah took the long wide staircase to the second floor. Her fingers gripped the white-spindled banister, and she couldn't help noticing how the dark wood on either side of the royal blue carpet gleamed. Dust didn't have a chance in Pamela's home. Rebekkah walked past the first bedroom, which belonged to Pamela and Alex. Jonathan's bedroom was the last one on the right. Next to his bedroom, was where Kimberly, his nurse, stayed when she had to. The other two bedrooms in the hallway had been converted to guest bedrooms.

Jonathan's door was open, and Rebekkah felt the same fear and hope she felt every time she entered his room. Fear he would be gone   truly dead—and hope that this would be the day he would come out of the persistent vegetative state he had been in since the accident, throw his arms around her, and they would stitch their old life back together. But in her heart Rebekkah accepted that even if by some miracle that did happen, their old life was gone, forever.

Pamela and Alex still held out hope their son would come back to them. They couldn't bring themselves to take out his feeding tube, or send him to a hospital that specialized in severe brain injuries. They had the means and the money to keep him at home, so they did. Pamela sometimes confessed to Rebekkah that she feared they were being selfish by holding on to him, but every time they discussed pulling out his feeding tube and letting nature take its course, Pamela became so overwrought that Alex didn't have the heart to insist.

As usual, guilt stabbed her conscience as Rebekkah pulled the chair closer to Jonathan's bed and sat. She wasn't here because she was still in love with him. Her love for him had very gradually changed to affection. Now he was more like another brother to her. Even though she was still angry with Avram, he was her husband, and it was him she loved. These moments with Jonathan were a shelter, a refuge, when things got rough. She could share her deepest secrets and fears with him. She prayed somewhere inside he heard her and felt her there with him.

His eyes were closed. That meant he was probably in a sleep cycle. It had been strange visiting him at first. When his eyes were open, they would move and stop randomly. He sometimes smiled or cried. Kimberly had explained to Rebekkah that, in reality, Jonathan could no longer think, reason, or relate to his environment. It was only because his brain stem was still intact that he retained his motor reflexes, heart rate, respiration, and blood pressure. But he would never recognize anyone again.

Rebekkah leaned forward and rested an arm across the blue cotton blanket. He was so thin and pale. His muscles had atrophied, and even his brown hair had faded. He was a shell, his spirit long gone. She wondered if he would have wanted to be kept suspended between life and death like this. They had never discussed anything like it during their engagement. There had been no reason to.

She sometimes agreed with Pamela, that it was selfish of them, herself included, to want to keep Jonathan here in his bedroom, a shrine that his parents, siblings, and she could visit. The Mindell's used to include Rebekkah in their discussions about Jonathan, but as she was married to another man now, she felt she had no right to help decide the fate of her ex-fiancé.

Rebekkah stood, and wandered to the window, peeking out the blinds. "I'm still not pregnant. I don't even think Avram wants kids. I'm so angry at him." She turned back to the bed. "You must like that I can finally visit you without crying my eyes out." She straightened his blanket for him, even though there was nothing wrong with it.

Rebekkah placed her lips on his cool forehead then sat back down, resting her head on his chest for a moment. When she picked up her head, his eyes came open. His clear blue eyes, like his mother's, looked right into hers. He blinked then grimaced.

"Jonathan? Jon?" Rebekkah grabbed his hand, and jumped up, for a second thinking that he had really made his way back. In the next instant she sank back into the chair, knowing the reaction was what Kimberly had told her, automatic behavior that didn't require any functioning of the thinking part of the brain. She should know that by now, but she felt fresh hope every time it happened.

"Sometimes, I really believe you can hear me," she whispered.

His room was unchanged. Still decorated with posters of his favorite team-the New York Giants, pictures of his family, and pictures of Jon and her together. Kimberly played music for Jonathan on a small CD player that sat on a bookshelf still filled with his college textbooks. Sometimes Kimberly sat in his room with Pamela and Alex, and they all watched TV. Kimberly was a godsend and so devoted to her charge.

"What do you think I should I do? Avram won't get tested. I want a baby. It's so frustrating. I love him, but he's so stubborn. He treats me as if I'm twelve half the time. I don't want to divorce him, but I want a baby so much. Every time I see a woman pushing a stroller, or comforting a child with a scraped knee, I get so jealous."

Jonathan groaned and closed his eyes again.

Rebekkah found herself grinning. "You want me to stop talking, is that it? Or are you telling me I should hang in there with Avram for a while? I intend to, but this time I'm not about to let this go away like he wants."

Rebekkah gave him one more look. "I'll be back." She squeezed his arm lightly. "Wait for me, okay?"

"How's our boy doing?" asked Pamela when Rebekkah joined her in the living room.

"He's good I think. He looks peaceful."

"I like to think your visits mean something to him." Pamela offered Rebekkah the plate of brownies. "These are sinfully delicious. I'm sure I'll ruin my dinner, but I don't care."

Rebekkah ate hers in two bites. "Delicious," she pronounced. "I hope my coming helps him in some way. I don't know if he appreciated listening to me talk about Avram. It's hard to realize when you're looking at him that nothing's registering."

Pamela nodded in agreement. "I find myself talking to him about things I never would have if he were...alive. You've never told Avram you come see Jonathan, have you?"

"No. He wouldn't understand. He's a little possessive. He hates when other men notice me. Not that Jonathan is noticing me. I know it's probably wrong of me, but I need to see him sometimes. And you and Alex of course." Rebekkah took another brownie.

"Maybe if you told him you wouldn't feel guilty about coming. He might surprise you and be supportive and understanding," Pamela offered.

Rebekkah almost choked. Avram would be more understanding if she told him she wanted to become a female wrestler. But she knew Pamela's advice came with good intentions. She checked the time and pulled out her cell phone. "I better call a taxi. Thank you for the brownies."

Pamela wrapped a couple of brownies in a napkin and stood. "Here, take one for the ride home. You're welcome here anytime. Think about what I said. I don't want to pry into your relationship with Avram. I'm glad you found him and I can tell you love him. Just remember, sometimes dishonesty comes back to haunt us."

"I know. I promise to think about it. Give my love to Alex, okay?"

"I will. Talk to you soon, I hope."

"You will," replied Rebekkah. She leaned in for Pamela's good-bye hug.

Rebekkah had just finished a turkey sandwich and the last brownie Pamela had sent her home with when the doorbell rang. She opened it to find a well-dressed woman standing there. "Yes?"

"Good afternoon. I'm Cindy Gates-Barber. Is Mr. Gelles at home?"

"No, he's not. Was he expecting you?" Rebekkah asked.

"He said he would be here." The woman scowled as if Avram not being at home had put a severe damper on her day. "He wanted me to bring his wife—"

"Here's his car now," interrupted Rebekkah, surprised at seeing Avram pull into an empty space across the street. What was he doing home so early?

"Oh good," gushed the woman. She turned and watched Avram get out of the car, her hands folded primly in front of her, the toe of one shoe tapping against the cement in a staccato rhythm.

Seconds later, Avram joined the woman at the front door. "Ms. Barber. I'm glad I made it in time. Come in, come in."

His eyes briefly met Rebekkah's as she stepped aside to let Avram and his visitor in. He brushed a kiss on Rebekkah's forehead.

"Who is this? "Rebekkah managed to whisper in his ear.

"Sweetheart, this is Cindy Gates-Barber. Ms. Barber, this is—"

"This must be your lovely daughter," Ms. Barber effused.

A laugh escaped Rebekkah as Avram scowled. It was probably her low cut jeans and her Hard Rock Café t-shirt that made the woman think she was Avram's daughter. As amused as she was, Rebekkah tried to stifle her laugh for Avram's sake.

"She's my wife," Avram ground out.

The woman clutched at her chest as her face turned a bright shade of red. "I'm so sorry...I didn't realize. I thought...I'm sorry..."

Avram was still glaring at the poor woman, so Rebekkah decided to put her out of her misery. She held out her hand. "It's okay. Rebekkah Gelles."

"Mrs. Gelles. So nice to meet you." Her head swiveled between Rebekkah and Avram, her face still a warm pink. Her free hand fussed at the buttons of her blouse. She made Rebekkah think of a fish flopping around on dry land.

"Why don't we sit down in the living room," Avram suggested, ignoring Rebekkah's questioning look.

As soon as they were settled, Ms. Barber, once again all business, pulled out a glossy brochure. "As I told you when you came by my office, Mr. Gelles, this condominium won't last long. The owners have dropped the price to three million seven hundred and fifty thousand.

Rebekkah couldn't believe her ears. She couldn't sit silent another second. "Wait a minute. You're a real estate agent?"

"Well, yes. Mr. Gelles told me you were thinking of moving to Manhattan and asked me to come by with a brochure of my best listings for you. This one will be perfect for growing family. It has three bedrooms and—"

"I'm sorry Ms. Barber, but I—"

The woman held up a hand to stop Rebekkah from speaking. "Please, call me Cindy. We're going to be working together on finding the perfect home for you, and I think this is it right here in my hand," she waved the brochure under Rebekkah's nose, "no need to be formal."

Rebekkah smiled sweetly. "I need to speak to my husband in private, Cindy. Would you excuse us for a few minutes? Would you like some water or ginger ale?"

"No, thank you. I'm fine. Please, take all the time you need. I'm not going anywhere. Here, take at the brochure. Once you look at it, you will love it," replied Cindy flinging an arm across the back of the couch and crossing her legs.

Rebekkah took it out of Cindy's hand and got up. "Avram?"

Reluctantly, he stood. "Excuse us, please."

Rebekkah took his hand and dragged him across the hall, through the kitchen, and into the dining room, leaving Ms. Barber out of earshot.

"Why is a real estate agent sitting in our living room?" Rebekkah hissed.

Avram hung his head for a second then placed his hands on either side of Rebekkah's face. "Sweetheart, I thought we would move to a bigger place, that's all. It's a better neighborhood, the best schools, and business-wise, a better address. You know, better for my image."

"I don't want to move. I love our neighborhood now. What's wrong with Park Slope? What's wrong with your image, and which one of us is going to school? My parents are within walking distance, my friends are here, and we were just talking about expanding the attic."

"If we move, we won't have to do that. You can convert one of the bedrooms to your studio. You can't be tethered to your parents forever."

Rebekkah bristled. "I am hardly tethered to them. They never come without an invitation. I don't go over there every day. Your funeral home is minutes away. What do you mean by 'a better address'?"

"Mark and I are thinking of expanding. I want to build the business, make a bigger name for myself. And Mark, too of course," he added hastily. "I want Gelles & Bender to be *the* place to have a funeral."

She was dumbfounded. "You want to be the Donald Trump of funeral homes? People mourn at funerals; they're a solemn occasion. They want a personal touch, reassurance that you really care about what they're going through. You, Mark, and Amy do a wonderful job of doing that now."

"Look, let's just listen to Ms. Barber. You're going to love this condominium. I know it. Please, for me," Avram begged.

Fine," Rebekkah relented. "I'll go listen, but only because it's rude to leave a guest waiting. We'll talk about this later, but I don't want to move."

Rebekkah followed Avram back to the living room. She couldn't wait until this woman left. How dare he consult a real estate agent without even mentioning it to her? She would never do such a thing.

She glanced at the brochure Cindy had insisted she take. It was a beautiful condominium she admitted to herself, but so was their current home. So what that it was bigger. Did they need bigger? Who spent millions of dollars on a home? They couldn't afford this. They couldn't even afford the taxes. Avram must be out of his mind. She couldn't even concentrate on what Cindy was saying.

Finally, she stood to leave. "It was so nice meeting you, Mrs. Gelles. I hope you and Mr. Gelles will look at this soon. It won't last long. How about this Saturday?"

"We don't conduct business on Saturday," Avram informed her. "We're Jewish."

Cindy wasn't deterred. "Sunday, then." She dug in her bag and pulled out her phone and began typing on the tiny keyboard.

Avram guided her to the front door. "I'll discuss it with my wife and get back to you."

As soon as the woman was gone, Rebekkah headed to the bedroom. Avram came in seconds later. "Did you like it?"

She sank down on their bed. "How can you consider moving? You never consulted me, never asked me if I wanted to move. Marriage is a partnership, Avram. Tell me again how we would pay for that condominium?"

He sat beside her and put an arm around her shoulder. "The business is doing very well. I have money put away. We can do this."

"I thought you liked this neighborhood. We bought this brownstone soon after we married. Now you want to sell it?"

"I think we're ready to move on, that's all."

Rebekkah jumped off the bed and leaned against her dresser, facing him. "I'm not. You want to expand the business, but you haven't yet. I'm still angry and hurt that you won't consider fertility testing. Why should I be so eager to do what you want?"

Avram wrinkled his brow and looked hurt. Rebekkah refused to melt the way she always did when he looked at her like that. She waited.

"I'm sorry, sweetheart," he finally said. "You're right. I should have consulted you. In my haste to provide the best for you I went overboard. I just want to take care of you."

"I know." She went over to Avram and held his head to her breast and caressed it. "I know you want to take care of me. But I want to be your partner. I don't want you to make decisions for me. For us. Big ones, I mean."

He kissed her palm. "It would be a good move, Rebekkah. It's near B'nai Torah. I want to start attending there. I've mentioned this before."

She'd hoped he'd forgotten. "They're Orthodox," she replied, as if he didn't know. "I don't know if we would feel comfortable there. I wasn't brought up that way and neither were you. At least that's what you said."

He leaned back and his eyes made a slow journey from her face down to her thighs. "I want us to be more devout. Look at you in those tight jeans and small t-shirt. You're so sexy, Rebekkah Gelles. But I don't want you looking that way for other men. Only for me. No wonder that woman thought you were my daughter. Can't you try and be more modest?"

Not this again, she thought. "You want me to only wear long sleeves and long skirts? I have long skirts I wear sometimes. I don't want to do that all the time."

"How about a compromise," he came back with. "No pants, but the skirts don't have to be long, just make sure they are below the knee."

"There is nothing wrong with the way I dress. What's gotten into you? You never complained about my clothing when we were first married."

"You're so beautiful. I don't want other men to ogle you."

"I love only you. If men ogle me, I don't notice and I don't care. I can't be someone I'm not. Even for you. I agree not to wear tight jeans and skimpy t-shirts outside our home, but that's it. I'll do modest, but fashionable. Looking nice is important to me." She looked him in the eyes. "I shouldn't even be agreeing to anything you want. I'm still angry at you for not agreeing to fertility testing."

"Rebekkah." Avram's voice held a thousand dark warnings. "You know my feelings. They haven't changed.

Pray, and you will be surprised how happy God makes you. Your womb is in God's hands." With that he left the bedroom.

She didn't follow him. Instead she climbed up on their bed, leaned against the headboard, and hugged a pillow. Were the reasons he gave her for wanting to move and become more religious true? It seemed like was trying to control every aspect of her life, and separate her from the people who were important to her. She wasn't going to let him do that, not until she had what she wanted above all else: Children. It wasn't as if she had given Avram reason not to trust her. She could be religious without being covered from head to toe.

They barely spoke the rest of the day. Rebekkah hated that the wall between them seemed to be growing, but she couldn't allow herself to give in to his demands. It was after midnight when he joined her in bed. She awoke from a fitful sleep as soon as the mattress shifted and she felt his warmth beside her. Despite their recent issues and their age difference, their sex life had never been a disappointment to either of them. Refusing him was going to be more difficult than she thought, Rebekkah acknowledged as she remembered her plan to not make love with him.

As if reading her thoughts, Avram turned toward her and his lips brushed her neck. One of his legs covered hers, and she could feel him hard already against her bottom. She bit her lip. This definitely wasn't going to be easy. Her body wanted nothing more than to open up to him, despite her frustration and anger. Besides, how was she supposed to get pregnant by not having sex? It would

64

only be for a little while, she told herself. He had to come around and agree to be tested. She shook his leg off. "Not now," she mumbled. "I'm trying to sleep."

Rebekkah held her breath, wondering if he would turn her over and slide between her legs anyway, but he gave a frustrated growl and turned over. She hated being devious, but if it worked she would make it up to him once she became pregnant.

FIVE

Rebekkah's finished painting had finally dried. She signed her name in tiny script at the bottom right of the painting like a true artist then took it to Ullman's Art Supply and chose a beautiful frame for it. She considered it her own now, and had been pleasantly surprised at how easy finishing it had been, the brushes taking on their own lives in her hand.

Her stomach clenched when she heard the key turn in the front door. Avram was home for lunch. They hadn't discussed moving since the realtor had been to their house a few days ago, but she had a feeling the subject wasn't over. Luckily, he had been busy at work since then, sometimes not getting home until she was asleep.

"You really did a good job," he remarked as he came into the dining room and paused to look at her painting. "You seem to have some talent after all."

"Thank you," Rebekkah answered. Their conversations had been stilted since Cindy had paid her visit; they sounded like they were actors reading lines in a play.

"What are you going to do with it?"

"I thought I'd give it to Ima, so she can hang it up."

"I'm sure she'll love it." Avram pulled out a dining room chair and sat. He reached to pull Rebekkah closer.

She stepped away from him. "I got my period yesterday, remember?"

He scowled as his arm fell. "I guess you mentioned it. It's not like we've had sex lately, anyway. You're never in the mood anymore, even when we're in bed together."

She grabbed the roll of tissue paper she was going to wrap the painting in. "How can I be in the mood when there are issues between us we need to iron out? Suppose I pray to God about my womb, as you put it, and nothing happens?"

"Everything's fine with our relationship, so stop looking for cracks. If you pray and nothing happens? Then it means God doesn't want you to have children. Now please, no more about that, I don't want to hear it. "

"I don't believe that's God's will," she said, ignoring his plea. "It seems to be more your will. Avram, I have to be honest with you. If I'm not pregnant in three months— that should give God plenty of time to answer me, don't you think—and you refuse testing, I don't think I can stay married to you."

Avram's mouth opened and he blinked. "Why are you saying that again? So you really would divorce me?"

"I don't want to—"

"Then don't," he cut her off. "I can't imagine a life without you. I don't believe for a moment you would be happy without me." He studied her then frowned. "Or is that all I am to you? A father for this baby you're so obsessed about. How can you be so foolish as to demand God answer you on your timetable?"

Rebekkah stayed calm as she spread out the tissue paper and laid the painting on it. "First of all, I don't believe God is against testing. Second, that isn't all you are to me." Suddenly, an idea came to her. She stopped what she was doing and sat in the chair opposite Avram. "What about adoption?"

Avram made a disgusted sound in his throat. "Where did that come from?"

"I just thought of it. If I don't get pregnant we could adopt. We could make sure the mother was Jewish, so there would be no fear of the baby not being Jewish. You can't object to that."

Avram look flustered before he responded in a tone that dared Rebekkah to continue the discussion. "Absolutely not. I don't want a child who isn't mine. I'll never agree to that."

"How can you say that?" Rebekkah was appalled. "I'm adopted, so are Lilly, Ben, and Sam. You know that. Ima and Aba consider us their children."

He looked up and glared at her without answering.

She shook her head. There was no talking to him. She pushed her chair back. "I'm taking the painting to Ima now. You want me to make you lunch first?"

"No." He didn't even look at her. "I'm not hungry."

Rebekkah gathered up the painting and said nothing more before she left. On the walk to her mother's house she suddenly remembered the present she had ordered for Avram ages ago. Their fourth anniversary was next week. She had been so thrilled about her choice back then. Now, she was afraid their relationship was coming to a crossroads, and she wondered if there would be anything to celebrate. If he never came around she would have a serious decision to make.

"It's absolutely gorgeous, Bekkah," Shira exclaimed when Rebekkah showed her mother the completed painting. "You're amazing. Your great-grandmother would be so proud of you."

Rebekkah beamed. "I've decided to sign up for lessons. I can't believe how relaxing painting is. I love it."

"That's a magnificent idea," Shira said. "You know, I read a notice when I was in the library the other day that they're having an art show. Why don't you enter this?"

"I saw it, too, but I don't know if my work is good enough for an art show," Rebekkah said. "I thought you'd want to hang it on your wall."

"I'd love too, but you should definitely enter it. What have you got to lose?"

"I guess you're right." Rebekkah sat on the couch. She would enter it in her great-grandmother's name if she could, and give her full credit

"Are you okay?" asked Shira, her brow bunching in concern. "You seem preoccupied."

Rebekkah picked at a piece of lint on her skirt before the words rushed out. "Avram refuses to go for fertility testing. He wants us to move to some fancy expensive condo in Manhattan we can't afford, and he wants us to go to B'nai Torah. It's Orthodox, by the way, and he's decided I should dress more conservatively."

Shira arched an eyebrow at Rebekkah, her mouth widening in a smile. "Is that all?"

Rebekkah jumped up. "Isn't that enough? I don't need a fancy condo, and I like the way I dress. He makes all these demands on me and refuses to do the only thing I ask of him." She waited for her mother to stick up for her and agree with how unfair Avram was being.

Shira sat, pulling Rebekkah down with her. "Do you think maybe you're pushing too hard about having a baby? Avram loves you so much. It's clear he only wants the best for you."

"That's what he keeps telling me. But I don't want to move so far away."

Shira laughed. "We do have transportation. It's not like we would never see you again. Avram is so wise, Bekkah, you should listen to him." Shira's face suddenly clouded. "You do love him, don't you?"

"Yes. It's just that ..." Was she indeed making too much out of the moving? The testing? Was she supposed to go along with everything Avram wanted? She didn't believe marriage was supposed to be like that.

"Then don't give poor Avram a hard time," Shira admonished.

"I'm not trying to, Ima, but he thinks I should pray about my not being pregnant. He thinks it's my fault, and that it's between me and God."

"Listen to me," Shira said, putting a hand on Rebekkah's knee. "It would be a blow to any man's ego if he couldn't father children. I bet he's afraid it's really his fault, and he doesn't want to find out. Instead of fighting him, make him feel special, show him that he's the center of your universe. He'll come around. I know it. You be good to him, he'll be good to you. And I have lots of orthodox friends who are perfectly happy. It doesn't sound like the end of the world."

Rebekkah sighed. She was hoping her mother would understand, but she knew Shira was more inclined to gloss over her children's problems than to face them. She wanted everyone to be happy, and couldn't stand when any of them were in emotional or physical pain. Her parents were so grateful that Rebekkah had found love with Avram; they had no desire to hear criticism of him.

"This isn't because you're still pining over Jonathan, is it?" Shira interrupted Rebekkah's thoughts.

"No." Rebekkah finally answered. "I'm not pining over him, Ima. This has to do with Avram. I know he isn't Jonathan. I love him for who he is. I just want to be pregnant."

"I'm glad you love him. I know whatever he wants is best for you."

Rebekkah knew that subject was over for Shira. She nodded toward the painting. "I think I'll take this over to the library and enter it now."

"I know it's going to win first place. I'm so excited. It's next Monday, you know, only four days away

As usual, the library was full of patrons when Rebekkah walked in. She went downstairs as the sign directed her, into a meeting room where pieces of art sat propped up against each of the walls. She hoped hers had a chance.

"Hi, I want to enter this painting in the show," she told the woman behind the desk.

The woman pushed her glasses up on the nose and picked up a pen. "Hello there. Just one?"

"Yes. My great-grandmother started it years ago, and I finished it. She died before I was born."

"How lovely. That you finished it, I mean." The woman took Rebekkah's name and other information she needed. "Does it have a name?"

"A name?" Rebekkah repeated.

The woman pointed toward the painting. "Your painting there. Does it have a name?"

"I hadn't thought about that." Rebekkah leaned the painting against the woman's desk. She un-wrapped it and turned it so the woman could look at it. "I don't know."

"It's gorgeous," the woman told Rebekkah. "So real. I feel like I could step right into it. It doesn't have to have a name."

"But I think it needs one," said Rebekkah. "How about *Bridge at Night*?"

"Hmmm." The woman chewed her pen. "I think the figure cloaked in red is pivotal to the painting. She looks very mysterious."

"*Figure in Red* then?" asked Rebekkah.

The woman slapped a hand on her desk. "I like it. Yes, I really like it." She took an index card and carefully printed Rebekkah's name, along with the painting's name on it, and slid it into the corner of the frame. "You're all set. Good luck, Rebekkah."

"Could you add my great-grandmother's name also?"

"I don't see why not. What is it?"

"It's also Rebekkah. Rebekkah Ruth Kantor."

The woman added it to the card. "There you are."

Rebekkah grinned. "Thank you."

She was on cloud nine when she left the library and stopped at Ullman's Art Supply on the way home. She signed up for lessons and, once again, Bill helped her with supplies. When she went up to the cash register she had artist's grade paints, four different brush types, and stretched and primed cotton canvas. She couldn't wait to start her lessons and to paint something else. When she arrived home, she was surprised to see Avram still home.

"Did Ima like the painting?" he asked.

"She did, and suggested I enter it in the art show the library's having, so I took it down there."

"I hope you won't be disappointed if you don't win."

"I won't be disappointed," she assured him. She wondered why he always had to be so negative before saying an encouraging word to her.

"What's in the bag?" he asked her.

"I bought more canvas, and Bill helped me pick out other supplies," Rebekkah replied, emptying it out on the table.

"Bill?" asked Avram.

She glanced up at him. "He and his wife Edith own the shop."

"I see. I hope he's not showing excessive interest in you."

"Of course not. Where did that come from?"

"I've seen men checking you out. I don't like it, that's all."

Rebekkah opened her mouth, but Avram had moved on, and arguing with him wasn't something she felt like doing at the moment.

"There's a reason I'm still home," he said. "I thought you would be back earlier.

Rebekkah stopped sorting through her new tubes of paint and looked at him expectantly. "Something wrong?"

"I told Cindy we'd meet her at the condominium."

Rebekkah froze. "You're determined to move, aren't you?"

"It will be better for us. I promise. Trust me, you'll fall in love with it. Cindy's sure this place will go quickly. Another couple has asked to see it, but I want it. It's perfect. I don't want someone else snatching it from us."

You mean snatch it from you, thought Rebekkah. Their home was her pride and joy. She felt safe and comfortable here. Avram had given her free reign, and she had taken tremendous care in decorating and choosing the right paint colors and furniture. Their house fit her like a favorite old t-shirt.

"Please, don't fight me on this," he implored.

She couldn't say why she didn't refuse. Maybe it was the look on Avram's face, or the fact that she didn't have the strength for an argument. But it didn't matter how many fancy condos they saw, she wasn't going to move to a place they surely couldn't afford.

Forty-five minutes later, they pulled up in front of a pristine white high-rise with a green awning over the elaborate front door. They were lucky enough to park right away. When the doorman tipped his hat and greeted them with a big smile, Rebekkah noticed how Avram assumed an air of superiority, as if it were somehow beneath him to greet the man. She smiled back and hoped her friendly greeting made up for Avram's cold shoulder.

The elevator whooshed them up to the eleventh floor. Cindy was already in the condo and greeted them like long-lost favorite cousins, but Rebekkah knew her only interest was unloading this place.

She dutifully followed Cindy and Avram, who were so deep in conversation they seemed to have forgotten she was there. As she walked through the various rooms, she admitted to herself that the condominium was gorgeous enough to be in a home magazine. But something was off. Then it came to her. It lacked warmth. It was all angles and starkness. The white walls made it sterile. She hated it. She couldn't imagine toys scattered around the floor, or curling up with a good book by the fireplace as she did in their home now. She even hated the huge chrome refrigerator that hummed in the kitchen.

"What do you think?" Avram came up behind her at the end of the tour. "Perfect, isn't it?"

"What if I refuse?" she whispered, wishing Cindy would give them some space instead of hovering practically on top of them.

"Refuse what?" Avram asked.

"To move?"

"Tell me you're kidding. Why would you? Most women would be thrilled to have the chance to move to such a prestigious address."

"I'm not most women."

"Why don't I leave you two alone for a moment?" Cindy finally said, throwing a wink at Avram that Rebekkah couldn't have missed.

Rebekkah wandered to the window. She couldn't imagine living here. "We can't afford this."

76

"If that's your only concern, I've worked out the numbers and we can. Our brownstone will go for a good price."

"Yes, but we have a mortgage on it. I don't want to owe money."

"Let me worry about the expenses. That's my job. I run a successful business, which you know. I know what I'm doing."

"I need time to think about it. We have to talk." Rebekkah glanced at Cindy's back. "Privately."

But there was no conversation on the way home. The way Avram slammed through each gear in their Mini Cooper told Rebekkah he was too angry to even think of discussing why she hadn't agreed to buy the condo that afternoon.

"I'm going to the funeral home," he announced as he pulled up to the curb to drop her off. "I'm so disappointed in you. I want to give you the best of everything, and you don't appreciate any of it."

Rebekkah paused as she stepped out of the car. "I do appreciate it. I just want to discuss things with you. You refuse to do that. You dictate, and I'm supposed to go along." Not waiting for his reply, she slammed the car door then watched as it disappeared around the corner.

"What do you have planned today while I'm away working?" Avram asked.

Rebekkah turned from the stove where she was making pancakes for them both. "I have shopping to do."

He nodded. "I'm sorry about yesterday. I would've said so last night, but you were sleeping when I got home from work. I shouldn't have sped off after I dropped you off. But I don't like that you think I'm a dictator. How can you think that?"

"All I ask is we talk about big decisions," she explained.

"I'm not a dictator. I'm trying to provide for you. For us. You didn't consult me about this interest in painting you've developed."

"It's not the same thing. I didn't say you were a dictator. I said you dictate." Rebekkah slid four pancakes on Avram's plate and two on her own.

"I'll do better. Please, will you trust me? As soon as you get used to the condo you'll love it. Give me this one. I deserve something for all my hard work, for making my business a success."

She sat, poured syrup on her pancakes, and dug a fork into them. Interesting he hadn't mentioned Mark, or Amy's hard work.

"I promise I'll discuss every little thing with you in the future," he continued.

He didn't get it. "Not everything. The big things. Like buying a condo. Or an airplane."

Avram didn't respond and concentrated on eating. Leaving half his breakfast on his plate he jumped up a few minutes later. "Have fun shopping. I've got to go."

She didn't try to stop him. Apparently, the issue was settled for him. Trying to talk about it again now would have the same effect as banging her head against the wall. Somehow, she would have to make him understand. When he wasn't busy going off to work.

She finished her breakfast, and half an hour later was headed to Jay Street in downtown Brooklyn near Borough Hall. Cufflinks, a gold bracelet, and Star of David on a simple gold chain stashed in a drawer since the day Avram and she had met remained stored in elegant little boxes stamped with the gold imprint of Gerson & Roth Jewelers. He never wore them. She'd never thought to ask why, but he must like the store, so that's where she had gone to order his anniversary present. A Rolex. As she thought of the watch, the words her mother had spoken popped into her head: *Instead of fighting him, make him feel special, show him that he's the center of your universe.*

The jeweler was only minutes away by subway in a neighborhood where she and her friends frequently shopped. Not lately, she lamented for a few seconds, but Rebekkah was familiar with all the stores. She knew a diamond from exclusive Gerson & Roth was as good as one from Tiffany. She pulled open the front door and joined the line already formed in front of the counter.

"Can I help you, miss?" the clerk asked when her turn arrived.

"Yes, please. I'm here to pick up a watch. My name is Rebekkah Gelles."

A thin statuesque blonde in a cobalt blue suit with a plastic curly key bracelet around her wrist was watching her. Studying her intently was more accurate. Did she have her shirt on backwards? Food on her face from breakfast? Was her lip gloss smeared?

"Right away," the clerk said.

She admired the sparkling diamonds and stones in the display case as she waited, avoiding the women's probing stare. When the clerk returned he flipped open the elegant navy blue box so she could inspect it. It was gorgeous, much fancier than anything she would pick out for herself. A part of her couldn't wait to see his face when he opened it. He wouldn't expect her to buy it. "Can I see the engraving?"

"Of course." The clerk lifted the watch out of its box then held it toward her. She forgot about the woman as she read, "To Avram, Happy Fourth Anniversary. Love, Rebekkah."

"Perfect," she pronounced and started away from the counter as soon as the clerk had slipped the box into a navy blue and white striped bag and handed her the receipt.

"Excuse me, Rebekkah Gelles?" a female voice called.

Rebekkah turned to see the woman who had been studying her minutes before striding across the store. She waited.

"I couldn't help overhear," the woman said. "The name you had engraved on the watch. Avram Gelles."

"Yes, why?"

"I'm Ellen Roth Page." She held her hand out. "My family owns this store. I'm rarely at this branch, I'm always at the one in Manhattan." She paused to smile. "I'm rambling. It's a bad habit. You'll think I'm forward for intruding on your day, but he must be your husband."

Rebekkah shook the woman's hand. A strange sensation crept down her neck. "He is." She allowed herself to be guided to a quiet corner at the front of the store.

"The watch is beautiful." Ellen smiled. Her eyes grew wide. "Wow. This is ironic. I think I was married to Avram. I knew as soon as I saw the name on your special order, it had to be him. Can we go in the back and talk? I'm glad he re-married. Does he still own Gelles & Bender?"

Ellen's words were like a punch to Rebekkah's stomach. She tried absorbing them, but her brain spit them back up. "I don't understand. You were *married* to Avram? He never said he was...he never mentioned you."

Ellen brought both hands up to her mouth, so it looked as if she was praying. She shook head. "Oh my God. You didn't know. He never told you? God forgive my big mouth."

Rebekkah felt oddly detached. She barely registered the bag holding the watch dropping to the floor. It seemed incredible she would run into a woman who claimed she was once married to Avram. Then again, this neighborhood was home to many Jewish people, so maybe it made perfect sense. Only, it didn't make perfect sense. How had this woman been married to Avram? When?

Rebekkah's mind raced, she couldn't find her voice. She remembered Avram's Gerson & Roth boxes. Maybe they had been presents from Ellen. Her world had tipped upside down. She was afraid she would throw up at Ellen's feet. "I have to get out of here. Now."

"No, wait. Please!" Ellen handed her the bag with the watch in it, then wrapped her fingers lightly around Rebekkah's wrist. "You're pale. You don't look well."

Rebekkah shook her head. "No! I can't stay. It can't be the same man. I don't want to hear anymore. I have to go." She took a step, but Ellen didn't let go, and dizziness made the store tilt at a strange angle. Ellen's mouth moved again, but all Rebekkah heard was buzzing in her head. She grabbed the counter near them to steady herself.

Ellen put an arm around Rebekkah's shoulder. "Please. Come with me. You can sit for a few minutes. I'll get you some water. You're so pale. I feel you trembling."

Like a robot, Rebekkah followed Ellen to the back of the store and waited for her to speak.

"Stay here. Please, don't go. I'll get some water."

Rebekkah nodded as she sat down. Avram had been married to this woman? He had shared her bed, made love to her? It had to be a different Avram. But Ellen had known Avram owned the funeral home. Avram Gelles wasn't a common name.

82

Ellen returned with the water and handed it to Rebekkah. She took a sip because it was something to do. She didn't want to think what this meant to her marriage. Not that he had been married before, she could deal with that. But the fact that he had never told her. What else was he hiding?

"I feel horrible," said Ellen. "I never dreamed you didn't know."

Rebekkah finally looked at Ellen. Avram's first wife. Or maybe there were more. Maybe Rebekkah was number three or four. "It's not your fault. No, I didn't know. He never said anything about being married before."

"His middle name is Joel, after his grandfather. His birthday is February 3rd," Ellen recited slowly. "He has a small birthmark on the inside of his right thigh and a scar from an appendectomy."

Rebekkah nodded. "It's the same Avram."

"I know. I'm so very sorry for upsetting you. Do you want to talk?"

"What happened to your marriage?" whispered Rebekkah.

"It lasted for six years. He was twenty-two and I was twenty when we married. It was so long ago; maybe he put it out of his mind. I never think of him either, but I saw the special order, I wanted to meet you. See how he was."

Ellen's voice faded, and a rush of blood pounded in Rebekkah's ears. Six years wasn't so short a time. You didn't forget six years of your life. She gripped the sides of the chair. Why hadn't he mentioned Ellen to her? She had told him all about Jonathan. Wasn't that something you discussed with someone you loved?

"What happened to your marriage? Did you have...did you have children with him?" Rebekkah asked.

"At first, neither of us wanted children. One day, I decided I definitely did want children after all. It's all I thought about. Avram decided he definitely didn't. I'm sure you know he loves to be the center of attention. He told me he wouldn't share me with a child. He wanted to be the only thing in my life." Ellen paused before continuing. "Avram's all about...well, Avram. Although, he's not without occasional charm and I did love him. At least I thought I did. But, I'm sure I'm not telling you anything you don't already know. We grew apart over the issue of children. I divorced him. How long have you been married?"

Rebekkah could barely breathe. Anger and hurt bubbled up and spread inside her. *I decided I definitely wanted children after all. Avram decided he definitely didn't.* "Almost four years."

Ellen studied Rebekkah. "You have some color back in your face. That's good. You don't want children? Ah, one of those career-first women then, climbing the corporate ladder. No time for diapers and bottles. You're a perfect match for Avram. I don't harbor any ill feelings toward him. He is who he is. At least my story had a happy ending. I got re-married and now have six children. I'm still married to my second husband."

"I do want children, a lot of children," Rebekkah cried, unable to stop herself. "I don't have a career. Being

84

a wife and mother is all I want to do." She didn't know why she continued to sit, spilling out her private life to this stranger, but she couldn't seem to get up and walk away.

It was Ellen's turn to pale as her eyebrows rose and her mouth formed a surprised O. "Then you don't…" She closed her eyes then opened them slowly. "I've upset your life enough as it is in the last few minutes."

"I don't what?" asked Rebekkah, grasping Ellen's forearm. "You were going to say something. What could be any worse?"

Ellen squirmed in her chair and murmured something Rebekkah didn't catch, then ran her fingers through her bangs, causing then to stick out at pointy angles. "I know it's not my business, but it's obvious you don't know anything about this. How old are you? If I wasn't sure it was pretty much impossible I would think you were his daughter."

"Twenty-five," Rebekkah replied quickly. "What were you going to say? If what was impossible?"

"I don't think I…"

By this time Rebekkah was sitting so close to the edge of her chair that another inch and she'd be on the ground. "Please, just say it."

"God forgive me if this is wrong of me, but you so obviously want children." Ellen paused and played with her wedding ring. "You'll never be pregnant. Not by Avram, anyway. He's had a vasectomy."

SIX

Rebekkah slumped back in her chair as the shock of what Ellen had said coursed through her. She almost reached out and slapped her, but it wasn't Ellen's fault. A vasectomy meant Avram would never be a father, and he'd known it all along. He had deliberately lied to her!

"I'm sorry. When I realized he hadn't told you...You're so young. I...I couldn't not tell you. You would be waiting and hoping to get pregnant, not knowing it could never happen with Avram."

Rebekkah jumped up. She didn't want to be here. She wished she had come for Avram's present at any other time. But then she would never have known. Her thoughts collided with each other and she forced them aside to focus on Ellen. Avram's ex-wife. "It's okay. I'm not angry with you. Please, let me go now." She grabbed the bag with the watch in it.

Rebekkah fled through the front of the store, then down the sidewalk, weaving through the throng of pedestrians. She could hear Ellen calling to her to wait, but she didn't care. The bag holding Avram's watch felt like a lead weight. She wanted to toss it in the nearest trashcan.

When Rebekkah arrived home she grabbed a step stool and went straight to the bedroom. She planned to hide the watch deep in the closet. She didn't care if she gave it to him or not, but she couldn't return it with the engraving on it. She climbed up on the stool and began re-arranging the boxes already there, looking for a hiding place for the watch. When her arm knocked a shoebox that had been lying in the corner to the floor, it made a loud thud. She climbed down.

What was inside this one? She wondered. Sometime she had to clean out the closet, but not today. Today, she had to confront Avram on his lie. She shivered remembering her conversation with Ellen. She slipped off the box's cover and peered inside. Buried in newspaper was a gun. Her stomach dropped as her heart raced. She knew nothing about them, but she didn't want one in her house. It was heavy and menacing. An ugly dull gray. What was Avram doing with it? Another thing he had never mentioned. Why did he feel he needed a gun? It scared her. Was it loaded? What if it had gone off when it dropped? She carefully put it back. She didn't know why, but she didn't want him to know she had found it.

When Avram arrived home hours later, Rebekkah was sitting on the couch in the dark living room, swaddled in a blanket. She waited for him to find her.

He switched on a light and rushed over, squatting in front of her. "What's the matter? Why are you sitting in the dark? You look like a ghost. Did someone die, sweetheart?"

Rebekkah stared at the man whose name and bed she shared. The man who was supposed to be the father of her children. The man she thought she knew. She was the one who felt dead. Her lips chattered as she spoke. "I picked up your anniversary present today. At Gerson & Roth."

Avram rubbed her thigh in a way that was meant to be comforting, but Rebekkah flinched at the contact.

"I'm sure I'll love it. What happened? Don't tell me you were in a robbery."

"No."

Avram's hand snaked farther under the blanket and he enveloped hers with it. "My God, you're freezing. I want to know what's wrong. Why were you crying?"

Her eyes filled with new tears. She felt so alone. Did Avram even love her?

He handed her a tissue. "Talk to me."

She wiped her cheeks. "I met a woman there."

"You met a woman? Doesn't sound so bad."

She looked away from Avram and withdrew her hand from his.

"Did she hurt you? What did she want?" he pressed. "Obviously she upset you."

Rebekkah's stomach lurched as her heart squeezed. "Her name is Ellen Roth Page. She said she's your ex-wife."

Avram's reaction wasn't what she expected. His concern melted away, he sprang up, sat by her, and tried to gather her to him "Is that all?"

"Is that all?" Rebekkah all but shrieked as she shrank away from him. "You never told me you were married before."

"I didn't tell you because it didn't occur to me," he began explaining. "It wasn't that I was trying to hide anything. It wasn't important. It has nothing to do with my love for you." He appeared to be searching for the right words. "My life started the day I fell in love with you. When I met you no one else mattered. It doesn't change how much I love you. It wasn't a good marriage, sweetheart. I don't like to even think about it. It was nothing like I have with you. I was young and stupid. We both were."

"So stupid you had a vasectomy and neglected to tell me?" she managed to get out before sobs choked her.

Avram blanched and the color drained from his face. "Jesus Christ. Is that what that bitch said?"

Rebekkah didn't think Ellen deserved to be called names, but she couldn't get any words out to defend her. She nodded.

Avram jumped up and paced back and forth. Finally, he came back to the couch and sat, hauling Rebekkah, blanket and all, into his lap.

She tried to resist, but he was too strong for her.

"Rebekkah, listen to me." He tilted her chin so she was looking into his eyes. "I did not have a vasectomy. Do you hear me? I didn't have a vasectomy. You have my word. Please believe me. Ellen is…unstable…she's mentally ill."

Rebekkah pulled his hand away. "She sounded perfectly fine to me. Why would she say that if it wasn't true?"

"I told you, she's ill. I don't care about her right now." His arms tightened around her "All I care about is that you believe me. I didn't have a vasectomy. Tell me you believe me."

Rebekkah wavered. She wanted to believe him, but what reason did Ellen have to lie?

"Don't look at me like I've just beaten you."

The anguish in his eyes seemed real. Was Ellen crazy as Avram was trying to convince her she was? Rebekkah had a terrible headache from crying. She wanted to believe him, but could she?

Avram continued to talk. "Ellen was obsessed with me. She couldn't accept that we had grown apart, wanted different things in life. She would follow me, show up at my work, and call me all hours of the night. Sit in front of my house in a car. She sent dead flowers to women I dated. Put dead animals in their mailboxes. I finally took out a restraining order on her."

She still didn't know whether or not Avram was telling the truth. "I want you to get your sperm tested."

He gently slid Rebekkah off his lap and got up. He pulled an envelope from the briefcase he had dropped in the middle of the floor when he came in. "Our anniversary is next week. I wanted to save this until then, but here."

Rebekkah took the envelope and opened it. It was full of papers. She pulled them out and began reading. "You bought the condominium."

"Yes. Happy anniversary. It's yours."

Her eyes filled with tears again. Not tears of happiness, but tears because Avram didn't understand that she truly didn't want to move, even though at the moment, she couldn't have cared less where she lived. More telling was that he hadn't replied to her request to have his sperm tested. If he really wanted her to believe him, he would have jumped at the chance to prove his ex-wife wrong.

Avram pulled the blanket away from Rebekkah and sat beside her. "I promise. One year. If you aren't pregnant I'll do whatever you say. Get tested, do in vitro, whatever you want. Give it a year. You have my word of honor. I'll even have a contract drawn up that if I break my promise, you can divorce me immediately. I'll leave the condominium and let you live there. I'll even continue to pay the mortgage for you."

She wanted to believe him, but…

As if sensing her indecision his hands came up to cup either side of her face. "I can't lose you. I can't live without you. You're everything to me."

"But if you're willing to do all that in a year, why not now?"

"Testing is expensive, as are babies. Now that we are the proud owners of a condominium on East 72nd Street, we should build up our bank account before we have a baby. A year, Rebekkah. That's all I ask. I'll give you what you want. I'll give you a hundred babies."

Rebekkah examined the papers in her hand then almost passed out. The monthly mortgage payment was eighteen thousand four hundred and forty one dollars. "How on Earth are we going to afford this? Have you lost your mind?" The figure was mindboggling.

"We'll be fine," he assured her. "I'll take care of it. So, do we have a deal? Give me one year to build up a little money in case we do need testing?"

She couldn't believe he was being so cavalier about the monthly mortgage payment on this dream condominium of his. She knew he made excellent money, but that was an insane amount to pay every month. She couldn't fight with him now about it, it was too late. "What if I get pregnant before a year is up?"

"Then you'll have the perfect life with a husband who adores you and a baby that, hopefully, will look like his mother."

"What about what you said about being too old for children?" Rebekkah reminded him.

"I'll learn to deal with it. I want you to be happy."

She wanted to believe him, but why did this feel like a business deal they were making: An expensive condominium for him, in exchange for a baby for her.

"You believe me, don't you? I need you to believe me."

Rebekkah waffled. Ellen didn't seem weird, or mentally ill. Of course, being mentally ill wasn't the stigma it used to be, and a lot of people functioned very well with medication and therapy. She tried to think.

"At least promise me you aren't going to leave me," he asked.

What was done was done. There was nothing she could do about the condominium now. Rebekkah looked around their cozy living room, the bookcases that lined the walls. She would miss this place. "I'm not going to leave you tonight. That's all you get."

"I'll take it. I'll let you decorate the condo any way you want."

"I need some time." He sounded so eager to please. But her emotions were still in turmoil and she needed time to sort them out. "I want to believe you, but I can't understand why you wouldn't tell me you had been married before. It's not as if I would have held that against you."

"I'm sorry. I promise I'll never again hold anything back from you. There will be no secrets between us."

Rebekkah thought of Jonathan and felt a twinge of guilt. But Avram wouldn't understand if he knew she still saw Jonathan. That was different, she rationalized. It wasn't as if Avram didn't know about him at all. "I'll try. That's all I can give you. I can't believe you wouldn't tell me you had been married, then I run into a woman who says she's your ex-wife and you never wanted children."

Avram hugged her to him. "Shhh. I wish I had done things differently. I should have told you, now I see that. But I wouldn't promise to have testing if I had had a vasectomy, would I? And I do promise. A year from today. If you aren't pregnant, we have every test there is, until you are."

Rebekkah allowed Avram to pull her to her feet. He hugged her to him and his mouth descended on hers, forcing it open. Suddenly, she remembered and tore her mouth from his. "My period! My God, Avram. How could we have forgotten?"

Avram's hands tangled in her hair. "I want you, Rebekkah. It's too late, we've already touched. We'll ask forgiveness on Yom Kippur. I need to make love to you. Don't make me wait."

"I can't. Not now." Strangely, she wanted to have sex with Avram, even desired him, despite the fact she was still upset and on her period. She had decided to believe him, but she still needed to think all of this through. "If you don't keep your promise, I promise I will divorce you."

"I know," Avram whispered. "Will you come to bed with me? I need to be inside you. I don't give a damn about your period right now."

"No. I need some time."

Rebekkah stayed in the spare bedroom until her period ended. But the night she came home from the

94

mikveh she still couldn't make herself join Avram in their bed. He had been patient with her questions, but she could tell he wanted her back in their bed, and their life to go on as it had.

"How long are you going to go on punishing me?" he asked her one evening as they sat watching TV.

"I'm not punishing you," she argued. "I'm going to work on my painting now."

"No. Not tonight." He grabbed her arm as she walked by. "I've been very patient. I know you've been upset, but it's been two weeks since your period ended and you still sleep in the spare bedroom. I think you prefer your art to me."

"That's not true. I'm not punishing you." Rebekkah rubbed her arm.

"What are you doing then? You come to work with me and barely look at me. I think you're avoiding me. You're too wrapped up in your art lessons and the new painting you've started. We're moving in six weeks and you haven't started packing."

"I'll try and do better."

"Damn it, Rebekkah, you sound like a robot. I don't want you to have to try. I want the woman I married. The happy, sweet, sexy woman I married."

"I'm trying, Avram. I really am."

"All I ask is that you join me in our bed. If you don't want me to touch you, I won't."

"I'll think about it. Right now I need to paint." She didn't wait for his answer, but she could feel the heat of his eyes on her back as she left the room.

That night, Rebekkah approached their bed and waited. Avram was reading and didn't speak. He seemed to wear a perpetual frown since she had confronted him about Ellen. Still, she saw his eyes light on her breasts and go lower, to the dark shadow between her legs, starkly visible through her thin nightgown. She climbed into bed and after a few minutes he turned off the light.

She realized after a time that he wasn't sleeping, either. She reached for him under the sheet. He was already hard and lust rode up from Rebekkah's belly to her chest, suffocating her. She moved her hand slowly, and Avram groaned. Life fluttered back into her heart. She sat up and pulled her nightgown over her head and straddled him. Rebekkah cried out as she welcomed him, felt him stretch her soft membranes, and soon she was deep in the familiar rhythm that had been so lost to her.

His seed exploded inside her within a minute. Rebekkah's own release was locked away somewhere inside her, but it didn't matter. Soon, she slid from Avram and went into the bathroom and washed herself. She had put the conversation with Ellen out of her mind. One year, Avram had promised her. She would go for testing and if he refused he would be out of her life.

Rebekkah was so excited she could barely contain herself. She tried to keep her attention on Mrs. Singer and

96

the wrinkled statement the woman had spread out on the table in the conference room at Gelles & Bender, but concentrating wasn't easy.

Yesterday, the library's director had called her, giving her the good news that not only had the painting she shared with her great-grandmother won first prize, the owner of an art gallery that had helped judge the show wanted to see her. She had taken the painting with her to her gallery. Rebekkah and Avram had gone out to dinner to celebrate.

They had started packing boxes for their move. Even though she still didn't want to leave the home she was in, she was glad that she and Avram seemed to have their relationship more or less back on track. He had adored the Rolex she had finally given him for their anniversary and wore it constantly. But his promise to her was always in the back of her mind.

"And...? What's wrong with my account?" Mrs. Singer demanded. The sound of her knuckles rapping on the wooden table dragged Rebekkah back to the present.

Rebekkah felt bad feeling so happy in front of a woman whose face was splotched with grief. She examined the statement and handed it back to the woman. Mrs. Singer was right. There was a ten thousand dollar discrepancy between the initial deposit five years ago and the current statement. Her heart lurched.

"I'm sure there's an explanation, Mrs. Singer," Rebekkah assured the woman. Although she'd love to know what it was, too. "I'll see if Mr. Bender, or Mr. Gelles, can speak to you."

"I gave you people fifteen thousand dollars. Mr. Bender, that's who I want to talk to." The woman shook the statement at Rebekkah with a trembling, vein-laced hand. "He tells us, 'It's such a marvelous thing to do. Pay for your funerals before you go.' That's what he tells Mr. Singer and me. So we did. Now you're telling me I have five thousand dollars left to bury Mr. Singer?

"The best I want for my husband. Not the bottom of the line. He drove a Cadillac, you know." Her voice shook with grief, but she went on. "Nothing but the best for my Herbert. Not the plain wood. I'm not saying that model is not nice, Mrs. Gelles." The woman paused to sniff. "But I wanted the top model. Like Herbert's Cadillac. You understand?"

"Of course I do, Mrs. Singer," Rebekkah assured her.

"I don't have ~~any~~ enough money now. What am I supposed to do? You people took my money!" Her stern expression crumbled, and tears flowed down her face. She blew noisily into a tissue.

"Please don't worry, Mrs. Singer. I'm sure it's only a clerical error."

"I don't want to know from an error," she lashed out. "Where's Mr. Bender? He's the one who talked us into this. The funeral is tomorrow." Fresh tears tracked down Mrs. Singer's cheeks.

Rebekkah thrust the box of tissues at her and stood up. "I'm so sorry, Mrs. Singer. I'll get Mr. Bender for you right now. Please, don't worry, it will be fine." Rebekkah hoped she sounded more confident than she felt. She couldn't imagine what the problem was.

Mrs. Singer covered her eyes with one hand and nodded, dismissing Rebekkah with a wave of her other hand.

Rebekkah hurried to Mark's office. The door was closed. She knocked then turned the knob. Locked. Exasperated, she found Avram leaning back in his chair, staring at a blank computer screen. "Mrs. Singer is in the small conference room. Her pre-paid funeral expense account is down ten thousand dollars," she whispered. "She needs it for Herbert Singer's funeral tomorrow. She's apoplectic, and I don't blame her. Where's Mark?"

"I'm right here, Rebekkah."

Rebekkah jumped. He had materialized like a ghost. "Mark, what's going on? Mrs. Singer is beside herself. There's money missing from her—"

"Really?" he interrupted. "That's not good. When I set up these accounts—"

"I'll take care of it," Avram broke in. "I've transferred some assets from our clients' pre-paid funeral expense accounts to a lucrative hedge fund. Mrs. Singer probably hasn't gotten a statement from them yet. That's all. No need to panic. Her husband handled all the finances. You think a woman her age knows what she's looking at when it comes to money?"

Mark frowned. "I didn't know you did that."

"I meant to tell you about it, I just forgot," explained Avram.

Rebekkah walked back with Avram so he could talk to Mrs. Singer. Then she gathered her things, wishing she

99

could stay to see that things were properly sorted out, but she had an appointment. She pulled a business card out of her purse. Kain Galleries, it read. The owner was Cairenn Kain, and Rebekkah was meeting her in a little over an hour.

Kain Galleries was in downtown Manhattan, near Rockefeller Center. Rebekkah opened the thick glass door and looked around in wonder. It was like being in a museum.

"Hello," a tall woman with long, curly red hair glided toward her. "Can I help you?"

"Hello." Rebekkah smiled at the woman. "I'm looking for Cairenn Kain. I'm Rebekkah Gelles."

"You're Rebekkah?" Cairenn's eyes traveled from Rebekkah's head to her toes. "Not what I expected. I thought you'd be older, more sophisticated."

Rebekkah opened her mouth to respond, but Cairenn began talking again.

"I absolutely love your painting. There is something so incredibly haunting about the lone figure in red on the bridge. I pictured her as a heart-broken woman contemplating her married lover. Or better, the lover she can never have. Very dramatic."

Rebekkah hadn't thought of the woman she had added to her great-grandmother's painting in that way, but if Cairenn wanted to interpret it that way, so be it.

"I think it will bring a tidy price. You will let me sell it for you, won't you?"

"You really think someone will buy it?"

"Of course. Why else would I want to see you?"

"I can't take full credit for it."

Cairenn frowned. "You didn't paint...what's it called? *Figure in Red*, right?

"I painted most of it, but my great grandmother actually started it years and years ago."

"How interesting. You did a smooth job. Are you planning on doing anything else?"

"I do have something started," said Rebekkah.

"How far along are you?" demanded Cairenn, as she waved to someone entering her gallery.

"About a quarter of the way through."

"By the end of the month then?" asked Cairenn.

"Yes, I think so."

Cairenn rubbed her hands together. "Good. Can't wait to see it. In the meantime, I thought I'd display *Figure in Red* over there." She pointed to a well-lighted corner of the gallery.

"That looks fine," said Rebekkah, not knowing whether or not that was the best or worst spot in the gallery.

"I'm so glad to meet you. You seem like a reasonable person." She made a funny face. "So many artists I deal with are high strung and temperamental."

"Nice meeting you too, Ms. Kain," said Rebekkah. She couldn't believe her painting was going to be in a gallery. She would be more amazed if someone bought it. Rebekkah hoped her mother wouldn't be upset at not getting the painting back.

"Call me Cairenn," the gallery owner interrupted Rebekkah's musings. "I'm sure we'll hit it off."

"Thank you, Cairenn, for doing this. I'm thrilled."

"I have a really good feeling about you, Rebekkah. I think you're going to be famous."

"She already thinks you're going to be famous?" asked Avram that evening when Rebekkah told him of her visit to Kain Galleries.

"I think she was kidding, but it's so exciting. Now I really have to finish the painting I started. She wants to see it at the end of the month."

"Don't forget we're moving in a few days," he reminded her.

"I know. I hate to say good bye to this place."

She had been to the new condo a few more times, and still hated it. She prayed that she would be able to turn it from cold and austere to warm and comforting. She hadn't met any neighbors yet, but she knew the doorman's name was Howard, and he was extremely polite and knowledgeable about the area. She had made chocolate chip cookies a few days ago and taken Howard a batch, much to Avram's consternation.

SEVEN

Rebekkah studied her latest creation. The image of a cottage sitting on a lake had come to her in such vivid detail she was going to ask her parents if they had spent a family vacation at a cottage like it when she was little and the memory had been buried until now. She wasn't exactly sure she liked the name she had picked. *Cottage* wasn't very exciting, so if Cairenn had a better idea, she was willing to listen.

She couldn't believe that almost three months had passed since she and Avram had moved. She still wasn't pregnant, but her anxiety about it had subsided a little. She tried not to think of the scene with Ellen, but if it crept into her mind, she convinced herself all over again that Avram would never agree to fertility testing if he had had a vasectomy. Not that she wanted to rush her life away, but knowing that in nine months she could collect on his promise to get tested if necessary took her mind off the fact that she still didn't like their new home.

They had yet to meet any of their neighbors. It was as if they were the only two in the building. The closest thing she had to a friend here was Howard. He always wore a smile and had a kind word. He helped her with her bags when she came home from shopping as if it was his greatest pleasure. She had apologized for Avram's unfriendly behavior, but Howard assured her it was no problem.

Rebekkah felt a little ashamed that she had barely done any decorating. Since Avram had agreed to go for testing she really should try, for his sake, to take an interest in the condo. It was he who had told the movers where to place the furniture because she really hadn't cared where it went. He encouraged her to go shopping for all new furniture if she wanted to, but she hadn't been able to muster any interest for it, even when her mother enthusiastically volunteered to go with her. Shira couldn't understand Rebekkah's attitude. Her whole family had been overwhelmed at their new home. She had half expected them to kiss Avram's feet they were so enamored of him.

She was surprised Avram hadn't complained about her lack of enthusiasm. He had been so busy, planning the expansion of the funeral home with Mark, he apparently hadn't noticed. Ever since her run-in with Ellen he had backed off demanding they attend an orthodox synagogue, and he had even stopped criticizing the way she dressed. It was as if God had thrown Ellen in her path for a reason that turned out to be a blessing. Avram had sure done an about-face since then and was going out of his way to be solicitous to her.

Between her painting and his long hours, she barely saw him. What good did it do to have a nice home if you had to kill yourself working trying to keep it? Rebekkah wondered. When she suggested that he and Mark take on another funeral director Avram had vehemently shot the idea down. He probably hadn't bothered to mention it to Mark or Amy.

The only room Rebekkah had furnished and claimed as her own was the room she now sat in, her art studio. Since the move, her time had been taken up with her art lessons and painting. She loved painting and enjoyed her lessons. Her teacher—Bill, the art store owner's daughter—told her she had a natural talent that couldn't be taught and had praised the homework Rebekkah duly completed for class.

At first, Avram complained about her making the long trip back to the old neighborhood, but she stood her ground. She missed the streets she loved, and looked forward to her once-a-week lessons. She had delivered her own first painting to Cairenn right on time, just as she'd promised. Cairenn had loved it and demanded to see more. Rebekkah had already given her three more, and *Cottage* would be ready to give to her in a couple of days or so.

She thought about her great-grandmother's other paintings. Her mother hadn't taken them to the show at the library after all, and Rebekkah wondered if Cairenn would like to see them. Why should they gather dust in the attic? One of these days she'd go get them. Ima would be so happy if they were sold in a gallery. Maybe she'd take them without mentioning to her mother. Then if Cairenn were interested, Rebekkah could surprise her mother. Cairenn wanted to see Rebekkah that afternoon as a matter of fact.

Whatever the reason for her call, Cairenn had sounded very secretive and serious and refused to discuss it on the phone. Rebekkah had time to change and stop to see Jonathan before going to the gallery. She smiled thinking of Cairenn who certainly was demanding, but her bark was worse than her bite. She was growing very fond of the woman. Of course, that meant she would be a little late getting to the funeral home, but she was just going to help Katie file and do inventory, so it wouldn't be a big deal.

Rebekkah straightened her studio and went to one of the spare rooms that served as their temporary master bedroom. If nowhere else, Avram wanted all new furniture for the real master bedroom. Their old stuff, as he called it, suddenly wasn't good enough. The master bedroom was huge, with a little alcove that would be perfect for a newborn to sleep in until it could be moved to its own bedroom. Right now, Avram had his computer in there and used it as his home office. He had shaken his head in disbelief when she professed that she actually preferred the smaller bedroom they slept in now. It was so much more intimate and cozy. She didn't understand why they needed new furniture when the bedroom set they had was perfectly fine.

She quickly changed for her meeting with Cairenn and was about to walk out the front door when the phone rang. "Hello?" she answered.

"This is Vinnie. Is Avram there?"

"No, he's not. Can I—"

Rebekkah frowned at the loud click in her ear. How rude this Vinnie, or whatever he had growled as his name, was. Avram didn't know any Vinnie, or at least he had never mentioned him. She pushed the irritating incident out of her mind, and by the time she took the elevator down to the lobby, her thoughts were on the day ahead of her. Since Avram had taken the car she would have Howard call a cab for her.

Howard was behind the lobby counter when she stepped out of the elevator. His face lit up as she approached him. "Good morning, Mrs. Gelles. Beautiful day, isn't it?"

Rebekkah looked out the window where light drizzle splattered the glass and chuckled. "If you're a duck."

"Ah, but I have a feeling you're going to have a beautiful day in spite of the rain."

"I hope so. Can you call me a cab?"

Howard grinned back. "Nope."

"Thank—What? Did you say no?"

"I did," Howard replied.

"Why?" Rebekkah glanced down at the counter where the phone was. "Is something wrong with the phone?"

"No."

She frowned. "Howard, I really have to go, can you—
"

He held up a finger and Rebekkah paused in mid-sentence. He reached into a drawer then withdrew his hand slowly, dropping a set of keys on a black leather BMW key fob on the counter. He pushed them toward Rebekkah.

She gave him a questioning look.

"Go on. Take them."

She was thoroughly confused. "Why?"

"They're yours."

What was he talking about? "Mine? They aren't mine. I have my keys."

"Mr. Gelles left them with me last night. He told me to make sure you got them today." Howard smiled at her. "I believe your husband bought you a new car. Don't you want to see it?"

Rebekkah gasped. Her eyes went to the keys, then to Howard, then back to the keys. "Why would he do that? We have a car."

Howard's eyes twinkled. "She's a real beauty. Red BMW 135i coupe."

Her favorite color. "Where is it?"

He inclined his head to the door leading to the garage. "Garage, level 2, space 34. Right next to your other space. You and Mr. Gelles are lucky that space was open. You're going to love her."

Heart racing, Rebekkah picked up the keys. When she'd first met Avram she knew he was successful, but she had the impression that he was happy with their home, their small neighborhood, having a wife who didn't need Gucci purses or Manolo Blahnik shoes. Now all of a sudden he was throwing money around as if they had a vault full of it.

Rebekkah wasn't sure she wanted to live this kind of life. She preferred to curl up with a good book, and now she had her painting, which she loved more every day. She wasn't even thinking about the money she might make, she just loved the creative process. Avram was slowly turning into someone she didn't know. Where was this money coming from? He was the one who paid all the bills. He gave her an allowance, but he got their bank statements and credit card bills at work, so she never saw them.

She had no idea how much money he made, or what their monthly bills were. She didn't even know what color their checkbook cover was. That had to change. Admittedly, her relationship with Avram had been a distraction from losing Jonathan at first, but even when she grew to love him, she hadn't bothered asking about how their bills got paid, or who was going to do it. She had handed her life over to him, letting him set the tone of their marriage. She didn't understand why a shiver quivered through her now, but she didn't want to be kept in the dark any more. She needed to talk to him about all of this.

"Mrs. Gelles?" Howard's voice snapped her back to the present. "You okay? You look upset. You want me to walk you to your car?"

She smiled at him. "No, it's okay. I'm in shock. I had no idea that Avram was going to do this."

"You're a lucky lady. He told me he wants people to see you only in the best."

Rebekkah's hand tightened on the keys. Was that how Avram had put it? Did he mean she was on display for him? Her car was nothing but a reflection on him? "Yes, I am...lucky. Thank you. Have a great day, Howard."

He tipped his hat. "You, too. Enjoy that car now."

"I will. Thanks." Rebekkah stepped through the door leading to the garage and pulled out her cell phone. While she waited for the phone at the funeral home to ring she changed her mind and snapped it shut. She should wait and talk to him in person.

She made her way to the parking space and her breath caught when she saw the gleaming red paint and tan leather interior. The car was stunning. Maybe Avram was trying to buy her love? She hadn't talked about divorce again since he had given her the one-year promise, so why would he think he had to do that? Maybe he did it because he loves you, she told herself.

Rebekkah unlocked the car, pulled the door open, and slid in. Breathing in the rich smell of new leather she caressed the steering wheel. She should at least call Avram to thank him. She pulled out her phone again. "Katie, hi. It's Rebekkah. Can I talk to Avram?"

"Sorry, Bekkah. He's not here. He was for about an hour then left without saying a word."

She hated bothering him on his cell phone during work hours, but she hit the button that would connect her with him. No answer. Oh well, she had tried. She'd have to thank him later.

She turned on the car and looked everything over while the engine purred. It had one of those fancy dashboards that she'd probably have to study for several days. Or ask a six year old, she thought and giggled. She'd bring her favorite CDs to put in the car during the weekend and figure it all out then. Avram would help her. She decided to put off seeing Jonathan that day. She missed Pamela and Alex, and felt guilty about not having seen Jonathan for longer than she liked. That might seem ridiculous to some people, but she still couldn't turn her back on him completely. And she couldn't imagine Pamela and Alex not being in her life. She put the car in reverse, and as she carefully backed out of the parking space, her thoughts shifted to her meeting with Cairenn.

"Hi there, sweetie." Cairenn strode across the floor to greet Rebekkah as the door to the Kain Art Gallery closed behind her. "I have the best news for you." She linked one of arms with Rebekkah's. "One of your paintings sold. I know, I could've told you over the phone, but I wanted to see your face."

Rebekkah stopped breathing as she stared open-mouthed at Cairenn. "Really? I can't believe it. "Already? Wait till I tell Avram. Which one?"

"*Piano Practice,*" said Cairenn. "I knew it would go fast. I'm so happy for you. Come here." She enveloped Rebekkah in a hug. "After my commission, that'll be five hundred sixty dollars for you."

Rebekkah was amazed. She'd never dreamed one of her paintings would sell that fast, or for so much. At least to her it sounded like a lot of money. It was incredible. "I don't know how to thank you."

"Oh please, I don't want to hear from that. You're the one who did the work. It means you have real talent. I thought you'd have another one in tow."

"I just finished one. I'll bring it in."

"Can't wait to see it. I told you I had a good feeling about you. My instincts are never wrong where art is concerned."

"So am I supposed to paint a certain amount for you?" Rebekkah asked. She didn't remember seeing that spelled out in the contract she had signed.

"No, no." Cairenn assured Rebekkah. "Don't worry about doing that. You're not a machine. Go at your own pace. I've had a lot of people look at *Figure In Red*. I bet that'll go next."

The door opened, and both women turned as an older, well-dressed couple came in.

"That's Mr. and Mrs. Thornton," Cairenn whispered. "They made a huge purchase last week and they're here to pick it up, so I need to talk to them. If you want to stick around this won't take long."

"No, you go ahead. I'll see you tomorrow with my next painting."

"Good." Cairenn gave Rebekkah a big grin as she walked her toward the door. "Thanks for coming down, and congratulations."

"Thanks again for the good news," Rebekkah said and gave Cairenn a final wave.

Rebekkah was floating on a cloud, and when she got to her car she hoped Avram was at the funeral home.

She spied their Mini Cooper as she pulled in to the Gelles & Bender driveway. Choosing a parking space away from the other cars she made her way into the building.

Avram was talking to Katie. When he turned and saw it was her he rushed over. "Well? What do you think? I bet you were surprised. Were you? "

"A little," she teased as she steered him further away from Katie. "Of course I was surprised. But I think it's too much. I love it, but you didn't have to give me something so extravagant." Rebekkah grabbed his shoulders. "Guess what? I was just at the gallery. I sold a painting. Can you believe it? I sold a painting already! Cairenn said a lot of people have been looking at one of my other paintings. I can't believe it! It's so unreal."

Avram stepped back and crossed his arms, looking as if he were going into a major sulk. "You seem more excited about selling one silly painting than your new car. It's not every husband who can buy his wife an expensive BMW."

"It's not every husband whose wife sells a painting at a gallery," Rebekkah retorted. "It's not a silly painting. I appreciate the car, it's amazing, but it's made me realize something. I don't know where our money goes, or how much we even have. I don't see any of our bills. I'm concerned about this spending spree you've been on. The condo, the car, you want new furniture."

He cleared his throat and, though it took an effort, his frown disappeared. "I'm sorry. I know your painting's not silly. You don't have to worry about our finances. You have me to do that for you. I love taking care of you and providing you with the best. Now, what do you want? A new dress? Some shoes? Perfume? Make up? I've given you credit cards to use, just don't go too crazy."

She hated clothes shopping, and the only makeup she liked was lip-gloss. Perfume she loved, but that wasn't the point right now. Did Avram really know so little about her? "I don't want a new dress or shoes. Stop treating me like a child. I want to know about our finances. I don't even know how much you make."

"It doesn't matter how much I make. Good grief. Why does it seem that the more I do for you, the more you complain. Is there nothing I can do to make you happy?"

Despite her frustration, Rebekkah felt contrite. Did she sound like an ungrateful shrew? Still, Avram was skirting the issue. "I am happy. I was happy without moving and without a new car. Where is all this money coming from suddenly?"

Avram blinked and looked askance for a second before answering. "We've always had enough money, but business has been really good and we're working on expanding."

"Are you saying more people are dying than ever before? People are supposed to be living longer these days."

"I'm saying the economy doesn't matter, people always die."

She supposed he had a point. "All I want to do is sit down, go over our finances, see our checkbook, and know what's going on."

Avram touched her nose with the tip of his finger. A habit she found condescending. She resisted the urge to slap it away.

"Fine. One day we'll sit down and talk about it. I promise. But right now, I need to go back to work." He kissed her. "Congratulations on your sale."

Rebekkah wound her arms around his neck and kissed him back. "Thank you. I do love the car."

He gave her a parting hug and she went back to Katie. "We're working on filing and inventory, right?"

"I have most of it done. I can take care of the rest of the filing tomorrow." Katie looked around and then leaned toward Rebekkah. "There's something I need to talk to you about."

"What is it?"

"I found some statements by mistake, in Mark's office."

"What kind of statements? How did you find them by mistake?"

Katie looked around again before she answered. "I went into Mark's office to get a book that Avram wanted. It was on the top shelf so I had to get the ladder."

"Katie, I can hardly hear you," said Rebekkah. "Why are you whispering?"

"Because, I don't want anyone else to hear me."

"I think you're safe," Rebekkah responded, glancing around the empty foyer.

Katie chewed on her lip. "It was a book on talking to children about Jewish funerals."

"Okay. And?"

"Statements fell out of the book."

"Did you ask Mark or Avram about them?"

Katie shook her head. "No, I'm afraid to. I mean, why would these statements be in a book on the top shelf so out of the way?"

"I have no idea. What kind of statements? What did they look like?"

"I made copies and put the originals back," Katie told her and reached for her purse. "I don't know what they mean. I thought if I gave them to you, you could ask Avram."

She took the folded papers from Katie's hand and unfolded them. They were bank statements from New York Independent Bank & Trust. It was the bank where Gelles & Bender's pre-paid funeral expense accounts were kept, that much Rebekkah knew. The name on the first one was Isadore Kushner, and there was a deposit of seven thousand dollars two years ago into his pre-paid funeral expense account. Three months ago, there was a withdrawal of the seven thousand, including some accumulated interest. His account now had a zero balance.

Rebekkah scooted around to the other side of the computer. She hit a few keys. Mr. Kushner was still alive according to the funeral home, so where was his money? Of course, his funeral could've been handled by someone else, but why leave the money in his pre-paid funeral expense account?

There was another statement from the same bank, for Rose Koski. Two years ago there was a deposit of five thousand dollars into her pre-paid funeral expense account. Her account also had a zero balance, and Mrs. Koski was still alive and well. At least Gelles & Bender hadn't buried her.

There were more statements in the bundle, but the balances were whole. She agreed with Katie it was odd. "I'll ask Avram tonight. You haven't mentioned this to anyone else?"

"No," replied Katie.

"Do me a favor and don't, okay? I'm sure there's a logical explanation."

"I won't," Katie promised. "I hope it's nothing serious."

"Hmmm, me too." Rebekkah tucked the statements into her own purse.

There could be a logical explanation, but what was it? Why would someone keep statements in a book? If there was something strange going on, why would Mark leave them here where they might be found? She couldn't believe either man would do anything to damage the business, or their relationship. Amy either.

That evening after dinner while they were relaxing in the living room, Rebekkah asked Avram those same questions when she showed him the copies of the two statements.

"Where did you get those?" Avram demanded after examining them.

"Katie said they fell out of the book you asked her for. Did Mark put them there?"

"I don't know. It's odd, I'll admit that. Mark's my best friend and partner but..."

"But what?" Rebekkah prodded.

"Nothing. I'll find out what happened." He ran a hand through his hair.

She laid a hand on his forearm. "Do you think Mark has something to do with this money disappearing?"

"No. There must be a reasonable explanation."

"Did you maybe also transfer their money to that hedge fund you mentioned?"

"What are you talking about?"

"You know. Remember when Mrs. Singer was so distraught because her money was missing? You said you transferred her account to a hedge fund."

Light dawned in Avram's eyes. "Oh her. I forgot about that. No, I didn't transfer these people's money anywhere."

"I'm nervous, Avram." Rebekkah scooted next to him.

Avram put his arm around her as she kicked off her shoes and tucked her feet underneath her. "No need. I trust Mark. It could be a bank error, you know. I'll take care of it."

Rebekkah watched as he got up and stuffed the statements into his pocket. She wished she had made another set of copies for herself. For the second time that day, a shiver went through her. She thought about calling him back so they could discuss their finances, but that would have to wait. She couldn't deal with any more surprises today.

EIGHT

The next morning Rebekkah swirled her oatmeal around with a spoon as she sat in the kitchen. Avram had been very sweet last night, making love to her before they had drifted off to sleep. The bank statements were still on her mind. She believed Avram would look into it, but she was uneasy. Maybe she could call New York Independent Bank &Trust and ask to see the pre-paid funeral expense accounts. But since she had nothing to do with them the bank probably wouldn't answer her questions. It had been Mark's idea to offer pre-paid funeral expense accounts, but she couldn't very well go to Mark and ask to see all of them. Avram wouldn't appreciate it, and although she liked Mark a lot, she didn't get a warm and fuzzy feeling from him. It would be best to let Avram handle it.

She tried to imagine who would steal from Avram and Mark. All of their employees, at least the ones Rebekkah knew, seemed like nice, loyal people, and she couldn't imagine any of them doing something so awful. She was worried for Avram and Mark.

She was rinsing her bowl when Avram came up behind her, wrapped his arms around her waist and nuzzled her neck. "You're up early."

Rebekkah turned around and kissed him. "I forgot to tell you. A man named Vinnie, at least that's what I think he said, called for you. He was rude when I told him you weren't here. He hung up on me."

Avram cleared his throat. "What did you tell him? Did you tell him where I was?"

"No, all I got out was that you weren't here. Then he slammed the phone down. Who is he?"

Instead of answering, Avram picked up the bottle of antacids sitting on the counter, shook one into his palm, then popped it into his mouth.

"Who's Vinnie?" she repeated.

He swung open the refrigerator door and grabbed the orange juice. "Some guy who wanted to work for us. We turned him down. He wasn't happy about that."

"How did he get our home number?"

"I don't know. Those things are easy to do now. You can find anyone if you try hard enough. If he calls again we'll change our number." He abruptly changed the subject. "I'm going to be gone a couple of days to a convention, sweetheart. Why don't you have Lilly come stay with you?"

This was the first Rebekkah had heard of Avram going to a convention. Before she could speak, he started talking again. "I would love to take you with me, but it'll

121

be boring. Minneapolis. You don't want to go to Minneapolis."

"I would if you asked me to," Rebekkah replied. She would miss him, despite their issues. This was the first time they had been separated since their marriage. It hurt a little that he didn't want her to go.

"It'll be all business. I'll have hardly any time to spend with you."

Rebekkah's eyes filled with tears. It was hard to tell which of them was more surprised.

Avram gathered her to him in a hug. "Don't cry. It's not even three whole days. I'm leaving next Tuesday and I'll be home Thursday." He kissed the top of her head.

Rebekkah wiped the tears from her cheeks. "I'm being silly. I have plenty to do. I want to start another painting for Cairenn, and I need to take the one I recently finished to her."

Avram withdrew from their embrace. "Painting is taking a lot of your time. I think it's turning into more than a little hobby, eh? I thought you would want to pick colors or wallpaper for the rooms, and choose new furniture. All you seem to care about is your painting.

The spiritual atmosphere of any Jewish home is a reflection of the woman's efforts. I want us to start having Shabbos dinner and inviting people over. I want to see you spending Fridays making challah and cooking a big feast."

He what? That was news to her. They never had Shabbos dinner at their home, they always went to her parents' house. She had insisted on doing that even after they moved. She loved being there with her whole family. Avram had acquiesced once he realized she wouldn't have it any other way. He had never been very social. He had a lot of business acquaintances, but he wasn't a man who liked to bond with other men. He and Mark played golf occasionally, and went to baseball games, but otherwise, his time was divided between work and her.

"I'll try and come up with some ideas while you're gone," Rebekkah promised. "I love painting, Avram. I'm still thrilled that I sold something." The truth was her art took precedence over working on the condo. She'd get to decorating it sometime soon.

"I'm thrilled for you, but first you are my wife. It's not so much to ask that I come first with you. Is it?"

She hated when Avram sounded petty, and she was getting tired of always having to convince him that her interests were no threat to their relationship. It was as if he didn't want her to have any outside interests. He wanted her to revolve around him like the Earth revolved around the sun. He complained so much when she saw her friends, she gradually withdrew from them in an effort to keep harmony in her marriage.

Rebekkah remembered the book club she and her best friend, Molly, had joined at the library months ago. It hadn't taken Avram long to start complaining that her reading was taking too much time from him, although that was so untrue it was absurd. How could it be true when they met in the afternoon when he was at work? He thought the books the club picked were ignorant and silly. His cutting remarks had finally made her quit the club. But she wasn't going to stop painting.

123

"You do come first. It's not as if I'm going to suddenly forget we're married," Rebekkah argued. "Since you're home this morning, can we talk about our finances?"

Avram looked annoyed then smiled. He threaded his hand through her long hair and held her neck. "Sweetheart, you don't have to worry about the finances. Let me take care of you. That's my job as a man."

Rebekkah met his gaze and didn't answer.

"Okay. I can see this isn't going away. What exactly is it that you need to know?"

"How much money do you make? What's the balance in our checkbook? What's our credit card debt? Are you saving for retirement? I signed the check over to you from the sale of our other house. Did you put it in the bank?"

"Is that all?" he asked dryly. "I don't know how much I make. See my accountant at tax time and ask for my Schedule C. I have about nine hundred fifty thousand dollars in our checking account. Of course I'm saving for retirement. I paid cash for your new car. Yes, I put the money from the sale of the house in the bank. It went toward this place. I'll have to get back to you on the credit card debt."

Rebekkah swallowed. Was it her imagination or was Avram's hand tightening on her throat? She stretched her neck, and his hand loosened. She relaxed. Maybe it had been her imagination. "Thank you. I just want to be aware of what our finances are."

Avram nodded. Then without warning his mouth descended on Rebekkah's so hard their teeth collided. She tried pulling free. He ignored her struggle. As his left hand held her head still, his right hand squeezed her backside. His fingers dug into her tender flesh. She squirmed against him trying to get free. What in God's name was he doing? When he finally released her she tasted blood. He had bitten right through the skin on her lip.

The only sound was their harsh breathing. Rebekkah bolted from the kitchen, but Avram was right behind her. When she reached their bedroom, she tried to shut the door on him, but he forced his way in.

"Don't touch me." She hissed backing away. Her heart twisted as she remembered the gun she had found. What had he done with it?

Avram held his hands up in surrender. "I won't. I just want to talk. Oh my God. What did I do? I'm sorry. I'm so sorry. Please, forgive me. I don't know what got into me. I got so excited. I wanted to make love to you so badly. Please, trust me. I want you to be happy with me, with our life together. I went crazy. Your questions mean you don't trust me to take care of me. Don't you know how much I love you?"

"Love me? You can say you love me and scare me like that?"

"I know, sweetheart. I know. Please, tell me you won't leave me. I'll never do that again."

Her thoughts and her blood were churning. He hadn't actually assaulted her, and deep in her heart, she didn't think he really had meant to hurt, or frighten her. Had he?

He was still standing in the doorway. "Say something."

"Don't ever do that again. I'll leave you—"

"No," he cried. "Don't say that. You can do anything to me but that. I can't lose you, Rebekkah. I can't live without you. Tell me how to make this right."

"I'd like to be alone for a while." She grabbed her nightgown and pillow off the bed. Her teeth chattered as she strode past Avram. She made sure not to brush against him.

"Where are you going?" he asked.

"To the spare bedroom. I'm going to sleep in there for a while. "

"Don't do that. I'm sorry. I lost my head."

Rebekkah stopped in the hallway. "It was more than that. You were an animal, out of control. Maybe it's a good thing you're going to that convention. We need some time apart."

"I know this isn't an excuse, but ever since we got married I feel like I'm living in Jonathan's shadow, that I'm your second choice. Even when we make love I don't feel as if you're there with me. I want to do everything to take care of you, but I still feel as if I'm failing you somehow."

"That's absurd." Rebekkah marched into the spare bedroom and sat on the bed, pulling the comforter around her. She scooted until her back was resting against the wall. Her teeth had stopped chattering, but she was still cold to the bone.

126

Of course she wondered what her life would be like if she and Jonathan hadn't been in that accident. She didn't believe in pre-destination, but ever since that terrible day she wondered how engaged God was in any of their lives. In a split second, Jonathan's life was over and hers was shattered. Could God have reached out and prevented the accident? Why did some people get to be with the love of their lives and some didn't?

"Is it absurd? Are you still in love with him?" Avram had followed her to the spare bedroom. "I don't want to share my wife with a man, who for all intents and purposes, is dead."

His cruel words pierced her. Why was he bringing up Jonathan now? "No, I'm not in love with him. Don't drag him into this, Avram. This is about you. I didn't ask for all these material things you seem so bent on giving me. There is only one thing I want. A baby, yet you've manage to somehow get around that."

"I promised you I would go for testing, didn't I?"

Rebekkah didn't respond. She didn't feel like getting into that again. She wanted to be left alone. She couldn't think about anything but Avram's confusing behavior.

"Can I sit with you?" he asked. "I am sorry. I give you my word that will never happen again. Can you forgive me?"

Rebekkah stared out the window. It wasn't her nature to hold a grudge, yet she couldn't let him off the hook so easily. A few minutes ago he had been a frightening stranger. "No, I don't think you need to sit with me. Please, go to work. I want to paint and be alone."

"What happens now? How can I make this better?" he persisted.

"Please! Give me a little breathing room. I don't want to talk about it now."

When Avram realized she wasn't going to say anything else he finally turned away. Rebekkah stayed huddled in the blanket until she heard him leave. She went into the bathroom. Her lip didn't look as bad as it felt. And he hadn't tried anything else. Still, she couldn't believe how aggressive he had been. Even when they made love he never got so assertive that he hurt her.

She stripped and turned on the shower. When the water was as hot as she could stand she stepped in and closed her eyes. The water stung her lip, and she let out a sob. This would never have happened if she had married Jonathan. He was so gentle and kind. How could she be in love with someone so opposite everything Jonathan was? She washed her hair and soaped every part of her body.

She hadn't been lying when she told Avram she didn't know if she could forgive him, didn't know how he could make this better. How could she stay married to him if she couldn't forgive him? She turned off the water and stepped out of the shower. She dried and went into the bedroom. After she dressed she reached for the phone. Molly would understand how she felt.

Half an hour later, she was at Molly's house. Thankfully, Avram had left without incident.

"He was that aggressive? What a jerk. I know he's your husband, but still." Molly wiggled on the couch,

128

trying to get comfortable. "Yikes, I can't even breathe." She patted her swollen stomach. "I hope this kid comes soon." Her eyes scanned her living room "Sorry about the mess. Right now I can't help it, and I don't even care."

"Your home is delightful, and the baby will be here soon," Rebekkah assured her. Even with her complaints, her best friend was obviously in her element. Her skin and hair shone, and she looked blissfully happy among the books and toys scattered around. Her two oldest children were engrossed in Big Bird on the TV screen, and the other three were in the kitchen playing with their miniature kitchen set.

Rebekkah was so envious of Molly's cluttered house, and the four pairs of little sneakers lined up on a plastic tray beside the front door. She thought of her own mostly neat and organized, quiet home. She'd trade it in a minute to have the clutter and chaos her friend had. Her heart squeezed as she thought of the babies she so desperately wanted. Her life felt empty without them. She focused on Molly. "I don't think Avram would really hurt me."

"He did hurt you. He hasn't hit you has he?" Molly asked.

"No, never," Rebekkah replied.

Molly switched gears. "Do you think he's upset because you visit Jonathan?"

"He doesn't know," admitted Rebekkah.

"Why do you keep seeing Jonathan? Is it because you think he's going to rise up and life will continue as it was?"

"I used to wish for that," Rebekkah said. "I don't anymore, I'm past that."

"I know it's none of my business, but it seems that it would be better for all concerned if the Mindell's took Jonathan's feeding tube out."

"Just let him die?" Rebekkah couldn't believe Molly had made such a suggestion.

"He's not exactly alive now. His condition doesn't seem to be doing you, or his parents, any good. I can imagine how Avram would react if he knew you still visit him. Bekkah, why do you really go see him? How can you let go and have a real marriage with Avram if you're still in love with a vegetable."

"How can you say that to me?" Rebekkah all but screeched. "He's not a vegetable, he's a …"

"A what?" Molly prodded. "I'm sorry, Bekkah, I didn't mean to hurt your feelings, or disrespect Jonathan. You know I loved him and was horrified when I heard about your accident. And believe me, I am in no way defending what Avram did. Right now I could strangle him, but don't you think he senses that you still love Jonathan?"

Rebekkah gave a short laugh. "That's funny, Moll. He said almost the same thing to me after what happened. But I don't love Jonathan, at least not like I did. I do love Avram. Why would I have married him?"

Molly shrugged. "You aren't that naïve. People get married for a lot of reasons. Some have nothing to do with love. I'm not suggesting that you don't love Avram, but that you're still emotionally invested in Jonathan. You can't accept that Avram isn't Jonathan."

"I didn't realize you had a degree in psychology," Rebekkah mumbled.

Molly laughed. "I don't. You and Jonathan were two peas in a pod. You had the same values, liked the same things, read the same books, voted the same way, and even finished each other's sentences. Did you guys ever have an argument?"

Rebekkah stared into space as she thought. "I don't think so."

"Boring, boring, boring," sang out Molly. "At least Avram and you have passion. I think you're trying to recreate what you had with Jonathan, using Avram. "

"I'm not," Rebekkah insisted. "Of course I loved Jonathan. Why would I deny that? I can't change that he was part of my life."

"I know you did, but he wasn't perfect. I mean, how do you know he wouldn't have gotten fat, lazy, and slept with old Rabbi Chevan's wife?"

Rebekkah had to laugh thinking of the retired rabbi from the synagogue's wife. "She's at least eighty-seven years old."

"I'm just saying," replied Molly, "don't bury Avram because you have Jonathan on a pedestal."

"I had to come over, didn't I?" grumbled Rebekkah.

"I'm glad you did. Do you feel better?"

Rebekkah nodded. "A little. Should I forgive him?"

"I can't tell you what to do. You have to follow what your heart is telling you." She clutched her chest. "How could you drag yourself away from that beautiful new condo and the BMW?"

"I don't care about them. Seriously. What if it were you?"

Molly looked around to make sure none of her brood was in earshot. "I'd kick his ass, parade around in clothes from Victoria's Secret, and withhold sex for a month or so. Then probably go on a major spending spree."

Rebekkah laughed at the picture her friend presented. She made the answer seem so easy.

"Do you want to divorce him?" Molly asked.

"I don't know. I don't want this to become a pattern."

"So one more time and maybe you leave him. Make sure he knows that," Molly advised.

Rebekkah didn't tell her about Avram's ex-wife, or his promise to get tested in a year. She was still too upset about what had happened that morning to start discussing that. She hated to leave her friend's cozy house, but she couldn't sit here all day. She had a lot to think about, and this afternoon she had to take Cairenn *Cottage* like she said she would.

"I didn't expect to see you here so soon, sweetie," Cairenn said. "What happened to your lip?"

Rebekkah brought her hand up self-consciously. "I bit it." She didn't want to burden Cairenn with her story of what really happened.

"Ouch! I hope it heals soon," Cairenn said.

"It will, thanks." Rebekkah set *Cottage* down and laid it against the wall. It was comforting being in the gallery, she loved it here. "I wanted to get it to you as soon as possible. I have to go get more paint, and I'll be ready to start another."

Cairenn laughed. "Don't burn yourself out. It's okay to take a break now and then."

"I guess you're right. I need to do a little decorating at the condo."

"Then do it. I'll still be here when you're done. I have three of your pieces here already. Come here." She grabbed Rebekkah's hand and pulled her to the other side of the counter. "I want to you to hear something." She pulled a letter from an envelope and read a paragraph:

We would like to feature the Kain Gallery, and some of your artists and their work in an upcoming issue of *National Art World*.

"Isn't that exciting?" said Cairenn. "There's more, but that's the important part."

"That's great, Cairenn. I'm so happy for you."

133

"Be happy for you, too," Cairenn said, stuffing the letter back in its envelope. "You're one of the artists who'll be featured."

Rebekkah didn't know what to say. Her art in a magazine? "Are you sure my work is good enough?"

Cairenn stared at her, mouth open. "Really? You can't be serious. How can you doubt your talent? Would I have you here if you weren't good? I'm picky you know. I don't take everyone."

Rebekkah didn't know what to say. She was stunned. She couldn't imagine her art being in a magazine. The whole thing seemed like a dream.

"They may want to interview you," Cairenn said.

"Interview me?" Rebekkah asked, already nervous. "I wouldn't know what to say."

Cairenn laughed. "Just be yourself. So tell me. You're eager to start another painting. Any ideas?"

"I want to do a self-portrait."

"Interesting. I love it, actually. But as I said, take your time, okay?"

"I will," promised Rebekkah. "There's something I want to ask you."

"Sure. Go ahead."

"My mother has more of my great-grandmother's paintings in her attic. I thought maybe you'd like to see them. I don't want credit for them, of course. But maybe you could show them under her name."

Cairenn stuck a pencil behind her ear and studied Rebekkah while she thought. Then her face broke out in a huge grin. "That may be a marvelous idea. What's her name?"

"Rebekkah Ruth, same as me. I was named after her."

"That could make an interesting show. That's great, sweetie. Whenever you can, bring some in. I'll take a look."

"Thanks, Cairenn. If you do accept them, I'm not going to tell my mother. I want to surprise her."

"Does she paint, too? Imagine what a display that would be."

Rebekkah laughed. "No, she doesn't. I'll leave you alone now. I can't wait for the magazine article. Sounds so exciting."

"*National Art World*'s letter says they want to come in a few weeks to take pictures, so that gives you plenty of time to get me a couple of more pieces, doesn't it?"

"I can do as many as you want."

"A couple will do it," Cairenn assured her.

Rebekkah felt much better after she left the gallery. She would forgive Avram she decided, but just this once.

NINE

Rebekkah stared at the large box Avram held out to her. "Another present?"

He grinned. "Did you forget I'm leaving for my convention tomorrow? I got you a gift since we're going to be apart. And to make up for our little spat, as it were."

Setting her paintbrush down on her easel, she reached for the box. "The car was enough present to last for a few years."

"Nonsense," he replied.

Avram's always giving her gifts lately made her uncomfortable. She wished she could accept his generosity, but hated the feeling that his presents seemed to come with strings attached. She pushed aside her negative thoughts, pulled at the big blue bow then tore the shiny paper off, her curiosity growing.

The box had some weight to it and was rather large. A fur coat?

Sheitels by Chayka the box read. Her heart plummeted. She pulled the cover off, hoping the contents had nothing to do with the wigs for which *Sheitels by Chayka* was so famous. Her fingers separated the layers of pink tissue paper to reveal thick dark brown hair. Avram hadn't forgotten about wanting to be more religious after all. Words clogged in her throat.

"Don't you like it?" Avram probed, looking disappointed at her lack of reaction.

"It's beautiful," she choked out, holding the mop of hair up for a moment before dropping it back into its tissue paper nest, "for another woman. I told you before I don't want to wear a sheitel. It's not who I am." She didn't even like the color, so unlike her own.

Avram squatted in front of her, placing his hands on either side of her thighs. "Who are you? A famous artist? Come on, you sell one painting and think you rule the world."

She flinched as if he'd slapped her. "I do not." She bit her tongue before she told him she had sold two. Cairenn had called that morning to tell her *Cottage* had sold for a whopping seven hundred and fifty dollars. Rebekkah now had her own checking account she put her art money into. She hadn't told Avram about it. She was grateful he hadn't asked what she did with her earnings. He probably thought they were selling for next to nothing. She had to face the fact he didn't care about her love of art, or her talent.

"Whatever," Avram dismissed the specifics. "Can't you stop being so damn stubborn? I told you I want us to be more religious."

"We don't need to be Orthodox to be religious. My parents are religious, and my mother and sister don't wear wigs. Aba would have a fight on his hands if he told Ima to wear a wig." The image made Rebekkah smile. "I'm not saying it's wrong for all women, just for me.

"We've already had this discussion. Besides, shouldn't actions determine one's religiosity, not a mode of dress and whether or not you wear a sheitel? I only wear that ugly scarf when I go out because you want me to. That should satisfy you."

"It's not ugly." Avram sprang up and frowned down at her. "It covers your hair, so other men don't look at it and think sexually about you. Modesty is about dignity. The Torah in shul is kept private. It's taken out not as a display, but to impart the deepest wisdom. Modesty is a gift and a validation of your ability to assess what you want to share about yourself, and when."

Rebekkah made no effort to suppress a loud, exasperated sigh. He lectured her as if she ran around in a bikini every day. She hated when he got on his religious high horse. The totally absurd image of men swooning with lust at the mere sight of her natural hair almost made her laugh aloud. "You want me to wear this every time I go out?"

"Why else would I have gotten it?" Avram snapped. "Do you know how many contacts I can make at B'nai Torah? It's a huge synagogue. Daniel Wexler, who runs that private equity firm, Lucentia Trust, goes there. I want to hook up with him. He's a multi-millionaire. Have you heard of him?"

"No," Rebekkah replied, not caring.

Avram drew his mouth into a thin line. "At least you remember me saying I wanted us to go to B'Nai Torah, don't you?"

Unfortunately, she did. So much for him forgetting. "I don't wear jeans and my t-shirts when I go out."

"It's a small start," Avram acknowledged. "Living a religious life isn't a burden, it's the only way God will answer your prayers for children."

Not that again. Rebekkah fought the urge to make a face. She started to reply, but Avram jumped in. "You know Mark and I are expanding Gelles & Bender. I want our clients to see that we are religious men of honor and trustworthy."

She stared at him. "That doesn't make sense. You're both already trustworthy, and not every Jew that you take care of at the funeral home is religious. It seems being more observant is all about your own image and impressing people."

"No," he argued. "I don't mean that."

Rebekkah laid the box with the wig in it on the floor. "Then what do you mean?"

He smiled, all malice gone from his expression. He bowed his head. "You'll think I'm crazy."

"No, I won't. What is it?" Rebekkah coaxed.

"What if we don't become Orthodox and God refuses to look favorably on my business, or on your desire for children?" he whispered. "I'm afraid of that. I want you to be like the women in the Torah."

Despite herself, Rebekkah was touched by the vulnerability in his voice. One minute he sounded like a tyrant, the next like a young boy begging for approval and assurance. She often wondered about his childhood. What he had shared with her about it was vague; maybe this need for approval stemmed from some incident when he was small.

She went to him, even though she was still annoyed, and put her arms around his neck. "That's not true. You're a good man. You don't have to go to B'nai Torah, and I don't need a sheitel to impress God, or anyone else. It's only our business how we choose to observe."

He met her eyes. "Then you'll do as I ask and wear it. God wants us to obey his laws. There is no excuse not to."

Rebekkah dropped her arms and made a frustrated noise. More and more Avram was starting to sound like a wild-eyed religious fanatic, tuning her out when she didn't give him the response he wanted. She didn't believe God wanted her to hide her body and wear a wig.

She tried again. "Many modern Orthodox women don't wear wigs. They wear tasteful jeans, have jobs, and are still modest and religious. I'm religious now, so is my family, and you know it."

Avram grimaced in displeasure. "I don't care about other women. You're refusing to cover your hair with the sheitel?"

Rebekkah wouldn't allow him to force her into skirts to the ground and blouses up to her neck and down to her wrists. Wearing a sheitel was definitely out of the question. "Yes," she found the strength to say. "Please, take it back. I promise I'll wear my scarf, as I have been when I go out, but no more. If you want to go to B'nai Torah, go yourself. I'll go with you sometimes, but not always. I'll meet you part way."

"Part way? What does that mean?"

"Part way is dressing as modestly as I feel comfortable doing and wearing a head covering when I go out with you. Notice I said head covering, not sheitel. I'll have Shabbos dinner here sometimes as you mentioned you want to do, but I still want to go to Ima's and Aba's, too, sometimes. "

Avram shook his head in disbelief, marched over to the box and snatched it from the floor. He folded the tissue paper back around the wig and jammed the cover back on. He waved the box in the air. "It's not enough. As my wife you should build me up. You're a girl still tied to your parents. I thought we wanted the same things."

She wanted to laugh at his theatrics.

"Don't think God will listen to your prayers while you refuse to obey Him."

She sobered, reeling back from his venomous tone. It wasn't God she wasn't obeying, it was Avram! She didn't bother to reply. At least he was right about one thing: They didn't want the same things.

Not that this should be such big news to him. She had made it clear she hadn't wanted this big condo. She hadn't begged for a BMW, even though she admitted to herself that she loved it, or the fancy jewelry he had lately decided she needed, but Avram spun it to appear that she was the one being difficult. She was convinced his desire to appear more religious had very little to do with worshipping God and a great deal more with his own self-image.

Even with the anguish in her heart, Rebekkah suddenly realized that she hadn't told Avram the news from Cairenn. She prayed God he'd be happy for her and it would derail their argument. "I had some good news from Cairenn."

"What?" Avram finally grumbled.

He sounded so uninterested, her elation evaporated. How could she feel so alone with her husband but a few feet away? "She got an invitation from an art magazine called *National Art World*. They want to feature her gallery, and some of her artists and their work, in one of their issues. That includes me. I can't believe this is actually happening to me. I have to finish a few more pieces for her. That's why I've been sequestered in my studio."

Avram startled her by crushing her to his chest in a hug. His mouth came down on hers and he plied her lips apart with his for a lengthy kiss. "I'm so proud of you," he said when their kiss ended. "I truly am, but—"

"But what?" He was about to ruin it, she could sense it.

142

"Your painting… this…" he gestured his hand around while he tried to come up with the words he wanted. "This career you've found. It's taking the place of our marriage."

Rebekkah threw him an incredulous look. "It is not. I wouldn't even call it a career."

"You want it to be, don't you?" he accused.

"I hadn't thought about it that way. I'm good at it and I love doing it."

He didn't look convinced. "I don't know. Your art will be in a magazine? What does that mean? Will you become famous and think you're too good to be my wife? Will I have to be Mr. Goldman? You'll be supporting me, instead of the other way around, as it should be? Your place is as my wife. I don't like all these changes. I don't want a famous wife."

"No!" Rebekkah cried. "It doesn't mean any of those things." She chewed her lip and tried to think of another subject. She decided it was as good a time as any to confront Avram with something that had been bothering her ever since he had given her the BMW, and divulged how much money was in their bank account. "Tell me why we have to wait another nine months before you agree to fertility testing. You said at the time it was because testing is expensive, but you have medical insurance. And you managed to buy me a BMW. I looked on-line so I know how much they are. You said we should build up our bank account before we have a baby, yet you told me our bank account has nine hundred fifty thousand dollars in it. Why can't we afford a baby now?"

143

Avram pulled her against him again and kissed the top of her head. "You want children, you want to be famous. What do I want? Two things: A wife who is devoted to me, devoted to God. Yet, you can't do that."

She wasn't surprised by his reaction, but Rebekkah wrenched away, staring mutely at him.

Avram continued talking, as if unaware of how disturbed she was. "You want to concentrate on your painting now, right? I gave you a promise, and I intended on keeping it…" He cocked an eyebrow at her.

"Intended? What do you mean *intended?*" Rebekkah tried unsuccessfully to squash the wave of panic rising from her stomach. "You're not going to—"

Avram held up a hand. "I didn't say that. I'll keep my promise to have fertility testing if you come to B'Nai Torah and cover your hair. I need a modest, virtuous wife who will stand my side no matter what. My children will need a virtuous mother."

She trembled so hard she couldn't form a sentence. Avram took it as a sign she had capitulated. He grabbed her shoulders, squeezing too hard, gave her a shake then smiled at her. "Think how much joy you'll experience if God answers your prayer for a child. Then we won't need to get tested. You'll be like the women in the Torah I told you about before, and you'll be *Eshet Chayil, A Woman of Valor.* I will have a faultless wife. We are going to do everything according to God's perfect will. Not by the dictates of science."

She pulled away from his hold and rubbed her aching shoulders. She turned her back on him. He sounded almost crazy. The first few lines from *Aishet Chayil* played in her mind. Avram recited the entire poem that concluded the Book of Proverbs to her before every Shabbos meal, as her father did to her mother. That's where Avram got the idea, but he was twisting its meaning to gain advantage over her.

An accomplished woman, who can find? Her value is far beyond pearls.

Her husband's heart relies on her and he shall lack no fortune.

She does him good and not evil, all the days of her life.

His voice broke into her thoughts. "Even if we do get tested, what if there is something wrong with either of us? I've told you repeatedly, I don't believe in conception through science. Surely we won't have to wait long for God to do his work, eh?"

She was trapped. She was afraid of what he might do if she argued further.

"Come help me pack. I'll take you to dinner, and when we come home I'll make love to you all night."

"Wait." She reached out, grabbing his arm. "You're blackmailing me. 'Become as observant as I demand or I won't get tested.'"

Avram cupped her chin with his palm. Rebekkah fought the urge to tear away from him. "Sweetheart, I'm not blackmailing you. Marriage is give and take. I've given you this beautiful home, jewelry, a car many people only dream of owning, financial security, and I let you follow your dream and paint. In return, I want obedience. I want what's best for you."

She shuddered at those words. "Tell me Avram, what's the bottom line? If I don't wear the sheitel, don't go to B'nai Torah, and I'm not pregnant in nine months. Will you or will you not get tested?"

"The way you put it sounds so cold. I promised you I would get tested, *if it was necessary*. Now it's all up to you, right?" He kissed the top of her head and strode out of the room as if he hadn't a care in the world.

Rebekkah didn't think her legs would hold her. How could he say it was up to her? She plopped down at her easel, but she wasn't in the mood to continue painting. She was sick to her stomach. Nothing about her marriage was turning out the way she'd imagined.

That night when Avram crawled into bed with her, Rebekkah cringed. She had been tossing and turning, unable to sleep. A dark feeling seeped through her, a poison she couldn't rid herself of. They had spoken little to each other through dinner, and while she cleaned up he had stayed in the living room, glued to the television and his newspaper. Even though tonight she had no desire to have him inside her, when his hand move over her hip and cupped her breast, she didn't push him away. It would bring another fight. He nudged her onto her back and slowly his hand crept under her nightgown.

"You don't want me?" Avram whispered as he

146

peeled off her panties. "We're going to be apart for a few days. I thought you would be eager to make love."

She didn't answer, and of course, he didn't notice. He prodded her legs open, and not bothering to give her pleasure first as he usually did, he entered her. The earlier dark feeling came to her again, but seemed less poisonous.

Rebekkah squeezed her eyes closed. His heavy body suffocated her. His noises of passion irritated her ears. The smell of him was overpowering. For the first time in her marriage she wanted him to be finished and to get off. She forced herself to move under him the way he liked, letting him think she was as aroused as he. Her fingernails grazed the skin on his back and she urged him on with her body while softly moaning in his ear.

When Avram climaxed, Rebekkah accepted his kiss goodnight and waited. It would only be a few minutes before he would be fast asleep. When his breathing became even, she slid out of bed and went to the shower, keeping the glass door open a bit so the steam filled the bathroom. Goose bumps rose on her skin as she soaped between her legs and down her thighs. If she hadn't conceived, maybe it would be for the best.

The dark feeling stayed with her. The feeling that she was no longer sure about her marriage, or sure she wanted Avram to be the father of her children after all.

The afternoon after Avram left for his conference, Rebekkah couldn't wait to go see Pamela. She had called her mother first to talk about Avram's attitude, and how upset she was. Shira still believed Rebekkah should listen

147

to Avram, insisting he must have her best interests at heart. Shira sounded as if Avram had given her a script to read. Rebekkah gave up. She adored her mother, but her head was buried in the sand on this one.

Now, as she and Pamela sat side-by-side, watching Jonathan, Rebekkah felt more at peace than she had at any time in the last few weeks.

"What did Shira have to say about Avram's behavior?" Pamela asked after Rebekkah had poured her heart out to her.

"That I'm being ungrateful and silly. I can't talk to my friends, either. I hate admitting this, but I'm jealous of their loving, young husbands and sweet children. They won't want to hear my problems. They'll think I'm crazy if I complain while I'm living a life of luxury. Avram hates when I see them anyway. He has no interest in meeting their husbands. I think because he has no real friends, except Mark, he wants the same for me. I barely even talk to any of my friends anymore, except occasionally on the phone, and I can't remember the last time I did that. Molly is the only one I'm still close with."

"It sounds as if you don't think Avram really loves you."

"I thought he did, but lately his love is …I don't know, twisted. I don't think he loves me the way a husband should love his wife."

"You aren't really happy with Avram, are you? I can sense that."

"I don't think so, not anymore. I don't know if I love him." It was a relief to say the words out loud to someone else. As if doing so made it irrefutable and final. Rebekkah laid a hand on Jonathan's leg. He felt even thinner than the last time she'd come.

"Have you thought of seeing a counselor?" Pamela asked.

Rebekkah snickered softly. "Avram doesn't believe in it. I'm sorry. I shouldn't come here with my problems. I've done nothing but talk about myself, and you've been so kind to listen. I just wish Ima would understand. I say one negative thing about Avram and she shuts down."

"Darling, you know you're welcome any time. I don't mind listening. Shira cares deeply, but as a mother it's hard to see your child hurting. You don't always have the words to make it better."

"She listens to some things, but I think she wants to believe Avram and I have a fairy-tale marriage. I wanted to believe it too, but we don't."

Pamela laughed, pulled a tissue out of her pocket and handed it to Rebekkah. "No one does. I don't even want one, to tell you the truth. How boring that would be."

"You have a point," Rebekkah agreed, and decided she had taken up enough of Pamela's time. Whatever decision she made about her marriage she would have to make alone.

An hour later Rebekkah entered Gelles & Bender. "Hi, Katie, how's—" Rebekkah stopped short. "What's wrong?"

Katie was standing in the corner of the reception area with her hands folded under her chin, her eyes wide as saucers. "Come here," she whispered.

Rebekkah heard loud voices coming from one of the conference rooms. She hurried over to Katie. "Who's yelling?"

"It's Mr. and Mrs. Baker. They're in there with Mark."

Rebekkah briefly pondered why Mark wasn't away with Avram since Amy was more than capable of running things, but right now she was more interested in what was going on in the conference room. "Why are they yelling at him?"

"Mr. Baker wrote a letter to New York Independent Bank & Trust, about his account. They told him his money had been withdrawn, that they had received a letter from him."

"What?" Rebekkah squeaked.

"They came in about a half hour ago, demanding to see the owner, yelling that Gelles & Bender were crooks and we'd stolen money from them. What do you think is going on? Did you ever talk to Avram about the statements I gave you?"

"Yes. He promised he'd talk to Mark, but never said anything more about it."

"I was going to go to lunch now. I need a break. All this emotion and shouting is giving me a headache. Do you mind going through the mail while I'm gone?" Katie asked.

Rebekkah's mind was reeling from what Katie had said. "Of course not, take your time."

Rebekkah settled at the reception desk and began sorting the mail. The loud voices suddenly ceased. Within minutes Mark came out with an older couple. He ignored her while he walked them to the front door. She could only hear snippets of their hushed conversation.

When Mark turned around he marched straight over to her. "Where's Avram?" he asked, not bothering to greet her. "He won't answer his fu...damn cell."

Rebekkah paused, letter opener in mid-air. "At the conference in Minnesota. You didn't know that?"

Mark ran a hand through his hair. "Sorry. I didn't mean to pounce on you, Rebekkah. Conference? I don't think he's at any conference."

"Where else would he be?" She was puzzled by his reply.

"I have no idea, but there's no conference he needed to attend, and we have problems. He should be here. I'm late for a meeting. If you talk to Avram he needs to call me, right away." He pushed away from the reception counter and strode off into his office.

Rebekkah swallowed. No conference? Then where was Avram?

A few minutes later, Mark came back out, sliding into his suit jacket. "You okay here by yourself for a while? Amy will be in soon."

Rebekkah assured him she would be fine.

Mark's words echoed in Rebekkah's head. He had to be mistaken. Why would Avram say there was a conference if there was no conference? She took out her cell phone and dialed his number. He didn't answer. She slid the phone back in her purse, not bothering to leave a message. He would see that she had called.

She wandered into Avram's office and sat at his desk. She tried a drawer, knowing it would be locked, and was stunned when it opened. Avram always locked his drawers, without fail. He was adamant about his privacy. He didn't like anyone in his office, even Mark or Amy.

She couldn't believe she was snooping. What was she hoping to find? All she had was a feeling that she might find something to explain what was going on. Avram had teased her about her intuitions, but they were real.

The drawer only held pens and paper clips, nothing very interesting. She slammed it shut. You can stop now, she told herself. Instead, she opened the bottom drawer. As she flipped past the carefully labeled client folders that seemed harmless, the drawer rolled open farther.

TEN

Rebekkah spied a checkbook all the way in the back. Strange place for a checkbook, she thought.

She reached for it and had it open before she could stop herself. She flipped through the register. The last dates entered were for various household bills before they'd moved. The last entry showed a balance of a little over three hundred dollars with no date. Where was all their money? The big balance Avram told her they had in the bank? How on Earth was he going to pay bills with this? She couldn't call the bank since her name wasn't on the account, and confronting Avram was out of the question.

As Rebekkah returned the checkbook, her hand brushed against something soft against the wall at the back of the drawer. She reached and tugged at a folder until it came loose. It must've slipped from the drawer above, she thought as she flipped it open. It looked like letters in one-pocket and bank statements in the other. She rifled through them. Before she lost her nerve and Katy or, God forbid, Mark or Amy came in, she scooped up the papers and headed to the copy machine.

Rebekkah raced through the lobby of her condo building when she got home, barely taking time to greet Howard. She went straight to the bedroom, dumped her purse, kicked off her shoes, and took the letters and statements she had copied out of her purse and threw them on the bed.

She hopped up on the bed after them and, stacking pillows behind her, snuggled into the covers. She thumbed through the letters first. There were about fifty of them, all written by Gelles & Bender customers to New York Independent Bank & Trust, asking that their accounts be closed, the checks issued to them, but mailed to Gelles & Bender. Rebekkah felt blood drain from her face.

With a sense of dread, she remembered the statements for Rose Koski and Isadore Kushner that Katie had found. Avram had insinuated that maybe Mark had something to do with the money disappearing, but he hadn't mentioned it after that day. Could Mark be embezzling money? If he was, why was Avram covering for him? He could be gathering evidence against Mark, Rebekkah supposed. But then why would he endanger the business like that while Mark did something criminal? Her thoughts splintered like the glass in a kaleidoscope.

She turned her attention to the bank statements going to the same people whose letters requested their monies be disbursed. Something didn't look right. She wished she had Mrs. Koski's and Mr. Kushner's statements to compare to these. These didn't look the same, she was sure of it. She leaned her head back on her pillow, wracking her brain for a way to ask Avram about these without letting him know how she'd found them. The phone beside the bed jangled, startling her.

"Hi, it's me." Avram's voice sounded in her ear.

Rebekkah's heart slammed against her ribs. She was afraid for a moment he could see exactly what she had been reading. "Hi."

"I'm calling to let you know I'm going to be a couple of more days."

"Avram, Mark's looking for you. Money's missing from the Baker's pre-paid funeral expense account. He told me there isn't any conference. Where are you, really?"

The silence extended so long Rebekkah thought she had lost the connection. Finally, Avram laughed, but it sounded forced to her ears. "Sweetheart, of course I'm at a conference. I bet I know what happened. Sheesh, I've been so busy lately. I wanted to reinvest the … I…and…spoke to…"

Rebekkah strained to hear him. "Where are you calling from? I can barely hear you. What's all the noise? Sounds rowdy for a funeral home convention."

After another burst of noise there was silence. "Sorry. Is this better?"

"Yes, at least I can hear you. What did you say?"

"Wasn't important. I'll call Mark and calm him down. It's just a huge misunderstanding."

"Why would he say there's no conference? Why didn't he go with you?"

"He forgot that I told him, obviously. Besides, it's not a huge conference. It's not like we both could have attended."

"Oh," was all Rebekkah could think of to say. Mark could have attended and left Amy in charge, but she kept the thought to herself.

"I hope you aren't too lonely, I'll call you tomorrow, okay?" He lowered his voice. "I miss you. I wish now you had come with me. I have a nice, big bed and no one in it but me."

"Maybe next time," she replied, her mind wandering to the scene at the funeral home today, and the statements she had copied.

"I have to go. I love you."

"I love you, too," she said automatically. "Bye." How easy it was to say those words, even when she wasn't at all sure she still meant them.

Rebekkah's had just finished breakfast the next morning when the phone rang. "Hello?"

"Someone's broken into the gallery!"

"What?" The panic in Cairenn voice pushed all other thoughts from Rebekkah's mind.

"Oh my God, Cairenn. Are you all right? Did you call the police?"

"I'm okay, just in shock. There's glass all over. The police should be here soon. Can you come? Am I calling at a bad time?"

"Not at all," Rebekkah assured her.

Cairenn made a noise that was between a sob and a hiccup. "You're always so agreeable. If I called you at three in the morning you'd deny you were sleeping. I can't believe this. I've been in this gallery for twenty-five years. Nothing like this has ever happened before."

"I'll be there as soon as I can. I'm so glad you're all right. That's all that matters. Wait outside for the police and don't go back in there." Rebekkah heard a faint siren growing louder through the phone.

A police car, and another car that looked like an unmarked police car, were parked at the curb in front of the gallery when Rebekkah arrived. Cairenn was talking to a uniformed police officer on the sidewalk, her arms flailing like a windmill. A crowd had gathered, and the officer was trying to disperse them while interviewing Cairenn.

Rebekkah caught Cairenn's eye, and waited while the officer talked to her friend. As soon as he finished, Cairenn came to Rebekkah, linking her arm with hers. "I feel awful. I'm just so glad you're here. All four of your paintings we had on display, and the one in the back for the *National Art World* layout, are gone. I'm so sorry. Only your self-portrait is left. It was in the storeroom, so the burglar must not have seen it."

"Oh no!" Rebekkah gasped.

"Of course, everything's insured, but all the work you put into them. It just rips my heart out." Cairenn pulled a tissue from her pocket and dabbed at her eyes. "They took all the cash in the cash drawer. Thank God it wasn't much. My lap top, too."

Rebekkah wrapped an arm around Cairenn, her eyes tearing. What would this mean for Cairenn? Would the gallery have to close? Could her friend survive losing so many paintings? She hoped so. The gallery was her life.

Then there were her own stolen paintings. The *National Art World* layout was important to both of them. They had worked so hard preparing for it. Rebekkah had spent long hours on the pieces she wanted for the layout. Now what? She didn't voice her fears out loud. For now she just wanted to calm her friend down.

"Don't be upset. It's not your fault. I can paint more." And she would. Her art was a part of her now, like an arm or leg. It was how she expressed herself best. Her dreams and thoughts flowed out of her like a swollen river spilling over its banks, and came alive on her canvasses.

"I just can't believe this. Why now? This show was going to be so good for you. For both of us," cried Cairenn, shaking her head in disbelief.

"I know." Rebekkah gave Cairenn a hug. "Don't worry, we can get through this."

Cairenn blew out a breath. "There's a detective inside. He wants to speak to you. I told him you were on your way. The other artists aren't here yet."

Rebekkah followed Cairenn into the gallery, hoping the damage wasn't too great.

"Detective, the artist I told you about is here," Cairenn called out to a man standing at the back of the gallery.

Rebekkah watched as the detective made his way toward them. Cocky and self-assured were the first words that popped into her mind. The artist in her noticed his dark eyes, flawless olive skin, the angle of his cheekbones, and masculine jaw line. Faint lines fanned out from his eyes. A scar rose above his left eyebrow. That, and his slightly crooked nose, saved his face from being too pretty. His jet-black hair was slicked back, reminding her of a seal's wet coat.

"This is Rebekkah Gelles, Detective Rossi," Cairenn said.

The woman in Rebekkah noticed right away that, even though he wasn't smiling—in fact, he was closer to scowling—he was an incredibly good-looking guy. He was so close that she could smell the clean scent of soap mingled with the faint smell of cologne.

Rebekkah realized he was speaking to her, and took a step backward. His presence sucked all the oxygen from the room. Something dark and sexual radiated through his chilly demeanor. "I'm sorry, Officer, I mean Detective—"

"Detective Rossi. Dominick Rossi," he ground out, his espresso-colored eyes boring into hers.

Rebekkah stared back longer than was necessary, or polite. "I'm sorry, Detective Rossi, what did you ask me?" She had been so busy staring at him she was embarrassed to realize that he'd continued talking and she had no idea what he'd said.

"Is there anyone who might have a grudge against you? It's Mrs. Gelles, right? Or, are you a Ms.?" he spat out.

"Mrs. Gelles," Rebekkah clarified.

He scribbled in his notebook and grunted something unintelligible.

"A grudge?" Cairenn cut in. "Who would have a grudge against her?"

The detective's expression didn't change. He ignored Cairenn, and his eyes remained fastened on Rebekkah. "No enemies then? No one who might have something to gain by stealing your art?" The look in his eyes turned accusatory. "How much insurance are you going to collect as a result of this theft?"

Rebekkah stared at him, astounded. Was he serious? She didn't appreciate his insinuation.

Cairenn found words first. "Listen, detective, instead of standing here asking stupid questions, you should be out trying to catch the scum who did this."

Rossi took a second to shoot a hostile look at Cairenn before returning his attention to Rebekkah. "Mrs. Gelles, would you mind answering my questions yourself?"

His good looks aside, Rebekkah didn't like him. He reeked of macho arrogance. "Of course the paintings are insured. I don't really know for how much. I'll have to check my policy. It's new."

Rossi's eyes darkened to almost black as he continued to scrutinize Rebekkah. She returned his stare. He wasn't going to intimidate her.

She was relieved when he finally blinked first, turned abruptly to Cairenn and barked a question at her. "Any suspicious people lurking around lately?"

"I answered these questions for the policeman outside. Can't you go," Cairenn waved a hand at him, "*do* something?"

"Now you'll answer them for me. Anyone look suspicious to you?"

"No. Well, maybe the man who came in by himself."

"What man?" Rossi made a speed-it-up gesture with his finger.

"I don't know his name. I guess you might call him suspicious. He was dressed...I don't know...kind of funny," said Cairenn, her brow scrunching as she spoke.

"Funny how?"

Cairenn thought for a few seconds. "Amish-like. Black pants, plain white shirt, long beard, a funny top-hat."

"Amish-like? I suppose he had a horse and buggy outside?" The detective's lip curled into a half-smile/half-sneer.

Rebekkah flinched at the sarcasm even though it wasn't directed at her. "Detective, please. You sound as if this is all her fault."

The detective cut his eyes at Rebekkah, clearly not pleased at her interruption, but he turned it down a notch.

"I'm trying to piece together what happened. Go on, Ms. Kain."

"He looked around for quite a while. I had other customers come in a few minutes after he did, so I didn't pay a lot of attention to him. He seemed interested in several pieces, but left without talking to me."

Rebekkah walked around as the detective spoke to Cairenn. She stared out the window at the traffic going by; people unaffected by what had happened here. The cash drawer was still open. She went over to it, wondering if she should close it. Her toe kicked something on the floor under the drawer. She bent down and picked it up. It was a matchbook from Borgata Hotel Casino & Spa, Atlantic City. On the cover was written one word: Vinnie. There was also a phone number.

She glanced over at the detective. He was still talking to Cairenn. She should call him over and show it to him. It might be a clue. But she stayed frozen where she was. Vinnie was the name of the man who'd called Avram that day. She would have felt silly about making the connection, but for one thing. It stuck her suddenly the handwriting was Avram's own distinct printing.

I must be losing my mind, she thought in the next second. There was no way that Avram had been here. Was there? He wasn't interested enough in her art to come to the gallery. Cairenn had never even met him. She tucked the matchbook inside her purse, ignoring her clamoring conscience. She headed back toward Cairenn and the detective.

"Did you set the alarm when you left last night?" Rossi was asking Cairenn.

162

Cairenn paused and shifted from one foot to another. "I didn't have it on. A man from the alarm company called late yesterday afternoon. He told me to turn it off, they had to run tests He said he would call to tell me when I could turn it back on, but that it might be a couple of days."

The detective's eyebrows rose. "Did you call back to verify the call was actually from the alarm company?"

"No, I just thought—"

"You 'just thought'," he interrupted. "Pick up the phone and call your alarm company. I guarantee no one called you from there. Then turn the alarm back on."

"You're saying it was the burglar?" Cairenn cried.

"Bingo."

"Why would—"

"How many employees do you have?" he interrupted.

The man has no patience, thought Rebekkah. What a sweetheart this New York City's finest was. She glanced at his ring finger and reddened when he caught her. It was bare and no tan line. If he wasn't married, she could see why, with that abrasive personality.

"None, I do everything myself," Cairenn answered, her own voice laced with impatience.

The detective asked a few more questions, took their addresses and phone numbers, pulled two business cards out of his pocket and handed one to both women. His fingers brushed Rebekkah's when she reached for hers.

She jumped. They were hot against her own, the contact almost intimate. His card fluttered to the floor.

Her face flushed and she froze. The detective bent down and picked it up, and slowly held it out to her. His fingers came nowhere near hers this time.

"Thank you, that was clumsy of me," she said.

"If either of you thinks of anything, call me. I'll be in touch, Ms. Kain." Even though he was addressing Cairenn, the detective's eyes remained on Rebekkah. Did he think she was some kind of criminal? This time she blinked first.

She dropped the detective's card into her purse, glad when he walked away. She turned to Cairenn. "I don't like him. Now, what can I do for you? Tell me what you need."

"I'm going to call my alarm company right now. After that… I don't know where to start. I…"

Rebekkah took Cairenn's arm, and gently guided her past the police milling about. "I know. Call the alarm company then let's go to that shop down the street. Have some tea. The police are going to be here a little while, so we have time. My mother says a cup of tea always makes a person think more clearly."

Cairenn called to the detective that they would return shortly. He glowered in their direction, barely acknowledging them. Rebekkah wondered who had peed in his cereal that morning. She couldn't think of a worse occupation for a man with his temperament to go into, except maybe teaching kindergarten. She put him out of her mind as they exited the gallery.

As they drank their tea, Cairenn pulled out a notebook. "I guess I should write down everything I have to do."

"What do you want me to help with?" Rebekkah asked, eager to be of some assistance.

"When we go back, can you call a locksmith? I'll call the insurance company."

"I'll do whatever you want."

Cairenn put her cup down and smiled. "Thank you. You're sweet, Rebekkah. Not like some of my other artists – temperamental, selfish and sensitive. I knew I could depend on you. Please don't change when you become really famous."

Rebekkah laughed. "I won't." Then she turned serious. "You aren't going to have to close the gallery, are you?"

Cairenn pasted on a smile and put down her cup. "No. At least I hope not. But please tell me you have some pieces at home we can at least use for the *National Art World* layout now. We've got only about a month until the show."

"Let me think about it," Rebekkah said.

After paying their bill, they walked back to the gallery. Once the police wrapped up their business they ensconced themselves in Cairenn's office.

"About replacement paintings," Rebekkah said, "I have one done and one on the easel. But I can paint more.

I'll bring them in once things are cleaned up and back to normal."

Cairenn smiled again. "Thanks. That sounds great. I'd better call the insurance company. You have to call yours."

Rebekkah reached over to her purse and pulled out her cell phone. "I will, in a minute. You have a locksmith you want me to call?"

Cairenn gave a rueful laugh. "I don't have a personal locksmith. Can you look one up? Wait, my laptop is gone. I guess you can't. Let me see if I can find a phone book around here."

She dug around in a few drawers and finally produced one.

Rebekkah paged through it and chose one to call. She was about to pick up the phone, but Cairenn stopped her.

"I can handle all this. Let me get organized and I'll make my phone calls. Why don't you go home? There isn't really anything else to do. It's my problem."

"If you're sure. I certainly don't mind staying."

Cairenn nodded. "I'm sure. Call your insurance company. Thanks for being here. I know we haven't known each other long, but I feel as if we've become good friends already."

Rebekkah reached out to Cairenn and hugged her. "I'm glad we are. I've learned so much because of you."

Cairenn hugged her back. "You're a peach. I'm glad I found you."

Rebekkah left and made her way to the car. Detective Rossi was watching her, but she ignored his dark gaze. Guilt racked her again for not giving him the matchbook she'd found, but she had to know for sure if it belonged to Avram, even though she was sure it had to because of the handwriting. Odd that none of the policemen there had found it.

If it did truly belong to Avram…the implications were too great to contemplate. His words echoed in her mind, *"I don't want a famous wife."* How far would he go to make sure she never became famous?

What about the strange statements and letters she had found? Was Avram committing some kind of crime? The thought was mind-boggling. She thought back to the beginning of their relationship. When had the first lie appeared? At least that she was aware of. It came to her quickly.

As soon as she arrived home, she booted up the computer and typed in Gerson & Roth. Rebekkah's hand was sweating as she pushed the buttons on her phone. "May I please speak to Ellen Page?"

"I'm sorry, she's in our Manhattan branch," the person on the other end informed her. "Would you like the number?"

"Please."

Rebekkah scribbled the number then ended the call and tried again. "May I please speak to Ellen Page?"

"Ellen speaking."

Rebekkah's mouth was dry and her hand trembled. "Ellen, this is Rebekkah Gelles. I'm Avram Gelles's wife. Do you remember me?"

"Rebekkah, of course I remember you."

Ellen's voice was so warm Rebekkah calmed immediately. This didn't sound like a woman who might do the things Avram accused her of. Of course, she couldn't really know for sure, but something told her Ellen was perfectly sane. "I need to see you. I hope you don't mind me calling."

"Of course not. I've often wished I'd run into you again. I even thought of calling Avram's funeral home and asking how to reach you, but I wasn't sure you would even want to speak with me."

"I probably wouldn't have," Rebekkah admitted, "but I need to now."

"I can send my driver for you. Would that be okay?" Ellen asked. "Or is Avram there? I'm guess he isn't, or you wouldn't be calling."

"He's out of town. I don't want to put you to any trouble. I can drive."

Ellen laughed. "It's no trouble. Besides, if I don't give Oscar enough to do, he just sits in my kitchen, flirts with the cook, eats and gets fat. Are you free this afternoon? How about three? I'll be home by then."

Rebekkah laughed then gave Ellen her address. "Thank you. Tell Oscar I'll be downstairs waiting."

168

When Rebekkah was settled in Ellen's blue and white living room, which was bigger than any single room Rebekkah had ever seen, Ellen asked her maid to bring them tea. "Or would you like a Coke or something?"

"Whatever you're having," Rebekkah replied, not wanting to be a bother.

"Two iced teas then, Alma," Ellen told the maid as she tugged her skirt down and sat facing Rebekkah. "What made you call me?"

Rebekkah didn't know how much to share. There was still that possibility Avram had been telling the truth about the woman beside her, but all her instincts were screaming he wasn't. "A lot of things have been happening. Avram's told some lies. I wanted to hear more about his…his vasectomy."

Ellen's maid came silently back into the room, and delivered the tea to the two women.

"Thank you," they said in unison.

"I have proof." Ellen's fingers brushed Rebekkah's arm. "I can prove beyond a shadow of a doubt that Avram Gelles had a vasectomy."

ELEVEN

Rebekkah stared at the benefits statement from *Allied Health Insurance*, dated August 12, 1993.

Ellen unsuccessfully tried to squelch a laugh at Rebekkah's incredulous look. "Sorry for laughing. You're thinking: *Why would she still have this?* It's a curse. I keep everything, including my grade-school report cards. In this instance, thank God I do. Read."

In a little more than five seconds Rebekkah knew the detailed cost of Avram's vasectomy. How could he have made such a life-altering decision at twenty-seven? She had dismissed people having out-of-body experiences as silliness, yet now she was having her own. The condo, her BMW, the funeral home bank statements, the burglary at Cairenn's, the matchbook, all swam in her mind in a perfect, bizarrely connected circle.

"Are you all right?" Ellen leaned forward. "Please don't faint on me."

Rebekkah glanced up at Ellen. Unlike the first time she'd met Avram's ex-wife, she had no desire to run away. Given her relationship with Avram lately, she shouldn't be so surprised at proof positive of his treachery. But suspecting your husband wasn't the man you thought you married was one thing, seeing actual proof, another. She managed a wobbly smile. "I promise I won't faint. This is why you left Avram, isn't it?"

Ellen leaned back in her chair, crossing her legs. "Partly. At first, when he confessed, or should I say bragged about his vasectomy, I told myself it didn't matter. We were young. I didn't want children, either. Problem is, I soon changed my mind, as I mentioned the first time we met."

"Yes. And Avram didn't," Rebekkah put in.

"He laughed when I shared my desire with him. I begged him to reverse his vasectomy. He refused. I asked him to consider adoption. He refused."

Rebekkah sucked in a breath. "He convinced me you had lied about his vasectomy. He promised me he would have fertility testing in a year. God only knows what he planned to tell me once a year was up. He also told me he wouldn't adopt."

Ellen made a disgusted sound. "You poor thing."

"You said it was partially the reason you left him," Rebekkah continued, now eager to hear everything Ellen had to say. She twisted her engagement and wedding rings on her finger, picturing tossing them from the Brooklyn Bridge.

"It was," said Ellen, interrupting Rebekkah's fantasy. "Before I go on, I'm glad you called. I was worried about you that day we met." She glanced at her lap for a few seconds. When she looked up her brow was furrowed, and her eyes troubled. "The dark times with Avram would've probably been enough to make me eventually divorce him, even if we had children.

"As I told you the day you and I met, he had his charm, but the darkness was ugly. He certainly didn't make it easy to leave him, believe me. Not because he was desperately in love with me. It was all about ego for him. I mean, how dare I leave him, right? Laughing in my face about wanting a baby was the proverbial straw that broke the camel's back."

Rebekkah committed Ellen's words to memory, saying nothing as she waited to hear more.

Ellen picked up her glass and took a sip. "He never physically abused me, but his mood swings weren't pleasant. His abuse is emotional, subtle. It happens so gradually you don't realize what it is until it's too late. He didn't want me to have friends, or see my family."

Rebekkah listened intently. The words sounded so familiar. "I don't see my friends now, either. I don't understand why friends and family are such a threat to him. Is he that insecure?"

"Apparently. My universe shrank while we were married. Someone who really loves you encourages you to be true to yourself and your dreams. They don't stomp on them."

Rebekkah shifted, nodding in agreement. "I paint, but I'm pretty sure Avram hates it. He'll compliment me then throw in a jab." She covered her face with her hands and shook her head. "Ugh, I'm such an idiot. I thought he loved me." She uncovered her face, and told Ellen everything about Jonathan, marrying Avram, and now, the certainty she no longer loved him. "How could I have married him? Fallen for someone like this?"

"You are not an idiot," Ellen interjected. "Avram is. We both started out thinking we loved him. He messed everything up. You loved Jonathan deeply then lost him. Avram was there afterward at the right time, that's all. Maybe it was just too soon for you to get involved. Don't blame yourself."

Rebekkah picked up her glass and swallowed the last of her tea. "I'm glad I came over. I guess I should go and figure out the mess that my marriage has turned into."

Ellen got up with Rebekkah and draped an arm around her shoulder. "I have faith in you." She walked Rebekkah to the door, and summoned her chauffer on the intercom. "Call me, anytime. I'd like to see you again, if that's not too strange for you. Just a minute, be right back."

She returned a minute later with pad and pen in hand. "Give me your number. Maybe we can meet for lunch and an afternoon of shopping when things are sorted out for you. At the very least, please make sure you let me know how everything turns out, Rebekkah."

Rebekkah smiled as she printed her cell number. "I love shopping and eating. I think we'll become good friends." Here smile faded. "If you hadn't talked to me that day…"

"Don't think about it," Ellen told her.

Rebekkah made small talk with Ellen's chatty chauffer on the way home, but her mind was on confronting Avram. The vasectomy was reason enough to divorce him, but if he had broken into the art gallery, she wanted him punished. She was trying to imagine what might have driven him to commit such an unthinkable crime, if indeed he had, when Detective Rossi's question popped into her head. *"Is there anyone who might have a grudge against you?"* Would her husband go that far?

As much as she disliked his macho attitude, she had to call the detective. She reached into her purse, and her fingers closed around the matchbook. She still felt guilty withholding evidence. When Oscar dropped her off she thanked him, and hurried up to her condo. She dug out the detective's business card and chose his cell phone number.

"Why didn't you show me this earlier today?" Detective Rossi tossed the matchbook on the desk, laced his hands behind his head, leaned back in his chair, and studied Rebekkah.

She squirmed under his scrutiny, taking a few seconds to look around. His office was stark, and the gray metal desk he sat behind had seen better days. There were no pictures anywhere, just manila folders stacked neatly to one side, and a computer. "I ...

"You what?" he barked.

Rebekkah concentrated on not letting him intimidate her. "I was scared."

Straightening up, he frowned at her. "Of what?"

"That it might belong to my husband," Rebekkah replied.

Detective Rossi's frown disappeared. "Why would that scare you? Hasn't he been at the gallery with you? If it's his, maybe it fell out of his pocket."

Rebekkah chewed her bottom lip. She wasn't crazy about the detective, but she needed him. He was her chance to find out who Vinnie was, and if Avram was the one responsible for the burglary.

"Mrs. Gelles, I asked you a question," he reminded her.

Rebekkah's head snapped up. "He's never been to the gallery with, or without, me. I took a call for him from a man named Vinnie not long ago. He hung up on me when I told him Avram—my husband—wasn't available." She pointed to the matchbook. "The name on the matchbook is Vinnie."

Detective Rossi waited a few seconds. "That's it, Rebekkah... Mrs. Gelles? I think there's more than one Vinnie in the world."

Rebekkah hardly noticed his use of her first name. "It's Avram's handwriting. I recognize it because it's so distinct, unique. I think he resents my interest in painting. He's afraid I'm going to be famous." The detective's going to laugh me out of his office, she decided, and that will be the end of that.

She was wrong. He leaned toward her. "You think he stole your art to sabotage you?"

Rebekkah rose and paced, aware that he was watching her. "I don't know. Can you find out who this Vinnie person is?"

Detective Rossi relaxed in his chair. "I'll get back to you."

"I think Avram dropped the matchbook while he was robbing the art gallery. I think he was the one who called Cairenn and told her to turn off her alarm," Rebekkah blurted out. She expected the detective to really laugh at her this time, or make a comment about watching too many cop shows. "The only thing…"

"Is what?" Rossi pressed.

"He's at a convention. He's been there for a few days. So how could he have? It's impossible, isn't it?"

"Do you know for sure he's at a convention?"

She opened her mouth to answer, but realizing the implication of the question, closed it. Of course she didn't know. He could be anywhere. Hadn't Mark said there was no convention?

"Can I call you on the number you gave me earlier?" Rossi asked.

"Yes, it's my private cell number," she told him.

"I'll be in touch."

She had been dismissed, but she hadn't any more to add anyway. "Thank you. I appreciate it."

He was already typing on his keyboard and didn't respond.

Rebekkah got into her car, and sat for a moment after starting it up, turning on her favorite Keith Urban CD. Another thing Avram didn't like: her music taste. She waited for the tears to come as she thought about her marriage ending, but they didn't. Avram's betrayal hurt nonetheless, and the depth of his deception was difficult to accept. She wondered if they had ever truly loved each other. If only Jonathan and she had been able to have the marriage they both wanted.

She felt empty, her life washed away like sand being swept from the beach to the sea. She loved being a wife, but now she was sickened and shamed that she might be married not only to a liar, but a criminal. She stared out the windshield, her stomach churning with anxiety as she thought about confronting Avram about his vasectomy. She had no plan yet, no idea of how he would react.

Worse, she was afraid he would try and convince her she had imagined his name on the statement, or that Ellen had manufactured it herself, and it was a fake. As much as it exasperated her to admit it, a tiny slice of her was afraid she'd let him convince her. She was about to pull into traffic when her phone chirped.

"Bekkah," Cairenn's voice wailed the minute she answered the call. "*National Art World* just called. They want to do the photo shoot in two days! Oh my God, what are we going to do? Of course I told them no problem. I must be out of my mind! But two days, I can't—"

"It'll be fine, we can do it," Rebekkah cut in.

"What's the matter? You don't sound right."

"I'm fine. We can do this." Rebekkah forced herself to sound cheerful for her friend. "You'll see. I'll bring you the paintings I have in my studio."

"You'll let me show your gorgeous self-portrait?"

Rebekkah laughed. "I'll let you."

"I have to call my other artists right away. Talk later, sweetie."

"Okay," Rebekkah responded to dead air. At least she was still excited about the magazine coming. She tucked her phone away and pulled into the traffic mess.

Rebekkah let herself into the condominium a half-hour later. Kicking off her shoes, she sank her feet into the plush tan carpeting. She would never decorate this place now that she knew she wasn't going to stay in her marriage. As she rounded the corner into the bedroom, her heart stopped.

Avram. He turned, and Rebekkah's eyes went to the piece of paper in his hand. She stood still as a rock, her mouth dry. It was one of the statements she had found at the funeral home. She must have missed one when she hid them. Her eyes slowly went from the statement to Avram's face.

He dropped the paper on the bed and strode to her. Rebekkah forced herself not to shrink back.

"What kind of greeting is this?" he whispered in her ear as he hugged her. "I've missed you. Haven't you missed me?"

Was he toying with her? Surely, it was clear how the statement got here, but she took his lead. "Of course."

He retrieved the statement from the bed. "I see you found these."

"I was...looking for something for Katy, I...thought these statements looked unusual and wanted to take a closer look." Her face grew hotter by the second. Why didn't he drop the charade and get angry?

He ran a hand through his hair and his shoulders slumped. "I didn't want you to find out. I guess it was God's will I left the drawer unlocked."

"You aren't angry?"

He shook his head and sank down to the bed, looking deflated. "No, I'm glad you found them. I wanted to protect you from all this. I'm afraid Mark is embezzling from the funeral home. I've suspected for a while. So far he's been able to cover his tracks, but he has to know it won't end well. I can't believe my best friend..."

"Are you sure?" Rebekkah cried, hoping she sounded sufficiently distressed. She didn't believe him for one second. The performance he was giving stunk to high heaven. "Why would he do that? Why aren't you confronting him?"

"I don't want you coming to work anymore," Avram pronounced, evading both of Rebekkah's questions.

"Mark said there was no convention. Where were you?" she demanded, wondering what he would come up with.

He stared at the floor, and after a pause, replied. "He was right. There was no convention."

Rebekkah waited, convinced he was making everything up as he went along.

"I went to see my family."

"You couldn't have told me this? Taken me with you?" Liar. Did he really think she'd believed he'd visited a family he rarely spoke about, and had never visited since she'd known him?

"I was afraid you would tell Mark where I was by mistake. I wanted some time away, hoping Mark would...I don't know...make a mistake while I was gone, leave a sloppy trail. I don't know what I thought. I didn't want you involved. Please forget all of this. I can handle it. It's devastating to me that my best friend could do this to me, to our business."

She refrained from rolling her eyes. His story made no sense. It was difficult to keep the disgust she felt for him from showing. She wanted to confront him about the robbery and the vasectomy, but now wasn't the time. Of course, if he was responsible for the robbery, nothing else would matter.

She didn't believe Mark would steal money from the funeral home. Nor Amy. She felt ill as the pieces came together in her mind. Was embezzling how Avram had afforded the condo, the BMW, and all the recent presents?

"I know you're upset about not being able to come to work," Avram's voice invaded her thoughts, "but you understand it's for the best. I'm only thinking of you."

Rebekkah smiled sweetly. "Of course I do. I'm glad you aren't upset that I found those statements."

He rose and came to Rebekkah, kissing her on the head. "I'm not. Just leave everything to me. I guess I'll unpack now."

"I'll be happy to leave it to you," she replied, then clapped a hand over her mouth. "I can't believe I forgot to tell you. Someone broke into the art gallery, and can you believe, most of the paintings gone are mine. Why do you think someone would do that? It's not like they're worth that much."

She watched Avram closely, but he didn't flinch. "She's so distraught. On top of that, *National Art World* will be here in two days. I need to gather the paintings I've done to replace the stolen ones. Thank God I have insurance."

Avram stopped unpacking and frowned. "What are you babbling about? What's *National Art World?*"

She wasn't surprised at his lack of comment on the break in. "You remember. I told you all about the magazine that wants to feature Cairenn's gallery, and some of her artists and their work. Including mine."

"Oh, that. I wish you both well," he replied, his attention back on his suitcase.

She crept from the room and made her way to her studio. She wasn't finished with Avram, but she would let things go until she came up with a plan.

Cairenn and Rebekkah made one last round to see that everything was in order at the gallery. A few minutes before nine the magazine staff and photographer arrived from *National Art World*, and the next two hours were spent in a flurry of photography and interviews with Rebekkah, Cairenn, and the other artists whom Cairenn represented. Rebekkah was pleased at how well it was going, and what good promotion the magazine article would be for the gallery.

"Oh Jesus, Mary and Joseph," Cairenn hissed during a break, slamming down her mug so hard that liquid from it sloshed on the counter. "Of all the times for him to come in here. Bekkah, would you mind speaking to the lovely detective? I can't deal with him today. He's been by a few times skulking about, never with any good news, only more obtuse questions."

Rebekkah followed Cairenn's stare, and her heart tripped when she saw Detective Rossi. She wondered if he had mentioned the matchbook to Cairenn. What would Cairenn think of her if Avram was behind the break in? She would probably drop her as a client. She had to talk to Cairenn later, and be truthful, before the detective said something.

She joined him where he stood in front of her self-portrait. Rebekkah's hair in the painting was loose, cascading down her shoulders in thick waves, magically catching the lighting in the gallery, making it look like spun gold. Her large green eyes, resembling wet moss, were magnets, drawing the viewer closer.

Rebekkah had perfectly captured the delicate angles of her own prominent cheekbones, the slight tilt of her nose, and the graceful arches of her eyebrows. Her full lips were curved up in a subtle smile that was barely visible unless you studied the picture for a minute or two.

"Good morning, Detective Rossi. Did you find out who Vinnie is?"

He didn't look at Rebekkah, and ignored her question. "That's you," he stated in a low voice. "You painted this one also?"

"Yes, I did."

"You're extremely talented, Mrs. Gelles."

"Thank you," she replied, fidgeting with the buttons on her sweater as a blush warmed her cheeks.

"What's going on today?" Detective Rossi kept his attention riveted on her portrait. "What's with the photographers and the woman with the laptop?"

"They're from an art magazine. They're doing an article and taking pictures for it." She lowered her voice. "Please don't say anything to Cairenn about the matchbook I found. Not yet, I don't want her to know it could be my husband."

Detective Rossi nodded slightly without looking at her. "I won't. I guess this is good publicity for the gallery, and you."

"Cairenn and I are really excited about it." Rebekkah glanced at his profile. His posture was perfect. He wore a dark blue pinstripe suit with a white shirt, and red tie. He was clean-shaven, and once again she vaguely smelled his cologne. His suit looked tailor-made, emphasizing his broad shoulders and muscular back. He didn't look like a detective to her–maybe an actor playing a detective on one of those police shows she favored, or a very in-shape athlete.

"Detective," she whispered, "did you find out who Vinnie is?"

"I was going to call you and talk to you about it."

Her brows puckered. That didn't answer her question. This conversation was strange. He kept addressing her likeness instead of her.

Rossi finally threw Rebekkah an enigmatic half-smile that revealed a deep dimple in his cheek and transformed his hard features. Then a shadow passed over his face and his smile disappeared so quickly she wondered if she had imagined it.

"Can you tell me now?"

He glanced at his watch. "Can we meet later?"

Rebekkah waffled. Avram would be at the funeral home until late, or so he'd said. It wasn't as if she was doing something wrong meeting with the detective. She shouldn't care anyway, but she was still Avram's wife. "When?"

He looked at his watch. "Four this afternoon?"

"Where?"

"You know Rosie's in Park Slope?"

"Park Slope?" Rebekkah echoed.

"Not upper-class enough for you?" he scorned.

"No, that's not it. I love Rosie's Diner. I used to live in Park Slope. I miss my neighborhood."

"Then I'll see you there," Detective Rossi replied.

"There's something else I need to ask you about."

"Save it for later. Don't forget."

She met his eyes, and neither looked away. She had the strange sensation of being alone with him over a small table for two in an intimate restaurant. That's what happens when you only read romance novels, she chided herself.

The spell was broken seconds later when he spoke. "Excuse me, I'm going upstairs and look around. We'll talk later."

Rebekkah went back to Cairenn, who was still mingling at the front of the gallery with a photographer from *National Art World*, who wanted to take a few more pictures and ask some of the artists more questions. His partner, the woman with the laptop, started to type.

By the time it was all over, Rebekkah was tired, but very happy, and Cairenn couldn't stop talking about how much the magazine had loved Rebekkah's work, and how great this would be for the artists involved, and for her.

Cairenn leaned against the counter, watching a few customers browse. "I can't believe he picked today to come back and ask more inane questions," she said to Rebekkah. "The detective, I mean. I guess I should be glad he's doing his job, but so far he's come up with zip. The good news is he bought a painting. Can you believe it? I never would have taken him for the artsy type. He looks more like an Italian mobster." She laughed. "How's that for stereotyping?"

Rebekkah couldn't have explained why, but her head turned to where her self-portrait had hung. Staring back at her was the stark, white wall. "He bought my portrait?" she asked, astounded. "Why?" She had let Cairenn show it, but she'd thought it unlikely anyone would buy it. She had planned on giving it to her parents on their anniversary.

"I don't know," Cairenn replied. "He was certainly taken by it. I tried to talk him into another one, but he was adamant, so I let him have it. Do you mind terribly? I'm sure we can buy it back if you do."

"No, it's okay. I don't want a confrontation with him." She wasn't angry at Cairenn. After all, she hadn't known Rebekkah had planned to give it to her parents. "I can do another if I want."

"It's a sale, look at it that way. It goes to show you can't really guess what people are into from their looks."

Rebekkah nodded absentmindedly. She was still unnerved by Detective Rossi buying her portrait. As soon as the magazine people left, she did, too. She hadn't said anything to Cairenn about the matchbook, deciding to wait until there was tangible proof of who was behind the robbery.

TWELVE

Rebekkah went home, nervous about her meeting later with Detective Rossi. Avram and she had said little to each other since his return, which was good since she had so much to think about. Thank God he hadn't tried having sex with her. The thought turned her stomach.

She threw open her closet door, but there was no need to change clothes just to see the detective. The navy blue dress she had on and the ballet flats were good enough. He wasn't a date she had to impress.

Rebekkah wished she could talk to her parents about Avram's lie and her other suspicions, but she wouldn't tell anyone until she'd decided what to do. And she had no idea where to begin. She was afraid to confront Avram about a divorce just yet. Should she move out first? Call an attorney first?

She went into the bathroom and lifted her brush to her hair, still thinking. Dark circles shadowed beneath her eyes and she had lost weight. She needed direction. Rabbi Weissman, she thought with a flash of hope. He could help her. Her cell phone rang from the bedroom, and she put down her brush to go answer it.

"Mrs. Gelles?"

Rebekkah recognized Detective Rossi's deep voice. "Yes, this is Rebekkah."

"It's Detective Dominick Rossi. Would you mind if we met earlier? How about in an hour? Is that okay with you?"

At least he wasn't cancelling. "Not at all, that's fine."

"I'll see you at one then. I'll save us a table," he said, ending the call.

Rebekkah offered a silent prayer to God as she called the Beth Israel office. Please be able to see me today, Rabbi. God had listened. Rabbi Weissman would be available all afternoon.

"Hi, honey," Rosie herself greeted Rebekkah when she got to the diner. "Nice to see you again. You alone?"

Rebekkah smiled at the rotund woman with the blazing orange beehive. "Hi, Rosie. No, I'm meeting someone." She looked past Rosie's shoulder. Detective Rossi was seated in a back booth studying the menu.

Rosie turned. "Mr. Tall, Dark and Handsome, huh? What's Mr. Gelles gonna say about that?"

She blushed under Rosie's scrutiny. "It's business."

Rosie gave Rebekkah an exaggerated wink. "If you say so."

Ignoring Rosie's comment, she made her way to the back of the diner. Detective Rossi stood up when he saw her. He had traded his suit for a pair of faded jeans and a black t-shirt that molded to his chest and abs like a second skin. He looked like a model.

Other women in the diner were checking him out. Not that Rebekkah could blame them, she felt a little breathless herself. Even her grandmother would take notice. Rebekkah could hear her saying, "Now that one's got matinee idol good looks."

"Thanks for coming early," Rossi said, waiting until Rebekkah was seated to sit back down.

"You're welcome. I can't wait to hear what you found."

Rossi opened his mouth, but a waitress chose that moment to come up to their table. "You two know what you want?"

The detective deferred to Rebekkah. "Do you need more time?"

Rebekkah looked up at the waitress. "I'm ready. Just an iced tea, please." Usually she ate the Caesar salad, but she had no appetite. The diner wasn't kosher, so there was a limited choice of foods on the menu for her. Mostly she loved the place because of its fifties ambiance.

Detective Rossi raised his eyebrows. "You sure?"

"Yes, thanks."

Rossi turned to the waitress. "I'll have a cheeseburger, fries, and a Coke."

"Be right back with your orders," she told them.

Rebekkah scooted to the edge of her seat. "Please. Tell me everything you've found."

He met her eyes. "I will, but can I call you Rebekkah instead of Mrs.Gelles? Not exactly protocol, but it fits you better."

She couldn't have agreed more. "I'd rather you call me Rebekkah. My family and friends call me Bekkah sometimes."

"You're a Rebekkah. If it makes you feel more comfortable, you can drop the detective and call me Dominick, or just Nick."

"Dominick. That's a nice name." She smiled at him then grew serious. "Now, what did you find?"

"Vinnie Martino is a bookie."

She gave him a puzzled look. "A what?"

"A bookie."

"Which means?"

"He takes bets, like on the World Series, or Super Bowl, sports events like that."

She took the glass of iced tea the waitress had just delivered. "That doesn't make sense. Avram doesn't gamble."

"Maybe he was thinking about it," Nick replied before taking a huge bite out of his cheeseburger. He swallowed it within seconds. "Or maybe he does, and you don't know."

190

Rebekkah's head spun. "Does this mean he's responsible for the break in at the art gallery?"

"No."

She folded her hands in her lap. "Can you do anything at all based on the matchbook?"

"I can have a talk with him. I'm also going to give Mr. Martino a call."

Her shoulders sagged. She hadn't expected the detective to run out and arrest Avram this second, but she had hoped he'd have something more concrete.

"You sure you don't want something to eat? Half of my cheeseburger?" he asked.

Rebekkah bit back a smile, touched by his offer. So, he had a human side after all. "I can't eat that. I'm Jewish and keep kosher, but thank you."

"No problem. I hope it doesn't bother you that I'm..." He motioned to his food.

"No," she assured him. "Please, go ahead and eat. I'm not hungry anyway."

"You said earlier there was something else you wanted to ask me about," he asked between mouthfuls.

She played with the straw in her drink. "I need an opinion."

Nick took a gulp of his Coke, his eyes on Rebekkah's face.

"I don't have positive proof," she continued.

He forgot about his food and leaned toward her. "About what?"

"I think my husband is embezzling money from his funeral home, and trying to blame it on his partner."

Rebekkah could almost sense Detective Rossi—Nick—going into detective mode. He reached over to a slim briefcase lying beside him and pulled out a notebook and pen.

"Do you have to write all this down?" she asked.

A smile pulled at his lips. "If you want me to remember it, I do. Any idea why he would do this?"

"I think he's in over his head financially. He bought a condo for us on East 72nd I didn't think we could afford, he bought me a BMW that I didn't want, and he keeps giving me expensive jewelry." It was easier talking to the detective than she'd thought.

His eyes raked over her, his expression serious. "That bothers you? The fancy condo and gifts, I mean."

"Yes, I don't need a lot of fancy jewelry, and I loved our home in this neighborhood. I didn't want to move," she cried. "I admit the BMW's nice, but I'd rather have a little Mustang."

"That would be my preference. You don't seem to be wearing much of his jewelry." Nick glanced at the ring finger of her left hand, which was splayed on the table in front of her. "Not even the wedding rings you had on earlier today."

192

She hadn't realized she had taken them off. Not that it mattered, they meant so little to her now.

"What about that necklace? It's unusual. Is that a gift from your husband?"

Rebekkah's fingers went to the multi-colored beaded necklace. "This is a hamsa, the symbol of an eye embedded in the palm of an open hand. My parents gave it to me when I turned sixteen."

Nick abruptly changed the subject. "Does your husband have a mistress? You've already said large debts, and again, what about gambling?"

Rebekkah blanched. Avram with a mistress? "I don't know if he has a mistress. And I don't know if he gambles. Maybe he does. I've come to realize lately that I don't know much about him."

He stopped writing and looked up at her. "Is there anything else you want to tell me? Surely you know about your finances."

She fidgeted. He would laugh at her naïveté when she admitted how little she knew. "My husband handles all the finances. He keeps the checkbook and pays for everything. I have two credit cards. One for shopping and one for gas." She wondered if she was telling him too much.

Dominick let his notebook drop to the table then let the pen fall onto the notebook. He leaned back in their booth. He didn't laugh, but he scowled at her. "Excuse my personal opinion, but that's ridiculous. I find it hard to believe you wouldn't know anything about your own family's finances. What if you want to buy something and your card's maxed out? What if you want to go shopping with your girlfriends?"

She winced. He was right, it was ridiculous. "Avram gives me an allowance, and I've made some money from my art lately." It sounded lame, even to her.

He shook his head in disbelief and picked his notebook and pen back up. "Do you own part of the business?"

"No," replied Rebekkah. "He has a partner, Mark Bender. Can you talk to him?"

"What proof do you have that someone is embezzling?"

She told him about the statements, the missing money from some of the clients' accounts, and Avram trying to implicate Mark.

"Have you talked to Mr. Bender about this?"

"I didn't think of it. Should I?"

"Not necessarily. What if he is the one who's embezzling, as your husband said?"

Deep down Rebekkah didn't believe that, but she had no concrete proof. She leaned back in her seat. "What should I do?"

"I wouldn't do anything right now. Let me talk to him about the matchbook. The break in at the art gallery is my first priority. If he, or his partner, is embezzling, they won't get away with it forever."

Rebekkah was hoping there was something she could do to help, but supposed she had no choice but to follow Nick's advice.

The waitress came with the bill. Detective Rossi immediately scooped it up. "I'll have a talk with your husband about the matchbook and let you know how it goes."

"Thank you, detective…Nick." His name sounded strange, unfamiliar on Rebekkah's lips. She reached for her purse and pulled out her wallet to pay for her iced tea.

"No, I've got it. Put your wallet back."

"Thanks, and thanks for meeting with me." She slid from the booth.

"You're welcome."

She waited while he handed the cashier a credit card, then they walked outside together. "Did you take the subway? I'll be happy to drive you home. Or did you drive?"

Rebekkah was embarrassed when her eyes filled with tears. She blinked them back. What was home now? She didn't have a home. Certainly it wasn't with Avram. "I drove, but I have a meeting with the rabbi at my synagogue before I go home. I was thinking I might walk by my old house, but I've changed my mind. I think I'll just walk to the synagogue then I can return for my car."

He nodded as if he understood what she meant. Then she remembered something she had forgotten to ask him earlier. "You bought my self-portrait. Why?"

The detective actually looked embarrassed, which amused Rebekkah.

"It was a beautiful piece of art."

"That's all?"

He shrugged, looking sexy and sheepish at the same time. "There was something …Hell, I don't know, I'm not the poetic type. I liked it, I bought it. Would you like to see where I put it? If you have time, that is."

Was he asking her to come to his house? Rebekkah's heart sped up. "Do you live near here?"

"Close enough. Union Street. I moved in about three years ago, after my divorce. I'm surprised I've never seen you around if you lived in the same area. I would have remembered you. I'll drive you in my car then bring you back here, so you can get yours. I have to make a trip to the office later anyway so it's not like I'd be going out of my way."

Envy flooded through Rebekkah. Union Street was filled with lovely brownstones, just like the one she had lived in with Avram. She was wary, though, wondering what was behind his invitation. Yes, he seemed nice enough. But, for all she knew, he might have nefarious motives. She no longer trusted her own judgment. Hadn't Avram been a big enough mistake?

"You can trust me," he said, as if reading her mind. "It's not a pick-up line and I know you're married. I just thought you might like to see it."

Rebekkah was torn as she looked at Nick. There was no harm in what he proposed. On the other hand, she was still married, as he'd reminded her.

"I'll tell you what," he offered. "I'll give you my address. If it makes you feel better, you can drive over yourself. I'd kind of like you to see how great your painting looks hanging up."

When he had questioned Cairenn and her about the break-in, Rebekkah had found the man brash and annoying. Now, he seemed somehow different. She stopped analyzing his suggestion, and before she let herself think any more about it, she agreed to go with him.

He seemed pleased as he led her to a shiny, late-model red Camaro. He opened her door, and new car smell filled her nose. A heavy silver cross dangled from the mirror on a chain of white beads. She knew it was something that Catholics used for praying, and she tried imagining Nick praying with those beads, but the image wouldn't come.

He got in on his side, pulled his seatbelt on and slid on dark, wrap-around sunglasses. His presence seemed to fill the entire car. She felt odd being in the closed space with him. Not like a date exactly, but as if they were good friends going somewhere. She had only been with two men in her life, and she had been in love with each of them, or so she'd thought, not friends. For no particular reason all her good friends were always women. What would it be like if she and Nick became friends?

She turned to fasten the seatbelt, and as Nick turned right out of Rosie's she saw a man staring at her, his

197

mouth in a grim line. Nathan Peck, one of Avram's good friends from Beth Israel. She turned her head, ignoring his sour look.

Nick slowly turned right out of the diner parking lot. He had a CD playing, but it was so soft Rebekkah couldn't tell who was singing. "Who was that guy staring at you?"

"A friend of my husband's," she replied, hoping he wouldn't ask any more questions.

"Is he going to make trouble for you?" Nick's concern was evident on his face.

"No, there's no reason for him to." Nathan's stare had made her uneasy, but it was nothing to bother Nick about.

Nick looked at Rebekkah for a second then returned his eyes to the road.

"I'm not making you break any laws am I?"

"What laws?"

"You're Jewish. Are you allowed to be alone with a man who isn't your husband?"

That made Rebekkah smile. "Yes, I'm allowed."

A few minutes later, Nick parked his car and ushered her inside his brownstone.

She was stunned. This was so much her idea of a perfect home that it took her breath away. She stood in awe in the narrow entrance hallway, where a beautiful navy blue and yellow oriental rug ran the length of it.

To the left was what she surmised to be his living room. A dark hardwood floor gleamed in the sun. A huge grand piano took up most of the space, leaving only room for a large, flowered couch. Bookshelves lined either side of a small fireplace. To her right was a formal dining room with a huge crystal and pewter chandelier hanging over the dining room table and hutch.

"It's to your left," Nick said. "Above the piano."

Rebekkah's attention was diverted by a squat bulldog hurrying down the hallway, its tongue hanging out of an adorable, jowly face.

Nick kneeled. "Hi ya there, girl." The dog trembled all over as he stroked her. "This is Grace. I hope you don't mind dogs."

Rebekkah grinned, and she kneeled to pet Grace. The dog wiggled under her hand, her stubby tail wagging fiercely as she tried to get close enough to lick Rebekkah's face. "I love dogs."

"Do you have any?"

Her smile faded. "No. Avram doesn't like them. My parents have two yellow Labradors. We always had dogs in the house when I was growing up."

Nick rose. "Great dogs. My family always had dogs, too. All right, that's enough, Grace. Leave our guest alone."

Grace sat immediately. She panted, her dark eyes shining up at Nick with adoration. Rebekkah laughed as she also stood. She was in love with Grace already. "It must be hard for her to be away from you. She adores you."

Nick grinned down at his dog. "I'm a little fond of her, too. My elderly neighbor walks her for me." He glanced at the clock on the mantel in the living room. "She probably just got back from her walk. I'm not usually home now. Come on, I'll show you how your self-portrait looks."

She followed him into the living room. Her likeness was hanging above the piano as he'd said. She still didn't totally understand why he would want it. He didn't even know her. "It looks nice in here. But it's strange looking at myself hanging in your living room."

He smiled at her. "I guess it would be. You did an excellent job on it. The colors are so vibrant. I can see you have talent even though I'm not an art...what's the word? Art connoisseur." His smile faded and he looked worried. "It doesn't bother you that I bought it, does it?"

"No, I guess not," Rebekkah allowed. She wouldn't tell him she was going to give it to her parents. "I appreciate the sale. Do you play?"

He looked at the piano. "No, it was my mother's. I haven't been able to part with it."

She noticed a change in his demeanor, and wondered what had caused it.

"Do you want to sit down for a while? Can I get you anything? I don't have a lot, maybe some juice or water."

His home was quiet and orderly, and Rebekkah had no lingering fear that he would attack her, or some such thing. She smiled at him. "No, thank you, I'm fine. Tell me about your family," she found herself asking as she sank into his couch. Grace came to lie at her feet.

He joined her on the couch. "I have three brothers. Three of us are police officers. My youngest brother plays minor league ball. My mother, Angelina, died of cancer last year."

Sympathy rose in Rebekkah at the pain in his eyes. "How awful."

"Yeah, it was. I honestly think she died of a broken heart. She was totally devoted to my dad. He was a decorated police officer, and he was killed seventeen years ago. I don't think my mom ever recovered from Michael Rossi's death."

Nick had such a sad, faraway look in his eyes, Rebekkah felt like an interloper. The deaths of both his parents had obviously affected him deeply. "Is that why you became a police officer?"

"Not just family tradition," he replied. "My dad's murderer is still out there. He was shot during a bank robbery. The case is still open. I may never find out who killed him, but I want to put away as many bad guys as possible. For him."

She reached down to pet Grace. "I'm sure you do a great job."

"I try. I hope this isn't too personal, but what do you plan on doing if your husband is responsible for the break in at the art gallery and really is embezzling?"

Rebekkah frowned then her eyes drifted up to her likeness on the wall. "I'm going to divorce him. Not just because of that, but because of something else I've found out."

"If you need advice, or someone to listen, call me."

She agreed to do that then laughed as Grace gave a little woof, as if she were offering her support, too.

"Was your divorce hard?" Rebekkah could have bit her tongue. Of course it must have been hard, when was divorce easy?

Nick took no offense. "Oh, yeah. Felicia and I had been together since high school. I was as happy as I thought I could be when we got married. But I played for keeps. She didn't."

He had Rebekkah's full attention now. She loved hearing people's life stories. What shaped them, and made them who they were. His eyes held a faraway look, as if he was reliving that part of his life again.

"What happened?"

"She had an affair with her boss then left me for him. I never saw it coming. How stupid was that? Then again, I had no reason to suspect my wife would cheat on me. My parents had a great marriage so I thought all marriages were like that. We sold our house, and I moved in here. Would you believe she had the audacity to call me after she married the man she left me for, to tell me she missed me? I was disgusted. Besides, the love I had once felt for her was long gone, as cold as a bench in Central Park in the dead of winter."

Rebekkah digested what he'd told her. Maybe his earlier arrogance had been a cover for the hurt he had suffered. There was no arrogance in him now.

She hoped he had someone in his life now, but she didn't get that feeling. If she were anyone else, she would be interested herself. He was good-looking, sexy in his jeans that fit to perfection, and he smelled really good. More importantly, he seemed genuinely nice. But he wasn't Jewish, and she wasn't in the market for a relationship even if he had been Jewish.

Rebekkah was sure she'd never be "in the market" again. Losing Jonathan and now discovering Avram was not the man she'd thought, was too much. Could you ever really know someone else's heart? She hadn't known Avram's true heart, and Dominick hadn't known his wife's true heart.

"Are you seeing anyone now?" she asked.

"No. I haven't wanted to get remotely involved with anyone until…"

"Until what?" she asked when his sentence ended abruptly.

His eyes met hers then he looked out the window. "Nothing. Never mind, it's not important. Until was the wrong word, and I've talked enough about myself. I must feel comfortable with you because I'm never this long-winded. What about you? Are you sure your marriage is over?"

His openness demanded she tell her own story. "Yes. Very sure." She repeated the same story she had told Ellen about Jonathan and the accident, and how she no longer loved Avram. She meant to stop short of telling him about Avram's vasectomy, but before she knew it, that had spilled out too. "I feel like you do. I don't want to get involved with anyone. I don't know who to trust."

"You'll figure it out when the time is right," Nick told her. "Your husband sounds like a jackass."

Rebekkah had to smile at the seriousness with which he said that. She didn't think she'd figure anything out, but she didn't argue. "I better go so I can meet with the rabbi."

He jumped from the couch. "I'm glad you got to see where your painting ended up"

She smiled. "I'm happy it has a good home." She knelt on the rug and hugged Grace good-bye. She almost didn't want to leave, but she didn't belong here. She hoped Nick would find a good woman to love.

"Do you want me to take you back to Rosie's?" he asked as he held open the front door for her.

She shook her head. "If you don't mind, the synagogue. I'll walk back and get my car from there. It's not far."

"You really miss your old neighborhood."

"I do," she confessed.

The ride to the synagogue was quiet, Nick knew right where it was, but the silence wasn't strained or uncomfortable.

"Thanks for the ride," she said when they arrived at Beth Israel. "You'll let me know what you find about the mysterious Vinnie, and what Avram says after you talk to him?"

Nick rested his arm on the back of her seat. For a minute she thought he was going to caress the back of her head. It tingled in anticipation, but of course there was no reason for him to do that.

"I'll call you soon."

"Thank you." Rebekkah got out. When she reached the top step she turned before she swung open the front door to the synagogue. The Camaro was still at the curb. He waved through the window at her, and she watched as he drove away.

Maybe they could be friends. They had something in common. She could see he intended to keep his heart tightly locked away, just as she did.

THIRTEEN

"Good to see you, Rebekkah." Rabbi Weissman ushered her into his office. "Help yourself to the couch. I'll take one of my uncomfortable chairs that needs reupholstering." He chuckled. "Unfortunately, our leaky roof takes priority."

Despite her circumstances, Rebekkah smiled at him. There were only twelve years between them, and she was grateful or his outgoing, friendly, and laid-back personality. She situated herself on the over-stuffed plaid couch under the window and gathered her thoughts.

Rabbi Weissman sat opposite her, lifting his feet to rest on the coffee table. "What can I help you with?"

Rebekkah expected the words to come flowing out, but when she opened her mouth, she was suddenly tongue-tied.

"Relax," he told her. "You've known me for what? Eight years? I haven't bitten anyone yet. Unless you're about to tell me you've murdered someone, our talk is confidential. Now, why are you here? I haven't seen you in a while. You've been missed."

She lowered her eyes. "Avram wanted us to go to an Orthodox shul near our condo. I've missed being here, too." She blinked and looked up at her rabbi. "I don't know where to start."

"You must have quite a list," he joked before becoming serious. "This is cliché, but how about starting at the beginning."

"It's Avram. I've discovered recently he's had a vasectomy. I've decided to divorce him."

The rabbi took his feet off the coffee table and sat up straight, leaning toward her. "Have you talked to an attorney yet?"

"Not yet." Rebekkah shifted her position on the couch. "I wanted to see you first."

"I'm glad you're here. Have you talked to Avram?"

"No," she replied, "but I need to soon."

"How did you find out about the vasectomy?"

"I met his ex-wife, whom I didn't even know existed until recently. She told me. When I first told him about meeting her Avram convinced me she was lying and had mental health problems. I believed him since he promised he'd have fertility testing in one year if I wasn't pregnant." Rebekkah blinked back tears. "Then I saw Ellen, his ex-wife, again, and she showed me the insurance statement for his vasectomy. She doesn't have mental health problems, Rabbi. We've even becoming friends."

He rubbed his chin. "No wonder you're upset. You need to talk to him, Rebekkah. If you have irrefutable proof, he can't deny it."

She wouldn't put it past Avram to try. He could deny his existence and convince someone. He was very persuasive. "I know. I just…"

"You aren't afraid he'll physically harm you, are you?" The rabbi's eyes were troubled, and his voice was full of concern. "If you are, then move out immediately."

"I don't think he would," she answered, although she wasn't absolutely sure. His assertive behavior that day that now seemed so long ago. "I'm moving out today, as soon as I tell him I want a divorce. I'm sure my parents will love to have me home after I tell them about everything."

Rabbi Weissman nodded in acknowledgement. "I'm sorry you're going through this. You're aware once you obtain a civil divorce you'll still need to obtain a *get*, a divorce under Jewish law. A civil divorce has no religious validity in dissolving the marital ties of a Jewish couple."

He leaned back in his chair again. "Without a get, you can't remarry under Jewish law. If you do remarry without a get, any children you have in a subsequent marriage are technically considered *mamzerim*, illegitimate. They will not be accepted into many Jewish communities. I know some Conservative synagogues turn a blind eye to the acceptance of mamzerim, but the status of a mamzer is inherited for ten generations."

Rebekkah processed what Rabbi Weissman said. Most of it she vaguely knew, but it was good to have him be specific. How had her life become so complicated? She hoped Avram wouldn't give her a hard time about the get.

"Normally, I'd encourage, or even insist, a couple come for counseling before they contemplate a serious step like divorce, but Avram entered into the covenant of marriage dishonestly. I consider what he's done marital abuse."

"What if Avram refuses to give me a get? I've read about the *agunah*. The wife chained to her marriage because her husband refuses to give her a get." Nausea rose inside her at the thought of being trapped in her marriage. He must have given Ellen a get, unless Ellen wasn't Jewish. She made a mental note to call her again.

"Why don't we take this one step at a time? Confront Avram, get an attorney, and we'll talk about the get after your civil divorce. Anything else?" he gave her an encouraging look, full of sympathy. "Not that that's not enough."

She got up and wandered to his bookshelf, scanning the titles. She'd changed her mind about discussing the theft at the gallery, finding Avram's matchbook there, and that he might be embezzling from his own business. "No, the rest isn't important right now. I want to take care of this, first. I'll tell Avram I want a divorce. Then I'll get a lawyer."

Rabbi Weissman joined her. "Sounds like a plan. Please come back, so we can talk again. If you want, we can schedule regular appointments until your divorce is final."

She didn't feel as helpless knowing the rabbi was there for her. "I'll think about it. Thank you so much, Rabbi."

"You're welcome. I expect to see you soon." He tried looking stern, but she knew behind that look was a soft heart. He cared deeply about his congregation.

She wandered out of the synagogue into the sunlight. She missed this neighborhood full of trees, beautiful old brownstones, and children walking with their parents. Maybe somehow she could move back here. All she wanted to do was forget about Avram and their mistake of a marriage. What would she do for money? Her art wasn't bringing in near enough to support her yet, and nothing was in her name, only Avram's. Would he have to pay alimony?

Rebekkah was only a few blocks from her parents' house. She decided she might as well see if Ima was home. It was time to bring her parents up to date on Avram. But first, she had to go collect her car at Rosie's.

Twenty minutes later she was ringing her parents' front doorbell.

Shira swung the door open, her initial look of surprise transforming into a smile. "What are you doing in your old neighborhood?"

"I had to talk to the rabbi. I thought it would be a good time to come see you, too."

Shira waved Rebekkah inside. "Is anything wrong that you had to see Rabbi Weissman?"

"Can we sit?"

"I'd prefer it to standing for your entire visit. It's nothing serious, I hope."

Rebekkah didn't reply as she made a beeline for the living room. She dropped on the couch and waited for her mother to join her.

Shira pulled the kerchief off her head and shook her hair loose. "I've been cleaning. Sometimes I think it's all I ever do. Maybe we should get a smaller place. Now, tell me, what is it?" She clapped her hands together and beamed at her daughter. "Ah! You're pregnant."

"No, Ima." Rebekkah reached for a pillow and hugged it.

Shira's smile fell away. "I guess you wouldn't be talking to the rabbi about that. I'm disappointed. I know how much you and Avram want children."

Rebekkah snorted. "I do, but he doesn't, and never has."

Now Shira frowned. "What? Why do you say such a thing? He loves you. He wants a child with—"

"No!" Rebekkah cut her mother off. "Avram had—."

Rebekkah was chagrined when her father chose that moment to walk in the front door. She adored him, but preferred some alone time with her mother.

His face lit up when he saw Rebekkah, making her feel guilty for resenting his presence. "What a surprise, two of my three favorite women. All we need is your sister."

"Hi, Aba." She watched her mother go to him. He gave Shira such a deep kiss that Rebekkah looked away. Hadn't they just seen each other this morning? Envy pricked her for the second time that day. How wonderful to be so in love after all their years together.

Her mother whispered something in her husband's ear. David left the room, and Shira returned to Rebekkah. "Okay, so tell me. No more interruptions. I promise. Avram had what?"

"He had a vasectomy before we met, so obviously he can't father a child. Maybe he could if he reversed it, but I'm sure he wouldn't think of doing that. I don't want even want him to. I don't love him. I don't think I ever did. I don't know why I married him. It was a big mistake."

Shira's eyes widened. "Slow down, you're talking so fast. What are you saying? Is this true? Why would he do such a thing?"

Rebekkah told Shira about meeting Ellen and seeing proof of his vasectomy. Tears spilled down her cheeks, and she swiped them away. "Why did he marry me? I want to divorce him, Ima. I can't stay married to him. I don't want to live with him anymore. That's what I was seeing Rabbi Weissman about."

"Oh, my lovely daughter," Shira crooned as she scooted closer to Rebekkah and hugged her. "I'm sorry. I had no idea this would happen. If only your father and I hadn't pushed him on you. What did Rabbi Weissman say?"

Rebekkah pulled away to grab a tissue from the box on the coffee table, then repeated what the rabbi had said. "It's not your fault. How would you have known? You wanted me to be happy. How can I blame you?"

Before Shira could respond, Rebekkah's father came back in, throwing Shira a pointed look. "Can I come back now? If something's bothering my daughter, why shouldn't I know?"

Shira ignored her husband. "Bekkah, you'll move in with us. Go home get your things then come back. I'll get your bedroom freshened up."

The thought of curling up in her old bed filled Rebekkah with peace.

"What do you mean she's coming back here?" David demanded. "What's going on?"

Shira stood and put an arm around David's waist. "Avram can't father children. He had a vasectomy." She gave him a shortened version of the story.

"She needs to see lawyer first. She can't just walk out." David replied.

"I don't want her spending another night with him."

"You're overreacting. What she needs to do is—"

"Wait," Rebekkah cried. Her parents seemed to have forgotten she was there. "Avram doesn't know I saw proof. When he gets home later I'm going to tell him I want a divorce then I'm going to find a lawyer. I'll come back tonight. I promise."

Her parents seemed mollified. She decided not to tell them about her suspicions about Avram and the art gallery break-in, or the statements at the funeral home. Those, she had no proof of. Not yet. The funeral home wasn't really any of her business anyway, but if something illegal was

213

happening, she wondered if Mark knew. She felt so bad for their clients.

Her mother hugged her, kissing her on the cheek, and her father embraced her.

"I don't know how I'm going to pay for a divorce. Or live on my own," Rebekkah confessed, "But I'm going to find out."

"You make Avram pay for the divorce," Shira huffed. She exchanged a long look with David. "But you needn't worry. There's money."

"Shira..." David glared at his wife.

Rebekkah glanced quizzically at her parents. Even she noticed the warning tone in her father's voice. The air was charged with tension she didn't understand, but she didn't have the energy to worry about it.

Shira made a face at her husband. "I'm just telling her there's money."

"Not now," he retorted.

"Fine," Shira replied, turning away from him. "We'll see you later then? You will be back, won't you? I don't want you staying with Avram."

"We'll wait up for you," her father added.

"I'll be back," Rebekkah assured them as she reached out and hugged both parents. As she walked to her car, she thought about confronting Avram alone that evening and pulled out her phone.

"What's up?" Rebekkah's brother answered.

"Hi, Sammy. Are you busy later?"

"I don't think so. Why?"

"I'm telling Avram tonight I want a divorce. I don't want to be there alone. I found a gun in the bedroom closet before we moved. He doesn't know I know about it. Maybe he put it there thinking I would find it and be scared. It worked. I'm not sure where it is now, but he must still have it. When I tell him I want a divorce he's not going to take it well. I think he might be embezzling money, too. It's a long story. Please, can you meet me at the condo?"

"What? What's going on with him? Never mind, tell me later. Of course I'll be there. What time?"

"Thank you. I'm so glad. Seven? I have an errand to run."

"I'll see you then."

When Rebekkah pulled into the parking garage of her condo, she half-hoped Avram wouldn't be there, but there the Mini-Cooper sat. She gripped her steering wheel. He was a liar, and if he was a thief too, he might be dangerous. If only there were some way to make him think the divorce was his idea. Don't be silly, she told herself. That wouldn't work. In his mind he was happily married. Why would he want a divorce?

Slowly she climbed out of the BMW, dreading the confrontation. She greeted Howard at the front desk. She would miss seeing him every day, she realized as she waited for the elevator.

"Rebekkah?" Avram's voice called to her as soon as she closed the front door.

She went into the living room to find her husband sprawled in a chair, legs outstretched, tie loosed, and a drink in his hand. "Yes. Did you expect someone else?" She prayed he couldn't sense her nervousness.

Instead of responding, Avram reached for his cell phone from the end table next

to the couch. "I had an interesting text from Nathan Peck. Along with a photo."

She tried for nonchalance. "Yes, I saw Nathan today, scowling as usual."

"The photo is of you getting into a car with another man." Avram's tone was eerily calm. She wondered how much he had to drink.

"The man was Detective Rossi. He's investigating the break in at the art gallery."

"Why did you feel the need to meet him at Rosie's Diner?" His eyes narrowed with suspicion.

She squared her shoulders. "I wanted to see Ima, so he offered to meet me there."

"If you're having an affair I'll find out. I won't be made a fool of."

"An affair? I'm not dignifying that with an answer. You should know me better than that."

He jumped up, towering over Rebekkah. He walked a circle around her, as if looking for proof she had been intimate with another man. "It could happen. You're

216

young, beautiful, why wouldn't men desire you? Maybe if you wore the sheitel like I asked men wouldn't want you. I don't like people to see you with other men. I don't care who they are. It diminishes me, makes me look stupid, as if I'm not in control of my wife."

Rebekkah couldn't believe her ears. On second thought, yes she could. "You can rest assured I'm not having an affair. I've been a good wife to you, and you know it. Where's the trust, Avram? Where is the man I thought I'd married? You're losing it."

He grabbed her arm, jerking her toward him. "Why did he take your picture?"

She squealed and he let go. Her arm throbbed. Where was her brother? "Don't touch me. I wasn't doing anything. Ask *him* why he took my picture. What's wrong with you? You've changed. You're not the man I thought you were.

"My art is gone! Don't you care about that? Can't you think of me first before wondering why Nathan decided to take my picture? If I were you, I'd be more worried that a man is taking your wife's picture for no reason then what she was doing talking to a detective. Which is perfectly normal by the way, when a robbery occurs."

Avram opened his mouth, but the doorbell rang, distracting him. He narrowed his eyes at her again and grabbed the back of her neck. "We aren't finished yet. Get the door."

Please, please be Sammy, she prayed as she hurried to the door.

217

She opened the door and breathed a sigh of relief. Sammy! Thank God. She reached up and hugged him.

"You okay?" he asked, looking past her shoulder. "He's here?"

"Yes. I'm about to tell him. Thanks for coming. I didn't want to be alone."

"No problem."

"Well, who is it, Rebekkah?" Avram bellowed.

"Sammy," Rebekkah called, taking her brother's hand as they walked into the living room. Facing Avram was easier with Sammy. She had told Rabbi Weissman she didn't think Avram would physically harm her, yet hadn't he done just that?

"Sammy, what's up?" Avram greeted him, his tone now ultra-jovial. "This is a surprise. Sit down. Rebekkah, get your brother a drink."

"I'm fine standing. Bekkah doesn't need to get me anything."

"Avram, I'm filing for divorce," Rebekkah announced.

He stared at her, his face flushing a bright red. His head swiveled between Rebekkah and Sammy. "You're what? What's gotten into you? Because I thought you were having an affair?"

"No, because you lied to me. You had a vasectomy."

Avram shook his head and plastered a phony smile across his face. He reached for her. "Why are we

218

discussing this in front of your brother? It's personal. I don't understand why you're bringing it up. I told you—"

She stepped back. "Don't bother. I saw Ellen again. She showed me proof. You can't deny it. I'm packing and leaving. You won't stop me."

Avram sank into the chair, his head hanging almost between his knees. When he looked up the angry look was gone, and tears shone in his eyes. "Don't do this. I love you. You're my wife. Where did this come from? How can you leave me? I know you're not having an affair. I was just kidding. Please, sit. We can talk all about it. You don't know what you're doing, my darling wife."

Rebekkah was tired of listening to him. He made her sick. What a brilliant actor. Two minutes ago he was raging at her. "I've said all I have to say. Our marriage is over. I don't even care why you deceived me any longer."

"Because," Avram cried out, his voice cracking with anguish as he began to explain anyway. "I had to. The vasectomy was a mistake I made when I was young. How could I tell you? I wanted you. I had to have you. You're so beautiful, you make me crazy. You would never have married me if you had known."

"That's right," Rebekkah spat out. She trembled with anger. "I wouldn't have married you. Lying was despicable. What exactly were you planning to do once the year was up? Remember, you promised to get fertility testing?"

"I don't know," groaned Avram. "I would have thought of something."

She shook her head. He was pathetic. "Don't try to contact me. Sammy, I'll be done in a little while."

In less than a second, Avram's expression went from sadness to sneering. "If you leave me, you'll get nothing."

"Bekkah, don't listen to him. Get your stuff." Sammy tried to gently guide her out of the room.

She looked around. Was there anything she wanted? No. Especially the new stuff if it was bought with ill-gotten gains. "I'm taking as much of my own things as I can now. I'll come back for the rest."

She started for the bedroom. Avram followed.

Sammy blocked him. "Let her go by herself."

Avram glared, but Sammy was bigger, more muscular. "I want to talk to my wife—she is still my wife—alone."

Rebekkah hoped a fight wouldn't break out. She continued to the bedroom with Avram on her heels. Sammy brought up the rear.

Avram slammed the door shut on Sammy.

"Avram! That wasn't necessary," cried Rebekkah.

"Don't worry, I'm not going anywhere," Sammy yelled from the other side. "Rebekkah, yell if you need me."

Avram ignored her brother. "The BMW and the Mini-Cooper are mine, leave them here."

"That's no problem," Rebekkah said. He sounded like a spoiled child.

"Leave all your jewelry."

"Fine." She wouldn't miss it. She wanted no reminders of him.

"Until we're divorced I expect you to act like a married woman. You are still my wife. If you run around with other men I will not give you your divorce."

She nodded as if he actually had that power. Run around with other men! He didn't know her at all. She would agree to anything if it meant not seeing him anymore. His attempt to control her was sad, but scared her, nonetheless. She remembered the gun and dizziness washed over her. She threw her clothes into two suitcases she pulled out from under the bed.

"Where are your wedding rings?" Avram snarled.

She glanced up from her packing. "I don't see any reason to wear them."

"I expect them back, too, since they mean nothing to you. After all I've done for you this is what you do? Most women would be at my feet."

Rebekkah refused to respond. He was baiting her and she wouldn't bite.

"I still love you despite your behavior."

She almost laughed. *Her* behavior? She went on packing, feeling the heat of his eyes on her. With her packing done she headed for the door.

Lightning fast, Avram lunged for her. He yanked her arm so violently she thought her shoulder would dislocate. He squeezed her face with his other hand until tears gathered in her eyes. "You're a bitch. A fucking bitch. How dare you do this to me?

"We aren't through, Rebekkah," he hissed in her ear. "Watch your step. You'll never know where I'll be. You'll pay for crossing me. You're a whore. Get out of my sight."

She heaved, almost throwing up when he thrust her toward the door. She flung it open and fell into Sammy's arms. "I'm all done. I'm ready to go."

"Your face. It's bruised. Wait here." Sammy started toward Avram who had collapsed on the bed in a fetal position. He didn't even seem to realize they were still there.

"Sammy, no!" Rebekkah was terrified of what would happen if a fight broke out between the two men. "I'll be fine. Let's get out of here. Please, now! I'm so glad you were here."

He grabbed her suitcases. "You need to file assault charges, Bekkah. Hey, Gelles, if you come around Rebekkah again, I'll kill you."

Avram didn't move. She couldn't wait to leave the condo. Until she was safe in Sammy's car, she was petrified Avram would come after them with the gun and kill them both.

"Hello?" Rebekkah answered her phone after automatically making sure the number displayed wasn't Avram's. In the ten days since she'd packed her things and left, she'd counted fifty messages from him begging her to come back. He'd even come to her parents' house, but

222

she'd refused to see him. Her father told him if he returned they would call the police. She'd programmed her phone to automatically send his calls to voice mail. If that didn't work she'd have to change her number no matter how much of a pain that would be. So many people had this number. He'd left her alone for the past three days. Maybe that was a good sign.

"Rebekkah? Nick Rossi."

Rebekkah settled back on her childhood bed, happy to hear from him. Maybe he had good news. She could use some. She twisted around, trying to fluff the pillows behind her so she could lean against the headboard while holding the phone.

"Can you talk?" he asked.

"Yes. I've left Avram and moved into my parents' house. That's where I am now. It's not far from where you live. Do you have any news?"

"Good for you. I know that had to be difficult," he sympathized. "I spoke to Avram."

Rebekkah's heart quickened. "You didn't tell him I gave you the matchbook, did you?" She hadn't thought of that before.

"No, I didn't."

"What did he say? Was it him?"

Nick laughed. "He didn't confess if that's what you're asking."

She was off the bed now, a jumble of nerves. "What did he say?"

"That he had been to the art gallery once. He came by to surprise you and you weren't there. He said he must have dropped it then."

"He's lying!" Rebekkah cried. "Cairenn would have told me he'd been there."

"Yeah, he could be lying, but if she didn't know who he was, she might've just forgotten. I talked to her, showed her the picture of Avram you gave me when we were at the diner. She couldn't be sure if he had been in or not. She said she wasn't too good with faces."

Rebekkah let out a pent up breath. She supposed it was possible, but she didn't believe it. "Now what?"

"Don't worry, the case is still open. I'll keep you and Cairenn posted."

"Thank you, Nick, I appreciate that you talked to him."

He paused so long Rebekkah wondered if they had lost the connection. She was about to ask if he was still there when he spoke. "It's my job. You don't have to thank me. I have something to ask you, Rebekkah, but I don't want you to take it the wrong way."

"I won't. What is it?" She plopped back down on the bed.

"I've found something else out about him. I want to see you, rather than talk about it over the phone."

She swallowed. "Is it bad? When do you want to see me?"

224

Another long patch of silence. "It's not good, but that's all I'm saying for now. How would you like…how would you feel about taking a ride to Atlantic City with me?"

Rebekkah was taken aback. Nick sounded unsure of himself, as if he was asking her for a date, although she knew he wasn't. "Atlantic City?" That sounded intriguing. "Why there? What have you found?"

"I want to tell you in person. I'm not trying to hit on you. I know you're still

married—"

"Please stop reminding me," she cut in, wondering why Nick was having such a hard time speaking to her. His name came naturally now, and it fit him. "I won't be for long. I'm seeing an attorney tomorrow afternoon. If you have something to show me, I'd like to go to Atlantic City with you."

"Great." He sounded pleased with her decision. "Good luck with the attorney. Are you happy about being in your old neighborhood?"

"Very. I've missed it so much. It was Avram who insisted we move to the condo." She laid her head back on the pillow. "I'm not proud I'm getting divorced. I never pictured my life like this. I feel like I've failed somehow."

"I know what you mean, but you haven't failed, so stop feeling that way. It's not your fault. I'd run as far as possible from Avram. He gives off bad vibes. You'll be fine. We'll take our ride next week, that good for you?"

"I think so. I can't wait to see what you've found. Will we have time for the boardwalk and the beach?" she asked impulsively. It would be nice to get away, see the ocean despite the circumstances.

Nick's laughter was deep and warm. "I think we can manage that. I'll call you soon and let you know what day."

"I'll wait to hear from you," she replied, then said good-bye to him.

When she joined her parents in their kitchen, Rebekkah's thoughts lingered on Nick, his sexy laugh, his home, and on cute, cuddly Grace. Eventually, the fact she was looking forward to seeing him again—and not just because he had something to tell her about Avram— seeped into her consciousness.

FOURTEEN

Tightening her robe, Shira pulled out a kitchen chair and sat next to Rebekkah. "You look disturbed, sweetheart. I thought you'd be happy because Avram has stopped bothering you and you've filed for divorce."

"I'm happy about those things," Rebekkah assured her mother, as she took a bite of her toast. "I called Ellen to ask her if Avram gave her a get."

"I'm ashamed your father and I took being Jewish for granted for so long. It was Sammy's bar mitzvah, the same year you turned ten, that made us more serious about our faith. We started keeping kosher, going to services, keeping the Sabbath. Sorry, sweetheart, just reminiscing. So, this Ellen, did he give her a get? Is she married again?" Shira pushed her chair back, and went to the sink with her teacup.

"No, she's a Reform Jew. Reform Jews don't put importance on a get, so she didn't ask for one. Yes, she did get married again. Ima, what if Avram refuses to give me one? I won't be able to marry again. I'll be chained to him."

Shira's teacup hit the terra cotta tiled kitchen floor and shattered. Rebekkah jumped up. "Ima! Are you all right?"

She gave a little laugh. "I'm fine. I'll sweep it up. I'm so clumsy sometimes. Sit, sit, I can take care of it. You won't be chained to him, that I can promise you."

How could Ima be so certain? Rebekkah glanced at the clock on the microwave. She had paintings to take to Cairenn's. It was amazing she had time to paint and continue her art lessons with her life in such turmoil. She had gone back to the condo with Sammy when Avram hadn't been there to get her easel, painting supplies, and the china and silver her parents had given her. She had said a tearful good-bye to Howard who seemed sad to see her go.

Shira pulled another cup from the cupboard and made herself more tea. "Your father and I are leaving for Florida next week for three glorious weeks."

"I'm jealous. Where?" asked Rebekkah.

"Deerfield Beach." Shira sat back down, and covered one of Rebekkah's hands with hers. "Come with us."

She was tempted, but she was looking forward to her trip to Atlantic City with Nick and eager to hear what he had to tell her. "Thanks, Ima, but no. I don't want to be a third wheel, and I'm supposed to meet with Nick…Detective Rossi."

"A detective? Why? It sounds dangerous."

Rebekkah laughed at her mother's worried expression. "It's not dangerous. I have the feeling maybe

Avram's behind the art gallery theft, except I can't prove it. Yet, at least. I also think he may be embezzling money from the funeral home. Detective Rossi has done some investigating and has information for me about Avram."

Shira's mouth fell open. "Stealing and embezzling? You're joking, aren't you?"

Rebekkah assured her mother she wasn't then told her about the funeral home statements and missing money from the pre-paid funeral trust accounts.

"It all sounds like a movie. If that's true, thank God you've left him. I can't believe he fooled us into thinking he was so nice. He was always such a gentleman."

"He certainly fooled me," Rebekkah admitted. "I almost believe it was divine intervention that led me to meet Ellen."

"I can't fault you, maybe so," agreed Shira. "So. What are you doing today?"

"I have some art projects to work on and I have to take some pieces to Cairenn. I really need to get a job, but what can I do with a bachelor's degree in Philosophy? My lawyer had assured me Avram would have to pay some maintenance, but I don't care about that. I want to be free of him. Surely, if I pray about the get, God will grant it to me. He wouldn't have brought me this far to drop a stumbling block in my path."

"Everything will work out. Don't worry. Soon you will bring enough money in with your art that you won't need a job. God will bless you. I know it."

"Are you sure you'll be okay by yourself? I don't like you being here alone," Shira fretted the day she and David were leaving for Florida. Suitcases were lined up by the front door, and her father was trying to shepherd Shira out to the waiting taxi that would take them to LaGuardia Airport for their eight p.m. flight.

"I'm fine. If there's a problem I'll call Sammy, or Tilly, or Ben." Rebekkah ticked off her siblings on her fingers.

"The alarm, don't forget to set the alarm," cautioned Shira.

"I won't," Rebekkah assured her. "Go, have a good time. Send me a postcard."

She watched her parents get in the taxi then locked the front door. Nick had called yesterday. They were leaving for Atlantic City tomorrow. She turned on one of the smaller living room lamps and the TV. She wasn't scared, not with the dogs and the alarm, but she wished she had company. When the doorbell rang a few moments later, Rebekkah almost jumped out of her skin. Lucy and Mortimer sprang up and barked. She wasn't expecting anyone, and she prayed it wasn't Avram.

It was probably Sammy or Ben checking on her. Shushing the dogs, she looked out the peephole. Nick Rossi. She breathed a sigh of relief, but what was he doing here? She turned off the alarm and threw open the front door.

Their eyes met and held until Nick spoke. "Hi. I'm on my way home from work. You said your parents were leaving for Florida tonight, I wanted to make sure everything's okay."

She was surprised to see him, but his thoughtfulness touched her. "Do you want to come in?"

"I don't want to interrupt anything." He reached down to pet Lucy and Mortimer who were thrilled to have a visitor bring them new smells. "If Avram's been bothering you, I'll pay him a visit."

Rebekkah was amused at his serious expression. "You aren't interrupting anything, and Avram hasn't bothered me, lately." She led Nick to the living room.

He looked around. "Nice house."

"Thanks. I love it, too. It's almost exactly like yours. These are Lucy and Mortimer, by the way."

He took a seat on the couch. The dogs came over, and he gave them equal attention. "I should've brought Grace. She loves other dogs."

Rebekkah's heart thumped as she sat beside him. He could have called to make sure she was all right. "I can't wait to go to Atlantic City tomorrow. I'm dying to know what you found."

He stopped petting the dogs and looked at her. "I'm looking forward to it, too. I haven't been to a beach in a long time."

"I love the beach." She paused then said, "I've filed for divorce." Shocked that tears were welling up in her eyes, she got up and moved to the fireplace. Turning her back to him, she made an effort to compose herself. "You can't believe how good it feels to be away from Avram. That sounds like a horrible thing to say about your husband, but he turned out to be nothing like the man I thought he was."

"Not to trivialize what you're going through, but better you found out now than later, so you don't waste more of your life with the idiot."

He was right. She turned around. She was glad he had come over. Talking to him felt like the most natural thing in the world. "I'm afraid to ever trust again. How did you learn to trust after what Felicia did to you?" She hiccupped as she tried to stem the tears leaking out again. "I'm sorry." She tried to give him a smile. "I don't know why I'm crying. I'm actually very happy." She was mortified at being so emotional, but Nick didn't seem bothered by it.

He got up off the couch. "Don't apologize for having feelings. I was a mess after Felicia left, until I saw, like you did with Avram, she had turned into someone I could never love. I didn't believe I could ever trust a woman again. But truthfully, Rebekkah, since my divorce, I haven't met a woman I care enough about to ask myself whether I can trust her or not. Until you."

He said the last sentence so softly Rebekkah convinced herself she imagined it.

"Why don't you come here?" Nick asked gently.

As Rebekkah stepped toward him, he reached out and took her hand, drawing her against his chest. She didn't fight it, breathing in his scent as she laid her head on his broad shoulder. A perfect fit. She was barely conscious of her hands spreading across his muscled back. Nick held her for what seemed an eternity. He was so warm and solid. The moment was intoxicating, surreal. She didn't think about how wrong being in his arms was for her. Right now, she needed someone who understood.

She tilted her head up at him. Emotion flickered across his face. Rebekkah felt as if they were the only two people on Earth, and her mouth went dry realizing he was about to kiss her. Her heart went from thumping to pounding.

She stopped thinking when he paused, then took it upon herself to close the small space between them, her lips joining his. Her stomach did a free fall, a small sound escaped her throat. Then, her mind closed to everything but Nick and his mouth against hers.

They swayed together, in their own little world. With effort, he tore away first, running his hand through his hair. "I'm sorry, Rebekkah. I promise it won't happen again. I just wanted you to feel better. I…"

His husky voice sent shivers up her spine, and warmth spreading through her. She felt as if she had been dropped into one of her favorite romance novels. But he was right, it wouldn't happen again. "It's…it's all right." Shaken by the kiss, she didn't know what else to say. She wasn't sorry it happened. It seemed to be something they both needed at that moment. But that's all it was, a moment.

She wasn't divorced yet. She couldn't think about getting involved with anyone, especially someone who didn't share her religious beliefs. As much as she liked

Nick, she couldn't even casually date a non-Jewish man. "I want us to be friends. I don't want you to think I do this with…" Rebekkah blushed, but she wanted him to understand. "Avram's the only man I've had …been with."

He held her shoulders and his eyes searched her face. "I didn't think you did. I don't either. This was between you and me. No one else."

Rebekkah nodded, grateful he understood.

Nick cleared his throat and squeezed her hand. "Walk me to the door. We have a big day tomorrow. You hear from Avram, or he shows up, call me."

She did as he asked, relieved the atmosphere in the room was returning to normal.

"Get some sleep. I'll pick you up at nine tomorrow morning," he said as she opened up the front door for him

"I'll be ready. Goodnight, Nick. I'm glad you came by."

The way he looked at her made Rebekkah weak in the knees. It would be the easiest thing in the world to reach up and kiss him again.

"Me, too," he finally said.

She watched until he got into his car, then closed the door and turned the alarm back on. She stared at the space in the living room where they had kissed. She wasn't thinking of just the kiss, but that she hadn't thought of Jonathan the whole night. She hadn't thought about him every day since she left Avram.

After a night of tossing and turning, Rebekkah stared at the clothes in her closet the next morning, trying to decide what to wear. A dress would be too formal. She went through her drawers, finally settling on white shorts and a yellow cross-front top. It was liberating to wear shorts, something Avram, of course, had frowned on. She loved having her legs bare in the summer. She would wear sneakers, she decided as she made her way to the shower, in case they did a lot of walking.

She was ready way before nine and anxious to leave. She took the dogs out for another quick walk before calling her sister, Lilly, and asking her to come by and take them out later. She had no idea how long she and Nick would be away today. She gave herself a last look in the hallway mirror. Her long hair hung down her back. As usual, she hadn't bothered with make-up except lip-gloss. Satisfied, she headed for the kitchen and grabbed some snacks: two apples, cookies, cheese and crackers, and bottled water. She hoped that would be enough. She stuffed them into her beach bag along with her towel and sunscreen.

Nick was right on time. Rebekkah called good-bye to the dogs, set the alarm, and followed him to his Camaro. He was wearing black cargo shorts, a red polo shirt, and sneakers. As usual, he looked like a model and smelled delicious. Rebekkah pulled the seatbelt across her chest and fastened it and tried not thinking about their kiss last night. She wondered if he'd thought about it, too.

"I brought snacks," she told him as he pulled away from the curb.

"Good idea, thanks," he responded, grinning at her. "If you flip your visor down I have CDs up there. Why don't you pick one for us?"

She flipped the visor down and examined each CD. Nick certainly had a wide range of music taste. Since they were going to New Jersey she picked Bruce Springsteen.

He gave her a thumbs-up. "My favorite."

It was the middle of the week, so traffic wasn't bad. Rebekkah was so excited she felt like a kid going to Disneyworld. As Nick drove they talked about their lives growing up, their siblings, and she told him more about her life with Avram, and how money and status were the only things that seemed to matter to him now.

They talked about their childhoods, religions, music, politics, and discovered they loved the same baseball team. She told him all about Jonathan, too, and her visits to him. She was glad when he told her he would do the same thing in her situation.

When Nick pulled into a parking garage two-and-a-half hours after they'd left Park Slope, Rebekkah felt she knew more about him then she ever had about Avram, who was already beginning to feel like a distant nightmare. She was happy to have a day away from her problems, and she didn't know what she was more excited about. Seeing the boardwalk and ocean, or hearing what Nick had to say.

"I have a couple of lounge chairs in the trunk. Let's bring those and we can sit on the beach," Nick said.

Rebekkah agreed, and they walked the couple of blocks to the beach. The boardwalk was crowded, but that

236

didn't bother her as she breathed in the fresh ocean breeze. They managed to find a spot that wasn't too busy, and planted their chairs.

"I should've asked you if you wanted to walk the boardwalk first," Nick said. "Or go into one of the casinos. Personally, I'm not crazy about the casinos, but if you want to go, I'm willing."

"I've only been once. My parents and I went to one in Connecticut. I didn't see the appeal. I'm happy on the beach. I do want to get some salt water taffy, though, before we go back."

"You hungry now?" he asked as they got comfortable.

Rebekkah pulled off her sneakers and socks and wiggled her toes in the warm sand. "Not yet. The snacks will last me for a while. But if you are, I'll go with you."

"I'm not either, the snacks you brought will last me a while, too, but I wouldn't eat without you anyway. Can you eat seafood?"

"As long as it's not shellfish. I can eat salmon or flounder, fish like that."

Nick smiled. "Great. Before we go home, we'll stop at Lola's, it's a nice seafood restaurant. I think you'll like it."

Rebekkah grinned back at him. "Sounds good." She reached in her bag and grabbed her sunscreen, rubbing it on her arms, leg and face. She handed the tube to Nick.

"Thanks, but I'll be fine. I don't burn, I just tan."

"Lucky you." She wanted to go wading in the blue/green water. She could sit here for weeks, with the warm salty air caressing her skin. She didn't want to be anywhere else. She turned to Nick. "What do you have to tell me? I can't wait another minute to know."

He pushed his sunglasses to the top of his head. "Avram's here."

"What?" she squeaked, twisting her head around. "Where?"

"Sorry, I don't mean *here*, here. I mean in Atlantic City."

"Why? How did you know that?"

"I leaned on Vinnie Martino. He told me Avram's a big gambler, and he's here now at the Borgata playing in a high-stakes poker tournament. Don't worry, he isn't about to come to the beach.

"I had two reasons for asking you to come here. One, I wanted you to have the opportunity to see Avram if you wanted to, and the second is for purely selfish reasons. I thought you would like being away, and I wanted to spend time with you."

Rebekkah finally became aware her mouth was hanging open and closed it. "You asked me about him gambling, and you were right. I had no idea. I do like being away, it feels absolutely wonderful."

"There's more. About Avram, I mean."

"Okay, tell me. I want to know everything you've found."

"I have cousins who are cops in the next town from here. I also have friends who work in the casino industry. I asked for a few personal favors. Avram goes through big money. He's won big, then turned around and lost big, too."

Rebekkah was almost afraid to ask. "Do you know how much?"

Nick nodded. "In one week he blew through three hundred-grand. I'm sorry to lay this on you, but you have the right to know. The hotels comp him rooms, they encourage his gambling. So if he's embezzling from his own company, that's why. I asked around about his partner, but apparently he doesn't have Avram's problem."

Rebekkah was dumbfounded. The amount of money Nick rattled off was staggering. Poor Mark. If he didn't know about Avram's gambling he probably had no clue he might be embezzling money.

"He wasn't at a convention a few weeks ago, like he told you," Nick continued. "I looked into that, too. He was here, and he burned through twenty-one thousand dollars."

Rebekkah gasped. How had she not known? She thought about the checkbook in the drawer she'd found at the funeral home. He must have had another checkbook somewhere.

"Do you want to see him in action?" Nick asked. "He won't notice us."

She shook her head. "No. I have no interest in seeing him. I believe you."

"I have pictures back at the car of him at various gaming tables. I brought them because I didn't want you to have any doubt, and I figured you wouldn't want to see him."

She digested what Nick had told her. She had to go see Mark. It wasn't fair to him not to say anything. She was so glad Avram was on his way to being out of her life

"You okay?" Nick asked after a few seconds. "How 'bout we go for a walk on the boardwalk? We can talk about it some more if you like."

"I'm fine. It's a lot to take in, but I'm really glad you told me. Can we walk down by the ocean first?"

"Of course." Nick got up and held a hand out to Rebekkah to help her up.

They walked along the water's edge, talking about how Avram couldn't possibly get away with embezzling for long. She waded deeper, the foamy water warm against her thighs, which had already turned a light pink. Making a bowl with her hands she splashed the salty water on her face. She motioned for Nick to join her, but two little boys with a baseball had roped him into playing catch.

Rebekkah pulled a rubber band from her pocket and pulled her hair into a ponytail. Nick's laughter carried across the breeze, and she couldn't tear her eyes from him. He looked like he was having the time of his life with the two boys, and she briefly wondered why he and Felicia hadn't had any children. She would have to ask him. Already she felt comfortable enough with him to ask anything.

"That's enough, guys," Nick told the boys a little while later.

They ran to him, begging him to stay. He lowered himself to their level, and seemed to be having a serious conversation with them, until they all broke out in laughter. He high-fived both of them, ruffled their hair then jogged over to Rebekkah.

She gave him a smile. "You were so good with them. Did you and Felicia want kids?"

"I thought so. I love kids. Before we married she did, but once we were married she was suddenly worried about her figure and career if she got pregnant." He rolled his eyes in disgust. "I was working on changing her mind when she had the affair. At least I'm still young enough to be a father."

He'd told her on their drive that he was twenty-seven, two years older than she was. Next week, she'd be twenty-six and next month he'd be twenty-eight. They continued their sand and ocean stroll, with Nick scooping up shells and handing them to Rebekkah. They had gone about two miles, she guessed when they turned around and made their way back to their chairs, so they could put their sneakers back on before they went up on the boardwalk.

She found a store selling her beloved salt-water taffy, and stopped to buy a few boxes. Nick picked out some boxes of it, too, and insisted on paying for all of them no matter how much she protested. Felicia must have been crazy to have cheated on this man.

Rebekkah loved spending the rest of the afternoon in the sun and water, and chatting with Nick about anything and everything. All too soon, it was time to go back to the car, so they could eat. By this time they were both very hungry.

Nick was right. Lola's was magnificent, and her salmon was delicious. It was a perfect ending to a perfect day. Rebekkah watched Nick as he ate. She had assured him she didn't care if he ate lobster, and observing the look of bliss on his face, she was glad he'd believed her.

Rebekkah chose another CD for their ride home, but she must have fallen asleep, because before she knew it, Nick was sliding into a parking space on her parents' street.

"You sure you don't mind staying by yourself?" he asked, turning off the engine.

She yawned and stretched. "Not with the alarm and dogs." Rebekkah hated that their day had come to an end. She would have to spend more time at the beach. There were some nice ones on Long Island. Maybe Nick would come with her. She felt boneless and warm from their day together. She could still feel the salt on her arms, legs and face from the ocean, and she loved it. "Thanks for the news about Avram. I'm shocked, yet I'm not. Does that make sense?"

"Perfect sense," responded Nick. "Thanks for taking a ride with me. I had a great time with you. Despite the news I delivered."

"I'm glad you told me. I had a great time, too. Goodnight, Nick." She had had a better time with him today than with Avram on their honeymoon. She reached for the door handle, reluctant to leave, but she couldn't very well sit in his car all night.

"Rebekkah, wait."

She turned, looking at him expectantly. He was so handsome he stole her breath.

Nick managed to turn toward her, and slowly took her hand, threading his fingers through hers. Goosebumps rose on Rebekkah's skin. He did it as if it was second nature, and their fingers melded perfectly. "I'm afraid I'm falling for you, and I don't know what the hell to do."

FIFTEEN

Rebekkah tried to swallow around the lump in her throat. She couldn't have imagined a better day than today. She was attracted to Nick too, but her feelings for him couldn't lead to anything. It was hard to believe he hadn't found anyone to have a real relationship with since his divorce. He was sweet, considerate, fun to be with, a good listener, smart, and handsome. Her list of his attributes was endless.

"Do you feel something between us, or am I imaging this?" Nick's deep voice sent shivers through her.

Rebekkah glanced down at their hands. She didn't want him to let go. "You're not imagining it, but I can't go out with someone who isn't Jewish. It's too soon after everything with Avram, even if I could."

He slowly released her hand. "I know it's too soon. You're so easy to talk to and be with. It's like I've known you forever, everything just feels so right with you. Today was the best day I've had in I don't know when. I feel so connected to you."

Rebekkah nodded in agreement. "I feel the same, Nick." She paused. "Can we at least be friends?"

He leaned his head against the headrest, still looking at her. "I'll settle for friends, but I hope someday it can be more." He gave her a slow, heart-stopping smile, his dimples on full display. "Come on. I want to make sure you're safely inside."

How sweet he was. Rebekkah was afraid the only way they could be friends was if their attraction waned. She doubted that would happen if they continued to see each other. She'd never felt this kind of quick connection with anyone, even Jonathan. Certainly not with Avram, as it turned out. Looking back she couldn't believe she'd even thought she was in love with Avram. Nick stepped inside the house with her. Rebekkah switched on the hall light then turned off the alarm. She turned when he chuckled. "What are you thinking?"

"That we lived blocks away from each other when you and Avram lived on Garfield Place, yet we never ran into each other."

She smiled. "Maybe we did and we didn't know. How would we?"

"I think I would've known." He followed her into the living room.

She picked up a note from Lilly off one of the end tables. The dogs glanced up. Satisfied Rebekkah and Nick belonged there, they went back to sleep.

Nick looked around, and then walked into the kitchen and dining room. "I really don't like you being here alone," he said, joining her in the living room. "I should sleep on your couch."

She laughed, basking in his concern. "I'll be fine. What could happen?"

"I suppose. I guess I'm just looking for a way to extend our day together. You'll call me if you need anything?"

"I promise." Fighting her attraction to him would be hard. It made her sad. She really felt as if she'd known him forever. "Goodnight, Nick." She swung open the front door. Instead of going out the door, he framed her face in both his hands and kissed her.

Her arms naturally skimmed around his ribs and up his broad back, until she was holding on to his shoulders. As his kiss deepened, logic and thought flew from her mind and she responded, wanting their kiss to go on forever. She finally tore away first, embarrassed at how she had all but melted against him. "This really, really, can't happen."

Nick's breathing was as uneven as hers. "I know. I messed up. I couldn't help it. Forgive me."

She gazed up at him. "There's nothing to forgive. I didn't exactly fight you off. But I can't do this."

Giving her a last look that pierced her heart, he rubbed his knuckles softly against her cheek before pushing the glass door open. "Yeah, I know. Just friends, okay? Sweet dreams."

"You, too." Rebekkah managed to reply before she locked up.

Curling up on the couch, she pulled the pink and red afghan Shira had crocheted years ago around her. She couldn't keep kissing him. What was happening to her? The very last thing she needed right now was the wrong man in her life. God had blessed her with Jonathan. Surely, He would bless her again with the right man.

She had to accept it wasn't Nick. Maybe she'd have to tell him she couldn't see him at all. It wasn't as if she had to see him. If he had news about the break in at the gallery he could tell Cairenn, she rationalized. But the thought of never seeing him again filled her with immense sorrow.

She tried focusing on what Nick had told her about Avram and his gambling. When that didn't work, she tried focusing on her impending divorce, but her thoughts kept returning to Nick. She finally went upstairs and got into her pajamas. Her heart heavy, it was hours before she fell asleep.

"What's the matter, sweetie?" Cairenn chirped at Rebekkah the next morning when Rebekkah arrived at the gallery. "You look miserable. I've never seen you with such dark circles under your eyes."

Rebekkah had used her parents' Volvo station wagon to bring Cairenn four more paintings. She had been on a painting roll. She'd finally also brought the sketches her great-grandmother had done. She hopped up on a stool behind the counter and played with a pen. "I don't know."

Cairenn *tsk'd* at her as she pulled out her own stool. "Of course you do. Spill

Maybe talking to someone about Nick would help. Rebekkah wasn't sure any of her friends would understand her attraction to him. None of them had married out of the Jewish faith. Besides, she hadn't been a part of her old group in so long, she didn't want this to be the first thing she said to them. She was sure her parents wouldn't understand. Molly might. Pamela might. Maybe the next time she visited she'd confide in Pamela.

Rebekkah began with her marriage to Avram falling apart—leaving out her suspicion he was responsible for the theft of the paintings—and ended with Nick, and their mutual attraction.

"Wow." Cairenn exhaled noisily. "You've been a busy woman. When have you had time to paint?"

Despite her sadness, Rebekkah grinned at Cairenn's reaction. "I don't know what to do. I'm not sure we can be just friends."

"So, it's a big deal he isn't Jewish, huh?" Cairenn reached for an apple sitting in a bowl. She bit a chunk out of it and chewed.

Rebekkah nodded. "Yes. I wish it wasn't. I'm still married, anyway."

"What if you designate him a friend with benefits?" Cairenn gave Rebekkah a pointed look.

Rebekkah burst out laughing. "I don't think so."

Cairenn waved a hand at her. "I'm kidding. I think you should take one day at a time. Sorry, I'm not so good with advice, am I?"

"It helps just talking about it. I think I'll have to tell Nick I can't see him at all."

Cairenn's brow furrowed. "Is that what you really want? Won't that be hard to do?"

"Yes," Rebekkah admitted. "But I don't see another option. He deserves a woman who's free to love him."

"I hope you know what you're doing, sweetie. He sounds like quite a catch, despite being so tough when we first met him." Cairenn's eyes twinkled. "Too young for me, though."

Rebekkah stared out the window. "I hope I do, too."

Cairenn cleared her throat to get Rebekkah's attention again. "Why is the Jewish thing such a big deal?"

"The Jewish home is the most important part of Jewish life," Rebekkah began explaining. "It's more important than a synagogue. Even more important than the Holy Temple built by King Solomon. By marrying a non-Jew I end over 3,000 years of Jewish continuity, effectively cutting myself and my offspring off from what it means to be Jewish."

Cairenn's eyebrows shot up. "You do? All by yourself? You really believe that?"

Rebekkah's head bobbed up and down. "I do. My rabbi pointed out that interfaith marriages are twice as likely to end in divorce as same-faith ones. The—"

"Wait. Time out," Cairenn jumped in, making a letter T with her hands. "You're divorcing Avram. He's Jewish."

"I know. I'm not saying no Jews get divorced, just that it happens a lot more to Jews who marry non-Jews. When a Jew marries someone who isn't Jewish, our heritage is being sacrificed for the sake of personal reasons."

Cairenn was silent for a few minutes. "Wow, woman. You sound like an encyclopedia. Do you have a card in your wallet with all that stuff printed on it?" She hesitated. "Please don't take this the wrong way, but it doesn't seem as if you've had luck with Jewish men. Maybe it's time to experiment."

A smiled teased at the corner of Rebekkah's lips. "I see your point. But being Jewish is who I am, it's not a choice."

Cairenn became serious. "I just hope you're not making a huge mistake by telling Nick to get out of your life."

"It can't be a mistake." At least she hoped not, she added silently, even though her heart obviously disagreed. "It's for the best. Thanks for listening to me, Cairenn."

"Anytime," she responded, jumping off her stool. "So, where did your parents hang *Cottage*?"

Rebekkah blinked in confusion at the abrupt change of subject. "What?"

Cairenn frowned. "You didn't know they bought it?"

"I knew it sold, I just didn't know they were the buyers. When?"

"Hmmm." Cairenn stared up at the ceiling and scrunched her nose. "Right after you brought it in. Your mother clucked like a proud mama hen. They were amazed by the painting, actually."

Rebekkah found this odd. It wasn't a work of genius. "Maybe they gave it as a gift. It's not hanging in their house."

"Your mom went right to it. I remember her saying, 'She remembers it,' to your father."

Rebekkah thought back to when she had painted it. She'd wondered then if it was someplace she'd been. Seems she was right. She would ask her parents about it when they returned from vacation.

"I have something for you for your birthday tomorrow."

Hearing Nick's voice on the other end of her phone had Rebekkah grinning from ear to ear, even though she was going to tell him they couldn't see each other again. Her siblings had offered to take her out to dinner for her birthday, but she'd declined. She didn't feel much like celebrating.

She and Nick had spent a lot of time the last few days talking on the phone. Every time she thought they couldn't come up with another subject to talk about, they did.

"You didn't have to get me anything," she told him, at the same time eager to know what it was.

"I wanted to. I also want to make you dinner. Or, take you out. Whatever you want."

Rebekkah paused. It would be rude to say no. Besides, she didn't want to say no. It was probably the last time she'd ever see him. "You told me you're a good cook, so I'll let you show me."

"How about at seven tomorrow night? And don't worry, it'll all be kosher," he assured her.

Rebekkah's face would hurt if her smile grew any bigger. "I'd like that, Nick. Thank you. See you tomorrow."

"You look great," Nick said as he ushered Rebekkah into his house. He gave her a friendly hug, which she returned.

"Thanks. So do you." She'd chosen a pink flowered sundress and white sandals. She breathed in. The smells coming from his kitchen were delectable. So was his cologne. She hoped her stomach wouldn't grumble. She had been too nervous to do more than eat a banana and some cereal all day.

"Dinner's all ready. Spaghetti and meatballs—kosher ground beef of course— salad, Italian bread, and seven-layer cake from Shapiro's Kosher Deli."

Rebekkah loved Shapiro's. She was touched by Nick's effort.

He rubbed his hands to together. "Dinner, or present, first?"

Rebekkah laughed as she patted her stomach. "Dinner, please."

Their conversation flowed easily, and the food was so good Rebekkah all but forgot what she was going to tell him later. What would it be like to share her life with him like this every day?

She scooped up the last cake crumbs from her plate, even though she was stuffed. "You must know something about Judaism," she told Nick. "You knew to put the kosher food on paper plates."

Nick smiled and winked at her as he swallowed his last piece of cake. "I did some research. The Internet's an amazing thing."

"Thank you. It means a lot to me that you went to all this trouble."

Nick met her eyes and his expression turned serious. "It wasn't any trouble. I enjoyed making dinner for you." He got up and began clearing their plates.

Rebekkah got up, too. "Let me help you."

"Oh, no. I want you to feel at home here, but it's your birthday. No work allowed." He nodded toward the living room. "Why don't you go sit. I'll just be a few minutes."

"Okay." She wandered into the living room. Grace followed her, wiggling in bliss as Rebekkah stroked her.

Finally, Nick came in. He lit two candles, turned on a romantic Frank Sinatra CD, and dimmed the lamp. The only other light was the streetlamp filtering through the sheer white curtains. Sitting next to her, he produced a small box wrapped in turquoise paper with a thin, white bow.

Rebekkah's heart sped up. She recognized the Tiffany blue.

Happy Birthday, Rebekkah." He leaned in and kissed her cheek.

"Thank you. Thank you for this whole night," she told him, her trembling fingers pulling at the bow. "Oh, Nick." She pulled the sterling silver heart tag bracelet out of the box. The charm was engraved with a single R. Tears filled her eyes. "I love it." She was in love with him, too. No sense denying it any longer, but she bit her tongue before the words escaped.

He grinned at her. "I'm glad. Here, let me put it on."

She held her wrist out. It fit perfectly.

"It's delicate, just like you," Nick told her.

With Sinatra serenading them softly, and Nick looking handsome beyond words, Rebekkah was sure nothing in her life had ever been this romantic.

He switched off the lamp and took her hand. His thumb lightly caressed the back of it. He cleared this throat. "I told you when we got home from Atlantic City I was falling for you, remember?"

"Yes," she whispered. As if she could possibly forget.

"It's more than that." He paused, looking very serious again. "I'm in love with you."

Rebekkah's eyes filled with tears and her heart soared. It was torture not crying out *I love you, too.* Inexplicably, something Nick had said when he had talked about his ex-wife popped into her brain. *I play for keeps.*

She took his hand, loving the warmth and strength of it. "I can't accept your gift. I don't think I can see you again. Even as friends. It's too hard. I can't..."

"Love me?" Nick supplied, tilting her chin so their eyes met. The tenderness in his voice wrapped around Rebekkah's heart like a vine.

She shivered. How could she say goodbye to his man? "Oh, Nick. I'm not ready. I thought I loved Avram, but I didn't. Look what happened."

He caressed her cheek. "The bracelet's yours. No strings. Forget Avram. I can't let you to walk out of my life. You're in love with me, too. I know that."

She tried to harden her heart and failed. "Yes, I love you," she finally admitted, "but—"

"Shhh." He leaned toward her and his lips brushed hers.

Rebekkah readied herself for a deep kiss like the last one he'd given her, but he pulled back.

Instinct told her he was waiting for permission. As everything faded from her world except for Nick, she took over, framing his face with both her hands this time. She pulled him toward her. "I want this as much as you do," she managed to get out, right before his lips met hers.

Still kissing her, Nick managed to arrange himself over her as she stretched out on the couch. She closed her eyes and soon felt his bare legs against her own. Her body opened up as if she was made for him.

"Rebekkah, look at me."

She complied and was swept away as she completely surrendered her body, heart, and soul to Nick.

She could never wish that they hadn't made love, but she'd committed adultery. Her marriage to Avram was over, but in God's eyes she was a married woman. She had broken the sixth commandment: Thou shall not commit adultery.

Nick had pulled on his jeans and was now lounged across the couch. Rebekkah was ensconced between his legs, her back to his chest. His fingers slid through her hair. "I didn't plan to fall in love with you," he confessed. "I'm pretty sure I did the first time I saw you. I tried to forget you when I found out you were married, but I also know that some marriages never should have happened."

"You're not Jewish," she argued, her eyes closing. She was weak and satisfied and didn't want to move. She loved his hands tangling lightly through her hair.

He kissed the back of her head. "You're not Catholic. But I still love you."

"Nicky," Rebekkah started over, dropping her head back on his shoulder as she struggled to find an argument she could win.

"No one's ever called me Nicky before." He wrapped an arm around her waist. "No one else ever will."

Her heart breaking, Rebekkah tried to sit up

"Stay next to me," he commanded.

She sank back against his chest. How could she love him this much already?

"Don't make me apologize for making love to you."

The emotion in his voice made goose bumps rise on Rebekkah's arms. She was at a loss for words.

"We can't turn back to what we were before. Not now," he continued.

Reluctantly, Rebekkah sat up and maneuvered herself so she was straddling him. Not exactly ladylike, but it was too late to worry about that. "We have to. Can't you see what I've done? I'm still married. I can't be with you like this. It's wrong."

"You never had a real marriage with Avram," Nick reasoned, sliding his hands up and down the sides of her thighs. "I love you so God-damned much, but if you walk away I won't come after you. I'm not going to beg. How can you even consider walking away from what we are to each other?"

Rebekkah's heart wrenched in two. "How can you respect me?"

"I want you to be my wife someday. That's how much I respect you. How can you be loyal to a man who's lied to you, and maybe worse?" He moved from under her and stood. "You can do a background check on me from

257

the day I was born and you'll find nothing. You can read my emails, listen to my voice mails, interview my friends and my family, whatever you need to do to feel safe with me."

"Please, don't say you want me to be your wife. It can't happen." Rebekkah's eyes filled with tears.

"You can't walk out of my life," Nick countered. "I offer you my heart, my soul, my love, I want you to be a part of my family, and you want to walk away?"

"I have no feelings for Avram, or loyalty to him," Rebekkah cried. "I don't want to walk away from you. I have to. I didn't want to love you, either, but I do. You have no idea how much. But committing adultery makes me the same as Avram. No better."

Nick squinted at her in disbelief. He muttered a curse in Italian. At least Rebekkah assumed it was a curse from the dark look on his face. "Where do you get *that* from? You're nothing like him. Don't ever lower yourself to his level."

"Please, Nick," she begged. "Don't make this harder than it already is for me."

He squatted in front of her, taking both her hands in his. "You won't be married much longer, so that's not an argument against loving me. Couples have overcome bigger obstacles than religion. What if I convert to Judaism? Then you'll have no excuse. That's what you're looking for, isn't it? An excuse to walk away."

She gasped. "No! I've given you the reasons I can't be with you. I wouldn't ask you to give up your religion. Why would you want to convert?"

"Why?" Nick echoed, as if he couldn't believe her question. "To keep you in my life."

Rebekkah shook her head. "No. If you wanted to become Jewish you would've converted before you met me. Don't you believe your Jesus is God? On the way to Atlantic City you told me about the saints, and who the Virgin Mary is. You go to church whenever you can. Saint Anne's, right?

"You can't all of a sudden say that's not what you believe. A rabbi would see right through that. So would I. I don't want you to be someone you aren't."

She could tell from his expression he was wrestling with what she'd said. He just didn't want to admit she was right. He couldn't decide to be Jewish on a whim. She couldn't decide to be Catholic.

"People intermarry," he said as he stood up. "What we have is too good to just throw away."

Rebekkah took a shuddering breath. She had to do what was right for her. For him. "Nick, no Conservative rabbi will perform a marriage of a Jew to a non-Jew."

He gave a long, exasperated sigh. "Tell me you don't love me. That you don't want me. Speak those words, and you can go. We'll never see each other again. Ever."

The silence grew tense. "I do love you, but I'll learn not to. I'll stop. You aren't Jewish, I'm still married, and I don't trust my judgment right now. Please, please understand." Her heart broke again, and the look on his face cut through her soul. The silence grew so long again, Rebekkah wanted to jump out of her skin.

He finally held his hands up in defeat. "You win. I won't beg you. If you can't see we belong together, this is good-bye. For good. I can't not love you."

Nick's words stabbed her heart like tiny daggers. She slowly rose from the couch. The magical night was over. It felt as if her life was over.

He strode to his front door. He yanked it open so hard Rebekkah jumped, thinking it would tear from its hinges. "I'll wait until you're safely in the car before I close the door." He lowered his voice so she had to strain to hear him. "I'll always love you, Rebekkah. Watching you go is the hardest thing I've done in my life, including burying my parents. Good-bye. Be happy."

The anguish in his face was impossible to look at. He sounded close to tears, which hurt Rebekkah down to her feet. Her own throat was too clogged with emotion to speak. She didn't want to leave him, but it was best. Wasn't it? She glanced at Grace, lying quietly by the piano, which made everything feel worse.

She didn't dare look at Nick again as she stepped out into the night. The noise of his glass storm door clicking behind her was the loudest noise she'd ever heard. She climbed into her parents' car. Tears she couldn't bother wiping away flowed down her cheeks.

At home, like a robot, Rebekkah readied herself for bed. She should take a shower, but she didn't want to wash off Nick's smell, or the feeling of his skin against hers.

Walking away had been the right thing, she told herself for the millionth time since his door had closed behind her. If only her heart would accept that. If only every part of her wasn't in love with Dominick Michael Rossi.

SIXTEEN

"What's the matter, sweetheart?" Shira asked keeping her eyes on the turquoise sweater she was knitting.

Rebekkah looked up from her book. "Nothing, Ima." Her parents had been home from Florida for three weeks. Rebekkah had spent most of that time, as she did now, by herself, painting. They were letting her use her sister, Lilly's bedroom as a studio.

National Art World magazine had come out two weeks ago. Since then she had already sold four more paintings to people who'd read about the gallery, and seen pictures of her work. Cairenn was thrilled for her. Despite her sadness at losing Nick, Rebekkah was excited, too. Maybe she'd soon have enough money for a place of her own. And there was no need to look for a job.

Shira scrutinized Rebekkah over her glasses. "I haven't heard you flip a page for at least a half-hour. You spend too much time alone. Don't you want to go out with your friends? You never told me what happened when you and that detective went to Atlantic City."

Rebekkah's heart jarred. He was always in her thoughts, and she couldn't seem to erase him from her memory. It had been six weeks since she walked away from him, and it hurt as though it had happened an hour ago.

She spread her book face-down on the couch. Ima was right, she wasn't really reading. The words on the pages barely registered. "He told me Avram has a gambling problem."

Shira stopped knitting. "Oh, no. What are you going to do?"

"I'm already divorcing him, what else can I do? It's his problem. I want to talk to Mark, but I haven't had the chance." The truth was she hadn't been feeling well enough to talk to Mark. She'd been feeling weak lately. *Shvach*, as her grandmother would say.

"How about some tea?" Shira offered.

"Sure. You want me to fix it?" Maybe tea would help the queasiness in her stomach. She didn't exactly feel like throwing up, but close. Maybe the divorce was stressing her, but she doubted it since it would be final soon. She gave thanks to God that apparently Avram had decided not to contest it. And extra thanks that he hadn't harassed her.

"You sit. I'll pour," Shira said as she tucked her knitting away in its bag.

When Shira returned with their mugs of tea, Rebekkah blew on hers then took a big drink, which she almost spat out. "It's bitter. Did you put sugar in it?"

"Such a question! I know how you like your tea, for heaven's sake. The same way I do." Shira took a drink of her own tea. "Mine seems fine."

Rebekkah tried again with the same result. "I'll get a Coke."

When Rebekkah returned to the living room, her mother had most of her tea finished. "I was so involved with my knitting, I almost forgot. This is my bridge day with the girls. I have to go to the mall afterwards then I'll be home. You want to come along?" Shira grabbed her purse and made for the front door.

"Thanks for the invitation, but I think I'll stay here," Rebekkah called over her shoulder. Tucking her legs under her she finished her Coke. She shifted on the couch. Her jeans were a little tight. Maybe she should start running, or join the Jewish Community Center, so she could swim and take Yoga classes. Getting up, she headed for the kitchen. She took two steps, froze then changed direction.

She hurried up the stairs to her bedroom. Dumping her purse upside down on the bed, she rifled through the messy pile for her calendar. She flipped the pink cover open with trembling hands. Her last period was September 8th. Today was November 3rd. Her period was due today, and there was no sign of it. It was the second one she'd missed. How could she have not noticed missing two periods? Had she been that distracted?

Rebekkah's hand went to her belly while her mind reviewed the symptoms: her late period, the queasiness, the tea tasting funny, and her pants feeling tight. She knew enough about pregnancy to be worried.

Oh, Nick, she thought. She sank down on the bed. Feeling very sick now, she hurried to the bathroom. After washing up and brushing her teeth, she returned to the bedroom and tossed the items on the bed back in her purse. There was a drugstore not four blocks away.

Ten minutes later, Rebekkah stood in front of a myriad of pregnancy test choices. She prayed none of her friends, siblings, or God forbid, Nick, walked by. She read every box. Each claimed to be the most accurate. Finally, she made her selection, and checked out.

Glad she had the house to herself, she closed the upstairs bathroom door, slid out of her jeans, and stood barefoot on the cold black-and-white tiles. She ripped open the box, her fingers fumbling with the instructions.

Shivering, she tore the foil and removed the test stick. She continued with the directions then placed the stick flat on the sink counter. She looked at her watch and began timing two minutes. She turned her back on the test stick and gazed out the bathroom window behind the tub. She checked her watch. Thirty seconds to go. She pulled her jeans back on and checked her watch again. Time was up.

Rebekkah lowered herself to the side of the bathtub. She was pregnant! First, her dream of babies with Jonathan ended before it started, then came Avram lying about his vasectomy, and now she was pregnant by a man she loved with her whole being, but could never have. Now you choose to bless me with a baby? She silently asked God. Joy flooded her heart. God certainly worked in mysterious ways. She tried not thinking about her estrangement from Nick and how much she still loved him.

265

Rebekkah stuffed the stick, the box, and the instructions into the drugstore's plastic bag, and buried them in the kitchen garbage. She lay on the couch and tried to think. She needed to call her gynecologist. She didn't know what the future held, but she already loved the baby growing in her.

She allowed herself to rest for a few minutes then called Dr. Gavin's office. Securing an appointment for later that week, Rebekkah hung up, and traded her jeans for a pair of comfortable sweats. She couldn't believe Nick's baby was growing inside her, totally dependent on her for the next few months. She would do everything her doctor said so the baby would be healthy and strong. Already her arms wanted to hold it.

Nick had apologized profusely for not using a condom, but she didn't blame him. She hadn't been on birth control, either. Neither of them had acted responsibly, but there was no use agonizing over that now. A baby! Rebekkah couldn't believe her prayers had been answered like this. What else did God have in store for her?

Unable to nap, she went into her studio, although concentrating on anything but the baby was difficult. It was what she had always wished for. Her dream was coming true, even though it was definitely not in the way she expected. She picked up a paintbrush and tried losing herself in her latest creation, but it was hard. She was envisioning all the little clothes she would buy, along with adorable stuffed animals, and baby toys.

Rebekkah heard the front door open a few hours later. Soon, Shira was standing at the doorway to Lilly's room. Rebekkah looked up and forced a smile. "How was bridge and the mall?"

"I lost again, but loved the shopping. How's that coming along?"

Rebekkah leaned back, gesturing at her painting. A row of Park Slope brownstones. "Come see for yourself."

Shira gasped. "It's gorgeous." She squeezed Rebekkah's shoulder. "You have such talent."

"Thanks, Ima." Still reeling from the pregnancy test, Rebekkah hoped she sounded normal. "That reminds me. Cairenn told me a while ago you bought *Cottage*. Thank you, but I don't see it anywhere. Did you give it away?"

Shira sat on Lilly's bed and plucked at the bedspread. "No, I haven't decided where I want to put it. So, how long until you finish this one?"

"I'll probably have it done this week." She slipped off her stool and stretched. "What? Why are you looking at me like that?"

"You look...I don't know, different. I noticed it a few days ago, but didn't say anything. Of course, your father thinks I'm crazy." She laughed a little. "But what else is new. Is there anything you need to tell me?"

Rebekkah waffled for a minute. "Ima, I'm pregnant."

"Pregnant?" Shira shrieked. "But Avram had a vasectomy." Her shocked look transformed into a frown, then a smile. "When did this happen? Maybe he didn't have a vasectomy, then? Maybe it's a miracle? Like Sarah and Abraham? But you're divorcing him. Or are you reconciling? Oh, not that. Don't tell me you're going back to him. Not after what you've told me about him. Should I be happy for you? How long have you known? Oh my! I'm going to be a grandmother!"

Rebekkah refrained from rolling her eyes at the barrage of questions. She tried to find an opportunity to respond. Finally, she just jumped in. "Ima! Stop. Please. It has nothing to do with Avram. I just found out."

Shira opened her mouth and blinked. "Nothing to do with Avram?" Her eyes widened. "I need to sit back down."

Rebekkah joined her mother on Lilly's old bed. "It's Nick's. Detective Rossi."

"You slept with the detective?" Shira looked horrified.

Rebekkah almost laughed at the way that sounded. "Yes."

"Is he Jewish?" Shira brought a hand to her chest.

"No," admitted Rebekkah. "That's part of why I'm not going to see him again. That, and I'm still married to Avram, and I'm not ready for a relationship. I'm afraid of making another Avram mistake."

Shira went silent then looked askance at Rebekkah. "Are you going to tell Detective Ros...Nick?"

She shook her head. "I can't tell him. I don't want him to think he's got to be tied to me."

Shira's expression softened. "You're in love with him. I can see it in your eyes, in your face."

"Yes. But I'll get over it. I have to."

"If he loves you too he won't feel tied to you." Shira squeezed Rebekkah's knee.

Tears filled Rebekkah's eyes, and she brushed them away.

"Don't you think he has a right to know about his baby?" Shira persisted.

"Yes, if things were different, but they aren't. If I tell him, he *will* be tied to me, forever. I want him to find someone to be happy with."

"Even if it's not you?"

"Yes," Rebekkah fibbed. "I just don't want to know about it."

"I don't believe that," Shira declared. "Your face when you talk about him gives you away. You've never looked like that talking about Avram, not even Jonathan. Do you want to keep the baby?"

Tears welled in her eyes again. "Yes, of course I do."

"My first grandchild." Shira clapped her hands in delight. "I can't believe my baby's pregnant. Rebekkah, talk to this man. So you don't marry him, but again, is it right keeping this from him?"

"I don't want to ruin his life. Does he have to know?" Rebekkah dissolved into tears.

Shira put an arm around Rebekkah. They rocked a little together. "I doubt you'd be ruining his life if he loves you. Maybe he's wanted a child as much as you. I don't have all the answers. Let's talk to your father then ask the rabbi for his advice. Plus you need to see Dr. Gavin right away."

"I've already made an appointment," said Rebekkah, wiping more tears away. She took the tissue Shira whipped out of her pocket.

Shira walked to the window and stared out of it. "Life is such a twisted road sometimes."

"I was afraid you'd be really upset."

Shira whirled away from the window. "I feel bad for you. I know you wouldn't have been with Nick if you didn't love him. I want to help you make the right decision. You didn't think to use birth control maybe? Not that I'm not looking forward to this baby already."

Rebekkah blushed. "No. I know. How stupid. We didn't plan to make love. It just happened."

Shira nodded. "I guess it's too late to worry about that now. I better start dinner. Why don't you come down in a little while, keep me company? We can talk some more."

She nodded, allowing Shira to envelope her in a hug.

"It looks like all is well so far," Dr. Gavin informed Rebekkah. "Are congratulations in order?"

Rebekkah sat up as soon as her exam was finished. She had been coming to Dr. Gavin since she was eighteen. She was a caring and compassionate woman, and Rebekkah felt comfortable confiding in her. "My husband and I are divorcing. The baby isn't his. But yes, congratulations are in order. I love him or her already, and I'm keeping it."

Dr. Gavin snapped her latex gloves off while giving Rebekkah a reassuring smile. "You're about eight weeks along. You're due date will be around June 14th. When you're at twenty weeks we'll do an ultra-sound. We'll be able to tell you the baby's gender, if you want to know."

Rebekkah thanked her, and paid cash on the way out. She didn't know if she was still on Avram's health insurance, but she didn't want him to know anything about this.

Did she want to know the baby's gender? Rebekkah got into the Volvo. She fastened the seat belt and started the engine. A little boy with Nick's dark hair and eyes, and his smile flashed through her mind. He'd have her wrapped around his little finger.

Tears started again as she pulled out of the doctor's parking lot. She reached for a tissue and blew into it, then took a clean one to dry her eyes. The tears wouldn't end. She stopped at a traffic light and glanced at the car next to her. Nick! Her hands tightened on the steering wheel and her heart thumped. They were bound to run into each other sooner or later. Unless she moved far from here how would she keep the baby a secret?

He turned his head, and looked right at her. Even from a distance she could see the surprised look on his face. She took off as soon as the light turned green. She glanced in the rearview mirror in time to see his Camaro slide in behind the Volvo. Was he following her home? Her heart was still racing, but she concentrated on her driving, terrified of having an accident, hurting herself or the baby.

She pulled into a parking spot near her parents' house, relieved, yet disappointed that she no longer saw him. She was almost to the brownstone's front steps when something made her look toward the street.

Nick's car was double-parked right in front of her. His passenger window slid down.

"Rebekkah."

The intimate way he said her name made her long to go to him. He looked even more handsome than she remembered. She pictured an invisible string connecting him to her and the baby.

"You were crying back there, weren't you?"

"I'm fine, Nick," Rebekkah managed to reply.

"I hope so." He didn't drive away.

She couldn't just turn away from him. She waited. She should tell him about his baby. He was a good man. He would be a wonderful father.

"Come closer," he asked.

She went to the curb.

"I miss you."

His image blurred through her tears. "I miss you, too."

A car came up behind his and the driver blasted its horn. Nick looked like he wanted to say more, and Rebekkah's heart froze when he slowly drove away. She went to the front steps of her parents' brownstone, and sat, hugging her knees. The breeze was chilly, but she had mittens on, and had layered on a t-shirt and two sweaters that morning. The cold bite of the air felt good on her face.

Was she being selfish by not letting Nick know about his baby? How could she deny her baby its father? What if he somehow found out? He'd hate her. She couldn't live with that. She didn't want him to feel obligated to her, either. She laid her aching head on her knees. She had so much to decide, it was overwhelming. How would she explain to her child that she hadn't let he or she meet their father? Let them develop a relationship with him? She was treating him as if her were stranger, and he wasn't. She still loved him as deeply as ever.

"You should eat something," Shira called from the kitchen.

Food was the last thing on Rebekkah's mind. She wasn't at all hungry. "I know. I'll try."

"Soup?" her mother enticed. "Chicken and rice."

"Okay," Rebekkah agreed, mostly to make Shira happy. She was so tired all the time. Even her divorce becoming final the previous day, and knowing she soon would have her get did little to cheer her. Her mind was constantly on Nick and the baby. Her parents had been unusually quiet too, lately. A depressing pall had settled on the house, and she felt responsible.

"Do you want me to bring the soup in there?" called Shira.

Rebekkah threw the afghan off. It wasn't right for her mother to keep waiting on her as if she were a feeble old woman. "I'll come out."

She padded to the kitchen and sat. Her mother delivered a glass of milk and soup. "Thanks, Ima."

"It was nothing," her mother replied, running a hand down the back of Rebekkah's head.

Rebekkah thought of her conversation with Rabbi Weissman the day before. She'd told him about Nick and the baby. Now she wished she hadn't. He'd encouraged her to forget Nick and put the baby up for adoption. She would never do that. Her baby was a blessing from God, no matter how he'd been conceived.

It was all so complicated. She would have to live with whatever she decided for the rest of her life. Tell Nick or not. In her heart she knew what was right. She was taken aback at how adamant the rabbi had been that she shouldn't see Nick again. Just because he wasn't Jewish didn't mean he was evil incarnate.

"Ima?" Rebekkah's spoon halted in mid-air. "Are you all right? You haven't said much of anything lately. Neither has Aba." Her father had reacted to her pregnancy like her mother had. Surprised, but supportive. They both wanted what was best for her, and the baby.

Shira let out a troubled sigh and turned from the sink. "I have to talk to you."

"About what?"

274

Shira twisted a dishtowel in her hands. "Wait until you've finished eating."

"You expect me to be able to eat now?" Rebekkah laughed, losing the meager interest she had in her soup. "Is it that bad?"

Shira gave a half-smile, but at least it was a smile. "Not that bad. Go on, eat for the baby."

Rebekkah finished in silence then followed her mother into the living room. She stretched out on the chaise portion of her parents' sectional couch while Shira settled in her favorite recliner with her ever-present cup of tea.

"You've known since you were little that you were adopted. So have your brothers and Lilly."

Rebekkah nodded. This wasn't anything new. She didn't remember a time when she didn't know. Where was Ima going with this?

"I've never told any of you more than that. You've all asked through the years, but I refused any details."

This wasn't new, either. Rebekkah had asked about her biological mother many times as a child, but finally gave up as a teenager, realizing her parents weren't going to tell her. She'd grown out of her curiosity. Her parents were her parents, and she adored them.

"Your father and I decided maybe we should tell you more. This may take a while. Are you sure you're up to it?"

"Ima," Rebekkah practically huffed, trying to curb her impatience. "I'm pregnant, not on death's door. I want to hear it, no matter how long it takes."

"Okay." Shira took a deep breath. "I didn't want to give birth. I chose to adopt all of you."

This part was new to Rebekkah. "I don't understand. Why didn't you want to give birth?"

"I had the curse," Shira revealed, wrapping her arms around herself.

"What curse?" Rebekkah prodded.

"Cancer. My mother, three of my aunts, and some cousins all died of cancer. Ovarian cancer. I'm sure I told you that before. I didn't want to die, too. I had genetic testing for it. It was positive. I decided to..." Shira paused and took a drink of her tea.

"Have a hysterectomy," Rebekkah finished for her.

"Yes. I had a hard time finding a doctor to do this for me. Finally, my Uncle Alan's brother-in-law did the surgery. My uncle lost his wife, he understood how I felt. I didn't want to die from cancer, and I couldn't risk passing this defect on to any daughters I might have. I had both my ovaries and uterus removed."

Rebekkah couldn't speak. She hadn't expected this. She couldn't imagine volunteering to have a hysterectomy. "Why didn't you ever tell us?"

"I don't like to dwell on it. I have my beautiful children, and I didn't have to worry about passing a gene down to my daughters that could kill them."

Rebekkah digested this information. "Aba just agreed to this? Didn't he want children of his own?" She thought about her parents' marriage. Other than knowing they were introduced by her mother's best friend, they married soon after meeting, and they were devoted to each other, their personal relationship was a mystery to her.

"You are his!" Shira exclaimed. "Of course he wanted children, but he understood why I did what I did. As long as we could adopt, he didn't care. We were so lucky to get all of you. Please, don't say anything to your brothers and sisters. I may tell them, I may not. This is a special circumstance, otherwise I wouldn't be telling you."

Rebekkah wondered what was special about it, but decided to listen at her mother's pace, eager to hear more. "I won't say anything."

"Your adoption was arranged by a friend of your father's cousin. He was an attorney in Manhattan. A reputable one," she hastened to add. "He had a very glitzy office and two secretaries—"

"What was his name?" Rebekkah cut in, not caring about the details of his office decor.

"I don't remember. After all this time, how would I?"

If she adopted a baby, Rebekkah doubted she'd forget any details, but she kept that to herself. "I don't understand why you're telling me all this now."

"Because, sweetheart. I can't stand the haunted look in your eyes. You look and sound worse than you did after Jonathan's accident. At first, I thought it was the pregnancy, but it's because of Nick." She paused. "The rest of what I'm going to tell you will make it easier for you to be with him."

Rebekkah got off the couch. Feeling dizzy, she sat back down. "I'm confused. I've decided it's best not to be with him."

Shira smiled, but made a face. "Sometimes you're so impossibly stubborn, I find it hard to believe you don't have any of my genes. You love him, he loves you. Just because Avram turned out to be a mistake, doesn't mean every man is. You can't live the rest of your life in your bedroom."

"I don't intend to," Rebekkah bristled. "What does my adoption have to do with Nick?"

"The woman who gave you up for adoption wasn't Jewish."

SEVENTEEN

Rebekkah's head swam. "What? What are you saying?"

Shira started over. "Your biological mother wasn't Jewish. Rabbi Weissman would say you aren't Jewish, either. He would be right."

Rebekkah couldn't believe her own ears. "I *am* Jewish. Why would he tell me I'm not?"

"We never had a conversion ceremony for you. I know you feel Jewish, but you're truly not. Not without a conversion ceremony. Don't you see? The religious issue between you and Nick is gone."

Rebekkah stared at Shira. "Wait a minute. I can't believe this. All of a sudden I'm supposed to accept I'm not Jewish? I can't do that."

Shira continued as if Rebekkah hadn't spoken. "Don't misunderstand. I'm not wishing that you turn your back on our religion. Your father and I would love if you found a nice Jewish man to settle down with, but I can't stand your being so conflicted and upset. Obviously, walking away from Nick hasn't given you any peace."

Shira was beaming at Rebekkah, as if she had delivered her from all her distress. But this was more shocking than learning she was pregnant. Surely her mother could understand that.

"Go to him, sweetheart," Shira urged. "Tell him about the baby. You can't let what Avram did hold you back from living your life. If you do then he wins."

Rebekkah blinked in disbelief. "I can't just snap my fingers and stop being Jewish. How can you want, or expect me to do that?"

Shira bowed her head for a moment. "I don't, but your happiness comes first with me, above anything else."

Rebekkah still couldn't believe what Shira was saying. "Why didn't you have a conversion ceremony for me? Why didn't you just adopt a Jewish baby?"

Shira glanced out the window. "At that point in our lives, your father and I were Jews in name only. We didn't care about religion. Remember, I told you we became more religious after Sammy's bar mitzvah?"

"You could've had a conversion ceremony anytime," argued Rebekkah. "Why have you kept this hidden from me all this time?"

"You're right, sweetheart. Unfortunately, we never got around to it. As time went by, we pushed it out of our minds. You were our daughter. We're Jewish, so you're Jewish." Shira looked crestfallen. "It was wrong, and I'm sorry, but that's what we thought."

"What else do you know about my birth mother?"

"Her name is Elisabeth Mandeville."

Rebekkah's brain grappled with the familiar name.

"She's a well-known poet," Shira continued.

That's why the name was familiar. Rebekkah had studied poetry in college. One of Elisabeth's books had been required reading.

"She also teaches at Columbia," her mother added.

"She's my biological mother?" Rebekkah no longer had Elisabeth's book, but tried remembering a picture on the cover. She couldn't come up with a face.

"Yes, Elisabeth is your birth mother."

Rebekkah was still in shock. "How much do you know about her?"

"Quite a bit," Shira admitted. "Elisabeth became pregnant with you at seventeen. Before I go on, she always wanted you to know the full story, so I'm not divulging anything I shouldn't be. You were born just before she turned eighteen. I don't know anything about your birth father, except he was young, too. She never spoke of him."

"Everything I've researched says New York state adoption records are sealed," Rebekkah replied, frowning. This made no sense. "How do you know so much?"

"Because our attorney handled it, and we agreed to have contact with Elisabeth, so this was different."

"Was my adoption illegal?"

"No, not at all." Shira looked appalled at the suggestion.

"Weren't you afraid she'd want me back?" Rebekkah asked.

"We trusted her, and our attorney knew her family. Elisabeth was very open, kind, and very mature for such a young woman. She wanted the best for you."

"Did she ever want to see me?" asked Rebekkah.

"You did see her, once. Her grandparents had a cottage in upstate New York, on Seneca Lake. That's the cottage in your painting. You were eight when you were there, somehow you remembered."

"That's why you bought the painting, isn't it?" Rebekkah put two and two together.

Shira nodded. "Yes, I was so surprised when I saw it. You did a perfect job."

"I wondered when I painted it if I'd been there. It came to me so vividly. You took me all the way to upstate New York to see Elisabeth?"

"She invited us to see her, so we went. Your father and I used to go camping in upstate New York, we loved it up there."

Rebekkah watched as Shira got up and wandered to the window, then stared out toward the street, lost in her own thoughts.

"I don't remember meeting her." Somehow, Rebekkah had remembered the cottage, but nothing else. She didn't even remember being inside it.

Shira came over and sat beside Rebekkah. "It was a beautiful red-shingled cottage. I can't believe you remembered it in such detail. It had an old refrigerator that hummed all the time. The square linoleum on the kitchen floor was yellowed and cracked, but it had personality.

"There was a beautiful view of the lake. Your father showed you how to skip stones over the water's surface. You thought the thick green seaweed bobbing just underneath the water was mermaid's hair."

"Sounds nice. I wish I remembered something," replied Rebekkah. "How long did we see her?"

"It was just the one day. Your father and I did some sightseeing and a couple of days later, returned home."

"Weren't Lilly, Ben, and Sammy with us?"

"They had summer camp. You refused to go, so we did this instead."

"I don't remember her at all. I remember my other relatives on yours and Aba's side of the family." Rebekkah grew pensive.

"Remember when you first left Avram? I started to tell you there was money for you, but your father wouldn't let me say more?" Shira asked.

"Yes. I wondered about that, then forgot."

"Elisabeth sent money for you until you were eighteen. We didn't want to accept it. She insisted. She asked that we not give it to you until you turned thirty. We promised, but if you need it I'm sure she'd understand."

Rebekkah wasn't sure she understood anything. How could her adoption have been so open? All this time her parents had been in contact with Elisabeth Mandeville, yet said nothing to her. How could they feel she truly belonged to them with Elisabeth looming in the background?

"Was the money because she felt guilty for having given me up for adoption?"

"No, I don't think so. I think it was her way of somehow being involved in your life."

"But why would you *want* her involved? Didn't you feel like you were sharing me with her?"

"It's hard to explain, sweetheart. Maybe Elisabeth did feel guilty on some level, but I know she trusted us to take good care of you."

"Do you still talk to her?" Rebekkah thought their arrangement a little unorthodox.

"No, no. The only contact we had was when she sent money, and of course when we went to her cottage. Are you thinking of meeting her?"

Rebekkah thought for a moment. "I don't know. In the back of my mind I've always thought it might be nice. It's so much to take in. Then again, maybe Elisabeth wouldn't want me to make an appearance."

"I think she would be very happy to see you," said Shira.

Rebekkah fell silent for a while. "Ima, this doesn't mean I can be with Nick."

"Please think about it. You're being far too stubborn. At the very least you should tell him about the baby."

Rebekkah got up and was relieved she didn't feel dizzy still. "If we aren't going to have a future together then he doesn't need to know." Even as she said the words her conscience twisted. It was wrong to keep Nick's baby from him. But how could she share the baby and not her heart. She would always love him, of that she was sure.

Shira frowned. "What if he wants it?"

Rebekkah forced herself to stay calm. "I feel it's my decision, Ima."

"I think you're making a mistake. But why should you listen to your mother? I was hoping you'd consider going to him when I told you we never had a conversion ceremony for you." She gave a tight grin. "Listen to me, Nick's champion, and I've never met him."

Rebekkah had nothing more to say. She needed to be alone to sort out her thoughts. As much as she loved her parents, it was time to find a place of her own.

"Have you given any more thought to what I said about putting the baby up for adoption?" Rabbi Weissman asked as Rebekkah took a seat in his office a couple of hours later. She'd been lucky to find his afternoon open.

"All I've done is think," she assured him.

"I'm sorry for being so stern with you when we last met, Rebekkah. If you wish to keep the baby, of course that's up to you. You're an adult, and I'm afraid I was treating you as if you were one of my kids. But there's no future for you and Nick. Unless he converts, and you don't think that's an option. Is that still correct?"

"No," Rebekkah answered. "He can't convert, he believes in his religion. That's not why I'm here. Something else has come up."

Rabbi Weissman lifted his eyebrows, curiosity shining in his eyes. "Not anything bad, I hope. You've had so much to deal with lately."

Rebekkah got right to the point. "My siblings and I were adopted at birth. Ima recently told me about my biological mother."

"Really? She knew something of her?" Rabbi Weissman inquired.

"A little. She wasn't Jewish," Rebekkah told him.

"Your biological mother you mean?" the rabbi clarified.

"Yes." Rebekkah kept Elisabeth's name to herself. "My parents never had a conversion ceremony for me. Ima says I'm not really Jewish, either."

The rabbi let out a troubled sigh. "I'm afraid she's right. Converting a baby girl is so simple." The rabbi frowned as he grasped the back of his desk chair. "I find it hard to believe your parents failed to do that. They were wrong to let me marry you and Avram."

If her marriage to Avram hadn't turned out so badly Rebekkah would have been devastated that her marriage to him wasn't valid in the eyes of Judaism. Now, it was a blessing of sorts.

Rabbi Weissman's frown deepened. "What about your brothers and sisters? Are they in the same situation?"

Rebekkah hadn't thought of them. "I don't know. We didn't talk about their adoptions, only mine."

"I'll have to speak to your mother. Why did she decide tell you this now? Why not earlier? I don't understand."

She knew better than to tell the rabbi Nick was the reason. He surely wouldn't approve. "I was asking questions about my birth mother. It just came out."

"How upsetting for you," Rabbi Weissman sympathized. "I'm sorry to hear about this."

"Thank you, Rabbi. What happens to me now?"

"For one thing, you don't need a get, since you weren't Jewish to begin with. Had I known, I wouldn't have performed your marriage to Avram."

Rebekkah didn't know what to say. Obviously, the rabbi felt deceived by her parents. She didn't blame him, but even though what her parents had done was wrong, and hard to understand, she couldn't bring herself to be angry with them forever.

"Now my main concern," the rabbi continued, "is that you don't feel Judaism has turned its back on you. My suggestion is we develop a ceremony in place of the get to help you process the end of your relationship with Avram."

Rebekkah listened, although she didn't think a ceremony to help her process the end of her relationship with Avram was necessary. He was no longer her problem. She never thought about him.

The rabbi continued. "We can base it around the get ceremony so as not to shine the spotlight on a problem you didn't create, and make sure it gives you honor to your identity, which I know you must surely need at this time."

"I feel...I don't know, like an orphan. If I'm not Jewish, what am I?" She hadn't asked her mother what religion Elisabeth Mandeville was. She knew little about Christianity. Most of it she'd learned from Nick on their ride to Atlantic City.

"That's understandable, but not irreparable. In your heart and mind, you're Jewish. Unfortunately, that's not enough to make you Jewish. You obviously don't need to undergo any studying, but I'd like to take you to be immersed in the mikveh immediately, and get you a proper conversion. That's very important in order for you to feel whole, both for completing a stage in your life via the divorce, and as a Jew."

He sat opposite Rebekkah and leaned toward her. "If you keep the baby, I assume you intend bringing it up as a Jew. Unless you have a conversion ceremony before its birth, it won't be Jewish, either. I'm sure you don't want that."

She stood abruptly, wanting to be alone again just to think. "I'll think about what you've said. Thank you for seeing me."

The rabbi walked to the door. "My pleasure. Don't wait too long. I know you've been through quite a bit, but your conversion ceremony will take but minutes. As they say nowadays, it's a no brainer. Call Debbie in the office and she'll set up an appointment. I'll see you very soon then?"

Rebekkah nodded as she slipped out of his office. "I'll call her. Thank you, Rabbi."

She took the long way home, through the park, despite the cold. No snow had fallen yet. Chanukah was only two days away. She was about twelve weeks pregnant. At her last visit with Dr. Gavin she'd heard the miracle of her baby's heartbeat.

The park was almost empty, which was fine with Rebekkah. She sat on a wooden bench and looked up at the brilliant blue cloudless sky. Her mother was right, not all men were like Avram. It was silly to think she could never trust again. He was her past. She wouldn't let him dictate the rest of her life.

Relishing the feel of the sun on her face, Rebekkah closed her eyes and tilted her head back. She was at a crossroads. She had choices. She could choose to be with Nick, she could choose to be Jewish, or not be Jewish.

She could choose to forgive herself for the night she spent with Nick that gave her this precious baby growing inside her. She had acted like a silly child instead of a grown woman when she had walked away from him. Now, embarrassment flooded through her.

She could go to Nick now, and tell him she wasn't Jewish, after all. Tell him she loved him with all her heart.

Had her mother indeed handed her a gift, telling her she wasn't truly Jewish? If she didn't have a conversion ceremony, she would never be Jewish. How would it feel give up a religion that was part of who she was, just to be with Nick? She tried not thinking about God's reaction.

Rebekkah opened her eyes, blinking in the bright sun. She wanted Nick to know about his baby. How could she have ever considered not telling him? It wasn't fair to keep such a big thing from him. She wanted to see him again. Maybe things could work for them.

She left the bench and began walking across the expanse of short, brown grass. When she got to the other side of the park, she crossed the street. Rebekkah had been passed the Episcopal Church that now stood in front of her many times. Of course, it had meant nothing to her.

She slowly went up the steps of the church. She pulled at the large, red wooden door, half-expecting it to be locked. It wasn't. Rebekkah's heart thumped. It was the first time she'd ever been in a church. She found herself in a little vestibule with a gray slate floor. She wondered if anyone would chase her out.

To the left were descending stairs, in front of her a glass door. She opened the door and stepped into the church itself. The smell was familiar. It was the same smell of old prayer books she noticed in Beth Israel.

She was struck by the quiet. It was peaceful, too, just like Beth Israel. The entire church was carpeted in red. There were pews, not unlike Beth Israel. There was an alter with a cross on it at the front of the church. Rebekkah knew that area as the bimah, the platform in the synagogue on which stands the desk from which the Torah is read.

She imagined Episcopalians didn't call it a bimah. There was also a lectern that looked much like the one the rabbi used. But the synagogue certainly didn't have a huge cross suspended from the ceiling with a man on it.

She waited to see if she felt any emotion, any connection to this place. She didn't. It was as foreign to her as another planet. It would be hard to cast Judaism aside. How could she fit in with Christians? For Nick, she wanted to try. Of course, just because Elisabeth wasn't Jewish didn't have to mean she was Christian. Maybe she was a Buddhist or something like that.

She was surprised the church also had a *ner tamid*, the eternal light hanging from the ceiling, just like all synagogues had. Since no one had come out to object to her presence, Rebekkah took a seat in one of the pews.

She picked up the Holy Bible from the rack attached to the pew in front of her. She paged through it, feeling guilty and curious at the same time. She noticed many of the books from the Torah. There was also the New Testament. She read from it for a while, but soon felt like a trespasser.

Tucking the Bible back in its place, she pulled out The Book of Common Prayer. She opened it up and paged through that, too, stopping to read here and there. Most everything she read referenced Jesus, but there were also psalms, some of the same psalms as in the *Siddur*, the prayer book at Beth Israel.

This church seemed very liturgical, just like the synagogue, only the prayers were nothing like she was used to. Words she didn't recognize like Advent, Epiphany, Whitsun week popped up at her. The only ones she knew about were Easter and Christmas.

She slid that book back in its place and looked around again. The stained glass windows were beautiful, but she didn't feel as if she belonged here. It was difficult to accept that maybe Christianity, not her beloved Judaism, was her background.

If she was a Christian, like Nick, she'd have to believe Jesus was divine, the Son of God, as Nick believed. Rebekkah couldn't imagine believing that. It was blasphemy to think of a virgin giving birth to God. She could barely think such a thing.

She believed Jesus had existed, but he wasn't God. No one is God, except God. *Sh'ma Yisrael, Adonai Eloheinu, Adonai Ehad.* Hear, O Israel: The Lord is our God, the Lord is one. In her head, Rebekkah recited the first part of the Sh'ma, the affirmation of Judaism and the declaration of faith in one God.

Strange she felt so peaceful and relaxed here. She was sure God probably dwelled here, also. She didn't think Christians were bad, or that they didn't believe in God. They just weren't Jewish.

After a while, Rebekkah got up. Sitting here had helped clear her mind. Like Beth Israel, this church was a little oasis away from the daily grind of living. Before she talked to Nick, there was someone else she'd decided to see first. Please wait for me, Nick, she prayed silently.

Rebekkah was glad no one was home when she arrived. She went into the little office her father kept and impatiently waited while the computer booted up. Once it did, she entered her search for Columbia University.

Clicking through the various pages she finally came to the English Department faculty. There was an endless list of names in a column to the left. She found Elisabeth's name and clicked on it, holding her breath in anticipation.

Assistant Professor of English and Comparative Literature Romantic and Victorian poetry; poetry and poetics; English literature and the classics.

Rebekkah stared at Elisabeth's face. Her dark hair was parted in the middle and pulled back, and she wore a big smile for the camera. Like Rebekkah, it didn't look as if she wore much make-up. Behind the tortoiseshell rectangular eyeglasses her eyes looked brown.

She tried to see herself in Elisabeth's prominent cheekbones and fair skin. Rebekkah thought she looked more like Ima. It was near impossible to grasp Elisabeth had given birth to her, not Ima. Ima would always be her mother, no matter what. She read the rest of Elisabeth's biography and found her email address at the end. Was email the best way to contact her, or should she just show up?

Rebekkah tried to put herself in Elisabeth's shoes, and thought about her own baby. The longer she carried the baby, the more attached she felt to it. She didn't judge Elisabeth's decision, but she could never put her baby up for adoption.

Finally, she decided to email Elisabeth. A million butterflies launched in her stomach as she pondered how to start. Rebekkah wasn't at all ready to pick up the phone and speak to her. They needed some warm-up time. She was a total stranger, after all. Despite Ima's assurance Elisabeth would be happy to see her, she was very nervous.

She started and stopped a dozen times before she had what she thought was a decent email. The worst that could happen was Elisabeth would ignore her. That wouldn't be so traumatic. She'd just go on with her life. She read and re-read her email, fidgeting in her chair. Just send it, she told herself. Stop reading it. It wasn't as if Elisabeth was going to return it with a grade. She leaned back and clicked on Send Message. Turning off the computer, she forced the email, and Elisabeth, out of her mind.

Later that evening, Rebekkah sat with her parents at V. Fong's, the best Chinese restaurant in Park Slope, picking at the rest of her chicken and broccoli. The restaurant was packed as usual, but since it was a Tuesday night, a table soon became available. That they were kosher was a bonus. Rebekkah ordered out of habit. Her mind was on Nick, telling him about the baby, and the bombshell Ima had dropped on her.

Her family ate here often, and she always felt comfortable in the cozy booths. A movement caught her eye and she turned to see Nick walk in with a woman. Rebekkah's appetite instantly evaporated. She could hardly breathe. She prayed he wouldn't notice her. Of all the places he could have brought a date for dinner, he had to come here?

He was smiling at his companion as if what she said was the most interesting thing on Earth. He looked happy. Rebekkah couldn't even think of another man, and not just because of her condition. How could Nick have replaced her so quickly? Had he forgotten he'd told her how much he loved her?

"What's wrong, Bekkah? Aren't you feeling well?" Her father's eyes were warm with concern. Ever since he'd found out about her pregnancy he'd treated Rebekkah with kid gloves,

acting more like a mother hen than Ima.

"It's nothing," she replied

"You usually go back for seconds and thirds." He motioned to her plate with a chopstick. "You've barely touched your food. You look white as a ghost."

"Are you all right, sweetheart?" asked Shira.

"Nick's here," she whispered, blinking back tears. "No! Don't turn around," she begged her father, barely in time.

Rebekkah's mother almost knocked over her water glass. "Where?"

"Behind you. Please, don't turn around," Rebekkah repeated.

"We can take this to go," her mother quickly offered, "if you want to get out of here."

Rebekkah shook her head. "No, it's okay."

Memories of her birthday with him rushed back. Memories of him kissing and making love to her on the couch. The way he'd looked at her, and how she felt in his arms. Seeing him with someone else made her sick, despite her earlier declaration to her mother she wanted him to be happy, even if it wasn't with her.

His friend was beautiful. Petite, with huge brown eyes, and glossy brown hair cut in a stylish bob. Rebekkah wasn't fat, but compared to the woman with Nick she felt not only fat, but frumpy in her old sweater, scuffed up riding boots, and her hair pinned up haphazardly to the top of her head. She hadn't even bothered with lip-gloss.

Nick was so captivated by the woman he paid no attention to anyone else. He hadn't noticed Rebekkah was but a few feet away. He'd apparently moved on. Without her. Her decision to go see him had come too late. She flashed back to his car pulling up to the curb, heard his voice telling her he missed her. He'd made a quick recovery. She bit her lip to keep from crying. She forced herself to eat, and tried to keep conversation going with her parents. She was relieved when dinner was over, and they made their way home.

She couldn't disrupt Nick's life now by telling him about his baby. She would raise it by herself. She would have her conversion ceremony, so her baby would be Jewish, too.

EIGHTEEN

Rebekkah tried not to feel disappointment when Elisabeth didn't answer her email right away. She was probably on winter break. Rebekkah's mind turned to other things. Like Nick. She wouldn't be able to see Elisabeth before seeing Nick now.

It was possible the woman with him last night was a relative. Whoever she was, Rebekkah had to put the ache in her heart aside. Nick had a right to know about his baby. She picked up her cell phone, her stomach fluttering with nervousness.

"Rebekkah." Nick answered so quickly it startled her. It was so good to hear his voice.

She jumped off her bed. "Nick. Hi." She tried to keep her voice from quivering. "I need to see you. I have something important to tell you."

"I'm glad you called." His deep voice was full of emotion. "I can't believe it's you. I've been waiting…I'll come get you. Where are you?"

Rebekkah paused. She hadn't expected him to want to see her that second, but it made her happy. "At my parents' house. I'll drive over."

"When?" he wanted to know.

"In a few minutes." The sooner the better. She glanced at her clock radio. Almost seven. It was already dark out. "Unless you're busy right now."

"Never too busy for you. I'll be waiting. Drive carefully."

Promising she would, Rebekkah hung up. She looked in the mirror. Would Nick notice she was a little plumper? She pulled a bulky gray sweater over her head then threw on her coat. Within ten minutes she pulled up to the curb in front of his house.

Seconds later, his front door flew open. Rebekkah stepped inside, and found herself in Nick's arms. "You smell so good," he whispered. "You have no idea how much I've missed you."

Rebekkah breathed a sigh of relief at being with him. There was no place else she would rather be. Reluctantly, she pulled away. "I've missed you, too. What I need to tell you is important."

"First..." He gave her a long, lingering kiss, and then took her hand. "Come in the living room."

Rebekkah slid her coat off, but stayed on her feet. Grace came right to her, and she bent down to pet her.

Nick laid her coat on the piano bench. "Do you want something to eat or drink?"

Rebekkah couldn't eat anything right now. She was much too nervous about telling him about the baby, not to mention worried about his reaction. She smiled. "No, I'm fine. But if you want something, go ahead."

"Let's talk first. You sounded so serious on the phone." He paused, looking as if he couldn't believe she was actually with him. "You have no idea how happy I am that you're here."

Rebekkah ran her lower lip between her teeth. "I just hope you're still happy when I finish telling you everything. First, I'm sorry for leaving you after we…we made love. It was silly to think I couldn't trust a man again, just because of Avram. I trust you."

"I'm glad," Nick said. "I'll never hurt you. Not intentionally."

She pushed the image of him and the other woman at V. Fong's out of her mind. "I believe you. Second, I don't regret making love with you."

He looked relieved. "I'm glad you've had a chance to think about things. You don't know how excited I was when you called."

"I'm glad." The nervousness in her stomach was back. "There's something else. A big something."

"Don't be afraid to talk to me." His eyes looked deep into hers. "There's nothing you can't tell me. Ever."

She'd gone over dozens of ways to tell him about the baby. Of course, none of them came to mind now. Please don't let me lose him because of this, she prayed silently. She wondered if God was listening to her these days.

"I'm...I'm pregnant. It happened when we made love."
She didn't want him to think, God forbid, it was Avram's
child. Or anyone else's.

Nick's jaw tightened. "You're pregnant?"

She nodded her head. She couldn't speak. Was he
angry? She couldn't tell.

Then a smile lit up his face. "Thank God! When you
called I was imagining all sorts of things. Like you were
going back to Avram, and for some reason wanted to be
nice by telling me in person."

He wasn't angry at all. What a relief. "I wouldn't have
kissed you like that if I had gone back to Avram. We're
divorced now. There's no way I would be with him again."

"You're carrying my baby," he whispered, closing the
space between them in one step. He enveloped her in his
arms, one hand cradling the back of her head against his
chest, as if she were precious and fragile.

Rebekkah felt him trembling, and hugged him back as
tightly as she could. She loved how solid and strong he
was.

After a long time, he drew away. Before his mouth
came down on hers again, she saw tears in his eyes. Tears
of happiness, she prayed. Sighing in contentment, she got
even closer to him as his kiss grew more urgent and
intimate.

"I'm glad Avram's out of your life," he said when
their kiss ended. "I want to take you upstairs and make
love to you so badly, but I'm going to wait until we're

married. I am going to marry you before the baby arrives. I want you to know that."

Her heart melted at his words. "I want to make love to you too. Nothing in my life has ever felt so right, or so good, but I agree with you."

She couldn't believe how perfect he was for her, in every way but one. If only she could accept not being Jewish. That was still so confusing. How could she dare believe someday they could be married? Accept Nick not being the perfectly nice Jewish husband she'd always dreamed of? But how many Jewish men would marry her since she wasn't Jewish now, and want to be a father to a baby that was a result of a one-night stand with a gentile? She felt guilty thinking that. She loved Nick with her whole heart. No other man would be a father to his baby. Why did religion have to be such a stumbling block?

"Why didn't you come to me sooner about the baby?" Nick questioned. "You must've known for months. How could you have kept this from me?"

"I know." Ashamed, Rebekkah looked at the floor then back up at him. "Please, try to forgive me. I realized whatever else is going on with me, you deserved to know about your baby."

"There's nothing to forgive. You're here now, that's all that matters. I'm sure it was a shock to you, too. It just hurts that you waited so long to come to me. You have to know there's nothing you can't share with me." He frowned. "So, what else is going on with you? Are you all right? Is the baby all right?"

She met his eyes, her heart turning over at how caring he was. "We're both fine. I just have some other things to tell you."

He splayed a hand across her belly. "I can't believe it. I'm having a baby." He hugged her again. "Come, sit down. Wait!" He held her shoulders lightly. "Is it a boy or a girl? When are you due?"

She smiled. "I'm due June 14th. Let's see, today's the 22nd of December, I'm about fifteen weeks. Dr. Gavin says she'll do an ultrasound when I'm between eighteen and twenty weeks pregnant. If I want to know, she'll tell me."

"We and us," Nick corrected.

"What?"

He grinned. "You said, 'If I want to know, she'll tell me.' Don't you mean, 'If we want to know she'll tell us'?"

Rebekkah laughed, thrilled at his immediate interest in their baby. "I stand corrected. You're really not angry?"

He guided her to the couch. "Are you kidding? There's no way I'd be angry. The shock's already worn off. I love you. I love that you're pregnant. I want both of you, very much. So, how do you feel about it?"

Rebekkah smiled from ear-to-ear as she always did when she thought about their baby. "It's what I've always dreamed of. I just never dreamed it would happen while I wasn't married. Or married to the wrong man, I should say. I was shocked, too. Now, I can't wait to feel it growing inside me, and to hold it in my arms."

Nick's grin grew. "I'm glad you feel that way. You'll be an awesome mother, Rebekkah."

Her smile faded a little. "I'm not sure how to bring this up, but I ate at V. Fong's last night."

"You did? Me too. I didn't see you. I would've at least said hello."

"I was there with my parents." She got up again, folding her arms against her body. "I don't want to sound silly, or petty, but you were with a woman. Of course, you have a right to be with anyone you want. I'm trying to say I don't want you to be tied to me only because of the baby.

"I can raise him or her by myself. Because if you're involved with..." She felt sick at the thought of him with someone else.

Nick's amused look turned into a smile. His smile turned into a laugh he tried to squelch.

"What's so funny?" she demanded.

"You really love me."

Rebekkah didn't understand what he was finding so amusing. "You knew that already."

"You thought I was on a date?"

"I didn't know what to think. That's why it was hard for me to call you tonight. I didn't want to interfere."

Nick became serious. "I want you to interfere. I've been on one date since you walked out on me. Only to prove I didn't care about you, didn't love you."

His admission hurt. "Did it work?"

He cocked an eyebrow at her. "Really? You have to ask?" He pulled her back down to the couch. "My brothers got tired of me moping around. Yes, I've told them all about you. Joey, the middle one, fixed me up with his girlfriend's roommate. I told her why my heart wasn't into dating. She understood, and encouraged me to go after you. I paid for dinner then drove her home."

"You don't like her then?" Rebekkah asked in a small voice.

Nick grinned again. "No, I don't 'like her', silly. I don't even remember her name. You're the woman I love. I've loved you since the moment I saw you. Don't ask me to explain it. I can't. When you left there was a big hole in my life. I couldn't believe I'd lost you."

"I'm sorry. My feelings for you overwhelmed me. They still do." Rebekkah felt immeasurably better that Nick had missed her as much as she'd missed him. "What would've happened if I hadn't called you tonight?"

Nick wasted no time answering. "I'd have given you another week then come after you. I don't want to live my life without you. By the way, the woman I was with last night wasn't a date. She's Lieutenant Daphne Crispino. It was business."

Relief washed through Rebekkah. "She's very pretty."

"Not as beautiful as you. Let's talk about our baby. Will you feel tied to me just because of the baby?"

"No! I didn't come just to tell you about the baby. I love you. I couldn't forget you no matter how hard I tried."

304

"I don't want you to forget me." Nick stared off into space, a smile on his lips again.

She laid her hand on his thigh. "What are you thinking? You have a very amused look on your face."

"My baby's Jewish because you are, right? I'm imaging my mother's reaction if she were alive." He looked at Rebekkah. "Don't get me wrong. Mom wasn't anti-Semitic, but she was Catholic down to her bones. Having a Jewish grandchild would be a bit of a jolt. She'd love it to pieces, though. Dad, too."

She laughed. "I can imagine she'd be shocked." She felt sad for Nick and his loss. "I wish I could've met your parents."

Her eyes went to the large Christmas tree sitting behind the piano. "I love your tree." It was beautifully decorated with a thousand tiny colored lights, and all kinds of delicate shiny ornaments. All she wanted to do was curl up with Nick on his couch and enjoy the romantic atmosphere. He spoke again before she could tell him his baby wasn't really Jewish. At least not at the moment.

"Thanks. I love Christmas. Are you hungry now? How about a sandwich? I can make tuna salad. You need to drink milk, right? How much milk do you want? Can you drink milk with tuna salad?"

Rebekkah was overwhelmed at Nick's attention. She giggled at the serious look on his face, and all the questions. "Yes, now I'm hungry. I didn't eat dinner, I was too nervous about calling you."

Nick frowned. "You have to eat. For yourself and our baby. Not that you don't know already. I don't want you to have any problems with the pregnancy. I ate dinner, but I can always eat again."

His concern touched Rebekkah. "So far no problems. Some morning sickness in the beginning, but not anymore. Tuna salad is fine. Yes, I can have milk with tuna salad. Please, let me help you. She got up with him.

"Are you sure you're up to it? Shouldn't you rest?"

"It's a sandwich, Nick." Rebekkah laughed. "I think I'm up to it." She followed him to the kitchen, Grace on their heels. They worked in intimate silence together.

"Have you thought of names?" Nick asked when they returned to the couch with their food.

"Not yet," Rebekkah admitted. "Ashkenazi Judaism has a custom of naming babies after deceased relatives. I was named after my great-grandmother. I don't think my brothers and my sister were named for any relatives, though."

"I like that practice," replied Nick. "Since you've been gone, I've studied Judaism. There's a lot about it I like. It's not so different from Christianity, you know. We worship the same God, we read the same Psalms in church. Your Tanakh is our Old Testament. We believe in the Ten Commandments. The first Christians were Jews. Everyone talks about Judeo-Christian values."

Impressed, Rebekkah listened intently to his list. "What else did you learn?"

"I like the concept of your Sabbath," Nick continued. "Taking a day to step back from the world and focus on God. Sorry, I didn't mean to go into lecture mode. Tell me more about the name thing."

She was touched he'd studied Judaism. "A lot goes into choosing a name. Naming a Jewish baby is not only a statement of the hope for what she, or he, will be, but also where he, or she, comes from.

"Naming a child after a relative who has passed away keeps the name and memory alive, and in a metaphysical way forms a bond between the soul of the baby and the deceased relative. But I'd like us to pick names together."

"Me, too," said Nick. "So, how did your parents react to your pregnancy? And about me not being Jewish? I really want to meet them."

Rebekkah swallowed a bite then took a big gulp of milk. He certainly made a good tuna salad. "That has to do with the other things I had to tell you. Remember I told you I'm adopted?"

"Of course I do."

"Wait till you hear this. Naturally, my parents always wanted me to marry a nice Jewish man. I, too, never imagined doing otherwise. Since childhood, I've had this image of my perfect Jewish husband. And our children. Then Avram turned out not so nice.

"I know that has nothing whatsoever to do with him being Jewish. But, as Cairenn pointed out, the Jewish husband thing hasn't worked so well for me. Jonathan and the accident, then Avram and his lies."

Nick laughed. "She has a point."

Rebekkah laughed, too. "When I told Ima and Aba about you and the baby, yes, they were a little surprised. Okay, a lot surprised. But not as surprised as I when Ima told me my birth mother isn't Jewish, which means I'm technically, and genetically, not either."

Nick ran a hand through his hair. His eyes grew large. "You're kidding. How can you all of a sudden not be Jewish? Why did she decide to tell you now? That must have been a real surprise."

"I know," Rebekkah agreed. "You're asking the same questions I did. I was more upset over that than being pregnant. I guess, like your brothers, Ima got tired of seeing me so distraught over you. She knew I was in love with you...am in love with you. She thought if she told me I'm not really Jewish, I would have no qualms about being with you.

"She is worried about your career choice, though. I think even more than you not being Jewish. She's afraid I'll spend my life worrying about your safety if I marry you."

"Do you worry about me?" Nick asked.

"I might," she teased. "But I have confidence you know what you're doing."

Nick studied Rebekkah's face. "How do you feel about not being Jewish? Does it mean you're fine now with being with me? Are your qualms gone? What do you do with that knowledge? Sorry about all the questions, but me not being Jewish is a big issue for you."

"I'm trying to be fine with it, but it's not easy. All I know is my life isn't working out the way I pictured."

Nick grinned at her. "Yeah, I'm guessing an Italian Catholic police detective wasn't at the top of your, or your parents' list, of eligible husbands."

Rebekkah returned his grin. Nick made even the most serious subjects easy to discuss. "The detective part would have been all right with them, but not the Catholic part. They want to meet you, too. Ima wants to have you to dinner."

"Tell them I'm looking forward to it. Your brothers and sister, too."

"Lilly, Ben, and Sam don't know anything about this," Rebekkah said. "They know about you and the baby, but not about me not being Jewish."

"I don't understand why you aren't Jewish if you're adopted parents are."

"It doesn't work that way. They should've had a conversion ceremony for me. They didn't."

"So your dilemma is, do I have a conversion ceremony and become Jewish, or do I not, and stay with Nick?"

Rebekkah took his hand. She brought it to her lips and kissed it. "Sort of. But I'm not going to walk away from you again. I just don't know how to make us work. I want my faith and I want you. Yes, to be Jewish I have to have a conversion ceremony, and immerse in the mikveh."

"There's no reason you can't have me and be truly Jewish, from my point of view. I don't want to change who you are. Is there anything I can do to help you figure things out?"

"That's sweet of you, but I have to figure this out myself."

He leaned over, and pulled her into a hug. "You will. Just remember I'm here if you need to talk. All I care about is having you near me."

"I know, and thank you." She paused and decided to share one more thing with him. "I actually contacted my birth mother with an email. She's sort of famous."

Nick leaned back and took a swallow if his drink. "Really? As in movie star famous?"

As she ate the last bite of her sandwich, he pulled her closer again, putting an arm around her. "No, not that famous. Her name is Elisabeth Mandeville. She teaches English at Columbia. She's written lots of poetry books."

"I don't read a lot of poetry. My taste in literature is non-fiction, mysteries, and police thrillers."

Rebekkah laughed. "Somehow I didn't think you sat around reading poetry."

Nick took her hand, threading his fingers with hers. "Not to change the subject, but you know we Christians don't think God is three different people. He's three-in-one. He's like the egg."

"God is like the egg?" Rebekkah couldn't wait to hear this one.

"An egg is the shell, the yolk, and the white," Nick continued. "One egg, but three different parts."

She nodded. "Makes sense in a weird sort of way."

"We can work this out," he assured her. "I was wrong to tell you I'd convert. At least without giving it serious thought. Religion means a lot to you. It means a lot to me. I don't want to take that away from our child. I have no problem with Judaism. It's love that's important. Do you know in Judaism sex is for the woman? A husband owes his wife food, shelter, and sex. Do you want to walk away from that?" He raised an eyebrow at her.

She laughed. He was so sweet. "Yes, I do know that. It's hard to shed the faith in my heart, the faith I've grown up with. How can I reconcile who I am with who you are?"

"Don't overthink it," Nick offered. "Our child won't be brought up without religion. We'll find a way."

Rebekkah squeezed his hand. "I hope so. I thought maybe it would be easy to just start being Christian. I went to the Episcopal Church across from the park to look inside. It was so foreign to me. I just need a little time to sort everything out. I don't even know what religion I was born into, really. I just know Elisabeth isn't Jewish."

"I want my...our baby to have a dad." Nick grazed his knuckles down Rebekkah's cheek. "I don't mean one who visits every other weekend. I want my baby's mother to have Dominick Rossi as her husband, Jewish or not. I know you need to sort out some things, but please don't shut me out of your life. Whatever we have to deal with, we'll do it together."

Rebekkah's eyes filled with tears. "I love you, Nick. I promise I won't shut you out. When I said earlier about my life not working out the way I pictured, what I didn't say was that what I have with you is better than anything I've ever imagined.

"But even though my brain has more or less accepted I'm not Jewish, my soul hasn't. I'm afraid I'd be lost without my faith. Rabbi Weissman keeps pressuring me to give you up. To have a conversion ceremony."

"Does he understand I don't want you to give up your religion? Neither do I want you to give me up. We're perfect together. Couldn't our child be brought up with both traditions? I think a Menorah would go nicely on the fireplace mantel beside the tree. Maybe I could meet your rabbi."

Rebekkah smiled. Nick was trying, but she was being pulled in so many directions. "All I ask is a little time to think about it."

He kissed the back of her hand. "I'm here for you, and the baby. Speaking of the baby, what do you want, a boy or a girl?"

"Do you want to know what it is, or should we wait until Rossi baby is born?"

"I like that. Rossi baby." He grinned and stared off into space while he thought about her question. "I want to know. I'll go with you to your appointment, so we can find out together. As a matter of fact, I'm going with you to all your appointments."

Rebekkah couldn't believe how happy she was. She trusted Nick with her heart, and with their baby. She would think about everything he said, even the God and egg part. But before she started any kind of life with him, there was something she needed to do. "Do you have time to go somewhere with me next week, or the week after?"

"Of course. Where?"

"It's time I returned Jonathan's engagement ring to his family. I'm ready to say good-bye to him."

Nick studied Rebekkah, taking a few seconds before he responded. "Will that be hard to do?"

Smiling, she looked up at him. "Not now. Jonathan is my past, a lifetime ago. My life is so different now. I'm different. I couldn't say good-bye to him when I was Avram. He never knew I went to see Jonathan.

"I see now that I held on to Jonathan because I wasn't truly happy with Avram. Even though I'd convinced myself I was, and that I loved him. It's time to let Jonathan go."

Nick drew Rebekkah in for a kiss. "I'll be happy and honored to go with you."

"Thank you. I'd like to keep his parents, Pamela and Alex, in my life. I love them."

"You should. I'm glad you want me to go with you."

Rebekkah closed her eyes, unable to stop smiling. Leaning against Nick she couldn't remember being happier.

NINETEEN

"I thought you told me Elisabeth wasn't Jewish so I could be with Nick." Rebekkah frowned at her mother. "You urged me to tell him about the baby."

She had been happily painting all morning. More of her paintings had sold, and a major New York City newspaper had done a feature on Cairenn's gallery, which included Rebekkah's art, in their glossy Sunday magazine.

She had enough money to move out, but that idea was on hold. Nick wanted to marry her before the baby came. Even though she hadn't given him a response, it made no sense to move on her own if they did get married. Since seeing Nick last night she hadn't stopped smiling. She was surprised now at her mother's subdued reaction that he knew about the baby.

Shira plopped on Lilly's bed. "Yes. I want Nick to know about the baby, and you to be happy. It's just that..."

"Just what?" Rebekkah put her paintbrush down, giving Shira her full attention.

"I don't know." Shira's fingers plucked at the bedspread. "I think I left you with the impression I didn't care if you turned your back on our religion. That's not true. I guess I didn't think past you going to Nick."

"I'm not marrying him tomorrow," said Rebekkah, smiling.

"But you want to marry him."

"Yes. But I don't want to choose between Nick and being Jewish. I have a lot to work out inside. I don't want to rush into marriage and go through another divorce. I couldn't deal with another divorce."

Shira raised her eyebrows. "You think Nick might be a mistake like Avram?"

"No, no. Not at all. I love him, Ima. More than I can describe. But I want everything to be right."

"I talked to Rabbi Weissman this morning, about not having you converted." Shira abruptly changed the subject.

"Is he angry with you?" Rebekkah hoped not.

"No." Shira made a face. "All right, a little upset, maybe. We had a long discussion. The air's cleared. He said you need to have a conversion ceremony very soon."

"What do you think I should do?" Rebekkah could use a little help.

"I know you love Nick, but I don't want him to take you from your family and faith. I want my grandchild to be Jewish. Will Nick convert?"

"No, Ima. I wouldn't force him. Neither does he want me to stop being Jewish." Rebekkah closed her eyes for a few seconds. "Why does this have to be so difficult? Even if I don't have a conversion ceremony, can't I still consider myself Jewish?"

"You need to convert."

"I love Nick. I didn't plan to fall in love with him, but I did. Now I'm pregnant, and I want to be with him. Maybe I want some time to see if I can get used to not being Jewish. It's all confusing still."

Letting out a sigh, Shira rose. "I guess I opened a can of worms. I can't make the decision for you. You're our daughter and always will be, no matter what. I've pushed the fact that we didn't have a conversion ceremony for you out of my mind since you're birth. Now it's all I think about."

"I'll figure it out. Don't worry."

"I don't think you can have it both ways. Without converting, no matter how you feel inside, you aren't Jewish. Won't you feel differently if you don't convert? You won't be given an aliyah when the Torah is read now."

Rebekkah did feel sad knowing now she couldn't be called up to the bimah for the Torah readings during the Shabbat service, but until she made up her mind about the conversion ceremony that's how it would have to be.

"Tell me. When are we meeting this man?" Shira sounded cheerful again. "Does he like beef stew? Maybe he could come for Shabbat dinner this Friday."

Rebekkah felt better. At least her mother still wanted to meet him. "I'll ask."

"Good. It's only two days away. Ask soon, so I can prepare." Shira got up, but lingered, as if something else was troubling her.

"What is it?" Rebekkah asked.

"Rabbi wants to see you. He wants you to meet someone." Playing with her wedding band, she avoided Rebekkah's eyes.

Rebekkah frowned. "Who?"

"He didn't say."

Rebekkah frowned again. "When?"

"Can you go this afternoon?" Shira came off the bed. "He made it sound urgent. I told him you'd call him first."

Rebekkah nodded. "Okay. Only to be polite. I can't imagine who he wants me to meet."

"That's all he said about it to me."

"Ima," Rebekkah called just as her mother got to the stairs.

Shira returned to Lilly's room. "Yes?"

"I emailed Elisabeth Mandeville. I hope you don't mind."

"I expected you'd want to see her. I don't mind. Did she answer?"

"I think she's probably on winter break. If I don't hear from her I'll let it go."

"I'm sure she'll answer," Shira responded.

Rebekkah reluctantly got up from her stool. "I guess I'll call the rabbi. See what time he wants to see me."

Shira nodded. Giving Rebekkah an encouraging smile, she went downstairs.

"Rebekkah, thank you for coming in," said Rabbi Weissman.

He had asked her to come right away, and she had, even though she hadn't felt like it at all. "Ima said you have someone you want me to meet."

"I do. He should be here any minute."

He? Rebekkah didn't have a good feeling about this. Who was this *he*?

"Have you decided when you want to have your conversion ceremony, and trip to the mikveh? We can get together tomorrow, then do all of it on Thursday."

Rebekkah responded honestly. "I'm not sure what I want to do. I love Nick. I love my faith. I'm hoping I don't have to give up one to have the other."

Rabbi Weissman frowned. "Unless Nick wants to convert I don't see how. I don't need to re-hash all the reasons interfaith marriages aren't ideal. That seventy-percent of them fail. Think of your baby. Don't you want it raised as a Jew?"

"Of course. I'm not saying I don't ever want a conversion ceremony, rabbi. I need a little time to think."

"Don't take too long. My advice is to tell Nick how important being Jewish is to you. How important having a Jewish husband is. That you want your baby to be Jewish."

Rebekkah opened her mouth to argue, but he wasn't about to let her break in.

"There's no reason he can't see his child, but right now you have to think of yourself, your conversion, and your baby. Don't let him sidetrack you."

She took a moment to gather her thoughts. She was frustrated he kept forcing the issue, and was beginning to resent it, but good manners, and respect for him, prevented her from lashing out. "Rabbi, I don't want Nick to be a visitor in his own child's life. He doesn't want me to stop being Jewish. People intermarry. Maybe that could work out. Even if I do convert."

"Rebekkah, I'm not against other faiths, but let's talk about your options." He glanced at his watch. "Say you don't convert, and marry Nick. Are you going to become a Christian?"

"No," Rebekkah said. "I can't see that. I feel no less Jewish just because my birth mother wasn't."

"But you are. We've discussed this before. Having a Jewish heart and Jewish feelings don't make someone Jewish. One has to be Jewish according to Jewish Law. You'll be left on the outside looking in. You could still attend religious services, and Nick would be welcome, too. But we aren't talking about him. We're talking about you."

Rebekkah didn't respond. She knew what he said was right; she would be on the outside looking in.

"Let's look at another option. You convert, and you marry Nick. Are you going to tell him he can't celebrate his religious holidays?"

"No, I wouldn't do that," she cried.

"You shouldn't. But your child will have no sense of what being Jewish really means."

Rebekkah's thoughts swirled around. There was a grain of truth in what Rabbi Weissman said, but she didn't want to live her life without Nick. What kind of God wouldn't understand that? "I don't agree with you totally. How do you know I won't run a Jewish home, and give my child an excellent sense of what being Jewish means?"

There was a knock at the door. "Just a minute," Rabbi Weissman called. He turned back to Rebekkah. "We'll put this discussion on hold. It's the young man I'd like you to meet."

Rebekkah was caught off guard. Obviously, Rabbi Weissman wasn't going to answer her question.

With an affected smile, Rabbi Weissman strode quickly to open the door. "Stephen, good to see you." He clapped the man on the back while slanting his eyes at Rebekkah. "This is the woman I told you about. Rebekkah Gelles. Rebekkah, this is Stephen Parker."

The rabbi draped an arm around each of their shoulders, grinning like a proud father. Rebekkah was afraid her breakfast was about to come back up. She knew exactly what Rabbi Weissman was doing. Matchmaking.

She blinked in Stephen's direction. His large wet lips were the color of dark pink chewing gum. They matched the pink splotches on his cheeks. His hair sprang from his head in thick, unruly curls. Even if matchmaking was what the rabbi had in mind, this was the best he could come up with?

"Pleased to meet you," Rebekkah said. She shook Stephen's hand, almost repulsed by his fat fingers. His hand was sweaty and hot against hers. She resisted wiping her own hand on her pants after their handshake. Wait until Nick heard about this.

Stephen was staring at her, transfixed. Had he never seen a woman before?

"I thought maybe Stephen could be a good friend, Rebekkah." Rabbi Weissman gave her a pointed look. "He's looking for a nice Jewish girl to settle down with."

Rebekkah's mouth fell open. "Rabbi, I am not looking—"

"Go, go. I want you two to have a nice lunch," Rabbi Weissman shooed them out as if he hadn't heard Rebekkah's protest. He had his office door firmly closed within seconds.

Stephen looked at the floor and mumbled something.
"Excuse me?" asked Rebekkah, trying not to take out her annoyance at the rabbi out on Stephen.

"I...I guess we could have lunch," he managed to get out.

It was the last thing Rebekkah wanted to do. She wasn't going to let Rabbi Weissman set her up this way. She sure wasn't about to go along with this scheme of his. "Let's go outside and talk."

Stephen followed right on her heels, reminding her of a faithful puppy.

They stopped on the sidewalk. Stephen blinked in the sun as he shuffled his feet. "What do you want to talk about?"

"Listen, I'm sorry Rabbi Weissman—"

"I've been looking for a wife for quite a while," he interrupted.

"I'm sure you're very nice, but I'm not interested in dating, or," God forbid, she thought, "marrying you. I'm sorry—"

"Right after your conversion we can start seeing each other," he interrupted again. "When are you doing that?" He frowned. "We should marry before your baby arrives."

Rebekkah gasped. Enough was enough. "You aren't listening. I'm sorry the rabbi mislead you. I'm not looking to be fixed up."

"Rabbit Weissman said you were converting. He thought we would make a good match."

"Hmmm, yes. I'm sure he did, but I'm in love with the father of my baby."

Stephen's scowl was replaced with a look of confusion. "I see. But you are converting, aren't you? How can you consider marrying a non-Jew?"

"That's not something I'm discussing with you. It's none of your business. I love the father of my baby. Nothing's going to change that."

322

"So, basically you've wasted my time," he announced, looking down his nose at her.

Rebekkah stiffened. "I didn't waste your time. This wasn't my idea."

"I was willing to overlook your...uh...little indiscretion." Clearing his throat, Stephen glanced in the direction of her stomach. "I was even willing to raise your baby as my own, along with the many others we would have. It seems you don't want to cooperate."

Maybe it was her hormones, but Rebekkah found this truly funny. Except the part about having babies with him. What had Rabbi Weissman been thinking? She looked at him through her lashes. "I may be having twins."

One of Stephen's fuzzy eyebrows shot up. "Oh...well then. I suppose I have no choice but to tell Rabbi Weissman this won't work. I'm looking for a Jewish wife I can be proud of."

"That's not me. At least not right now. I'm sorry."

"I don't think you are sorry. You don't care at all. I see no reason to talk anymore."

Rebekkah gave her biggest smile. "I don't either. I'm sorry this didn't work. I'm sure you'll find a wife who's worthy of you."

He licked his lips. "You're making a big mistake, but I'll tell Rabbi Weissman you aren't the one for me."

Rebekkah watched as he turned on his heel and headed back inside the synagogue. She hurried home before Rabbi Weissman had a chance to drag her inside, too.

Shira was gone when Rebekkah got home. She couldn't wait to tell Nick about Rabbi Weissman's strange attempt to fix her up. They'd have a good laugh over it. She went to the computer and turned it on. She logged in to her email account and was stunned to see Elisabeth Mandeville's name there. Her hand shaking, she opened the email.

Dearest Rebekkah,

Very surprised and glad to hear from you. I think my heart stopped when I saw your name! I've often wondered how it would feel if you did contact me. Of course, I told your mother I wouldn't interfere with your life and would never contact you first. It may not be a step you're ready to take yet, but I'd love to see you.

I'll leave that up to you. I have so many questions for you. I am so eager to see what you look like! I'm sure you have questions for me, also. Maybe you would feel more comfortable speaking on the phone. Please call me anytime you like. My cell phone number is 555-811-9002. I'm very glad you wrote. Hope to see you soon!

Best Wishes,

Elisabeth

Rebekkah stared at the screen. Her fingers reached out, as if somehow she could connect with Elisabeth through her computer. Was she ready to see her birth mother? Goosebumps rose on her skin, and a shiver traveled through her. Would her parents be hurt if she saw Elisabeth, despite Ima's assurance she didn't mind? She couldn't help but think they would. Rebekkah stared at the email. She typed her response and hit *Send.*

"Why don't you go into the living room and wait for Nick? You're making me nervous with all this pacing," said Shira.

Nick would be arriving any moment for Shabbos dinner to meet her parents. Her brothers and sister weren't coming since her mother didn't want Nick to feel as if he were on display.

The doorbell rang, making Rebekkah jump. She flew to the door and opened it. Nick was standing there looking incredibly handsome in a dark suit with a red tie. "Come in."

He grazed a kiss on her cheek then laid a hand on her belly. "How's my girl and Rossi baby?"

Rebekkah grinned. She had to find a way to marry this man. She loved him so much. "Good. I have a very funny story for you."

She closed the front door, and they made their way into the living room.

Shira rushed out from the kitchen, her apron still on, her cheeks flushed from cooking. "I'm Shira. Rebekkah's mother. You must be Nick." She held out a hand. "I'm so happy to finally meet you."

"I'm happy to meet you, too," Nick said. "Rebekkah's told me so much about you. These are for you." He held out a stunning bouquet of flowers.

Shira's cheeks flushed even more. "Thank you, Nick. How nice. I'll put them in water. Please, sit down. Would you like a glass of wine? Some water? I have soda and iced tea, too."

Nick sat. "Water's fine, thank you."

"Come, Rebekkah. Help me with the flowers."

"Be right back," Rebekkah called to Nick.

Shira laid the flowers on the counter and pulled a vase down from one of the

cabinets. "You didn't tell me how good-looking he was. My goodness. He looks like a model, just as you told me before."

Rebekkah grinned. "He's okay."

Shira tsk'd at her. "You're kidding, I know. I think he's a very nice guy."

"Based on his looks, and because he brought you flowers?" Rebekkah teased.

"I have a feeling. Go sit with him. It's rude to leave guests alone. Take his water to him, please."

Rebekkah sat next to Nick. "Ima's flustered. She's impressed with your good looks, and the flowers, too."

Nick smiled. "I'm glad. Now I just have to impress your father."

"I'm sure he'll like you. As long as you talk sports and not politics, you'll be okay."

"Did you tell them I want to marry you before the baby comes?"

"Not yet. But I'm pretty sure Ima knows you do."

He draped an arm over her shoulder. "I'm not going to pressure you."

Rebekkah squeezed his thigh. "I know you won't."

She told Nick about Elisabeth's email, then about the man Rabbi Weissman tried to fix her up with.

Nick gave a mock scowl. "Do I need to go talk to this Stephen guy?"

Rebekkah laughed. "No, I think he got the message loud and clear. I had a nice chat with him. I told him I wasn't in the market for a man."

"What did he say?"

"He apologized and admitted he shouldn't have done that. In his very next breath he said next time he'd find a more suitable man then he hung up on me!"

Nick laughed. "He's determined to find you a nice Jewish husband. I'd still like to meet him."

"Aren't you worried?" she teased.

Nick looked at her. "Nah. I know you love me. Besides, you're carrying my baby. I'd never let another man raise my child. Unless something happened to me and you re-married."

"Don't say that," pleaded Rebekkah. "I wouldn't re-marry. I can't picture loving anyone as I do you."

"I'm glad. If something does happen to me, I want you to marry my brother, Joey. That's a biblical thing, you know. He's almost as good looking as I am and I trust him."

Rebekkah laughed as soon as she figured out he was teasing her now. She prayed nothing would ever happen to Nick, but life had no guarantees. Their conversation was interrupted when Rebekkah's father walked in the door. Nick and Rebekkah both stood and went to greet him.

"Aba, this is Nick Rossi. Nick, my father, David Goldman."

Rebekkah watched as they shook hands, grateful her parents were willing to meet Nick.

Shira came out of the kitchen and gave David a kiss. "Dinner in fifteen."

David laughed. "My cue to change. Be down in a minute."

Dinner was delicious as usual. For the first few minutes, everyone was too busy eating to speak.

"I don't know how much Rebekkah has told you about our relationship," Nick said. "Her pregnancy must have been quite a surprise."

Shira put down her fork and smiled at him. "It was. But when Rebekkah talks about you, it's very evident how much she loves you."

"I love her, too," Nick responded. "She knows I want to marry her before the baby comes."

David looked intently at Nick. "Have you asked her?"

"No, I wanted to talk to you and Mrs. Goldman. I'd like your blessings to marry Rebekkah."

"Please," said Shira. "David and Shira."

Nick smiled. "I'll try and remember."

"There's no need to talk about me as if I'm not here," Rebekkah joined the conversation. "I love Nick, and I want to marry him. I know you thought you were helping me, Ima, telling me about Elisabeth, and the fact I'm not really Jewish, and maybe it will help. Right now though, I want to deal with that before I agree to get married again."

"I've assured Rebekkah I don't expect her to walk away from her faith," Nick said. He took her hand under the table and squeezed it.

Shira glanced at David before speaking. "I have to be honest, Nick. I want my grandchild to be Jewish, but more than that, I want Rebekkah to be happy. If she loves you and wants to marry you, we welcome you into our family. It's ultimately her decision."

"I agree," said David. "She's obviously in love with you, Nick. If she decides not to convert, and our grandchild isn't Jewish, we'll love him or her no less."

"Of course," echoed Shira.

"I don't think we need to discuss this to death tonight," Rebekkah said.

"No, I agree," said Shira as she got up to clear the table. "I'm so glad we met you, Nick."

"I am too, Mrs. Gold...Shira."

Shira brought in cherry pie and sat back down. "Have you ever been shot, Nick?"

"Ima!" Rebekkah exclaimed.

David laughed and put an arm around Shira. "My wife is nothing if not direct."

Nick smiled. "I understand your concern. No, I haven't been shot. I've only been a detective for a year. Before that I was with the mounted unit."

"That's right. Rebekkah told me you rode a horse. Do you miss it?" asked Shira

"Sometimes," Nick replied. "But I love what I'm doing now."

Their cozy dinner was interrupted by banging on the front door. Rebekkah's hand flew to her chest. Her eyes fixed on Shira's.

David got up. "I'll get it."

"Is everything all right? Shira? Rebekkah? You both look scared to death," Nick asked.

"It's Avram. I just know it," whispered Rebekkah. "I can feel it."

Nick was on his feet. "David, let me get it. If it is Avram, I don't want any of you to deal with him. A badge speaks volumes."

Rebekkah could tell her father was about to protest. He didn't like taking orders from someone else in his own house. She didn't want to see anyone get hurt, and was relieved when he agreed with a nod. She knew Nick always had a gun strapped to his ankle. God willing he wouldn't need it. Her heart thumped as he opened the front door. Her instincts were right. Avram stood there. She stood her ground with Shira a few feet away from the door, David stood right behind Nick

"I want to see my wife," Avram demanded.

"If you mean Rebekkah, she isn't your wife. You're not welcome here," said Nick.

Avram stared at Nick, his brow creasing. "Who the hell are you? Rebekkah belongs to me. She had no right to divorce me. She'll come crawling back soon. Where is she?" He tried peering around Nick.

Nick pulled out a thin wallet from his pants pocket and flipped it open. He shoved the badge in Avram's face. "Detective Dominick Rossi. You need to go, before I arrest you for trespassing and harassment. I'll make sure it's a felony conviction. If you come back here I'll skip the formalities and you'll deal with me, alone. It won't be pretty for you."

"You can't have me arrested," Avram muttered, his face red.

"Really." His eyes never leaving Avram he whipped out his cell phone.

Avram sneered at him and clenched his fists. "Yeah, okay, okay. I'm leaving, for now. I don't need to be hassled by a dumb cop. You have no right to stop me from talking to my wife. If she thinks she can divorce me and walk away she's got—"

In one swift movement, Nick tucked away his cell phone and seized Avram by his shirtfront. He hauled him in, so they were nose to nose. "Listen carefully, Mr. Gelles. I don't take orders from you. Rebekkah is no longer your wife. Got it? Erase her from your mind. I don't want you anywhere near her, or her family, again. I'll be watching you.

"My friends will be watching you. Not all of them play by the rules. You get what I'm saying? If you don't, you'll pay, and you won't like the price. Your choice. But you will never see or talk to Rebekkah again. Do we understand each other?"

Avram stumbled down the stairs and grabbed for the handrail as Nick let go of his shirt and shoved him away.

"If you're sleeping with my wife, you'll be the one who pays," Avram shouted over his shoulder, but he headed toward his car.

Nick waited until he drove away before closing the door.

Rebekkah swelled with pride. He was awesome. She hoped the fury in his voice would never be directed at her.

"Thank you. Oh, Nick you were so good. You even had me scared."

He hugged her. "You never have to be scared of me. No one is ever going to hurt you. Or your family."

"What if he does try to physically hurt Rebekkah?" Shira cried. "The baby…"

Nick went to her, and put an arm around her shoulders. "My degree had a concentration in Forensic Psychology, Shira. People like Avram are basically cowards. They intimidate through threats. They have no self-esteem. They use verbal abuse to scare and control their victims. They rarely resort to assault, or worse."

Rebekkah bit her lip, and said nothing about the times he'd grabbed her roughly. She didn't want to worry her mother, and she trusted Nick to take care of her. She didn't believe she would see Avram again.

Shira let out a nervous laugh. "I hope you're right."

David and Shira murmured their thanks. Rebekkah could tell they were impressed with him. Shira stared at him like he was her own personal hero.

"Shall we get back to dessert?" asked Shira after a few seconds.

Everyone made their way back to the dining room.

"If he shows up call 9-1-1. I'll ask that a patrol car swing by periodically. Just in case." Nick put his arm around Rebekkah and her. "Take out a harassment restraining order out on him tomorrow."

"First thing," answered David. "We should have done that when he was calling Rebekkah and sitting in his car outside waiting for her to come out."

Rebekkah was happy when she kissed Nick goodnight a couple of hours later. Her parents hadn't been too rough on him, and they seemed to genuinely like him. Thank God he had been there when Avram arrived.

She climbed into bed soon after Nick left, but tossed and turned in the dark. She couldn't stop thinking about the statistic Rabbi Weissman had quoted: Seventy-percent of interfaith marriages failed. She didn't doubt how much she and Nick loved each other, but were they living in a dream world with the deck stacked against them?

She reached over and switched on the light. She grabbed the novel she was almost finished with. Maybe reading would make her sleepy, and stop the thoughts tormenting her. A half-hour later she was still awake and convinced she and Nick would be headed for divorce if they married. She thought of their baby. If their marriage was doomed to begin with, how much harder would it be for their child to lose Nick's constant presence after having grown up a few years with him? It seemed she and Nick were growing closer every day. If they did end up divorced, how would either of them survive a trauma of another divorce? She had to think of what was best for all concerned.

TWENTY

Rebekkah pulled the shirt over her head then brushed her hair. She and Nick were finding out their baby's gender this morning. She didn't know which of them was more excited. Her negative thoughts of a few weeks ago had subsided. They would find a way to make their relationship work.

Her parents had rented a car and left early this morning for a two-week long trip to the Pocono Mountains in Pennsylvania. Rebekkah was glad to have some time to herself.

When the doorbell rang, Rebekkah trotted down the stairs. "You're early." She smiled as she met Nick halfway for a hug and kiss.

"I want to give you something before we leave. You look beautiful."

"Thank you. You look pretty good yourself." Today he wore a black and brown sweater with black dress pants. He always managed to make looking dangerous sexy, but she knew he had a tender heart for her and the baby.

"Your parents left this morning?"

"Yes, right before the sun came up. They've been acting strange. Ima, especially. She kept staring at me like she wanted to tell me something but couldn't."

Taking her hand, Nick led her to the living room. "I'm responsible."

"For them acting strange?"

"I'll explain in a minute."

"Is everything all right?"

Nick grinned. "It will be, I hope." He sat on the couch, bringing Rebekkah down with him. He pulled a black velvet box out of his jacket pocket.

Her heart sped up. It was the perfect shape for a ring.

"Rebekkah." He flipped open the box. "You're the love of my life. This ring is a symbol of my love. On my part, it's meant to be an engagement ring. Will you marry me?"

She looked down through a film of tears. It was a gold *Ani L'Dodi* ring. The Hebrew inscription meant *I am my beloved's and my beloved is mine.* "Oh, Nick. I love you so much. It's beautiful. I'll never take it off." She threw her arms around him.

He pulled back to look at her. "I know you still have things to decide, things to think about. That's why on my part it's an engagement ring. When you're ready to accept it as an engagement ring," he slipped it on the ring finger of her right hand, "move it to your left hand. I couldn't wait to give it to you. I want to know we belong to each other."

Her heart overflowed with love for him. "We do." She kissed him. "I don't want to lose you."

"You will never lose me."

"How did you know about this kind of ring?"

Nick smiled. "Remember last week when you went shopping with your sister for the day?"

Rebekkah nodded.

"It was planned. That's why your parents have been acting strangely. They knew I was giving it to you while they were gone. Your mom told me about the *Ani L'Dodi* rings. I loved them. They say so much in so few words."

"I want to marry you," Rebekkah said. "But I want everything to be perfect."

"It doesn't have to be perfect, it just has to be about us." He took her hand. "Not that I'm giving you any ultimatums, but promise me before this baby comes you're going to be Mrs. Nick Rossi."

"I promise." How could she not promise when she wanted that more than anything. She didn't know what she was going to do about converting, or if she was going to have to adapt to not being Jewish, which she was very afraid she could never do. But she couldn't live without Nick. Surely by the time the baby came she would figure out how to have both her faith and Nick in her life.

Her eyes closed as he kissed her. She longed to make love with him as their kiss grew. She remembered how

337

gentle his strong hands had been on her body. How she had felt being one with him. She wanted that feeling again.

"If we don't stop I'm going to carry you upstairs," Nick told her when their kiss ended.

She giggled and looked down at her expanding middle. "Really? I don't think you can."

"You may be right." His eyes darkened. "But I want you so much right now."

"I want you too, but we agreed to wait. We did agree?"

"Yeah. Unfortunately. Don't know what we were thinking."

"Besides, I don't look very sexy right now."

Nick grinned. "You look very sexy right now."

"I'm glad you think so." She changed the subject to get her mind off Nick's body joined with hers, and how he felt inside her. "We should get going. I can't wait to see if we're having baby girl Rossi, or baby boy Rossi."

She got up, stretched out her hand, and examined her ring again. She was touched he had gone to her mother for advice. "I still need to take Jonathan's ring back. I've been busy painting, along with being at the gallery. And you've been so busy working."

"I know. We should do that soon. How about next Thursday?"

"I'll call Pamela and see if that's okay for her. I don't want to hold onto it any longer."

Rebekkah and Nick arrived at Dr. Gavin's office with minutes to spare. She was so happy and proud he was with her. They had barely taken their seats when the nurse called her name. She led them both into a room and took Rebekkah's vital signs. "The doctor will be in shortly." She smiled at both of them then left the room.

Dr. Gavin entered seconds later. "Good morning, Rebekkah. Today's the big day."

"I can't wait to find out." Rebekkah could barely sit still. "This is Nick Rossi. He's my baby's father."

Dr. Gavin smiled as she shook Nick's hand. "So good to meet you. Are you ready to see your baby?"

Nick held Rebekkah's hand. "We can't wait. I just wish I could meet him or her in person now."

This time, Dr. Gavin did the scan herself. Rebekkah lay back, scooting her pants down. She had felt the baby move several times now, and was looking forward to meeting it in person.

Dr. Gavin applied the topical gel to Rebekkah's abdomen then moved a transducer around. "Ah, here we are."

Rebekkah stared at the ultra-sound machine. "Is it a girl? Is it a boy?"

Dr. Gavin laughed. "Well, yes. I'm afraid those are your only choices. Say hello to your son. Congratulations!"

Nick reached down and kissed Rebekkah. "It's our first look at our son."

Rebekkah swiped at tears of happiness. "We're having a boy. It's a boy! Hi there, baby." She reached out and touched the screen. "Your mommy and daddy can't wait to meet you."

"I'll leave you two alone," said Dr. Gavin. "Stop at the desk on your way out, I'll have a couple of pictures for you."

Rebekkah adjusted her pants and slid off the examining table. She turned to Nick and hugged him. "You really are happy?"

"Very. Wow. I have a son. We have a son!" He grinned at Rebekkah. "Let's celebrate. How about lunch at V. Fongs?"

"That sounds great. But don't you need to get to work?

"Later this afternoon. Right now I want to have lunch with my family." He kissed Rebekkah's forehead.

She frowned. "Are you still working on that murder?"
He paused while he handed Rebekkah her purse. "Yeah, but I'll be fine. Don't worry."

He didn't talk a lot about his work. When he did it was in general, never specifics. It scared her sometimes that Nick had transferred to organized crime right after the art gallery break-in, but she didn't voice her fears. She didn't want to be a clingy female. He loved what he did, and she had complete faith in him. Being part of the New York City Police Department was who he was. She couldn't take that away from him.

340

Rebekkah paid her bill and collected the ultra-sound pictures of the baby. She had already started a baby album for him. She would have loved a daughter to dress up, but a little Nick filled her heart with as much joy. She suddenly had the perfect name for him.

Nick was subdued as they drove to the restaurant. They held hands, but she felt tenseness in his fingers. She hoped he wasn't feeling anxious about fatherhood.

Rebekkah looked over the menu once they were seated. She was very hungry even though she'd eaten a good breakfast that morning. Luckily, the waitress came quickly to take their orders.

"Is something bothering you, Nicky?" she asked.
He smiled. "You noticed."

"I guess you aren't the only detective in the family. What is it?"

"I don't want to make it sound like this is a reason to get married, it's not. But the sooner you marry me the sooner I can put you on my insurance. I don't want you paying for your doctor visits."

She relaxed. At least it wasn't something major. "That's sweet of you. I have money. Ima told me Elisabeth's been sending them money for me until I was eighteen. I haven't used it yet, but it's there. My art is selling well, too. And Ima and Aba don't charge me rent."

"All good points," he acknowledged. "But this is my baby, too. It's not right that you're paying for your doctor visits."

"We can split the cost."

"No," he argued. "Sorry to go all macho on you, but in my mind I wouldn't be much of a man if I agreed to that. I'll pay for them."

She tried not to smile. She loved that Nick was so willing to take care of her and the baby, but there was no reason he had to pay for all the visits. Looking at his face, she knew, however, this wasn't an argument she would win. "Then I accept. Thank you."

"I'm glad that's settled. I have no intention of telling you how to spend your money, but I want to be responsible for my family."

This time she did grin at the earnest tone in his voice. Her heart melted with love for him.

The waitress came with their food, and they both ate in silence for a few minutes.

"I'd like to suggest a name," Rebekkah said after she swallowed the last bite of her eggroll.

"Go ahead. I haven't thought of any yet. I wanted to wait until we knew what we were having."

"Michael Anthony."

Nick stopped eating and looked at her. "After my father. You would do that for me?"

"For us. Yes. Our son will never know his grandfather. Your father's name is something we can give him."

Nick reached across the table, covering Rebekkah's hand with his. "Michael Anthony Rossi." Tears glinted in his eyes. "That means so much to me."

Rebekkah smiled. "I can't wait to see our Michael."

Nick's smile was even bigger than hers. "I can't either. We have a lot of planning to do. I love you so much."

"I love you. I'm so very glad you're my baby's father." She looked down at her ring. This was a time for celebration. The only people in her world right now were Dominick Michael Rossi and Michael Anthony Rossi. This wasn't a time to worry about decisions she had to make.

Rebekkah awoke early the next morning. She wanted to bring *Mikveh*, her latest piece, to Cairenn. She also needed to buy more maternity clothes. After dressing, feeding and walking the dogs, and eating her own breakfast she was ready for a nap, but grabbed her coat instead. Stepping outside, she pulled the front door closed then locked it.

When she got to the bottom of the steps she looked down the sidewalk in the direction of the Volvo and froze. Avram was pacing back and forth a few feet away. He was pale and gaunt, his short beard scruffy, and his clothing too big. He must be cold in the thin, dirty raincoat. What in heaven's name had happened to him?

Her adrenaline surged, and not in a good way. There was no one around, on foot or in a car. She could count on one hand the number of times that had happened. He saw her before she could run back in the house.

"Rebekkah. I thought you'd never appear. I've been walking back and forth for an hour." He buried his hands in his coat pockets. "I miss you."

Rebekkah forced herself to stay calm as she leaned her painting against a tree. She pulled out her cellphone, ready to dial 9-1-1. "I took a restraining order out on you. Get away from me. We have nothing to talk about."

He took a step toward her. She took two steps back. She was afraid if she tried running back inside he would follow. "Please, Avram. Just go. We're divorced."

"I'm in a lot of trouble. I need help. I came by to tell you I'm sorry. Sorry for everything."

"It doesn't matter anymore."

"I want another chance. I'll move back to this neighborhood. I'll adopt ten kids for you. I'll reverse my vasectomy. Please, you have to take me back. I can't make it without you. You're my last hope. You're the only one I have."

Rebekkah couldn't believe she had shared a marriage and bed with this man. The thought revolted her. She didn't hate him, she just wanted him to go away. Forever. "You don't *have me*, Avram. I won't take you back. Our marriage is over."

"I can't go to jail," he whined. "I won't survive without you."

Rebekkah was stunned as he twirled around in a circle, his raincoat billowing around him like a tent. He shook his fists in the air then dropped to his knees. Rocking back and forth, he pummeled his fists into the cement. "I can't live without you. I won't go to jail! You're the only woman I've ever loved. I screwed up, Rebekkah, but I need you. Let me come back. I'm begging you."

Rebekkah pushed 9-1-1 and spoke rapidly. Thank God Avram didn't notice.

He suddenly stopped beating the ground. Leaning back on his heels he looked up at her, his cheeks wet with tears. "I've lost everything. Don't you get it? I can't go to prison. I'd rather die."

Rebekkah shivered, her teeth chattering. She only had sympathy because he was a human being. But he wasn't her responsibility. If he had indeed lost everything, he had brought it on himself.

He pinned narrow bloodshot eyes on her and she watched in fright as his mood shifted from defeated to aggressive. His eyes shone with evil. "You're a bitch!" He spat as he stood. "I come here to give you another chance. You dismiss me like I'm nothing? You're my wife. You belong to me." He grabbed her painting.

"Avram, no," she whispered. Horrified, she watched him crash it over his raised knee.

"That's what I think of your art. All of it. 'Look at me,'" he mocked. "'I'm Rebekkah, the great artist.' You always thought you were better than I. You're nothing! You'll be nothing without me! It was me who took your art from that stupid gallery. I burned every piece. How come your smart detective didn't figure that one out? Guess he's not so smart after all. Ask Jimmy. But no one will ever be able to prove it now. It's all ashes. Ashes, ashes we all fall down."

How was she going to get away from him? He was truly crazy.

A police car came skidding to a stop at the curb. Two officers jumped out. The male office strode toward Avram, telling him to stay put. The female officer approached Rebekkah.

"I'm Officer Belinda Lamont. Are you all right? What happened? Do you know this guy?"

"He's my ex-husband. He was outside when I left the house and went ballistic. He destroyed my painting and threatened me. I need to sit down. I'm pregnant," she whispered. "I don't feel very well."

"Do you want an ambulance?"

"No, thank you, Officer Lamont. I just want to get away from him."

"How about if I come inside with you for a few minutes?" Her eyes met her partner's. He nodded.

"Yes, that would be good." The male officer was leading Avram toward the police car. Rebekkah shuddered. She watched him put the painting Avram had smashed in a bag. Tears filled her eyes at Avram's cruelty.

"Where's your kitchen?" Officer Lamont asked once they were inside. "I'll get you some water. Why don't you sit down."

Rebekkah sank down on the couch and directed her, inviting the officer to take some for herself. She was grateful for her kindness. She felt light-headed. Officer Lamont's questions seemed to come from far away.

Rebekkah assured Office Lamont that yes, she definitely wanted to file charges against Avram, and she waited for the officer to finish her report. When she saw the officer out she called Cairenn, who offered to close the gallery and come right over. Rebekkah thanked her, but she just wanted to take a long nap now. Nick would be beyond angry that Avram had come by, but she wasn't going to tell him about it until that night.

She lay down on her bed, but sleep wouldn't come. Instead, Avram's words haunted her. "Ask Jimmy," he'd said. Did she know a Jimmy? She bolted up, her heart racing. Yes, it had to be that Jimmy.

Howard's face wore a shocked expression when he saw Rebekkah come through the revolving doors of the condominium building where she'd lived with Avram. "Mrs. Gelles. What a surprise."

"Good morning, Howard." Rebekkah got right to the point. "Is Jimmy here?"

"Yes he is, Mrs. Gelles. Why?" He was clearly surprised to hear Rebekkah asking about the condominium's janitor.

"Howard, Mr. Gelles and I are divorced. Please, call me Rebekkah."

"I thought so after you moved out and he didn't go with you. I'll try to call you Rebekkah, but somehow that doesn't sound right."

"I'm asking about Jimmy because I need to know if he remembers getting rid of anything for Mr. Gelles."

Howard's eyebrows shot up. "It's funny you should ask. I don't mean funny laughter-wise, I mean strange-funny."

She swallowed. "Why?"

Howard looked around at the empty lobby, then his eyes widened. "You won't believe this, but it's true. Jimmy just told me today about a box Mr. Gelles had asked him to destroy in the incinerator a week or so after you moved out."

"Go on," urged Rebekkah.

"According to Jimmy, Mr. Gelles had him come up and get it. It was sealed with a bunch of duct tape. Mr. Gelles told Jimmy he wanted to watch, to make sure it got done. Jimmy told me Mr. Gelles got an important phone call right then.

"He told Jimmy to take the box down, but not to do anything until he, Mr. Gelles, I mean, got down there. So, Jimmy took it on down to the basement in the freight elevator."

Rebekkah's fingers gripped the edge of the marble counter. She leaned toward Howard. "Then what happened?"

"Jimmy's a good guy. He's slow, but he does a great job. He loves watching all those police shows. Some are filmed right here in New York. They've even filmed in a buddy of mine's house."

"Yes, yes, I know the ones." Rebekkah reigned in her impatience as she wondered where this was all going.

"For some reason, Jimmy got it in his brain that Mr. Gelles was up to something sinister." Howard chuckled. "All those police shows influencing him, I guess. Instead of throwing that particular box into the incinerator, he threw in a whole bunch of empty boxes.

"He shoved Mr. Gelles' box into a corner of the tool room. By the time Mr. Gelles got to the basement, Jimmy was burning the empty boxes. Mr. Gelles wasn't at all happy Jimmy had started without him, he really blew his top, but what could he do?"

"Is the box Mr. Gelles wanted burned still here then?" She nearly grabbed Howard's arm in anticipation.

"Sure is," Howard replied. "Jimmy got real sick right after Mr. Gelles asked him to do that. When he came back last week Mr. Gelles had moved out and—"

"Mr. Gelles moved out?" she interrupted

"Yes, ma'am. About two weeks ago. Anyway, Jimmy feels a little guilty about what he's done, and was wondering what to do with the box Mr. Gelles wanted destroyed. I didn't want to reach Mr. Gelles, obviously, and I didn't know how to reach you.

"That's what I mean by funny you should ask. Here we were discussing the box not an hour ago, and now you're here asking about it. Like *The Twilight Zone*. I wonder if God brought you here."

Rebekkah wondered the same thing. "Let's go see what's in that box, Howard."

Howard put up a sign indicating he would be gone for thirty-minutes. "Jimmy's downstairs."

She followed Howard to the freight elevator then to the incinerator room.

"Jimmy?" Howard called.

"In the tool room," a voice called.

Jimmy looked scared when he saw Rebekkah. "Are you angry at me for not destroying the box?"

Rebekkah smiled. "No, Jimmy. I'm very glad you didn't."

"Let's open it up," said Howard.

She stood back as the two men went to work.

A couple of minutes later, Rebekkah understood exactly why Avram wanted it destroyed. Howard stared at it, looking puzzled. Jimmy seemed disappointed it wasn't a dead body.

Howard turned to Rebekkah. "Do you know where these came from? Why would Mr. Gelles want Jimmy to get rid of these beautiful paintings? Are you okay, Rebekkah? Jimmy, why don't go see what Mrs. Nelson wanted. She was looking for you earlier."

Jimmy nodded, looking happy at being dismissed.

"I'm all right." Rebekkah ignored the nausea. "Please call the police, Howard. We can't touch any of these. They're... they're paintings I had in a gallery. They were stolen, so now they're evidence. I thought it was Avram all along who took them. Now there's proof it was."

"You poor thing. Why would he do something so heinous?" asked Howard.

She looked at Howard. "He's a sick man. I'm so grateful the box is still here. Jimmy should get a reward for solving this mystery. I'm going to bring something by for him. Let's go upstairs. Tell the police you need to speak to the detective in charge of the Kain Gallery break-in. It used to be detective Nick Rossi. Tell them what you've found."

Without touching the box's contents, Howard and Rebekkah returned to the lobby. For the second time that day, Rebekkah waited for the police to arrive.

Nick stared at her then hugged Rebekkah as tightly as he could. He had been at her house for about fifteen minutes and she had taken all that time to tell him about her day. "Why didn't you call me?" he murmured into her hair.

"I didn't want to bother you. I'm fine, now."

Nick held her at arms' length. "You don't look fine. You look pale. Your day sounds like a made-for-TV-movie. God forbid something like this should happen again, but if it does, you call me. Understand?"

"I promise I will. But I'm hoping it won't."

"I'll help you pack a bag. I want you to stay with me tonight."

"Nick..." Rebekkah searched his face. She wasn't sure that was a good idea, given their decision not to make love until they were married.

He kissed her. "I want you with me. Not here, alone. Besides, I clearly need to keep an eye on you."

She laughed, happy at the thought of not spending the night alone. "What about Lucy and Mortimer?"

"Bring them along. Grace will entertain them. I'll walk them when I walk her."

She grinned, "Give me ten minutes. I'll be all packed."

"I put you in my guest room," Nick said shortly after they'd arrived at his house. "But if you want to sleep in my bed, I'd like that."

"What if I can't keep my hands to myself?" Rebekkah teased.

He cocked an eyebrow at her. "I probably wouldn't complain. I'll walk the dogs then I'll be up, too."

She laughed. She loved being with him. She went to the guest room and put on her pajamas. After brushing her teeth she wandered into Nick's bedroom. His room was both masculine and warm at the same time. She pulled down the fluffy blue down comforter and slid between the sheets.

She drifted off to sleep within minutes. She barely woke when Nick got into bed with her and pulled her to him. Their baby gave a kick when Nick's arm folded around her tummy and his thigh rested protectively over hers. "Good night, my darling," he whispered.

"Good night," Rebekkah managed to reply just before she drifted off to sleep again.

TWENTY ONE

When Rebekkah woke up, Nick was no longer in bed. She scooted to his side. It was still warm. She breathed in his scent. How did they manage to spend the night together and not make love? Vague memories of his body against hers during the night made her shiver with longing.

She stretched, rubbed her hand over her growing belly then got up. After making the bed, she went into the guest bedroom to dress. When she got to the kitchen there was a note from Nick telling her he'd taken the dogs to the park. He'd left a paper bowl and plastic spoon out for her along with a box of cereal. Rebekkah smiled at his thoughtfulness.

She was in the middle of pouring her cereal when Nick came through the door with three happy dogs. Moving her hair to one side, he kissed her neck. "I've got to go in to work in about a half-hour, but stay here as long as you want." He went to a drawer and pulled out a key. "I had this made for you a while ago. You can come and go as you please."

She took the key. "Thank you. I feel safer being here than alone at my parents', even though you told me Avram hasn't been able to post bail yet."

Nick frowned. "I definitely want you to stay with me at night until your parents return. Why don't you call them to let them know you're with me. What are your plans, or do you just want to relax here for the day?"

Rebekkah took her bowl of cereal over to the kitchen table. "I'm meeting Elisabeth today. I almost forgot with all the excitement yesterday."

"Oh, that's right. I can't wait to hear how that goes. I'd come with you if I didn't have to work, but then again you probably want to see her alone. At least for the first time."

"I'm nervous and excited about meeting her. I hope it goes well."

"I'm sure she feels the same. I'll be thinking of you. My phone will be on, as usual. If I can't answer, I'll call you back as soon as I can."

Rebekkah got up. She wound her arms around his neck and kissed him. "I'll try to stay out of trouble."

It was just after nine when she got into the car and set the GPS with Elisabeth's address in Forest Hills. Snow was beginning to fall, but she loved it and didn't mind. At least it wasn't accumulating yet.

When Rebekkah arrived at Elisabeth's thirty minutes later she sat in the car for a few minutes. Now she wished Nick had come with her. What if Elisabeth took an instant dislike to her? She pulled on gloves then hurried through drifting snowflakes into the seven-story square brick building. Elisabeth lived on the fifth floor. Rebekkah stood in the foyer and pushed the little button next to 5-K. Elisabeth's apartment.

"Hello?" came a garbled voice through the metal speaker.

Rebekkah swallowed. "Elisabeth? It's Rebekkah "

"Great! Come on up."

The door buzzed, and Rebekkah went through. The small elevator was agonizingly slow. She couldn't believe she was about to meet her birth mother. She stepped off the elevator and found 5-K. She was about to ring the doorbell when the door opened. Rebekkah was thrown off-kilter for a second.

It was like looking at an older version of herself. She hadn't seen a huge resemblance when she looked at Elisabeth's picture on Columbia University's website, but it was definitely there now. Elisabeth looked a lot like Ima, too, which was strange. They could have been sisters.

They stared at each other for a few seconds. Elisabeth spoke first. "Come on in, please." The door swung shut behind Rebekkah. "I've pictured this day so many times." She hugged Rebekkah.

"Me, too." Rebekkah pulled back. She couldn't help staring. The eyes, the nose, the full lips, even the color of her birth mother's hair, all looked familiar.

"You're thinking we look alike. I see it, too. Here, let me take your coat," said Elisabeth. "I don't know if I'll be able to stop staring at you."

Grinning at Elisabeth's comment, Rebekkah handed over her coat. "Thank you. I know what you mean."

"You're pregnant!" exclaimed Elisabeth.

"I'm about twenty weeks. I just found out it's a boy." Her hand went to her belly. This woman was part of her baby. She adored her parents, siblings, and her other relatives, but now Rebekkah was painfully aware of what being adopted meant. She didn't share blood with any of her relatives. She didn't really belong to them. Elisabeth and her baby were related to her by blood. They belonged to her in a way no one else did, or could.

"I can't wait to hear all about you," Elisabeth said as she walked a few steps to a closet. "I was ecstatic when your email said you wanted to see me."

"I was so nervous emailing you. I wasn't sure how you would respond."

Elisabeth turned around. "I've always hoped for this day."

Rebekkah loved the apartment. A long eat-in kitchen painted in pink faced her, and a large living room was just to the right. There were floor-to-wall bookshelves covering two walls. Heavy pink brocade curtains covered windows on the remaining wall. The rug was a deep red. Very cozy. She loved the pink and red color combination.

Elisabeth took Rebekkah's hand as they walked down the short hall. "I'll give you a tour." She laughed. "It will only take a few seconds."

Her home wasn't huge, but she had decorated it with taste. It was warm and homey with just enough clutter.

There were two bedrooms, one of which was Elisabeth's study. The bathroom was straight out of the fifties; black, pink and mint green tiles.

"I love this bathroom. I also need to use it," Rebekkah said.

"Take your time." Elisabeth patted Rebekkah's back. "I'll be in the living room."

When Rebekkah joined Elisabeth she was overwhelmed at all the books on the shelves. "I love to read. This is heaven. I studied one of your books in college."

Elisabeth smiled. "Did you like it?"

"Yes. It was the first poetry I'd ever read. Have you read all these?"

Elisabeth tilted her head, her eyes taking in the shelves. "Just about. I don't watch a lot of TV. I have a small one in the bedroom, but as soon I start watching I fall asleep."

Rebekkah laughed. "Lately, that's been happening to me, too."

Both women settled on the couch facing out from one of the bookshelves. "Tell me about your baby and husband. Is this your first?" Elisabeth asked.

"I'm not married," said Rebekkah.

"Oh, I'm sorry. I shouldn't have assumed. Stupid of me."

"No, it's okay. I was married. My husband turned out to be a jerk. We're divorced."

Elisabeth's brow furrowed. "I'm so sorry."

"But I am in love with my baby's father. He's asked me to marry him."

"Best wishes, then. He's good to you?"

Rebekkah grinned. "Very. His name is Dominick Rossi. Nick. He's a detective."

"I hope I can meet him someday." Elisabeth paused and studied Rebekkah. "I can't believe you're sitting here. I don't know how involved you want me to be in your life. I don't want to push."

"I can't believe it, either. I love my parents very much. And my brothers and sister. I don't want to hurt them, but I want to get to know you. I want to know about my father, and how you met." Once the words started spilling out, Rebekkah couldn't stop them. "I want to know everything about both of you."

"And I want to be involved with you as much as you'll let me. I don't expect to take your mother's place. I've thought of you most every day since the second you were born, but I have no right to call you my daughter. Even though in my heart you always will be. It wouldn't be fair to Shira, who I'm sure is a wonderful mother."

Rebekkah readily agreed. "She is. My father is a wonderful father."

"Do you remember seeing me when you were eight?" Elisabeth asked.

"I'm an artist," Rebekkah said. "I actually did a painting of your cottage. But I don't remember meeting you, I'm sorry. Apparently, the cottage stayed in my subconscious. Ima and Aba, that's what I call my mother and father usually, bought it."

"You're an artist? How lovely." Elisabeth laughed. "I can't draw a stick figure."

"I show my art at the Kain Gallery. Cairenn, the owner, has become a good friend. I'm happy to say I've sold quite a few pieces."

"That's great, Rebekkah. I'm so happy for you. I'd love to come to the gallery and buy one."

"I'll paint something for you. I'll make sure it goes with your décor."

Elisabeth laughed. "I don't know that I have a *décor*, but I'd absolutely love one of your paintings."

"I'll start on it this week." She paused. "It feels strange we know nothing about each other."

"I know what you mean. Where shall we start? You first."

Rebekkah settled back on the couch, and brought Elisabeth up to speed in short time. "So you see, my life was pretty normal until Jonathan's accident. Then my marriage to Avram turned out to be a huge mistake. I'm pretty sure he's embezzling from his funeral home. Just yesterday I found evidence he was the one who broke into Cairenn's gallery and stole my art a few months ago."

Elisabeth frowned. "That's awful. What a jerk. I'm glad you're rid of him."

"It seems he has a gambling problem. Nick discovered that."

"So, you met Nick while you were married to Avram?"

Rebekkah nodded. "Yes, but we didn't have an affair or anything. When the Kain Gallery got broken into he was there investigating. I didn't like him at first. He was brash and unfriendly."

"What changed?" Elisabeth brought her knees up toward her chest and hugged them.

"I saw a different side of him when I talked to him about the break-in. We fell in love rather quickly." She looked at her belly. "And here we are."

"Oh, Rebekkah, I'm glad you're happy."

"There's a problem. At least I'm making it into a problem."

Elisabeth looked alarmed. "It's not the baby, is it?"

"No, the baby's fine."

"I remember the feeling I had being pregnant with you. I had a name all picked out." She turned serious. "Even though I knew I couldn't keep you."

"I won't talk about the baby if it bothers you, Elisabeth."

"No, no. It's fine. You've had a happy life. That's all I care about, and now you're here. I want to hear about your baby. But go back to the problem you mentioned."

Rebekkah stood and arched her back. She walked to the bookshelf and faced Elisabeth. "My parents are Jewish as you probably know."

"Yes, I do."

"I thought I was Jewish, too. Let me back up. The night Nick and I conceived our baby, I left him." She counted the reasons on her fingers. "I didn't think I was ready for a relationship, I felt guilty for making love with him when technically I was still married to Avram even though our divorce was imminent, but mostly because he isn't Jewish."

"How did he feel when you did that?"

Rebekkah gave a half-smile, half-grimace. "Not real happy. Then Ima told me because you aren't Jewish, I'm not. She thought by telling me, I'd feel free to love Nick. When I spoke to my rabbi he confirmed in order to be Jewish I need to have a conversion ceremony."

"But you still don't feel free to love Nick, is that it?"

"I still feel Jewish. I can't just stop being who I am. I love the holidays, the traditions. I love being in the synagogue worshipping God. I think I want to have a conversion ceremony, but I don't want to lose Nick." Rebekkah sat back down. "It's so confusing. Do I sound crazy?"

"Not at all," Elisabeth assured her. "But why do you have to lose him? I confess I'm not religious at all. I only know the basics about Judaism."

"My rabbi said that seventy-percent of interfaith marriages fail. I admit that's very scary to me. He's encouraging me to find a nice Jewish guy. He fixed me up with one." Rebekkah rolled her eyes.

Elisabeth laughed. "I'm guessing you didn't like the guy."

"Not at all."

"Just because some marriages fail, doesn't mean yours will."

"Nick says love is the most important thing. He says we can make it work. We can blend our two traditions."

"He sounds like a wise man."

Rebekkah frowned. "What if we can't make it work?"

"What if you can? He's not the one saying you have to make a choice between him and Judaism, is he?"

"No. That would be me."

"Is he religious? Does he have a problem with you formally choosing the faith you were brought up with?"

"He's Catholic. He goes to church, but he says our religions aren't that different. He wants me to do what's right for me, as long as I don't shut him out."

"It seems to me that he accepts you being Jewish, you feel Jewish, want to keep being Jewish, and want your baby to be Jewish. Am I right so far?"

"Yes," Rebekkah agreed, grateful for Elisabeth's understanding.

"Not to be stupid, but what exactly is the problem?"

Rebekkah looked at Elisabeth. "My rabbi is pressuring me to convert, and all of a sudden Ima is concerned Nick may take me away from my family and faith, and she wants her grandchild to be Jewish.

"I always thought I'd marry a nice Jewish man. I feel an allegiance to my religion although it really isn't mine now. I feel I'm letting thousands of years of Jewish tradition down by marrying Nick. I'll be adding to the problem of Jews not marrying Jews."

Elisabeth shifted her position. "No one can make this decision for you. Listen to your heart. You'll find a way, but it has to be your way. Not your mother's, not your rabbi's, or mine, or anyone else's. But honestly, I can't see a major religion that's survived so much for so long toppling because you marry a non-Jew."

Rebekkah laughed. "You sound like Cairenn. She said kind of the same thing. I'm sorry for going on about myself."

"Don't be silly." Elisabeth dismissed her concern. "I love talking with you so openly. But before we go on, you must think I'm a terrible hostess. Do you want some iced tea, water, or a Coke? I'll make us lunch in a little while."

"I could use a Coke if you don't mind. I don't drink a lot of them since I've become pregnant, but once in a while it hits the spot."

"Great. I'll be right back." Elisabeth jumped up.

Rebekkah got up too and studied all the books Elisabeth had. She'd never heard of most of them. She'd love to be surrounded by so many books.

"I'm back," announced Elisabeth. She handed Rebekkah a glass filled with Coke and ice. "Do you have a name picked out for your baby?"

"Michael Anthony. For Nick's father. He was a police officer, too. He was killed on duty."

Elisabeth winced. "How sad."

"It's very sad. His mom died of cancer. Now I'd like to hear your story," said Rebekkah. "How you met my father, and who he was. Did you ever marry him?"

Elisabeth sat down. "No, we never got married. I still see him, though."

Rebekkah was surprised. "You do?"

Elisabeth nodded. She gazed at the floor before continuing. "This is ironic. You're sort of in the same situation I was, but opposite."

"I can't wait to hear everything," Rebekkah said.

"I met Gabriel Posen when we were both sixteen. We fell in love. I was off limits because I wasn't an Orthodox Jew. His family was extremely strict. One-and-a-half feet in the old world, and half-a-foot in the new. They had a girl all lined up for him. He totally disliked her.

We met at the Metropolitan Museum of Art. He wanted to escape his upbringing for a while. He began taking trips to different places around the city, trying to absorb other cultures and lifestyles. His parents didn't know. Fast-forward. We're seventeen, deeply in love, I'm pregnant." Elisabeth had a far-away smile on her lips.

Rebekkah was enthralled. "What happened when you told him about me?"

"He wanted to marry me. Of course, his parents and family freaked out. There was no way in hell, excuse my language, they'd let him marry a *shiksa*. They sent him to his grandparents in Israel. I cried for weeks. I wanted to kill myself, but I had you to think of."

"They sound mean. Did his parents know you were pregnant?"

"Yes," Elisabeth replied softly. "They wanted nothing to do with me, or you. They didn't care I was carrying their first grandchild. To them I was nothing. Dirt to be swept away."

Rebekkah imagined how hurt Elisabeth would have been. Their reaction hurt her on Elisabeth's behalf, and she didn't even know them. "When did you decide to put me up for adoption?"

"As soon as Gabriel's parents forbade him to marry me. I couldn't keep you. I desperately wanted to, but my parents weren't rich. I wanted to finish high school then go to college. I knew the best thing was finding a good home for you. People who could give you everything I couldn't."

"Ima said a friend of my father's cousin arranged the adoption."

Elisabeth nodded. "Not so much a friend. Gabriel's parents shocked Gabriel and me before sending him away by insisting on finding you a Jewish home. God knows why they cared, or what was in their heads, but since they promised they'd find a good home for you, my parents and I listened."

Elisabeth looked up at the ceiling. "Let's see if I even remember. Gabriel's father, Nadav Posner, was a colleague of Bryce Kenzer, your father's cousin. They were both attorneys. Bryce confided in Nadav that your parents were looking for a baby. They took care of the adoption. I was lucky because your parents wanted to stay in contact with me and, later, they were willing to let me at least send money for you.

"Thank you for that, by the way," said Rebekkah. "I appreciate it."

"You're very welcome. I was so happy when I got to see you when you were eight. But I had no intention of being a regular presence in your life. I thought that would confuse you. I'm not sure I agree with all these open adoptions now."

"Why didn't Gabriel fight to marry you?" Rebekkah frowned.

"He was seventeen. What could he do? His parents would have disowned him, sat Shiva because he would have been dead to them. When we told them about my pregnancy, I promised them I would convert if they allowed Gabriel to marry me. They laughed, saying the Jews didn't want me. I found them backward and unforgiving."

Rebekkah's heart ached for what Elisabeth had gone through. "But you still see Gabriel."

"I'm not proud I do. He's a married man with eight children."

Riveted by Elisabeth's story, Rebekkah was on the edge of the couch. "Did he marry the woman his parents wanted him to?"

"Yes. Her name is Rina. He feels a responsibility to her, and to his children, but he doesn't love her."

Rebekkah wondered if that was true, or if Elisabeth just wanted it to be true. It was such a strange story. "Then why couldn't he have divorced her, and married you once he was an adult? He could've done what he wanted."

"Guilt, obligation, fear of being ostracized by his friends and colleagues, fear of losing his family. Gabriel is not a strong-willed man. He's weak. He needs his family's approval. It wasn't as easy as he thought to shed his religious beliefs.

"Even if I converted as an adult, I felt even he wouldn't accept me as a pure Jew, although there is no difference between someone born Jewish, and someone who converts. I detest that attitude in him. Yet, I'm still in love with him. He's in love with me. I settle for what I can have.

"I stopped questioning a long time ago. I don't want anyone else. He comes two or three nights a week. Sometimes he manages a weekend. I don't know what he tells Rina. I don't ask. We talk, listen to music, watch movies, he cooks for me. Things a real married couple does."

Rebekkah assumed they shared her bed, too, but she wouldn't dare ask such a personal question. "Did he ever wonder about me?"

"A little. Not like I did." She smiled. "But he didn't carry you for nine months. He didn't feel your little stretches and kicks, see the outline of your foot or elbow pressing against my belly. I wasn't even showing when he left for Israel. When he returned to the United States and tracked me down, we were twenty-seven years old."

"You never married anyone?" Rebekkah was amazed Elisabeth still loved him, but she understood and felt sad for Elisabeth and Gabriel.

"No. I've dated lots of men, but no one measures up to Gabriel. I'll never love anyone else."

Rebekkah was fascinated by Elisabeth's story. She had more questions, but maybe she should save them. She didn't want to pry too deeply when they'd just met. There would be other visits. They could keep learning about each other.

Elisabeth got up. "I don't want you to go through what I did. If you and Nick are in love, then be his wife. If God is supposed to be a loving God, He will look favorably on your marriage, and bless it. From what I know of the Bible, I don't think Sarah, Abraham's wife, was even Jewish in the beginning. Neither were Ruth and Esther. So you're like them." Elisabeth patted Rebekkah's leg. "Not bad company to be in."

"You're right, they weren't. I'll think about everything you said." She felt sad Elisabeth had only fleeting moments with Gabriel, that he was a married man, but she had no right to judge her. She didn't even want to. But it wasn't the life she wanted with Nick.

The rest of the morning they talked about Rebekkah's art, and Elisabeth's life as a professor. Time flew by for Rebekkah.

"How about some lunch?" Elisabeth offered.

"Sounds good. Please, let me help you." She followed Elisabeth into the kitchen.

"There's nothing you need to help with. Sit. I should have thought of this before. Do you keep kosher?"

Rebekkah nodded. "Yes, but I don't want to be difficult."

"Please, you're not difficult. I made salad with tomatoes, olives, carrots, celery, and cucumbers. My salad dressing has a kosher symbol on it. Is that a good start?"

Rebekkah smiled. "That's fine, and more than enough for me."

"Are you sure?" Elisabeth's head disappeared inside the refrigerator. "Let me see what else I can find."

Rebekkah pulled out a chair and sat. "That really will be enough."

Elisabeth placed two bowls full of salad on the table. "Would you like a glass of milk?"

Rebekkah laughed. "I'm sorry, but Ima and Nick are always trying to get me to drink milk. It's become quite comical."

Elisabeth laughed, too. "Sounds like it. You tell me what you want."

"Milk's fine. I like it, but it's as if Ima and Nick think drinking milk is the most important thing I could possible do for the baby."

Elisabeth brought over two glasses of milk. "I'm so glad you came today. I haven't told Gabriel I was meeting you, but I will. How would you feel about meeting him at some point?"

"I wouldn't mind. If he really wants to meet me."

"I'll let you know what he says. In the meanwhile, you and I have email and phones to stay in touch. I want to meet Nick, too."

"He offered to come today, but thought I might want to see you alone, first."

"That was considerate of him."

When Rebekkah finished her salad she helped Elisabeth rinse their dishes, and put them in the dishwasher. "I think I better go."

"So soon?" Elisabeth asked.

"We'll talk, or email soon," promised Rebekkah. "I don't want to take up your whole day. Do you have to teach later?"

"I have two late afternoon classes," said Elisabeth. She handed Rebekkah her coat. "Thank you so much for coming by. I'm proud of the woman you've become, and grateful your parents have been so wonderful."

Rebekkah hugged Elisabeth. "I'm glad I did, too. I want you to be part of my life, and my baby's life."

371

When Rebekkah got to the elevator she waved good-bye to Elisabeth as she stepped inside. Elisabeth had helped her see her choices much more clearly.

TWENTY TWO

"I hope you don't mind I waited here for you," Rebekkah asked Nick when he got home in the late afternoon.

"Of course not." He greeted her with a quick kiss and a pat to the belly. "I love you. I love that you're here. I want you here. Even when your parents come back, I want you here. For good."

She followed him into the kitchen. "You're going to think I'm really old-fashioned. I don't want to live with you. Not permanently I mean, without being married."

Nick turned and took her into his arms. Rebekkah initiated her own kiss seconds later.

"I have no idea now what I was going to say now," said Nick.

She laughed. "I guess I shouldn't have kissed you that way."

"That way was very good. I remember now. It's fine with me if you're old-fashioned. I don't respect women who hop into bed with every man they meet. Or, for that matter, men who do that. I'm not referring to us, we were in love already. So see, I'm just as out-of-sync as you are. I may look young, but my soul is at least eighty-five."

Rebekkah laughed. "I have to light candles tonight for the Sabbath. Sunset is in about an hour. Do you want to come home with me, then I'll make us dinner?"

"Best offer I've had all day. How are things with Michael? You both doing okay? It won't be too much for you to make dinner?"

"We're both fine. It won't be too much. I love to cook. Do you realize it will be the first dinner I've made for you?"

"I can't wait. Let's walk the dogs first then head over."

They snapped leashes onto Lucy, Mortimer, and Grace, bundled themselves up, then headed outdoors.

"How did your meeting with Elisabeth go this morning?" Nick asked as they made their way to the park.

"Really well. I was nervous at first, but in minutes it was as if we'd always known each other."

"It must have felt strange meeting the woman who gave birth to you." Nick took Rebekkah's gloved hand.

"It did. She told me she still sees my father, even though he's married and has eight kids. His name is Gabriel." Rebekkah stopped short.

"Are you all right?"

"They're my half-siblings. I can't believe it." She began walking again.

"Wow. I wonder if you'll ever meet them?"

"I don't really want to, to tell you the truth. I told Elisabeth I wouldn't mind meeting Gabriel, even though I don't think I'll feel as strong a connection to him as I do with her. He's Jewish by the way, but I'm still not because Elisabeth isn't. It's funny how her story is kind of like ours, isn't it?"

"Yeah, it is."

Rebekkah stopped again and faced Nick. "Promise me we will never end up like they are. Married to other people and loving each other in the shadows."

He framed her face in his hands. "Not a chance, babe. Not a chance."

Her hands covered his. "Good. I don't know how Elisabeth stands it."

"It is a little strange, I'll give you that. Do you think then you'll meet Gabriel at some point?"

"Maybe. Not that I approve of affairs at all, but I sort of sympathize with him. He's still torn between his religion and Elisabeth. They never resolved their differences."

"Do what you're comfortable with," Nick advised.

"Elisabeth wants to meet you. I told her all about you."

"I'd like to meet her, too. And Pamela, still. Are we on for next week to take Jonathan's ring back to her?"

"Yes, I called her. I didn't have a chance to tell her about you because she was on the way out the door. I'll bring her up to date when we see her."

"I want to ask you something," Nick said as he stopped to unhook the dogs' leashes. They could run free in the park for a few minutes since no one else was around.

"What is it?"

"I'd like to go to Beth Israel with you."

Rebekkah stared at him. "Really?"

He smiled. "Yes. I've read so much about Judaism, I'd like to go to a service."

"We'll go tomorrow, then." She was glad Nick showed interest in Judaism. She would be happy and honored to have him beside her at Beth Israel

Rebekkah hadn't been to Beth Israel for months. She had finally told Molly about her divorce and Ellen, but none of her other friends knew about her divorce from Avram. Partly, because he had discouraged her from talking to them, and partly because she had been on an emotional roller coaster lately and despite her divorce, still hadn't made time for them. She hoped they would forgive her. She wanted to re-connect with them. At least with a baby she'd be able to join in their baby conversations now. None of her friends knew about her status as a Jew, not even Molly. For now, she intended on keeping it that way.

Rebekkah explained the service to Nick on the ride to the synagogue the next morning. When they arrived, she handed him a yarmulke. Most synagogues had extras left over from bar or bat mitzvahs in a box for visitors to use.

"The prayer book we use has Hebrew on the right and English on the left." Rebekkah waited while he put on the yarmulke.

"You read Hebrew right to left, don't you?" asked Nick.

"Yes." Rebekkah grinned at his earnestness. "There are a lot of Jews who aren't familiar with Hebrew, so don't feel like anyone is going to notice, or care, that you're reading from the English side."

When they entered the sanctuary, Rabbi Weissman was standing at the bimah. Only a few other people were there. He came down and greeted Rebekkah. She watched for his reaction when she introduced Nick to him, but he smiled, shook Nick's hand, and welcomed him to the synagogue.

Rebekkah handed Nick a blue prayer book then took one for herself. Before things got started, a few women came and hugged Rebekkah, squealing with delight at seeing her again. They all eyed Nick curiously. She introduced him, but there wasn't time to go into any details. Even though she hadn't seen these women in months, they would always be her friends.

It was one of the things she loved about Judaism. Jews could go to any synagogue and be called to read the Torah. They would be totally accepted, an instant part of any Jewish community. With promises made that they all would catch up soon, Rebekkah turned her eyes to the prayer book.

She knew the service by heart and kept up with the cantor as he chanted psalms and prayers. This was her world, the way she worshipped God. Her focus in the synagogue was on God alone. She didn't just recite the prayers mindlessly. Every word meant something to her. They were on the Musaf Amidah for Shabbat. She glanced at Nick and helped him find his place.

Before she knew it, they were at the Torah service. Apparently, word had spread that she wasn't a Jew, because she received no aliyah, the honor of being called to the bimah to bless the Torah before the Rabbi chanted the Torah reading. She knew that would be the case, but it still hurt. She truly was an outsider. The only way to find her way back to her God, and her synagogue was to convert.

"How did you like it?" Rebekkah asked Nick as they drove home.

"It was longer than the services at Saint Anne's, but I liked it a lot. It's very liturgical, like the Catholic service just no mention of Jesus."

She laughed. "I hope you weren't bored."

"Not at all. It was touching and very spiritual. I feel renewed. As I said before, I love the concept of the Sabbath; a day of rest. I think everyone could benefit from that. I'd like to incorporate it in my own life."

She was happy he had been so comfortable beside her at Beth Israel. "Nick?"

"What is it?"

"If we get married—"

"When we get married."

Rebekkah smiled. "Okay, when. I'd like to keep a Jewish home."

"I have no problem with that. If you want we can move to a different house."

"No. I love your house. The first time I saw it I knew it was the kind of home I'd dreamt about."

"It could use a few feminine touches. So whatever you want to do is fine with me."

"I love decorating. We'll do it together."

Rebekkah left the warmth of her car, shivering as she walked the short distance to Pamela's townhouse. Even her heavy coat, hat, scarf, and gloves weren't sufficient protection from the frigid wind. Nick was supposed to meet her here. She was surprised there was no sign of him, but he had probably been held up by work. It was too cold to wait outside. She pulled out her cell phone and listened to Nick's phone ring then go to voice mail. She left a message that she was going into Pamela's home and she would see him when he arrived.

"Darling!" Giving her usual enthusiastic greeting, Pamela hugged Rebekkah, and welcomed her inside. "I'm so glad you called. It's been a long time. How are you? How are your parents, and Avram?"

"It has been a long time. I'm sorry. I've had so much going on. Wait until I tell you." Rebekkah unfastened her coat. "Ima and Aba are good. They're in the Poconos right now."

"How nice. Oh my! Rebekkah, are you pregnant?"

"Yes." Happiness filled Rebekkah's heart at she thought of Michael growing inside her.

Pamela hugged her again. "I'm so happy for you. You must be ecstatic after waiting so long. I'm glad you worked out your issues with Avram. Is he excited about the baby?"

She evaded Pamela's question for the time being. "I'll tell you everything, don't worry. How's Jonathan?"

"He's faded even further from us. It's time..." Pamela paused, her face shadowed by pain. "Time we all said good-bye, and took his feeding tube out. Let him go home to God."

Rebekkah swallowed over the lump in her throat. "I think you've made the right decision. I need to say good-bye and let him go, too."

"Go on up, darling. Kimberly's up there."

Rebekkah went upstairs, greeting Kimberly as she went into Jonathan's room.

"I'll leave you alone." Kimberly smiled at Rebekkah. "I'll be in my room if you need me."

She smiled back. "Thanks, Kimberly."

Rebekkah leaned over his bed. He was almost unrecognizable. She went over to his bookshelf and picked up a photograph of her and Jonathan when they'd first started seeing each other. How she had changed since then. They both looked so young, so earnest and innocent. So full of hope.

She laid it down then wandered to his bed. "Avram and I got divorced. I'm in love with a man named Dominick Rossi. I call him Nick. We're having a baby. I'm happy, Jon. Happier than I thought I ever could be. It's unbelievable.

"I've come to say good-bye." She blinked back tears. "I wish your life had turned out differently. I loved you very much, too." She reached down to kiss his forehead, nearly overcome with sadness. It seemed such a life changing moment—leaving behind the past and her first love for a future with the father of her child. "I'm grateful for the time we had together, Jon. May your soul be at peace very soon."

Rebekkah gave his room one last look then glanced back at his frail, unmoving body. There was nothing more to say, or do. Jonathan couldn't even hear her. She popped into Kimberly's room to say good-bye before joining Pamela downstairs.

"Was it difficult for you?" Pamela asked.

"A little, yes, but I agree with you—Jonathan deserves to be with God. It's not fair to keep him here."

"Alex feels that way too. It's just that when he's gone, he'll really be gone. Does that make sense?"

"It does. I totally understand."

"We're taking out his feeding tube next Monday. I'll call you about the funeral arrangements."

Rebekkah nodded. She felt so bad for Pamela and Alex. How hard it must be to bury a child, even an older one. Rebekkah couldn't imagine anything like this happening to Michael. She hadn't even met him, but she knew it would kill her. She took the small box that held Jonathan's engagement ring out of her purse. "It's time you had this back."

Pamela wiped away a tear. "Are you sure?"

Rebekkah nodded. "Very. It's not right for me to keep it. It belonged to your mother, Pamela. You should have it." Something stopped her from showing Pamela the ring Nick had given her. It seemed tacky to do so right now.

"I wouldn't mind if you kept it."

"No. I want you to have it."

Pamela smiled. "You may get it back once I'm gone. What else will I do with it? Now, tell me about this baby. How are you and Avram doing?"

"We're not," replied Rebekkah, getting comfortable on the couch. She told Pamela all about Avram, then about falling in love with Nick. She left out Nick not being Jewish, and her really not being Jewish, either.

Pamela's eyes widened when Rebekkah finished talking. "Stealing from his own business? How could he have lied about a vasectomy when he knew how much you wanted babies? You poor thing. He's obviously got issues. I can't believe it."

"I know. It was unreal to me, too," agreed Rebekkah. "He had the surgery some years ago." She retold the story about meeting Ellen.

Pamela stood up, holding her arms out to Rebekkah. "Come here."

Rebekkah got up and let Pamela hug her. "You were looking forward to Jonathan and me having children. I was, too."

"Who can know what life will bring. I'm happy for you. I want to be an honorary aunt to this baby. I thought you looked different, more serene and happy than when you were here last. I must meet Nick sometime."

Rebekkah smiled. "You were supposed to do that today. I've told him all about Jonathan. He was going to meet me here."

"You're not worried about him, are you?"

In his line of work it was possible something came up. He didn't have the type of job he could walk away from. Rebekkah certainly didn't expect him to check in with her every hour.

She wasn't the sort of insecure woman who had to know where her man was twenty-four hours a day. "Not really. Just disappointed. I called him outside, but it went to his voice mail. Are you sure you don't mind meeting him?"

"Don't be silly. I look forward to meeting the man who's given you such happiness."

Rebekkah gathered her purse, and put on her coat. "I better get going."

"I'm really sorry Nick didn't make it."

Rebekkah was distracted from answering Pamela by her ringing cell phone. "That's probably him now." But the number was unfamiliar.

"Hello?" Rebekkah motioned for Pamela to stay put when she started walking away.

"Can I please speak to Rebekkah Gelles?"

The voice was almost Nick, but not quite. "This is Rebekkah."

"Rebekkah, I'm Joey Rossi. Nick's brother."

She was puzzled. Why would Nick's brother call her? How did he get her number? "Joey, hi. Nick's told me a lot about you."

"He's told me a lot about you, too. I can't wait to meet you and Michael."

"Joey, did something happen to Nick?" Instinct told her this wasn't a social call and his voice sounded strained.

"He's been hurt, Rebekkah. He's in surgery now. He gave us all your number a while ago. In case..."

Rebekkah's heart and stomach constricted. *In case anything happened to him*, her thoughts finished Joey's sentence. Her fingers tightened around her phone. "Where is he?"

"Saint Mary's Hospital. That's where I'm calling from. I'll come get you."

"No, that's okay. I can get there. I don't want you to leave him."

"Make sure to save my cell number. Call me when you arrive. I'll meet you in the lobby. I'll give you details then."

She felt strangely calm. Her brain refused to accept the possibility of losing Nick. God wouldn't do that to her again. It was impossible to imagine him gone. If he was in surgery then he was still alive.

"You're white as a sheet and shaking. What's wrong?" Pamela asked as Rebekkah tucked her phone back into her purse.

Rebekkah focused on Pamela. It wouldn't be good for her, or the baby, to fall apart. "Nick's been hurt. That was his brother. He's in surgery at Saint Mary's."

"I'll take you there." Pamela rushed toward the closet.

"No, please Pamela, don't." Rebekkah followed her. "I drove here. I don't want to disrupt your day."

Pamela grabbed her coat, shoving her arms into the sleeves. "Don't be ridiculous. You're like a daughter to me. I wouldn't let my daughter go off by herself when she's just received bad news. I'm sure if Shira were home she'd insist on going with you. I'll tell Kimberly then be right down."

Rebekkah didn't argue. She wanted to get to Nick, and she really would rather have Pamela with her.

When they arrived at Saint Mary's, Rebekkah called Joey. She was relieved he picked up right away. Despite never meeting him, she felt a connection because he was Nick's brother.

"Rebekkah. Where are you?" he asked.

"Downstairs. By the couches right across from the elevator. I'm with my friend, Pamela."

"Be right there."

Rebekkah paced. She couldn't stop shivering. She remembered Shira asking Nick if he'd ever been shot. She never dreamed it would actually happen. "I should have described myself. All I can think of is that I can't lose him."

"I'm sure his brother will find us. Don't think about losing Nick. God willing, you won't."

Rebekkah turned when the elevator doors opened. For a moment she almost ran to the man stepping out, but he wasn't Nick.

"Rebekkah?" Joey asked. He sounded even more like Nick in person. He reached for her and she stepped into his hug. If she closed her eyes it would be Nick she was with.

"Yes, and this is my friend, Pamela."

"I'm glad to meet you both. Although I wish the circumstances were different."

"Me, too, Joey. Is he going to be okay?" Rebekkah asked. "What happened?"

"He was shot several times just above his bulletproof vest. He had gone into a house looking for a cell phone tied to the case he's investigating. Gunfire erupted. They had to do emergency surgery."

Rebekkah gasped. She had been so afraid Avram had been responsible. That he had shot Nick with the gun she had seen. Pamela put an arm around her and squeezed.

"My brothers are upstairs, too. We're waiting for him to come out of surgery. Let's get you two passes from the receptionist then we'll go up."

Numb, Rebekkah was grateful for Joey's take-charge attitude. She couldn't string two thoughts together right now. She and Pamela followed Joey into the elevator, which deposited them on the fifth floor. The stark white halls were eerily quiet, smelling like Pine-Sol, or some kind of antiseptic. Rebekkah shuddered, still stunned that she was here because Nick was here and hurt. It was unreal.

Joey introduced Rebekkah and Pamela to Nick's other brothers, Philip and Marco. They, too, seemed familiar to her. They all resembled Nick. They each gave her a hug and murmured words or encouragement.

Joey guided Rebekkah and Pamela to a couch.

"How long has he been in surgery?" Rebekkah asked.

"About forty-five minutes. They said it would be about an hour and a half." Joey covered Rebekkah's hand with one of his. "He's tough, Rebekkah. He's not going to leave us, or his son."

Rebekkah's lips trembled as she tried smiling at Joey. "It's so hard to sit here doing nothing, knowing his life is in balance. What if he...he..." Unable to finish the thought, tears streamed down her cheek.

"We can only pray that he comes out of surgery and recovers," Replied Joey. "I have faith he will."

Pamela draped an arm around her. She pulled a tissue from her purse and handed it to Rebekkah. "We're all praying for him. God will see him through."

She tried to take comfort in Joey and Pamela's words as she offered a prayer to God. Nick's life was in His hands.

She was amazed at how many police officers were already descending on the hospital to offer their support and comfort. Nick had more brothers than the ones he was related to.

Rebekkah tried not to stare at the clock on the wall, moving with agonizing slowness. She couldn't concentrate on the outdated magazines, or on the television perched high on the wall.

Just when she thought she couldn't stand the wait any longer, a doctor strode into the waiting room, still dressed in scrubs, his surgical mask hanging from his neck. "Dominick Rossi's family?"

They room went silent as a dozen faces consisting of family and friends, turned toward him. Rebekkah's heart thumped so hard, she could barely hear the doctor.

"We're all here for Nick. I'm his brother, Joseph Rossi."

The doctor shook Joey's hand. "Doctor McGill. Nick made it through the surgery. He'll be on a ventilator for as long as needed, but usually it's only overnight. Once we take him off the ventilator we'll move him to the transitional trauma room."

Everyone in the room seemed to breathe a collective sigh of relief as they thanked God that he had survived this far.

"Then he'll be okay?" Rebekkah interjected.

"Nick will be treated with antibiotics to prevent lung and wound infections, and of course he'll be given pain med," the doctor explained. "He'll be mobilized from the bed to a chair as soon as possible. This helps prevent pneumonia, and other situations we want to avoid. He'll begin respiratory therapy, initially with deep breathing exercises to help the lung stay inflated and heal more readily, and then to walking and strength building.

"With no complications he should be ready to go home in a week, rest there for a couple of weeks, return to part-time work for a few a while and be full speed by three to four months. The good news is that none of the bullet wounds affected any major blood vessels."

More sighs of relief rippled through the room and everyone started speaking softly to each other all at once. Rebekkah tried to listen to the rest of the doctor's words, but all she wanted to do was see Nick.

Once his patient was settled, Dr. McGill allowed Nick's brothers to see him for two minutes apiece. He wasn't awake yet. Joey was last to see him. When he came out he walked over to Rebekkah. "I explained to Dr. McGill you're his fiancée, and carrying his child. He's okay with you going in."

She took Joey's hand. "Thank you."

"No problem." He paused for a moment. "I can't wait to be at your and Nick's wedding. I'm counting on being best man."

She smiled. "I can't wait to be at my wedding to Nick, either."

Her eyes filled with tears again as she sat by Nick's bed. It reminded her of looking at Jonathan, except Nick was hooked up to a machine. "Please God," she whispered. "Don't take him away from me." Leaning closer, she whispered a more personal prayer. *"May the One who blessed our ancestors, Sarah and Abraham, Rebekah, and Isaac, Leah, Rachel and Jacob bless Dominick Rossi along with all of the ill among us. Grant insight to those who bring healing, courage and faith to those who are sick, love and strength to us and to all who love them. God, let your spirit rest upon all who are ill and comfort them. May they and we soon know a time of complete healing, a healing of the body and a healing of the spirit."*

Nick wasn't Jewish, and she really wasn't either, but it was the only prayer she could think of.

She touched his arm. Michael gave a kick. She spread a hand on her belly. "Don't worry, little guy. Your daddy is not going to die on us."

Pulling the ring Nick had given her off her right hand, she transferred it to her left. She found his hand under the blanket and held it. It was ice cold. That couldn't be a good sign. "You were right. Love is the most important thing. Before Michael arrives I want to be Mrs. Dominick Rossi. I'm not letting you leave me. Your son needs his daddy. I need you. I love you so very much. Don't you

390

dare leave me." Nick didn't stir, but she was positive his fingers moved against hers.

A nurse came in and smiled. "We'll take good care of him."

"Thank you," Rebekkah whispered. She leaned down and kissed Nick good-bye. "I'll be back very soon."

TWENTY THREE

Rebekkah climbed out of Pamela's car after assuring her she would be fine, "I'm so grateful you were with me."

"Anytime, darling. Call if you need anything. You're sure you don't want to stay with us tonight?"

"That's sweet of you, but no. You have Jon to think about. We'll talk soon." Rebekkah closed the door then waved good-bye as she climbed in her own car. Joey wanted her to come to his house with the rest of Nick's brothers later that night, but she had declined.

She would go to Nick's and take a shower. She hadn't wanted to leave the hospital at all, but Pamela convinced her to try and get some sleep. First thing in the morning, she'd return to the hospital.

She pulled her cell phone out to call her parents, but they were enjoying themselves. There was nothing they could do from Pennsylvania. She would call Elisabeth later. Her friends didn't know Nick, and her synagogue friends had only seen him last Saturday. She didn't feel entirely comfortable calling them. She was afraid they would ask a lot of questions, and she didn't feel like answering them.

Her heart sank when she opened Nick's front door. She missed him so much. It was strange knowing he wouldn't be walking in the front door soon. Three subdued dogs greeted her, as if they sensed something was wrong. She took them for a walk, her mind on Nick the whole time. Thank God he had come out of surgery alive. Surely, God would continue to look after him.

She made her way to the kitchen after her walk with the dogs. She picked up the mail that had been delivered through the mail slot in the front door, and stacked it on top of Nick's piano for when he got home. The newspaper she took to the kitchen. Maybe reading while she ate would distract her for a few minutes.

She had stopped at Freling's for roasted chicken and potatoes. She wasn't hungry, but she had to eat something. She found paper plates and a plastic fork and knife to eat with. Nick's presence was everywhere. She turned on the radio, gave the dogs hugs then poured their food before she sat down to eat her own dinner.

Once she began eating she realized how hungry she was. She flipped the *Daily News* over to the front page. She almost dropped her fork as she stared at the headline.

Brooklyn Funeral Home Owner Charged With stealing close to TWO mil.

Below the headline was a picture of Avram, trying unsuccessfully to cover his face with his arm as he was being led down the front stairs of the funeral home by two unidentified men.

Rebekkah's mind went back to his appearance outside her parents' home. His rants about jail and losing everything. He must have known he was going to be arrested. Rebekkah's heart went out to his clients, and to Mark. Unless he was somehow involved, too. Rebekkah flipped to page five to read the rest of the story, her brain reeling, her stomach in knots.

Avram Gelles has been charged with stealing from a funeral home he owns in Brooklyn. Prosecutors say 46-year-old Gelles embezzled close to two-million dollars between July of 2005 and May of 2011 at Gelles & Bender Funeral Home, which he owns with partner Mark Bender. The money was allegedly used for Gelles' gambling, and other personal expenses. Gelles is charged with grand larceny and tax fraud, among other charges. He faces up to thirty years in prison if convicted. His partner, Mark Bender has been quoted as saying he is stunned by this revelation. No charges have been brought against Bender, who seems as much a victim as the senior citizens Gelles robbed.

Gelles forged letters authorizing the closing of his clients' pre-paid funeral expense accounts then presented them at the bank where the accounts were held. The bank closed the accounts and issued checks payable to Gelles &

Bender customers. Gelles then presented fraudulently endorsed bank checks made out to Gelles & Bender customers, and deposited the proceeds in a bank account he controlled.

Rebekkah's eyes gobbled up the words, her appetite diminishing with every sentence. There was also a mention of his arrest for breaking into the art gallery, but the embezzlement charges overshadowed that story. She felt so sorry for Mark and the other Gelles & Bender employees. So many victims of Avram's lies and deceit. Her heart ached even more for the people Avram had stolen from.

She was sick that she had married such a man. He had thrown everything he had away, and now had no one. He would be an old man with nothing if he was alive at the end of his jail term. But it was what he deserved.

She reached for her cell phone and looked up Elisabeth's number. Rebekkah poured out what happened to Nick when she answered. A little more than half-hour later Elisabeth was on the doorstep.

"Thanks for coming," Rebekkah said. "I hope you didn't mind me calling."

"Don't be silly. I'm glad you felt comfortable enough to call me. Have you eaten lately? I picked up some cheese and a loaf of unbelievable French bread."

"You didn't have to do that, but it sounds good." Rebekkah led Elisabeth to the kitchen table. "Sit with me while I finish eating. I stopped at Freling's and got some chicken and potatoes earlier. There's plenty left if you'd like some. I'd love to try the bread and cheese later, though. It's only six o'clock and I feel as if it's midnight."

"You've had a very stressful day."

Rebekkah nodded in agreement then showed Elisabeth the newspaper, "That's my ex-husband."

Elisabeth read the headline then grabbed Rebekkah's arm. "Oh my God."

"Keep reading."

Elisabeth continued on then looked up at Rebekkah. "I can't believe it. You were right. He was embezzling money. You must be so glad you aren't married to him."

"Very," said Rebekkah. "I feel so sorry for those people. I can't imagine someone being so selfish, so evil."

"I know. Sometimes I can't even watch the news. You've really had a hard day. I couldn't believe when you called saying Nick had been shot. Did he wake up while you were there?"

"No." Rebekkah took a napkin and wiped the tears in her eyes. "Hopefully, when I go see him tomorrow he will be awake."

"I'm so glad he's alive."

"Me, too. It made me realize how dangerous his work is. But loving him means accepting a detective is who he is."

"Are these all his dogs?" Elisabeth asked.

Rebekkah managed to smile. "No. The big ones, Mortimer and Lucy, belong to Ima and Aba. Grace belongs to Nick."

"How cute they are."

"Nick and I both love dogs." Rebekkah finished the last of her meal. "Come on, we'll sit in the living room."

Elisabeth followed with the dogs close behind, but stopped in the doorway. "What a beautiful portrait of you. Did you paint it?"

"Yes. Nick actually bought it before we fell in love."

"Wow. Fantastic. I can't wait for one of my own. But don't worry about it now. You have Nick to think of."

"I'll start something soon for you. Painting is very relaxing."

Elisabeth sat next to Rebekkah. "I thought about what you were telling me the other day. Choosing between Nick and being Jewish."

"I want to spend the rest of my life with him. That much I know."

"I may have some happy news for you. There's someone I want you to meet. I don't know why I didn't think of him when you were at my co-op. He's a funny, kind, spiritual person. His name his Sean Beckman. He's a rabbi."

Rebekkah frowned. "Is he going to tell me I have to convert and forget Nick?"

Elisabeth laughed at the scowl on Rebekkah's face. "No. I think you'll be surprised. Will you see him?"

"I don't know. I'll think about it. Right now all I care about is Nick getting better."

"I don't blame you. But I think your religion means a great deal to you. You want your baby to be Jewish, don't you?"

"Yes," Rebekkah admitted.

"Sean is a Reform rabbi. He counsels and marries interfaith couples. I know you weren't raised reform, or were you?"

"No, I wasn't. My parents are Conservative. They're very strict now." She hadn't thought about Reform Judaism. They were usually more tolerant than the Conservative branch. Maybe Elisabeth had given her an answer to her dilemma.

"He's great. You'll love him, I know it."

"How did you meet him?"

"He teaches a couple of classes at Columbia. Yesterday I asked him about your problem. I didn't use names. I kept it very general. I left my purse on the staircase when I came in. Let me get it. He gave me his card in case you want to call him."

When she returned, she sat down, placing a large purse in her lap. "If I can find it in this mess."

Rebekkah laughed. "You remind me of myself and my purses."

"Honestly, I don't know why I put all this crap in here." After some rummaging, she pulled out a card and handed it to Rebekkah. "I'm sure he'll be happy to advise you on converting, and on marrying Nick."

Rebekkah read the card. It wouldn't hurt to talk to him. "Do you really think he'll be able to help?"

"I don't see why not. There are a lot of interfaith couples in his congregation. He performed many of their marriage ceremonies."

Rebekkah nodded. "Thanks. I think I will call him."

Elisabeth gave her a big smile. "Great. How about some bread and cheese?"

Rebekkah jumped up. "Good idea. I'll get it and bring it in."

"Would you like me to stay with you tonight?" Elisabeth asked between bites. "I don't have class until late afternoon tomorrow. I can sleep on the couch."

Rebekkah thought about Nick in the hospital and herself being alone here. She doubted if she would get much sleep. "I'd love that. I'll find a t-shirt of Nick's for you to sleep in."

"Great. We can talk some more, too. I promise I won't keep you up late. And I can come to the hospital with you tomorrow morning. I assume that's what you want to do."

Rebekkah nodded. "First thing after we have breakfast. I'd love if you came with me."

"I'd be honored."

Rebekkah and Elisabeth talked deep into the night. When she couldn't keep her eyes open any longer

Rebekkah went upstairs and got ready for bed. Cocooned in Nick's bed with the dogs around her, she fell asleep with thoughts of seeing Nick in a few hours filling her head.

Rebekkah and Elisabeth ran into Joey as soon as they stepped off the elevator on the fifth floor early the next morning. "How is he?" Rebekkah had to refrain from grabbing him.

Joey grinned and gave thumbs up. "Awake and complaining, so he's going to be okay. They took him off the ventilator a couple of hours ago then moved him to the transitional trauma room. He asked for you right away."

Rebekkah smiled back. "Thank God. This is Elisabeth. Elisabeth, this is Nick's brother, Joey."

Joey shook Elisabeth's hand. "Happy to meet you. I'm going with my brothers to go grab a bite to eat. We'll give you some time alone. He'll be happy to see you, Rebekkah."

"I'll sit in the waiting room," Elisabeth told Rebekkah. "Somewhere in this purse I may have some knitting I started. Take your time."

Rebekkah hurried to the nurses' station and asked for Nick's room.

"I'll take you," one of the nurses offered.

Rebekkah rounded the corner into Nick's room. As soon as he saw her, he reached for her. "I've been waiting for you. Come here."

She didn't need a second invitation. She hurried to the bed. Sitting on the edge, she hugged him the best she could.

"I'm so glad to see you. I've had a lot of visitors already this morning, but I wasn't going to be happy until I saw you walk in. Hey, don't cry. I'm going to be fine." He stopped a tear as it ran down her cheek. "I'm hoping I can go home soon."

"I was here yesterday. You were sleeping. Joey called me. Nicky, I don't know what I would do if I lost you. I love you so much."

"I'm not going anywhere. I love you, too." He glanced at her hand. "My ring. You have it on your left hand."

She smiled, feeling better now that Nick seemed out of danger. "We're engaged."

Nick let out a loud whistle that caused three nurses to run in. "I'm engaged!" he whooped the best he could. "This gorgeous woman has agreed to be my wife."

The nurses couldn't hide their amusement while advising him to calm down.

"Congratulations!" one of them whispered to Rebekkah on the way out.

Nick lay back on the pillow and held Rebekkah's hand. "My brothers are all impressed with you."

She tried to get as close as she could to him. "I like them, too. It's clear they certainly love you."

"They're all great guys, but don't tell them I said that. How about you and Michael Anthony? You both okay?"

"We're fine now that you're going to be okay." She couldn't stop smiling. "Elisabeth came with me. Do you feel up to meeting her?"

"I'd like that. I'm glad you aren't alone."

"Pamela was here with me yesterday, but I didn't want to bother her again. She has so much to deal with right now regarding Jonathan."

Nick's head hit the pillow as he closed his eyes and groaned. "That's right. I was supposed to meet you at her place. I'm sorry I let you down."

"You did not let me down. You were out doing your job. I know things occasionally can come up. I wasn't thinking about you getting shot, but I figured something happened. Elisabeth spent the night with me at your house. I hope you don't mind."

Nick opened his eyes as he struggled to get into a sitting position. He ran a hand down the back of her head. "It's your house, too."

She leaned down and kissed him. "Be right back."

She went to get Elisabeth, relieved that Nick was on the way to recovery. Many of Nick's friends had gathered in the waiting room for their turn to visit him. She hoped they wouldn't wear him out. He was already paler since she had gone in to see him. She would introduce Elisabeth quickly then let some others visit with him.

Nick stared, open-mouthed when Rebekkah brought Elisabeth in. "You guys look so much alike. It's amazing." He turned to Rebekkah. "I thought you looked like Shira, but you look like a clone of Elisabeth." He smiled at Elisabeth. "Thanks for coming with her, by the way. I'm really happy to meet you."

Elisabeth approached his bed. "Nice to meet you, too. I'm so sorry about your accident. Hopefully, you'll be totally recovered, soon."

"I will be. I want to come home to my bride-to-be." He winked at Rebekkah.

Rebekkah's insides started to un-knot themselves now that she could see Nick was going to be fine. She carefully got off the bed. "I'll let you have some other visitors. The whole New York City Police Department must be outside." She leaned down and kissed him. "I have some things I need to take care of."

Nick looked hurt when she said she was leaving. "Promise you'll come back later?"

"I promise."

"I definitely want to meet your Sean Beckman," Rebekkah told Elisabeth as they returned to Nick's house. "I think he might be the answer to my prayers."

"I think you'll be very pleased with him," Elisabeth replied looking happy with Rebekkah's decision.

"Babe, is everything all right?" Nick asked Rebekkah. He had been home for a week and was progressing nicely, but he was restless and itching to go back to work. He hated being a semi-invalid.

She still hadn't told him about Rabbi Sean Beckman, but this seemed like the perfect time. She had met him once, and Elisabeth had been right. Within minutes of meeting him at Temple Shalom in Queens, Rebekkah felt as if he completely understood her dilemma.

He assured her he would supervise her conversion, and once he met Nick he would determine whether or not he would perform their ceremony.

"Everything's fine now that you're home. There's a rabbi I want you to meet. Elisabeth told me about him."

"Not Rabbi Weissman?"

Rebekkah shook her head. "No. His name is Sean Beckman. A reform rabbi. He performs interfaith marriages."

Nick patted the couch beside him. "Sit with me. Sounds promising."

"I asked him if he would supervise my conversion. He said yes, and that once he spoke to you, he would decide if he felt he should marry us."

Nick took her hand. "Being Jewish is important to you. I'm glad you aren't going to give it up."

"You aren't upset?"

"Not at all. I fell in love with a Jewish woman. I don't know if I would love you if you weren't Jewish."

Rebekkah swatted at him. "Very funny. Even if Rabbi Sean won't marry us, we can have a civil ceremony. When you were in the hospital, I knew I had to be your wife, no matter what. Living without you is not an option for me."

Nick took her hand and squeezed it. "Let's go see Rabbi Sean as soon as we can."

Rebekkah immersed herself once in the mikveh at Mikveh Israel. After she and Nick had spoken to Rabbi Sean, she knew conversion, then marriage to Nick, was the path she needed to take.

Especially, when Rabbi Sean had explained that, in his opinion, a marriage of a non-Jew to a Jew could actually strengthen the Jewish community. It was often the non-Jewish spouse who knew more about Judaism; the non-Jewish spouse who attended religious services; the non-Jewish spouse who made sure their child had a Jewish education. He had ideas Rebekkah had never heard of, but they made sense to both her and Nick.

"Barukh atah Ado-nai Elo-henu melekh ha'olam asher kideshanu b'mitzvotav v'tzivanu al ha'tevillah. Blessed are You, O Lord, our God, King of the universe, who has sanctified us with His commandments and commanded us regarding the immersion," Rebekkah eagerly recited.

She immersed twice more and came out of the mikveh. She felt no differently than she had before her conversion ceremony, except now she could truly say she was a Jew. Naked in the mikveh, the water had cleansed and renewed her soul. Her heritage was sealed for good. She had never felt closer to God. It was the first step to restoring her Jewish soul before being united with Nick in marriage.

"As I said when we first talked, I do perform interfaith marriages," Rabbi Sean explained that afternoon. Both he and Nick had waited for Rebekkah while she was in the mikveh. Now the three of them were sitting in his office at Temple Shalom. "Now that Rebekkah's conversion is over, we can discuss this at more length.

"I don't do it for just any couple. We have to look at what these marriages mean for the larger Jewish community. Nick, you're a strong Catholic. At least that's what Rebekkah told me."

"I'm Catholic, yes," replied Nick. "But, not a closed-minded religious bigot. I've explained to Rebekkah Judaism isn't so different from Christianity. My religion came from yours. They're linked. Because of that, I feel God will support and nurture our growth as a family. Being Jewish is who Rebekkah is. It doesn't take away from who I am. She glowed after her conversion. She looked like an angel. Hope you don't mind the analogy. She's my life. I want to support her."

"How will you feel if your child is not baptized in the Catholic Church?" asked Rabbi Sean.

"The Catholic church is not perfect. I've studied Judaism quite a bit since I met Rebekkah. I'm open to the possibility of converting. Meanwhile, I don't want my child torn between religions." He caught Rebekkah's eyes as he took her hand. "I promise to raise my son in a Jewish environment, make sure he has a Jewish education. When he's thirteen I'll be at his bar mitzvah. Maybe I'll be Jewish myself by then. And have mastered Hebrew.

"Back to your question about baptism, rabbi. Is being a bar mitzvah not as good as being baptized? In God's eyes, I mean? Both tell God you trust Him with your child, no? That you intend to teach your child about God's ways."

Rabbi listened intently, but made no comment. Rebekkah was suddenly afraid he was going to turn them down. Nick spoke beautifully. How could Rabbi Sean not see and hear his sincerity?

"My parents are dead. Even if they weren't, I'm too old to worry about their approval," Nick continued. "They would've adored Rebekkah. I come from a family of Israel supporters. A family who understands the importance Israel and Jews have played in history."

"What about the rest of your family? How did they react knowing Rebekkah isn't Catholic?"

"I don't have a big family. My brothers and me, and my grandparents. I have cousins, but I don't know them well. They're spread around the country. My grandparents are happy for me. My brothers, too. They don't care if Rebekkah is green and has two heads."

Rabbi Sean smiled as he leaned back in his chair. "How will you feel about having a home in which Jewish, not Christian, holidays are observed? What about your belief in Jesus Christ?"

Nick thought about the question for a few seconds. "Jesus said, 'In my Father's house are many rooms; if it were not so, I would have told you. I am going there to prepare a place for you.' To me, that means there is room

407

for everyone. He won't love me less if I convert. He came to earth as a Jew.

"I'm not saying everything will be easy. I do love Christmas and Easter, but I love my Jewish wife and son much more. As Ruth said in the Tanakh, 'Where you go I will go, and where you stay I will stay. Your people will be my people and your God my God.'

"I'm proud my wife is passing down her rich heritage to our son. I'm eager to learn more about her holidays, and how I can participate. I want to help teach my son about his religion. Again, I may decide to convert. If I do, it will be before my son gets very old. Maybe you and I could discuss that separately."

Rabbi Sean smiled again. "The point of this is not to make you convert. I want to be certain you know intermarriage can be tough. I don't want you so blinded by love for Rebekkah you aren't seeing what may lie ahead."

"I don't expect Nick to give up his holidays," Rebekkah piped in. "Or what he believes. He can have the biggest Christmas tree he wants. I have no objection to attending church services with him. I'm not a religious bigot, either. Nor is my family. We have nothing against Christianity. I don't want Nick to give up who he is for me. After all, I wasn't really Jewish myself until this morning."

The rabbi laughed. "You have a point."

"I know my decision to support Rebekkah's religion will have an impact on my life, but I'm not so sure it will be a negative one," said Nick. " I plan to be on a lifelong journey of nurturing the spiritual growth of Rebekkah, myself, and our children."

"You've given some thought to this. I like your answers," replied Rabbi Sean.

"Thank you. I love God. I love Rebekkah. I intend to honor both."

"I feel the same," said Rebekkah.

The rabbi turned to his computer. "What day are you thinking about? Other than Saturdays I'm pretty much open."

"You'll marry us, then?" Rebekkah grinned. She wanted to jump up and down with happiness.

"You're both deeply in love. You've both thought about this. Nick, your comments and attitude impress me. Rebekkah, you could have turned your back on Judaism, embraced Christianity then there would be no reason for this conversation. You didn't. I admire your love for your religion, and for Nick.

"I hope to see you both in my synagogue from time to time. Nick, you're welcome at Temple Shalom whether you convert or not. We have other couples that are of two different faiths."

Rebekkah took Nick's hand. "I think we'd both like visiting your synagogue."

"She's right," agreed Nick. "I appreciate your talking to us and being so open. Thank you. You asked about a date for the wedding. How about tomorrow?"

"The rabbi laughed. "Spoken like a man in love. I'm really looking forward to doing your wedding."

"Tomorrow?" squeaked Rebekkah, laughing. "I need time to find a dress, plan the wedding. Give us six weeks, rabbi."

The wedding would be intimate. Family and close friends at Shira and David's home. As Michael grew inside Rebekkah it seemed the list of things she had to do before she became Mrs. Dominick Rossi grew right along with him. At least the marriage license part was done. They had gotten it the day after Rabbi Sean agreed to marry them. Rebekkah had immediately flipped open her official wedding notebook and marked that off her "TO DO" list.

Her mother, sister Lilly, and Molly were all helping. Cairenn volunteered to do the decorations, and Molly wrote and mailed the invitations. Nick's grandparents were coming from Florida. Rebekkah couldn't wait to meet them.

She invited Elisabeth, with Shira and David's blessing, but she wouldn't be involved in the wedding plans. Elisabeth wasn't hurt, she understood that pleasure belonged to the people who had raised Rebekkah so well.

Just when she felt everything might come together after all, Ima informed her that her aunts would not be attending.

"What?" cried Rebekkah. "I was looking forward to seeing them."

Shira set the cake she had just pulled from the oven on the kitchen counter. "You know my sisters love you."

"I sense a 'but' coming," said Rebekkah.

"They're upset about Nick not being Jewish, and you being pregnant before you're married. They don't think it looks right. They're afraid of what their friends will think."

Rebekkah pushed her hair away from her face, spread out her hands on both sides of her lower back and stretched a little. "You cannot be serious. Who cares what their friends think? They live in New Jersey; their friends don't even know me. Anyway, this isn't the 1950s. Things have changed."

"I know, sweetheart, but my sisters are from a different time."

"Different time?" echoed Rebekkah. "I know you're the baby of the family, Ima, but Aunt Nora is only ten years older than you, Aunt Susan twelve years older. They're not old maids. I guess you shouldn't have told them about the baby yet."

"I didn't think they would react this way. I'm sorry. I know you want their support. They love you, they just don't want to be gossiped about."

Rebekkah squinted at her mother, not believing what she was hearing. "So who's going to gossip?"

Shira sat down on a kitchen chair. "Your back hurts. Sit a few minutes. Who can explain what they're thinking? They know other relatives will be here, they feel you've embarrassed yourself. Embarrassed us, embarrassed the family. Which, of course, you haven't. Nobody else feels that way, so don't let it upset you, or ruin your day."

Rebekkah sat. "It's not going to ruin my day. I feel worse for you. They were going to help you with the food. I'll pitch in."

"You certainly will not. It's your wedding. Actually, Joey's agreed to help me."

Rebekkah's mouth fell open. "Joey? Joey Rossi?"
"Yes. He's apparently a good cook. And baker."

"Really? I had no idea."
Shira handed Rebekkah a cookie. "Milk?"

Rebekkah shook her head. "I'm confused. How did Joey's cooking skills come into a conversation?"

"I told Nick your aunts weren't coming when he was here the other day. He had Joey call me. He sounds just like Nick, doesn't he? So polite and sweet. I can't wait to meet him. So see? I'm good. I have lots of other help, so don't worry."

Rebekkah grinned, thinking of Joey helping out in her mother's kitchen. He must really have wormed his way into her heart.

The other problem that had cast a temporary pall over her joyous day was the way Rebekkah's friends from Beth Israel had reacted to her plans to marry a non-Jew and being pregnant by him. They still didn't know about her finding Elisabeth, and her own recent status as a non-Jew, so they viewed her choice to marry Nick something of a betrayal. A second holocaust, which Rebekkah found farfetched. She felt hurt and shocked, but eventually realized if they couldn't accept her choices, they weren't really friends. Molly had stuck by her, and had been fascinated by Rebekkah's conversion story.

She and Nick had been going to Sabbath services at Temple Shalom, and they both loved it. They were already making new friends there, and Rabbi Sean was becoming a good friend, also. All because of Elisabeth introducing her to him. The people at Temple Shalom accepted them and didn't question their relationship.

They wished them well on their upcoming wedding. She had met a couple of other women who were pregnant, too. They had invited her to join their New Mommy group and she was looking forward to it. They didn't care if Nick was Jewish or not, or if she was pregnant before she was married. It hadn't even come up.

"You better shop for a wedding dress before you can't fit into one, young lady" her father admonished with a mock frown as he walked into the kitchen. "Nick has his tuxedo all ready. I do, too."

In all the excitement, Rebekkah had forgotten one of the most important things. "Ima, you have to come with me."

"Of course. Try and keep me away. Do you want to go now? We'll have lunch out, too."

"That sounds good. I'll be ready after a trip to the bathroom."

When they were seated in the Volvo, Shira turned to Rebekkah after starting the engine. "Did you want to invite Elisabeth to come with us?"

"No. You're my mother. I like Elisabeth a lot. But she's a friend. I'm grateful she had me, but she's not you. This day belongs to you and me."

"I was with you when you picked out your dress for your first wedding. I thought maybe this one you would want to share with Elisabeth."

Rebekkah grimaced. "Let's not talk about my first wedding. I've erased it from my mind. I think Elisabeth would feel awkward stepping into any kind of mother role now. Besides, I want you to come."

Shira nodded as she smiled. "It's settled then."

"I can't even get this one zipped up. I'm too fat." It was the fourth store they had visited. Nothing appealed to Rebekkah. Not only was she fat, her face was breaking out.

"Please! You are not fat. This is a beautiful dress," exclaimed Shira.

"It's not the one."

"Forgive my rudeness, but are you pregnant?" asked the saleswoman

Rebekkah turned toward her. "Yes, I am. I'll never find a dress that fits."

The saleswoman smiled as she laid a hand on Rebekkah's arm. "We have a woman who designs maternity wedding dresses for us."

Rebekkah had to laugh. "Oh, Aunt Nora and Aunt Susan would just love hearing that."

Shira laughed too, rolling her eyes. "I can see them now."

"Can you please show me what you have?" Rebekkah asked.

"I'll be right back."

She returned with a rack on wheels filled with dresses. She pulled a lace one off and held it up.

Rebekkah shook her head. "Looks like a nightgown."

"No problem," the woman assured her. "We've just begun."

The next one she held up stole Rebekkah's breath. It was an off-white halter neck with triple layers of sumptuous looking fabric. The black velvet sash was detachable and gave the dress a regal look. "That's it! That's my dress! Ima, I've found it!"

"It's definitely you," agreed Shira. "It will show off your beautiful long neck."

"It is divine. Why don't you try it on?" suggested the saleswoman. "Come, I'll show you the dressing room."

Once in the dressing room Rebekkah slipped out of her clothes. Goosebumps rose on her arms as she put on the gorgeous dress. Her wedding dress! . The next time she wore it she would become Mrs. Dominick Rossi. She couldn't wait! She came out and Shira and the saleswoman collectively drew in their breaths.

"You look so beautiful," whispered Shira. "The perfect bride."

"I agree," the other woman spoke. "The dress was made for you. You're radiant."

Rebekkah felt herself blush. "It's hormones."

"It's a bride-to-be in love," gushed Shira

"I'll take it," said Rebekkah. She carefully handed the dress back to the saleswoman then changed back into her street clothes.

Before she knew it, her six weeks was down to one day, and Rebekkah was being called to bless the reading of the Torah at Temple Shalom the Saturday before her marriage. Tomorrow she would be a married woman. Again, she felt the warmth of the people at the congregation, and felt as if she belonged already. She didn't even miss her old friends. Nick was going to coach their kids' baseball team next spring, and she would join the Mommy Group when they returned from their honeymoon.

"Are you nervous?" asked Shira the next afternoon. She and David had come into her bedroom to walk her downstairs to meet Nick, so they could be married.

"No, Ima. I want this. More than anything."

Shira wiped away a tear. "You are a gorgeous bride."

"You certainly are," added David.

Rebekkah looked down at her stomach and laughed. "A fat bride."

"No," retorted Shira. "All I see is your beauty. That's all Nick sees. I love him, by the way. So does your father. And we already adore baby Michael."

Rebekkah blinked back her own tears then hugged her mother and father. "Thank you, Ima and Aba. For everything, and for always being here for me. For accepting Nick and all my decisions. I love you both so very much. Oh, look at the time. We should get downstairs. I don't want my groom to think I've gotten cold feet."

Rebekkah joined Nick under the *chuppah* - the canopy that covers the bride and groom during the wedding ceremony. She would never forget the look on his face when he saw her come into the living room. The way tears filled his eyes the same time hers filled. And he was beyond handsome in a black tuxedo. She couldn't wait to make love to him tonight.

Everyone else faded away except for him and the words Rabbi Sean spoke. Soon, Nick was slipping a gold band on her hand and reciting *"Harei aht mekudeshet li betaba'at zo k'dat Moshe v'Israel."* Thou art sanctified unto me with this ring, in the tradition of Moses and Israel.

They were having a double ring ceremony. When Rebekkah slipped Nick's wedding ring on to his finger she recited *"Ani L'dodi V'dodi li."* I am my beloved's and my beloved is mine. Just as it said on her engagement ring.

They were husband and wife! Standing under the chuppah with a renewed Jewish soul, Nick by her side, and a baby inside her she already adored, Rebekkah had never been happier.

Next, Rabbi Sean read the *Ketubah*, the traditional Jewish wedding document, marking the official agreement by Rebekkah and Nick to wed. She had designed it herself. An intertwined double scroll that formed a locking heart. The colors were brilliant and the pattern intricate. She called it *Two As One*. Soon, it would be framed and displayed in their home.

After everyone had gone home, Rebekkah dropped to her parents' couch. She looked down at the rings on her hand. She was truly Mrs. Dominick Rossi now. She thought Nick looked very sexy with his wedding ring on.

He soon came to sit beside her, draping an arm around her shoulder, and gathering her closer. "Happy?"

She grinned up at him. "Very. More than I ever dreamt possible."

He caressed the side of her face. "I hope I can put that look on your face every day."

"I love you, Nicky. So much."

"I love you, too, Mrs. Rossi." He lowered his voice. "I can't wait to be alone with you tonight."

Rebekkah's heart leapt. Exactly her thoughts. They were spending the night at Nick's, then flying to Buffalo tomorrow morning, so they could honeymoon in Niagara Falls. She sighed with contentment. Seven days with her husband all to herself.

She looked around at her family, mingling and laughing with Nick's grandparents and brothers as if they'd known each other for years. There was such warmth and love in this room. She leaned her head on Nick's shoulder and closed her eyes, willing this moment to last forever as she drifted to sleep.

Rebekkah opened her eyes as she tried getting comfortable, which she knew was impossible. She had been waking up off and on all night. Through the open blinds she could see the dawn starting to brighten the bedroom. She looked over at Nick. He lay on his side, facing her, sleeping soundly. She smiled. He looked so young and handsome. Her heart swelled with love for her beloved husband.

The pains seized her again. They were stronger now, and closer together. Michael Anthony Rossi was going to arrive today. She was certain of it. She was dying to hold him in her arms. She couldn't wait to see the child she already adored. Michael's bedroom was all ready for him, even though he would be spending his first few weeks in a bassinette in their bedroom.

More clothes than he could possibly wear filled his closet, and life-sized Disney characters took up an entire blue wall, courtesy of Marco, her talented brother-in-law. Evidently, Rebekkah wasn't the only artist in the family. She loved all of the Rossi boys.

Stuffed animals lined Michael's crib, courtesy of Ima, Aba, Samuel, Benjamin, and Lilly, who had a crush of her own on Nick, and wanted to know if any of his brothers were available. Nick had had Michael's first sonogram picture enlarged and framed. It now hung on another wall in Michael's bedroom beside a beautiful black-and-white profile picture of Rebekkah and Nick, her huge belly on

419

display. She couldn't stop smiling, thinking how lucky and blessed she was.

Before she reached over to wake Nick, she took a minute in the peaceful quiet to thank God. As He had done for her biblical sisters, Sarah, Rachel, and Hannah, He had answered her prayers. She had everything she could possible wish for.

ACKNOWLEDGEMENTS

Thank you to my agent, Frances Black, for taking a chance on me, E-lit Books for publishing me, Long Ridge Writers Group, who helped me find my writing voice, Kelly McClymer who worked with me on the premise that would become my novel, and Katherine Johnson who read, edited, suggested, and encouraged. For help in researching Judaism many thanks to my husband, Aaron, and also to Gloria Oren (who did double duty as a reader), Robyn Bavati, Andrew P. Hechtman, and Rabbi Yossi Pollak. For helping me research funeral home embezzlement, thank you, Lee Lofland and Joseph DeCicco. Thank you to Darrin Addams, RN, LPC of the Karen Ann Quinlan Foundation for his information about people in a persistent vegetative state, and to both Mercedes Rodriguez and again, my husband for answering my questions on New York City neighborhoods. And, thank you to author Matthew Dicks for introducing me to the wonderful world of Twitter.

CPSIA information can be obtained at www.ICGtesting.com
Printed in the USA
BVOW08s1844200814

363624BV00011B/121/P